I0780773

BROTHERS, HOPE & HEARTS

A SMALL TOWN FRIENDS – TO – LOVERS MYSTERY ROMANCE

HOPE & HEARTS FROM SWAN HARBOR
BOOK 3

SOPHIE BARTOW

CONTENTS

This book is dedicated to ...

My street team;
The Wall-Giennie Wicks-Delaney,
Connector Inspector- Linda Hagerty
Reactor Inspector- Jami Fenton
Plot Catcher- Barbara Berry
Sign Crew- Kate Semenyuk

The Clean-up crew: Cindy, Laura, Kim, Maggie, and Sylvia, whose feedback was valuable.
And my family, who are still waiting for me to clean the house.

Inspiration began,
when a lost girl fell for a lost boy

Two Hearts Press
An Imprint of LLIPSS, INC
Copyright 2020 by Sophie Bartow

Regular Paperback ASIN: B08HRKXHLR

Regular paperback ISBN: 978-1-965510-08-7
Large Print Paperback: 978-1-965510-01-8
Large Print Hardback: 978-1-965510-04-9
Regular Print Hardback: 978-1-965510-23-0

All rights reserved. No part of this book may be reproduced or used in any manner without written permission of the copyright owner except for the use of quotations in a book review. This is a work of fiction. Names, characters, and places are the product of the author's imagination or used fictitiously. Any resemblance to actual persons, living or dead, business or locales is coincidental. This book was updated, and new content added in January 2025.

Cover by Kate Semenyuk

Without hope, there would be no happy endnings.

FROM DARKNESS INTO LOVE

KITTENS, PUPPIES & LOVE

BROTHERS, HOPE & HEARTS

KISSES, FAMILY & HOPE

A TREE, MISTLETOE & A SUNSET

HOPE, HEARTS & FOREVER

THE MEMORY OF LOVE

THE INNOCENCE OF LOVE

THE FORGIVENESS OF LOVE

THE POWER OF LOVE

THE CHRISTMAS LOVE SONG

THE KISS OF LOVE

THE LESSONS OF LOVE

THE HEART OF LOVE

THE JOURNEY TO LOVE

Hope & Hearts Historical Novellas

GUIDED BY LIGHT - 1952

GUIDED BY HEART - 1964

GUIDED BY LOVE - 1969

WELCOME TO SWAN HARBOR- 1979

FINDING HER LOST HEART- 1983/1990

GUIDED BY A KISS - 1995

SOME RESIDENTS OF SWAN HARBOR

Liam Reade: Firefighter/Paramedic in New York City. Works at Queen's Court Medical Center, owned by King Industries.

Elsa Winters: She owns a pediatric practice in Swan Harbor and is best friends with **Emma Foster.**

Killian Reade: Detective for the Swan Harbor Sheriff's Department. Brother to **Liam Reade** and son of **Finley Reade,** who live in New York. Engaged to **Emma Foster**. Their story is told in **Kittens, Puppies & Love.**

Emma Foster: The owner and veterinarian of Swan Harbor Veterinarian Hospital. Daughter of **Ava King** and **Peter Foster** and engaged to **Killian Reade**.

Rusty Langley: He is a detective for the Swan Harbor Sheriff's Department and partner of **Killian Reade**. He is married to **Rene Langley,** and the father to **Roland.** His story is told in **The Power of Love.**

Rene Langley: She is the mayor of Swan Harbor, married to **Rusty,** and the mother of **Roland.**

Roland Langley: The young son of Rusty and Rene.

Dylan Prince: The Sheriff of Swan Harbor and married to **Molly Barnes Prince**. He is the brother of **Jessie** and the late James and son of the late Ruth and Robert. Their story is told in **The Innocence of Love.**

Molly Barnes Prince: She teaches first grade at Swan Harbor Elementary School and is married to **Dylan Prince**.

Grayson Hunter: Engineer at Hunter Construction and married to **Sadie Martin Hunter.** Their story is told in **The Memory of Love.**

Sadie Martin Hunter: The office manager of Swan Harbor Veterinarian Hospital and an accountant. She is married to **Grayson Hunter**.

Finley Reade: Owns a real estate business in New York City. Father of **Liam** and **Killian**. His story is told in **Kisses, Family & Hope.**

Ava King: Philanthropist and businesswoman for King Industries. Mother of **Emma Foster**.

Tyler James: He is a professional singer and owner of Siren's Song, a music club located on Swan Harbor's pier. He is the father of six-year-old **Bethany**. His story is told in **The Christmas Love Song.**

Sally Miller Patterson: Owner of Sally's Diner, the place to see and be seen in Swan Harbor. Sally is married to **Daniel Patterson** and mother to **Christian** and **Tracey.** She is also grandmother to **Julianna.**

Danny Patterson: Married to **Sally** and the head of neurology at Swan Harbor General Hospital. He is the father to **Christian** and **Tracey,** and the grandfather to **Julianna.** Their story is told in **Welcome to Swan Harbor.**

Captain Jack: Retired Naval officer and local legend of Swan Harbor, who gives out sage advice to the town's residents. He's the owner of Captain Jack's Fine Dining, located at the newly renovated pier in an old Spanish galleon. His story is told in **The Journey to Love.**

Welcome to Swan Harbor

A Haven of Hope for Lost Hearts.

ONE

QUICK NOTE: *If you enjoy* Brothers, Hope & Hearts, *be sure to check out my offer for more Elsa and Liam at the end.*
Happy reading!

New York City
Liam's Apartment
August 1
1:30 p.m.

Liam Reade was home. She could hear a sporting event on the TV—most likely watching a soccer match he'd already seen.

She'd been waiting in front of his apartment for ten minutes, and the door still hadn't opened.

He doesn't know you're here.

With a shaking hand, Elsa knocked. She tapped rapidly twice, rested a heartbeat, and then followed with two more rapid ones. Once she did, she could picture exactly what was happening inside.

He'd turn down the television and toss the remote onto the coffee table.

Then he'd glance around the room to see if he needed to put anything away. Finally, he would take the necessary steps to reach the door—for him, probably only four or five. Those were the benefits of having long legs.

After that ....

Elsa thought she was ready for the door to be yanked open—but she wasn't. It was impossible not to be affected when faced with six feet of deliciousness.

"Elsa." Liam's sexy baritone slithered along her skin. "Did we have plans?"

Don't stare at his bare chest.

"I'm sorry to drop in like this." She mentally patted herself on the back for sounding somewhat normal. "I, I need to tell you something."

Don't admire his flat abs exposed by the cut-off sweats hanging low on his hips.

"Come in."

He stepped aside, and as she entered, Elsa held her breath. She didn't want to smell his musky cologne or feel the heat from his body. If she did, it would be so much harder not to step close and bury her nose against his furry chest. That would make it too difficult to do what needed to be done.

"I'll not be long."

Unless ....

"It's fine, love. It's just Liverpool."

Her hands were sweating, and her heart was racing.

Liam waved toward the sofa. "Have a seat."

"Thanks."

Just spit it out.

"I ..." Elsa took a deep breath. "I came to say goodbye."

"Goodbye? Are you going on vacation?"

Told you he wouldn't remember.

"In a way."

"Elsa, love." Liam stroked the top of her hand with his long fingers. "What's going on?"

"I'm moving. Remember? I told you a month ago."

Liam's blue eyes darkened, and his brows drew together in confusion. She knew him well enough to know that he was trying to place the conversation.

"Moving? When? Where?"

She wanted to say something, but somehow, she knew words wouldn't matter. If he'd cared, he would have listened.

"I finished my residency." She stayed with the simple explanation. "But I got a better offer than Queen's Court."

"A better one?" Liam brushed his hands through his hair, a sure sign of agitation. "What could be better than working for Queen's here in New York City?"

Say it.

"It's a place where I'll have more control. I want a life, Liam. This allows me to see both office and hospital patients without working twelve to sixteen hours a day. Tate promised it was possible."

"Tate?"

"Doctor Tate Doolittle," Elsa explained. "Head of Swan Harbor General's pediatrics."

"Wait, you're moving to Swan Harbor?"

Ask me to stay.

"I am." Elsa forced herself to stand. "Anyway, I just wanted you to know before I ... well, leave."

"But." Liam glanced around the room, and there was almost a wild look in his eyes. "But ..."

Ask me.

"Liam." A buxom redhead stepped from the bedroom. "I hope you don't mind that I borrowed a shirt. Mine ..."

Elsa's mouth dropped open, and all she could think was he didn't wait long to find someone new. "I'm sorry. I should go."

"Wait," Liam began.

But Elsa wasn't in the mood to hear any of his excuses. Neither was she ready to meet his replacement girlfriend.

"I need to finish packing." She pushed past him and walked straight to the door.

"Elsa, wait," Liam called again, and this time, he lightly touched her elbow. "When are you leaving?"

"In a couple of days," Elsa shrugged. "It will depend on how long it takes to get everything done. I'll ..." Then she made the mistake of looking at him.

Liam's hands were curled into fists and held close to his side. His body was rigid, but it was his eyes that said what he couldn't say out loud.

I'm going to miss you.

Please stay.

I'm sorry.

"Take care of yourself."

At the last minute, she kissed him goodbye and rushed toward the door. She worried if he said anything, she wouldn't be able to hold back the tears clogging her throat. Before she could escape, Liam caught her wrist.

"Elsa."

Don't look.

"Look at me. Please."

Her heart twisted, but she knew herself. If she looked into his navy blue eyes that spoke volumes, she would be lost.

"I can't." Elsa tugged her hand free and hurried to the elevator.

The first tear fell just as the door closed.

Crap.

She couldn't cry over him.

It hurts.

He'd already moved on.

"You've done it now, Elsa," she muttered as she crossed the street into Central Park. "There's no going back."

LIAM SHUT THE DOOR AND, ON HIS WAY TO THE SOFA, SLIPPED A shirt over his head.

"What the hell was that?" Barbi came from the bedroom wearing one of his dress shirts and her jeans.

"What?" he asked, the nonchalance in his voice a perfect accompaniment to the 'neutral' question. So perfect he didn't think anyone could see beneath it.

But Elsa ...

Barbi dropped into a chair and tucked her legs beneath her. "Come on, Liam. You care for that woman. Why did you just allow her to leave?"

"Of course I care for her. We've been friends for a while and work for the same hospital."

"Cut the bull," Barbi snapped.

"I'm not—"

"It's just like Debi Monroe."

That name still had the power to create an ache in the center of his chest. However, his feelings at twenty-one couldn't be compared to what he felt now.

"This is nothing like that," Liam retorted. "Nothing."

Only because you refuse to ....

"Sometimes we have to let go of the past in order to move toward the future, Liam. You know that."

Just like Killian had done.

"Are you trying to knock some sense into Liam, Hon?" Justin, her husband of a year, entered the room. "You know he's too stubborn to listen."

"I'm beginning to remember that," Barbi grumbled. "But Liam, you really should set her straight. She thinks you and I ..."

"Look, it's no big deal. Do you want to grab a bite to eat?" Liam glanced from one to the other. "I'm suddenly hungry."

"You're always hungry." Justin laughed. "Right now, we should check on the clean-up crew at our apartment."

"Think they've started?"

Barbi sighed. "I hope so. We don't want to overstay our welcome."

"You're fine," Liam assured her. "I'm happy to help."

"We'll let you know if we need a place tonight. But Liam," Barbi's gaze met his. "Go talk to her. Tell her I didn't spend the night."

"But that would be a lie." Liam's blue eyes twinkled. "Wouldn't it?"

"Oh, you!" She flipped her hair over her shoulder and flounced out of the room.

"Does she always pout when she doesn't get her way?"

Justin laughed. "Don't ask me. You've known her longer than I have."

"You're married to her."

"True," Justin grinned. "In this situation, though, I agree with Barb. Talk to your lady friend. She deserves to know the truth."

Liam turned on the television sound, hoping Justin and Barbi would ignore him on their way out. He hadn't offered them a place to stay so they could dig into his psyche. It was all about helping a couple of friends because their place smelled like smoke. Nothing more, nothing less.

Are you sure about that?

What else could it be?

A way for you to bury your head and not have to deal.

Liam scoffed at his thoughts.

"We'll see you later, Liam." Barbi waved. "Remember what I said."

Once he was alone, Liam tried to watch the match, but he couldn't focus. Besides, Liverpool was ahead by three goals.

It has nothing to do with the score.

That's not true.

It wasn't long before he could no longer stand the quiet apartment and went looking for something to eat.

He meandered past Queen's Court Medical and the bar, O'Toole's. It was too late for lunch, too early for dinner, and he didn't have to work. Right then, nothing sounded interesting.

Face it, you want to see her.

Who?

That he could imagine his inner voice raising a brow in disbelief was unsettling. It was equally annoying that he could imagine its facial expressions. However, those were heavy thoughts he wasn't ready to deal with right then.

That's what you always do.

Do not.

Then, just to prove he was in control, he ducked into Nathan's. Even after eating a hot dog and fries, the same sense of needing to be somewhere remained. It felt like an invisible thread was pulling him, and where it was leading was beyond his control.

Liam hurried through Central Park to the Upper West Side. He took a right, then a left, and walked two streets over until he stood in front of Elsa's apartment building.

He'd been to her apartment many times since January. It was modern to his ancient, homey to his sterile, and he'd been completely enamored. Knowing that she was dangerous to everything he believed didn't seem to matter, though, as he'd jumped in with both feet. Could he let her walk out of his life?

You have no choice.

But was that the truth?

It's the only truth you're ready to hear.

Meaning?

Meaning sometimes we have to look inside to find the answers.
Like Killian did?
Yes.
I'm not suffering from the same issues as Killian.
Aren't you?
No! And even if I was, there's no Violet out there waiting.
True. But Elsa is waiting. Isn't she enough?

GUILT AT THE WAY SHE'D LEFT THINGS WITH LIAM CHASED ELSA all the way home. Yet, she knew she'd done the only thing possible. With her residency completed, she had to take care of herself. If that meant she had to tell a lie, then so what? He'd never know.

Are you sure?

She'd asked herself that question several times over the past few weeks. When she did, the answer remained the same. Yes.

Liam Reade had plenty of friends to keep him entertained and wouldn't come looking for her. It also appeared he had replaced her with a new friend.

Crap!

"I'm so not going there," she muttered, stacking the box on the cart.

Elsa took one last look around, left her keys on the table, and locked the door behind her. She'd told Liam she was leaving when everything was done. That she was leaving earlier than she'd anticipated, well ....

Since she was only taking a few suitcases and some boxes, it didn't take long to store them in the car. She'd just loaded the last box when the hairs on the back of her neck stood up.

"Going somewhere?"

Crap!

Elsa slammed the lid and turned to face Liam. "What brings you to this side of the park?"

LIAM TOOK TWO STEPS TOWARD HER. CLOSE, JUST NOT CLOSE

enough to make her feel like he was trying to intimidate her. "You didn't answer my question. I asked if you were going somewhere?"

"What makes you think that?"

"I saw you push your cart full of boxes out the back hall."

"So?"

"Why'd you lie?"

"Wha … What are you talking about?"

"Come on, love," Liam's voice dropped into a lower range. "Why?"

Several emotions flitted across her face, and she seemed to wilt before his eyes.

"Why do you care?" she asked instead of answering his question. "Did your new girl not give you what you were after?"

"My new girl?" Then he remembered Barbi's plea. "About that. Barbi isn't my new girl. I've known her forever."

"Forever?"

"Her brother was my best friend in high school. And," he took another step closer, "she's married to Justin. Remember? I told you about him."

A little pucker developed between Elsa's brows, and he could practically see the wheels turning inside her head. "Justin? Your old partner?"

"Yes. Barbi's first husband was a prat, and after he left, she was pretty messed up."

"So you introduced her to your old partner?"

"Yes."

"Why?"

Her question surprised him. "Why what?"

"Why did you introduce them to each other?"

"I don't know." Liam shrugged. "I thought they'd be good together."

"Oh. Well, if that's all, I need to return this cart."

Oh? He couldn't decide what she meant by using the word. It meant one thing to him, but something told him its meaning was more important to her.

"I'm still waiting for an answer."

"Which was?"

He wanted to grin because there was no way she didn't remember what he'd asked.

"Are you going somewhere?"

"I told you," Elsa replied. "I'm moving to Swan Harbor."

Liam propped his hands on his hips. "But you said, and I quote, 'I'm leaving in the next day ... or two.' I know sometimes I confuse things, but it's only been a few hours since you said that. Not," he popped his T, "a day or two."

"I told you when I got things done." She pushed the cart past him. "Well, I got things done."

"And so you're leaving—just like that?"

"I said goodbye," Elsa sighed. "I don't know what else you want, Liam." *For things to be like they were.*

"But why, love? Why are you moving so far away?"

"I," she began. Then, almost as if she changed her mind, she pulled her shoulders back and stood a little taller. "You're a smart guy, Liam. I bet you can figure it out. Now, I have to go. Look me up if you come to Swan Harbor to visit." Then she walked away.

Liam stared at her retreating figure, all the while rubbing circles in the center of his chest.

Heartburn. He blamed it on the chili dog he'd eaten. *Couldn't be anything else.*

Swan Harbor
Veterinarian Clinic
August 1
6:00 p.m.

Emma Foster was trying to focus on work, and checking Daisy and her puppies for worms seemed mindless enough. Yet, no matter how many times she reminded herself of what she was supposed to be doing, her thoughts kept returning to Elsa. Something was going on with her friend of over ten years, and for the first time in their friendship, their roles were reversed.

She'd first noticed the change in April when Killian said something about his brother. Since Liam had been seeing her best friend for months, the conversation was in what *wasn't* said. But when Elsa came to Swan Harbor in June, Emma could tell things were different. They hadn't talked, though. It left her with the question of how to help when her friend wouldn't share her burdens.

Sound familiar?

Yes, but …

No buts. What has Elsa always done when you weren't ready to talk?

Be there.

Exactly. When she needs you, she'll reach out. In the meantime …

I have a fiancé who …

The thought had barely formed when the air shifted, and the man who rocked her world invaded her space.

"Hello, Doc." Killian buzzed a kiss next to her ear. "Eww, what's that smell?"

"You're an investigator," she teased. "What does it smell like?"

"It smells like shi–"

"Puppy poop," Emma interrupted. "Be nice. I'm sure you've smelled worse."

"Aye, that's true." He sighed, and she knew he was thinking about cases he'd seen on the job. "But I don't relish getting a whiff of it every time I nuzzle your neck tonight."

"Oh?" She grinned, still feeling the need to pinch herself at how far she'd come in less than a year. "Were you planning on doing that tonight?"

Killian's blue eyes darkened. "As often as possible. Got a problem with that?"

"No." She kissed him. "I definitely don't have a problem with your nuzzles."

"Good." Killian placed his hands on her shoulders and turned her toward the door. "Now, go shower."

"But," she gestured at the mess scattered across her worktable. "There's stuff to be done."

"I'll clean." Killian kissed her ear. "You can reward me later. And …"

Emma slid her arms around his neck. "What else are you promising me, Killian?"

"I'll even start dinner."

"Oooh, a girl could get used to that."

His expression turned serious, and he brushed her hair over her shoulder. "I hope so. I just want to make you happy."

"You do, Killian," she replied breathlessly. "I love you, you know?"

Killian tugged her closer, aligning their hips. "Ditto, Doc."

"Ditto. What kind of declaration is that?"

"It's a ..." His phone buzzed. "It's Liam. Go. I'll see you upstairs."

Emma rushed through her shower, eager to hear what Liam had to say. She didn't think he was calling to 'just talk.' Something told her it had to do with what she'd been worried about for weeks.

When she walked into the kitchen, Killian was standing in front of the stove. He'd tucked a towel into the waistband of his pants and was rhythmically stirring the ingredients in a pot.

"You're making spaghetti with your world-famous sauce, aren't you?"

"Aye."

Emma leaned against the cabinet and waited for him to look at her. "What did Liam have to say?"

Killian didn't respond right away, which meant he was wrestling with something. The longer he remained quiet, the more concerned she grew.

"What has Elsa said the last few times you've spoken to her?" he finally asked.

"Wait a minute, Killian." Emma frowned. "Everything between them is okay, right?"

He sprinkled something else into the sauce and then offered her a taste.

Her eyes flared. "Oh, that's good. You changed the recipe, didn't you?"

"Of course," he teased. "A good chef never spills his secrets. Now, I laid out the vegetables for the salad for you. I'm going to make a bruschetta."

Since she assumed he was working his way around to what to say, she focused on the salad. It wasn't until he'd slid the bread into the oven that he looked at her expectantly.

"Did you know Elsa was moving?"

"Moving?" Emma's gaze collided with Killian's. "As in leaving New York City?"

"Aye."

Her thoughts traveled back to the last time she'd seen Elsa.

"You were standing there when she told Liam about her job offers. But as for taking one of them, she's been pretty quiet. Why?"

"She showed up at Liam's today and told him goodbye."

"Goodbye?" Emma dropped the knife she'd been using to cut the tomato and frowned up at him. "She's said nothing. Where's she moving?"

"Here, Doc." Killian hesitated while he pulled the bruschetta from the oven. "It seems your friend Elsa has left my brother and is moving to Swan Harbor."

Emma dropped into the chair, fighting her initial reaction. She really wanted to protect her friend and blame Liam, but where would that get them?

"Why's she moving to Swan Harbor?" Emma murmured. "Unless ..."

"Unless what?"

Killian flicked off the burners, drained the pasta, and prepared her a plate before she'd wrapped her head around her thoughts.

"Tyler."

"Tyler?" Killian repeated. "Tyler James?"

Emma smirked at the territorial tone in his voice. She knew at one time he'd worried there was something between her and Tyler.

"Yeah." Her gaze met Killian's. "At one time, Elsa loved him and thought he was the one."

A tic began pulsing on Killian's jaw as if he were clenching his teeth and working to hang on to his temper. "You don't think she's moving here to be with Tyler, do you?"

The low, menacing quality of his voice worried her. "I don't know."

"Bloody hell, Doc!" Killian stood so fast his chair fell over. "She's your friend. How can you not know?"

"Just wait a minute! Why are you mad at me? Did you ever consider the possibility it's Liam's fault?"

"Aye." He brushed his hand through his hair, causing it to stand in several directions. "And if it is, you'll blame me."

"Oh, Killian." Emma flew across the kitchen into his arms. "What are we going to do?"

"Same thing they did for us, love. Just be there for them. Now come here."

When their mouths met, something told her being on the 'supporting' side was going to be just as challenging as the relationship side had been.

TWO

Swan Harbor
August 1
9:00 p.m.

Elsa drove into Swan Harbor, Maine, at 9:00 p.m. on a Friday. The small picturesque town just north of Portland was alive with tourists, a factor she hadn't considered before leaving New York. When she drove past The Beachside Inn and The Lighthouse Inn, their no-vacancy signs caused her bravado to fade.

Crap!

Perhaps she should have called Emma, but in the end, did it matter? After all,—she'd failed.

Her directions led her around town and to the veterinarian clinic. From there, she followed the long driveway and parked in the back, next to Emma's classic yellow Volkswagen, lovingly called Elli.

She was fine until she turned off the car. That was when the enormity of what she'd done washed over her.

Crap!

'This isn't you. Chin up old girl,' her late father would have said.

"I can do this."

One foot in front of the other.

Once she made it to Emma's door, she knocked, using the same rhythm they'd created in college.

Three quick taps ... then a pause, followed by three light taps.

When no one immediately answered the door, she almost knocked again. Then she heard barking dogs, and the fog of despair wrapped around her.

Had her directions been correct? Emma didn't have dogs.

She's a vet. It's probably her patients.

The door flew open before she could knock again.

"Elsa?"

"I'msorryEmma," Elsa blubbered. "Ididn'tknowwheretogo."

"Emma, who the bloody hell's at the door?"

The voice, so similar to Liam's, sent her over the edge. She slid onto the top step and buried her face in her crossed arms.

Lost in her misery, it took her a while to realize Emma had joined her. "I'm sorry. I should have called."

"No, it's okay. Come on. Let's go upstairs."

"Are you sure?"

"I'm sure."

Every step was a struggle, and if Emma hadn't been helping, she would have ended up on the floor and not the sofa. She could hear Emma moving around and talking to someone, but when a cat jumped next to her, she allowed her thoughts to scatter.

Lethargy pulled her under, and the last thing she heard was, "Elsa's here, and it's bad. Bring reinforcements and ice cream," just before everything faded.

The Beach Shack
Swan Harbor
August 1
10:00 p.m.

Killian sauntered into The Beach Shack and slid onto the bench seat across from his partner, Rusty Langley. "Did I miss anything?"

Rusty frowned. "No, but why are you here? I thought you had plans with Emma."

"I thought I did too," Killian sighed. "She kicked me out."

"What did you do to make her mad?"

"Wasn't me," Killian grumbled. "The evening started with a call from my brother and went downhill from there."

"Wait," Rusty frowned. "So, Liam is being a cockwomble, and by extension, you're suffering?"

"I don't know." Killian shrugged. "We had dinner, and then Emma's friend showed up, and I was told to leave. Didn't even get to ask questions."

"Ahh," Rusty nodded. "Female solidarity. You'll get used to it."

"Female solidarity?" Killian groused. "What the bloody hell is that?"

"It's when something happens to one female, and all her friends have to rally around her. You'll be in the doghouse for a few days." Rusty grinned. "But it will pass. In the meantime, you can be my backup."

"I guess." Killian moved around on the hard seat, trying to get comfortable and yet appear relaxed. "What are we waiting for again?"

"A buy," Rusty sighed. "It's supposed to happen here sometime between ten and twelve."

"A buy?" Killian glanced around the room. While the crowd was different at night, it still seemed like a long shot. "What kind of buy?"

"A big one." Rusty lowered his voice. "Coke."

"Coke?" Killian laughed. "In Swan Harbor?"

"Shout it loud enough for the whole town to hear, will you?" Rusty retorted. "Yes, in Swan Harbor."

"Seriously?"

When Killian had worked in New York City, drugs were a part of the job. For some reason, though, he'd not thought about them being in Swan Harbor. If he had, it would have been cannabis cookies or brownies sold at school or sports bake sales. In a way, that made sense, especially since his and Rusty's cases were often bizarre. Panty thief, dog killer, cat thief, or bra thief— those he'd come to expect. Drugs, though, seemed almost too normal.

"Relax." Rusty leaned back in the booth and opened his newspaper, effectively shutting down the conversation.

Killian huffed, but with no reason to hurry home, leaned against the back of the booth, and waited.

What had gone wrong between Liam and Elsa? Was it something he had to worry about getting between him and Emma? They'd gone through a lot to be together, but since getting engaged, she refused to set a wedding date. Was he missing something that needed to be attended to?

"Head's up," Rusty murmured. "That could be our guy."

Killian refocused his attention and studied the individual Rusty had pointed out. He appeared to be in his early twenties, clean cut, dressed in jeans and flip-flops, but wearing an oversized trench coat. While a jacket usually wouldn't raise eyebrows in Swan Harbor, the temperatures lately had been too warm for so many layers.

"Stop staring at him," Rusty snapped, crinkling his newspaper as he turned the page. "We don't want him knowing we're on to him."

"Bloody hell, Rusty," Killian shot back. "I'm not a rookie."

"I'm well aware of that. But ..."

"Psst," the individual in question said, interrupting Rusty's reprimand.

Bloody hell, Killian thought, watching the young man unbutton his coat. *Does he have a gun?*

From the corner of his eye, Killian saw Rusty sit up straighter in his seat, as if he had similar thoughts.

"What do you need?" Killian made sure the butt of his gun was within easy reach.

"My, my," the kid said, looking around furtively. "My coke is crisp and cold." He sniffed. "Would you like some?"

His coke is crisp and cold? Why would announcing you had cold cocaine be a strong selling point?

"Cold coke?" asked Rusty.

"Sure." Their seller opened the right side of his coat. "See."

Killian's gaze flew to Rusty's, who was gawking at the inside of the man's coat. "*That's* the coke you're selling?"

"Shh," the man hissed. "I don't want everyone to know."

"But," Rusty gasped.

Killian relaxed his posture and sent the man a toothy grin. "What my friend is trying to ask is why are you selling coke inside The Beach Shack?"

"Come on, man." The seller slid onto the bench next to Rusty. "The owner of this dump doesn't like coke. Only sells that other stuff, so ... do you want some or not? I have Vanilla Coke, Cherry Coke, Orange Vanilla Coke, Lime Coke."

"No." Killian waved the man off. "I'm good. Rusty?" He tapped his partner's hand. "Coke?"

"Go." Rusty shook his head with disgust and flashed his badge. "Don't let us see you in here again."

Killian's cheeky comment faded when he saw who entered the building just as their 'coke seller' was leaving.

"Who's that with Hayden?" He tipped his head to where the younger man was standing, a brunette on one side, a blonde Killian knew, as Diane was on the other.

Rusty glanced across the room. "I think her name is Peyton. She works part-time at Sally's. Why?"

"I don't know," Killian murmured. "Something is going on with him. Just a gut feeling."

"You think it has to do with the company he's keeping?"

"I'd bet on it." Once Hayden had left, Killian slid out of the booth. "Now, it might be just me, but I think your tip was a bust."

"Stuff it," Rusty grumbled. "Let's go."

Killian followed Rusty out of The Beach Shack and waved him off. He needed to call Liam and let him know Elsa had arrived. Except based on the condition she'd arrived in and Liam's last comments, there was a disconnect somewhere. The question was, where?

New York City
O'Toole's
August 1
11:00 p.m.

LIAM STRETCHED HIS LONG LEGS UNDER THE TABLE AND TOOK A drink of his Guinness. This was more like it. Marissa, Candace, and Sherry on his right, and Penny and Kelly on his left. Women he'd been friends with forever, who expected no more from him than a little of his time. Just the way it should be.

If that's the truth, then why do you keep watching the door?

Just seeing who else is here.

Right.

Since he'd waved goodbye to Elsa, his inner voice was louder.

That's not quite what happened.

Shut up.

"Kim!" the women cried when a newcomer settled into the seat across from him.

"What have I missed?" Kim smiled at everyone. "Anything?"

"Liam ran Elsa off," Kelly stated.

"Off?" Kim frowned at Liam, then glanced back at Kelly. "As in, away from our group or …?"

"Off … as in, she moved out of New York," Penny added.

"But he won't say where," Marissa retorted, giving him a dirty look.

"Or why?" Candace offered her two cents.

"What did you do?" Kim tilted her head and pinned him with a blue-eyed stare that frightened most people.

"Why are you asking me?" Liam snapped. "I'm not the one who left."

"But you ran her off," Kim sighed. "I was afraid of this when I saw her in here with you the last time. You are such an ass."

When all the other women agreed with her, a feeling of consternation washed over Liam, but he wasn't sure why.

"How am I the ass?"

"It's just like Debi Monroe," Sherry whispered sadly.

"What the bloody hell do you know about Debi?" Liam barked.

"Barbi told us," Kim explained. "But I agree with Sherry. It's exactly like Debi."

Liam made a point of meeting each of the six women's eyes. "This is nothing like Debi."

"How can you say that?" Marissa hummed. "You pushed Debi away when she asked for more than you could give. Isn't that why Elsa left? Did she ask for more?"

"No!"

"No?" Candace echoed.

Elsa's comment about him figuring out why she was leaving still lingered in the back of his mind. Why had she gone?

"No," Liam repeated. "She didn't ask for more."

When the women exchanged looks, Liam had a creepy feeling they'd had an entire conversation. "What?"

"Another man," Kim nodded. "Has to be. Right, girls?"

"Another man?" He shrugged as if it was no big deal. "We're just friends." As soon as he uttered those words, the burning in the center of his chest started again. "Listen, while this conversation has been enlightening, I should go. Catch you all later."

Liam threw a few bills on the table and waved at several acquaintances on his way out. He could have stayed.

But you felt like you were missing something.

Like what? He'd been with friends.

Not the one you wanted.

Could there be merit in what they'd said about Elsa's leaving? Was there another man?

His phone buzzed, and when he realized it wasn't Elsa, disappointment rushed through him.

"Took you long enough," he answered, shoving his feelings aside.

"What are you talking about?" Killian exclaimed. "I'm not the one who cocked up."

Liam immediately went on the defensive. "How'd I cock up?"

"You called me, remember?"

"So, I did," Liam sighed. "Is she there?"

"Aye," Killian grunted. "Showed up a bit after 9:00 p.m., and my evening plans went pear-shaped."

Meaning she drove straight through, Liam decided, surprised as he knew how much she enjoyed meandering when on a road trip.

"But you like Elsa." Liam frowned. "How did she ruin your plans?"

"Let's just say my plans didn't include getting kicked out of my fiancée's home because you couldn't keep your girlfriend happy."

"She's not my girlfriend," Liam automatically corrected. "Except why do you say she was unhappy?"

"Oh, I don't know," Killian's dry tone came across loud and clear. "Perhaps it was the tears. But if she isn't your girlfriend, maybe she was crying over Tyler."

"Tyler?"

"Aye, Tyler," Killian repeated. "The bloke I thought Emma had a thing for last fall. Turns out it was Elsa who had a thing for him."

"Who the hell is Tyler?" Liam snapped, wondering why this was the first time he'd heard the name.

"Tyler James," Killian supplied. "Owns Siren's Song here in Swan Harbor. Nice enough looking, I guess. Maybe he's why Elsa was blubbering."

Elsa was crying? Why?

You know why.

"Maybe," Liam conceded. "Thanks for letting me know she arrived. I was worried about her driving that far alone."

Face it, man. You were worried about more than that.

Killian was quiet for several minutes, making Liam wonder what was going through his mind.

"I'll talk to you later. I'm getting another call."

"Don't be a cockwomble, Liam," Killian muttered before hanging up.

He wasn't being a cockwomble, was he? He was behaving the only way he knew how.

Are you sure about that?

Swan Harbor
Veterinarian Clinic
August 1
11:30 p.m.

Elsa heard whispering around her but didn't feel like opening her eyes to see who was in the room.

"Did she say anything?" someone whispered.

"No," Emma replied.

"Just came in, dropped on the sofa, and zonked out?" a second voice asked.

"Yes," Emma responded.

It was quiet for several minutes except for a moan here and there.

"She needs to open her eyes," the first voice murmured.

"Let her sleep," Emma came to her defense.

"But if she doesn't wake up soon," the second voice answered. "Her ice cream is going to melt."

"True," Emma agreed.

Elsa opened her eyes and immediately shut them again, when there were four pairs of green ones staring back at her. After a moment's hesitation, she tried again. Just as before, three human sets and one feline set watched her.

"Does everyone who lives in Swan Harbor have green eyes?"

"What?" Emma gave her a tub of ice cream.

"Green eyes," Elsa repeated, before digging into her ice cream.

It was quiet while she took several bites, and her brain added names to everyone. Sadie and Molly were voices one and two, and the feline was Millicent, Emma's cat.

"I'm sorry." Elsa shoved her hair behind her ear. "When I woke up, you were all staring at me with identical expressions. Plus, your eyes are all green."

"Well, to answer your question," Sadie smirked. "Only the women's eyes are green. The men all have blue eyes."

"Really?" Elsa frowned at Emma. "Killian's are blue?"

"Yes." Emma arched a brow. "Just like Liam's."

"Ouch," Elsa winced. "Way to bring the conversation to a screeching halt."

Emma shrugged. "Sorry. You've been asleep for several hours and—"

"We're dying to know what happened," Emma's friend Molly added.

"It can't wait until the morning?"

"No," Emma shook her head. "Remember what happened after the New Year's Ball?"

"I didn't make you talk," Elsa tried to give herself a way out.

"Come on, El," Emma scolded lightly. "You used that subtle guilt thing you do so well until I spilled, and you know what?"

"What?"

"I felt better, and everything happened as intended." Emma flashed her diamond engagement ring.

Elsa's thoughts spun as she crammed more of the ice cream into her mouth. "The guy wanted you ... and you wanted him."

"And you don't think Liam wants you?" Emma frowned. "Or did you move here for Tyler?"

"Tyler?" Sadie glanced at Molly, who shrugged. "Tyler James?"

"Yes." Emma nodded. "Tyler and Elsa met at summer camp when they were sixteen."

Sadie glanced back at Elsa. "Then what happened?"

"He was the first guy to touch her boob," Emma offered tongue-in-cheek.

"Emma!" Elsa cried. "Stop."

"You know, I can go on," Emma teased. "But El, you've acted weird since I saw you at my engagement party. Don't you think it's time to explain why?"

Could she?

"I've really made a mess of things," Elsa admitted. "Everything seemed to snowball, and ... here I am. In Swan Harbor, with no place to live, no job, and no boyfriend."

"This is going to be good," Molly grinned. "Anyone want chips and dip?"

"Reminds me of all those hen parties in college," snickered Emma.

"Me too." Elsa glanced toward the kitchen, where Molly and Sadie were giggling. "Looks like you've made some good friends here in Swan Harbor."

Emma laughed. "They're busybodies, just like you."

"You'd better believe it, sister." Sadie plopped down on the floor and crossed her legs. "Okay, Elsa, spill."

"It really started when Killian called and invited me to be a part of your proposal, and ... something inside broke."

"Broke?" Emma frowned. "I thought you were happy for me."

"No, no," Elsa apologized. "I'm incredibly happy for you. But something in *me* broke. It seems I wanted what you were getting. A man to love me, who wanted to spend his life with me."

"You didn't feel you had that with Liam?"

Elsa thought back on her relationship with Liam, "Putting a label on Liam and I was impossible. We were more than friends, but while his eyes and his actions said and did things *sometimes*, he promised nothing. After your engagement, I wanted those promises, and there were moments when I thought maybe, but ..."

"Is this where Tyler comes in?" Sadie asked softly.

Elsa felt a corner of her mouth quirk. "I won't deny that I looked the night of the engagement party."

"He is pretty fine," Sadie grinned. "But he didn't make your heart flip?"

"No."

"You've lost me, El." Emma reined the story back in. "We were talking at Sally's, and Liam walked up—"

"And I lied about having multiple job offers," Elsa admitted.

"You lied?" Emma grinned and repeated the statement, almost as if she couldn't believe what she'd heard.

"I know," Elsa acknowledged. "I don't lie."

"Nor lose your cool."

"And I did both."

"Then she stormed off," Emma added for Sadie's and Molly's sake. "Then Killian had to hold on to Liam to keep him from going after her."

"Really?" Elsa smiled. "He never told me that."

"It's the truth. But what happened while you were gone?"

"I ran into this quirky older gentleman and his dog."

"Captain Jack and Bandit?" guessed Sadie.

"Right." Elsa thought back to that night. "He told me I was lost, and he knew what I wanted."

"That sounds like Captain Jack." Sadie grinned. "Then what happened?"

"He led me back to the diner on a very circuitous route through Swan Harbor," Elsa murmured. "He told me that the heart wants what the heart wants, and I just had to listen. Then he took me to Sally's and introduced me to Tate Doolittle."

"Doctor Tate?" Sadie frowned. "I thought he retired."

"He did," Molly inserted. "But I heard the son was moving back home to take over. Right?" She looked to Elsa for confirmation.

"I'm guessing I met the son." Elsa hesitated a bit. "He looked to be in his forties or fifties and was talking to Ava."

"My mom?" A curious look crossed Emma's face. "Maybe he's her Flynn Ryder."

"Her Flynn Ryder?"

"Never mind." Emma waved away the question. "Go on with your story."

"Tate painted a picture of the perfect job, but I brushed it off. Then, Liam and I went back to the hotel ... and," her voice faded, unsure about continuing.

"And?" Emma prompted.

"My heart wanted, and I thought, this is it. Once back in New York City, though, everything changed."

"Wait," Sadie interrupted. "Are you saying before that night, you and Liam had never ...?"

"No," Elsa answered.

"Never?" Sadie prodded.

"No," Elsa sighed. "Maybe a little petting here and there. But our schedules were erratic, and I ..." She glanced sideways at Emma. "I'm cautious."

"Elsa prefers the once burned, twice shy attitude regarding men," Emma offered.

"But when the heart wants," grinned Sadie.

"I guess." Elsa hesitated to reorganize her thoughts. "In hindsight, I wish I hadn't listened. Maybe then I wouldn't be in this situation."

"I'm sorry, El," Emma murmured. "But what happened when you returned to New York?"

"I tried to play a con game and lost."

"A con game? With Liam?"

"Yes. I told Liam I wanted to move to Swan Harbor."

"What did Liam say?"

"He laughed." Elsa sniffed, remembering the conversation as if it were yesterday. "Told me I'd hate small town life and be on the first plane out."

"But how does he know that?"

"I don't know." Elsa glanced at the melting ice cream in her hands and sighed. "I even thought if I told him I was leaving, he'd ask me to stay."

"He didn't?"

"No."

"So now what?" Emma asked what Elsa was trying to figure out. "Do you want to go back to New York?"

The more Elsa thought about it, the more she knew she'd made the right choice. "No. I'm where I'm meant to be."

"How did you leave things with Liam?"

"I challenged him to figure out why I was moving." Elsa grinned. "Now, I need a plan."

"Lists are good." Emma snickered. "And you know how good I am with lists."

"Maybe I'll try it," Elsa decided. "Flying by the seat of my pants certainly didn't give me answers."

"Things will work out, Elsa," Sadie assured her. "You're in Swan Harbor now, where the heart always wins."

THREE

New York City
September 1
Early Morning

Liam slung his bag over his shoulder as he left his apartment. It was a warm day, yet something in the air said fall was just around the corner. And the new month reminded him he'd survived the first one without her.

It doesn't have to be this way.

Which wasn't quite the truth, because it did. He didn't know of any other way for it to be.

Since she'd been gone, his days were the same. Two days of twelve hours and a third of sixteen before having four days off. Those were the worst, as he found himself tempted to take a drive. But then what? He'd not changed, and if she'd found someone else, what was he supposed to do about it?

You tell her how you feel.

And that would be?

You lo ....

Liam's thoughts scattered when he glanced up to see a dark sedan heading directly for him. It roared past, giving him little time to jump back and press against a building.

Bloody hell, it was so close I could have reached out and touched it.

When it flew around the corner, Liam knew it was going to be bad even before he heard screams. He took off running toward the middle of the street, arriving in time to see the car plow through a group of people before disappearing.

"Paramedic! Let me through!" He noted three individuals down—two bicyclists and a pedestrian.

The agonized cry of a parent screaming, "Help my little girl! Please help my little girl!" had Liam changing directions and running toward a woman kneeling next to a fallen child.

"I'm Liam."

He dropped to his knees and did a cursory examination. While he would have preferred a fully loaded medical bag, he'd have to make do with the supplies he carried in his duffle.

"Let's see what we've got." Liam smiled at the mother and handed her his kit, thinking if he could keep her busy, she might remain calm. "How old is your little girl?"

"Seven," the mother sobbed. "Her birthday was in June."

Liam kept up a steady stream of innocuous questions, and the more the mother talked, the more he relaxed.

The ability to attend to several things at once alerted him of sirens in the distance. The police had also arrived to clear the traffic for the emergency vehicles. With that taken care of, he could focus on his patient.

She was lying on her side, her bike about four feet away. A pink helmet covered her head, but the impact with the street had pushed it up off her forehead, revealing pale blonde curls.

Just like Elsa's.

Her pulse was quick, and her breathing sounds were strong.

When Liam reached for his penlight, she moaned.

"What's her name?" he asked, while checking the child's pupils. Equal and reactive, another good sign.

"Daria. Her name is Daria."

The child whimpered and rolled over on her back, revealing blood and debris covering the left side of her face.

"It's alright, Daria." Then, needing something to remove the blood from the child's face, he pointed to the gauze pads. "Can you open those, love?"

The mother's hands were shaking so hard, it took her several minutes to get the package opened. "Sorry."

"You're fine." He dabbed gently at the little girl's cheek. "See that," he kept wiping at the blood, "it's just a little scrape."

The whimpers grew louder, and as he tossed one pad away and picked up another, Daria opened her eyes. Seeing her large, tear-filled blue eyes felt like a knife to his heart.

Elsa's eyes.

"Can you tell me where it hurts?"

"My arm," Daria tried to lift her left one and grimaced.

The unnatural way it moved told a story he was sure X-rays would confirm. She'd broken her upper arm and would wear a large cast for quite some time.

"I need you to keep it still, alright?" Liam laid it across her stomach. "Can you do that for me?"

"Hurts," Daria cried.

"I know, sweetheart. We'll get you to the hospital and they'll take care of you. Here they come now."

Liam glanced up to see Wade, Seth, and Rocco, men he trusted, rushing toward him with the stretcher.

"What do we have, Reade?"

He rattled off his findings regarding Daria's condition, but every time he tried to step back, the little girl clung to his arm.

"Go with me, please!"

"Alright." Liam took her right hand and laid it on top of her left. "Help me hold your arm still."

"Okay."

He could tell she was tough. Her lower lip trembled, and a few tears trickled from the corners of her eyes, but that was it.

"Ready?" Liam smiled at her as Seth and Wade transferred her to the stretcher and wheeled it to the ambulance. "Won't be long now."

He, Wade and Daria's mom climbed into the back, while Seth and Rocco hopped into the front.

As they rode the few blocks to Queen's Court, Liam couldn't stop wishing that Elsa was waiting at the hospital. The little girl deserved the best ... and damn if the best hadn't moved to Swan Harbor.

Swan Harbor
Elsa's Pediatric Practice
September 1
4:00 p.m.

Elsa glanced at the clock to see she'd been on hold for roughly twenty minutes, and she had a patient due anytime.

"Last patient is in room one," Audrey, her nurse of two weeks, reminded her. "Want to trade?"

"Sure." Elsa pointed to the boxes on her desk. "All we need is to exchange those adult tongue depressors for the pediatric ones. Shouldn't be that hard, right?"

"You wouldn't think so," Audrey agreed. "Need anything else after I take care of this?"

"I don't think so," Elsa replied. "You've been a huge help. Thanks."

"No problem."

She'd first met her nurse one afternoon while eating lunch at Sally's Diner. Emma had introduced her to Audrey, and one thing led to another.

With Audrey taking care of the medical supply problem, Elsa turned to her patient. She pulled the folder from the pocket next to the door and flipped it open.

Crap.

Bethany James.

Crap

In the month she'd been in Swan Harbor, she'd been lucky enough not to run into Tyler.

That's not quite true.

Okay, it wasn't the whole truth. She'd been on the lookout for him and made a point of going in another direction several times. Although, exactly why, she wasn't sure.

With a little lift of her chin, Elsa breezed into treatment room one. "Hello. I'm Doctor Elsa."

"You're pretty," the little girl giggled.

"And so are you."

The little girl's long dark hair and big brown eyes showed her to be her father's daughter.

"What brings you to the clinic?" she asked Tyler, working to maintain a neutral voice.

"Elsa, it's nice to see you again."

His eyes were just as dark and expressive as she remembered. And the slight drawl in his voice was still as smooth as butter.

"Tyler." Elsa tried again when he appeared to be lost in thought. "Bethany?"

"Sorry." He blinked several times as if to clear the cobwebs. "Runny nose, fever, a cough, and she's been tugging at her right ear," he rattled off typical symptoms.

"Okay, Ms. Bethany." Elsa picked up her stethoscope. "Can I listen to your heart?"

The little girl studied her with serious eyes for several seconds. "You can listen to Lila's first." She held up her stuffed kitten.

"Okay." Elsa placed the stethoscope on the stuffed animal's chest. "Listen closely. Thump-thump. Thump-thump."

Bethany giggled as Elsa had hoped and pulled the kitten away. "Now, my turn."

Elsa quickly checked the little girl's heart, throat, and ears.

"Does Bethany have a history of ear infections?"

"N-No."

"That's good, and all looks clear now."

"Lila's too?" Bethany held up the kitten for its ears to be checked.

"Of course."

But when she found nothing out of the ordinary, it caused her to wonder. Had Tyler really needed to bring the little girl in for a visit? Or was that an excuse?

"Just keep doing what you're doing," Elsa murmured, when walking Tyler and Bethany to the front of the clinic. "Give the office a call if she gets worse."

"Okay." Tyler knelt in front of Bethany. "Punkin, can you play with Lila for a second and let me talk to Doctor Elsa?"

Bethany tilted her head, and the look on her face was much more mature than one would expect from a four-year-old. "Sure, Daddy."

They took several steps away from the little girl before Tyler got to the point.

"I have a confession."

"Bethany isn't really sick." The surprise on Tyler's face had her chuckling. "I've been doing this a while."

"She liked you." Tyler smiled indulgently. "I'm glad."

"Was that why you brought her in? To see if she liked me?"

His dark eyes, surrounded by thick black lashes, once had the power to turn her inside out. But as their gazes held, her conversations with her friends were there, hanging out on the edges of her consciousness. Did he still have control over her heart, or did it only belong to Liam?

A ruddy hue dotted his cheekbones. "I think it's past time we talked, don't you?"

There had been a period in her life when she'd wanted nothing more than to hear those words. The longer she was in Swan Harbor, though, the more she realized her future wasn't on a map waiting for her to step into it.

Her future was under her control. It was hers to choose, to investigate and mold into what she wanted. While running from the tough conversations might be easiest, that wouldn't get her what she wanted. She had to be ready to let go of the past before she could move forward.

"I'd like that."

"Can I come by later tonight? Maybe around 8:30 p.m., after I get Beth to bed. I'm sure Lois and Rupert wouldn't mind staying with her for an hour or so."

"You know where I live?"

Tyler laughed. "It's Swan Harbor. Everyone knows where you live."

New York City
Queen's Court Medical
September 1

5:00 p.m.

NINE HOURS INTO HIS SHIFT, LIAM WAS SITTING IN THE DAYROOM, mindlessly scrolling through his social media. While he'd been busy, there hadn't been time for him to think about the events from earlier in the day. But with it quiet, his brain kept trying to connect dots in a way only it seemed to understand.

He'd returned to the EMS break room after leaving Daria and her mother with the pediatric orthopedist, to find two NYPD officers waiting for him. They'd asked multiple questions about the hit-and-run episode. Questions he'd not considered abnormal. However, after examining the overall tone of the officer's questions, a shiver slid up his spine.

"Are you telling me," Officer Brody asked, *"the dark sedan was aiming directly for you?"*

And then later in the conversation.

Officer Stevens asked, "Can you think of any reason someone might want to cause you harm?"

Him, no. Except was there a possibility someone could connect him to Ian Jones? That made his blood run cold. What should he do?

Protect your family.

He pulled out his phone and called Killian. It took several rings before his brother answered.

"Have you decided you're tired of being a cockwomble and are coming to claim your woman?" Killian quipped.

"Is that any way to greet your favorite brother?"

"You're my only brother," Killian pointed out. "And according to my fiancée, you're still in the doghouse."

"Emma's still mad at me?" Then because he couldn't help himself, broke down and asked, "How is Elsa? Is she working?"

Killian hesitated, and Liam waited for his brother's cheeky response.

"What do you want to hear, Liam?" Killian asked carefully. "Do you want me to tell you she's doing fine, and I've seen her out with several men? Or would you rather hear she still spends evenings with Emma, Sadie, and Molly, where they have quite the man-bashing time?"

"I don't know," Liam muttered. "But she's working, right? I hate the thought of her not being able to work."

"She's working," Killian volunteered. "Elsa isn't why you called, though. What's going on?"

"Are you sure about that?"

"I'm sure." Suddenly, a light went off in Killian's head. "Bloody hell, Liam! This has to do with what we talked about when you were here in June, right?"

"To be honest, I don't know," Liam admitted. "But hell, Killian. You're—"

"I'm law enforcement."

"Yes."

It had been three months since Liam learned someone Killian helped put in prison was looking for a way out. That could mean ....

"Tell me what happened."

Killian's straight-forward statement had Liam retelling the story. As he told it, he had to admit how paranoid he sounded.

"I'm sorry." Liam suddenly felt like the wanker his brother always accused him of being. "I must sound ridiculous."

"No," Killian assured him. "It's better to be safe. But remember, my undercover persona was Ian Jones, and he died in a fiery car crash. Only my captain knows I'm not really dead."

"If you say so, little brother," Liam grumbled. "When Officer Stevens asked if there was any reason someone would want to hurt me—"

"You immediately thought of me."

The disgust in Killian's voice was not something that had popped up lately, making Liam feel even more like a git for calling.

"Killian, this isn't your fault." Liam pointed out.

As an undercover officer with the NYPD for the better part of ten years, his younger brother had seen the seedier side of life. After moving to Swan Harbor and meeting Emma Foster, Killian had undergone a transformation. He'd found the better side of himself, and got the girl too.

"Well," Killian snapped, "if it's not my fault, whose is it?"

Liam took a deep breath and tried again. "Killian, I'm sorry. Kiss your pretty lady for me, and I'll let you know if I hear anything else."

"Wait, Liam. Don't go asking questions. Let me do some digging and I'll get back to you, alright?"

"Okay, but ..."

"I will, Liam," Killian promised. "I'll keep an eye on Elsa and Emma. Later."

Liam shoved his phone into his pocket, wishing he weren't thinking what he was thinking. But sometimes that sixth sense was a lot wiser than you thought.

Swan Harbor
Sheriff's Department
September 1
5:15 p.m.

KILLIAN SAID GOODBYE TO CAPTAIN WEAVER AND FOUGHT NOT TO throw his phone across the room.

"It's obvious you're holding onto your temper by a thread, so you might as well spill," his boss, Dylan Prince remarked.

"I heard part of your conversation," Rusty offered. "It seems there are one or two holes in the Killian Reade story."

"Aye, Mate," Killian winced. "Sorry about that. Might as well have a seat, Dylan, and I'll fill you both in at the same time."

Dylan's blue eyes clashed with his, and Killian wanted to kick his own arse. He should have known he'd not been able to run from everything that had happened.

"I worked undercover with the NYPD for almost ten years," Killian began. "In the beginning, the cases were simple, mostly drugs. Without this," he rubbed his hand across his jaw, sporting a few days' worth of scruff, "I looked young enough and easily mingled with the college kids. But I grew bored and started begging my lieutenant for the tougher assignments."

"Violet's case?" Dylan asked quietly.

"Hers came later," Killian explained, and then added for Rusty's benefit. "Violet was the little girl caught in the crossfire in my last case."

"Something tells me you haven't completely put that case to rest," Rusty guessed.

"You could say that," Killian agreed.

"Spit it out Killian," Dylan prodded. "Stretching out the story doesn't make it go away."

That he knew, as he'd tried to run from it for months. Until Emma. She'd given him a reason to change.

"Santora Callandra." Killian glanced back and forth between Dylan and Rusty. "Sound familiar?"

Rusty whistled. "When you do something, you don't do it halfway, do you?"

Killian's brows arched with surprise. "You know of Santora Callandra?"

"I may just be a lowly deputy in Swan Harbor," Rusty retorted. "But I do know a few things that happen outside our sleepy little town. Let me guess, Santora's out on bail."

"Not yet," Killian growled. "But his lawyers are trying to get the case tossed out on some cocked-up technicality."

"Damn," Dylan barked. "Does Weaver think it's a possibility?"

"He's like us," Killian sighed. "Hopes not, but realizes sometimes the good guys often need a little help, and a lot of luck, to come out on top."

"And what about your real identity?" Dylan asked. "Does he think there's any way for those dots to be connected?"

"That's what Liam's worried about," Killian answered. "Weaver tried to assure me my identity was safe, but I don't much care to leave things to chance."

"And neither do I," Dylan sighed. "But this is Swan Harbor. Strangers stand out—"

"Bloody hell, Dylan!" Killian interrupted. "There are still quite a few strangers sitting out there on our beaches."

"I'm aware of that," the Sheriff tipped his head in acknowledgment. "But we'll do our homework."

"This is Santora Callandra!" Killian barked. "One person lost their life because of me. I'll not have it happening again."

"Killian!" Rusty stood so quickly he knocked his desk chair over. "You're not the only one whose life a monster turned upside down. We'll get him, but only if we stay one step ahead of him."

There was a tone in Rusty's voice Killian had never heard before. So much so, it broke through his anger, and when he glanced into his partner's eyes, he could see the pain that was usually hidden.

"Who, Rusty?" Killian glanced at Dylan before returning to his partner. "Who did Santora take from you?"

Rusty righted his chair and dropped back onto it. "Wasn't Santora. But someone cut from the same cloth took my wife and daughter. Never again on my watch."

Dylan pinned his hard stare on both Killian and Rusty. "Do not ... I'll say it again ... do not go off half-cocked. We do this together. Do you hear me?"

Killian's jaw hurt from clenching his teeth.

"Aye."

He wouldn't go off half-cocked, but he also would do everything in his power to make sure his family and his town were safe.

FOUR

Swan Harbor
Elsa's Cottage
September 1
8:30 p.m.

ELSA WAS RUNNING LATE, SOMETHING SHE HATED—ESPECIALLY when she expected company. She'd just tossed her keys on the table when her phone buzzed.

> Emma: How did today go?

> Elsa: Today? Fine, why?

> Emma: Fine? Really?

Elsa frowned, feeling like she'd jumped into the middle of a conversation.

> Elsa: Why wouldn't it have been fine?

> Emma: Oh, maybe because you saw Tyler.

Crap.

Elsa: You know, there's such a thing as patient confidentiality.

Emma: Ha! This is Swan Harbor. Gossip often travels faster than cell service.

Elsa: It was actually okay seeing him. Our talks have helped. But how did you know?

Emma: Audrey mentioned it to Leroy, who mentioned it to Sadie, who told me.

Elsa couldn't help but chuckle at how her friend, Emma I-don't-let-people-close Foster, had changed so completely. She was no longer willing to allow life to pass by, and had jumped smack dab in the middle.

"And seems bound and determined to bring me along with her."

Elsa: That's some gossip chain you've got going there.

Emma: Oh, that's nothing. Wait till I tell you how I found out Tyler's on his way over right now.

Elsa: What?!

Emma: Yep. Hope you're ready for him, because he just turned onto your street.

Crap.

When she peered out her front window, she saw he'd just pulled into her driveway.

Elsa: They're good. He's here.

Emma: I'll expect details.

Elsa: Yes, Mother.

Something told Elsa that as soon as Tyler left, she'd be bombarded with questions.

She'd barely had time to wonder if she was ready when Tyler knocked.

"Hi," Elsa pushed open the screen door wide enough for him to enter. "How's Bethany?"

Tyler smiled, "She's fine. Listen, I'm ... sorry for making up an excuse to see you. I've just ..."

"It's okay," Elsa replied. "I was afraid it was going to be awkward, too."

"Is that why you've gone out of your way to avoid me since you moved to Swan Harbor?"

Elsa winced. "Noticed that, did you?"

Tyler grinned. "Well, Swan Harbor is a small town."

"I'm just now learning how small," Elsa laughed. "I heard you were on your way just before you pulled into the driveway."

"That doesn't surprise me. I'm sure it started with Lois and moved out from there."

Elsa thought about sharing who'd told her about his arrival. In the end, she decided those nerves racing around inside needed to be settled.

"Are you thirsty? Would you like a glass of lemonade?"

"You don't have—"

"No, no, it's okay. I'll be right back."

Once in the kitchen, though, she felt silly and hurried to return to the living room.

"Not that I don't enjoy catching up," Elsa decided to get right to the point. "But in my office earlier, I got the feeling you wanted to talk about something specific."

Tyler bent over, dropped his elbows on his knees, and clasped his hands together.

He's nervous. Why is he nervous?

"Why did you move here?" he blurted.

"What?"

"Did you move to Swan Harbor because of me?"

"Because of you?" Elsa echoed. "No Tyler. I can honestly say I didn't move here because of you." He relaxed, and Elsa grew even more confused. "Tyler, what's going on?"

"What do you know about my wife?"

"I know she died." Elsa shrugged. "And based on Beth's age, you had to be with her when we met in Illinois."

Tyler sighed. "Kara and I were dating, but I thought she knew I wasn't interested in doing serious. And then I saw you again, and I realized there was still something between us. When I went back home, Kara told me she was pregnant."

Elsa hissed. "Ouch."

"Yeah."

He brushed his hand through his hair and Elsa had to turn her head and blink away the tears. The motion reminded her of Liam, something she didn't want to get into with Tyler.

"We got married and Kara developed pre-eclampsia. But ..."

His voice faded, and a series of expressions crossed his face Elsa couldn't interpret.

"She didn't tell me how dangerous the diagnosis was," he continued. "When she went into labor ..."

A sense of profound loss flowed through Elsa at everything he and Bethany had gone through.

"Kara hemorrhaged, didn't she?"

"Yeah." Tyler stood and wandered around the room. "I hated her for so long," he admitted softly. "Blamed her for screwing up my life, Beth's, and then you were here and I ..."

"You what?"

She'd heard stories of where a wife dies in childbirth and the husband blamed himself. Possibly survivors' guilt—something not uncommon in situations such as his.

"When I saw you at Emma and Killian's party, you looked happy. Were you?"

"Yes." She hesitated a beat, wondering how much to say. "And then Tate offered me an amazing opportunity. It was so good, I couldn't turn it down."

"And the guy?"

"Liam is back in New York."

"Do you love him?"

"Why does it matter?"

"You deserve happiness." His dark eyes seemed to scrutinize every movement, and Elsa fought to maintain a neutral expression. "I want you to be happy."

"And if I had moved here for you?" Elsa watched the color drain from his face. "You don't think you could make me happy?"

"Oh, Elsa. I wish. But you deserve so much more than I can give anyone right now. I need to focus on Beth."

"I see that. You can rest easy, though. I didn't move here for you."

"Good."

Elsa frowned. "I feel like that should offend me."

"Sorry." He grinned, and she got a glimpse of that sixteen-year-old boy she'd met so long ago. "But you never answered the question. Do you love Liam?"

"He doesn't love me," she replied instead.

"Bull ... hockey," he spit out.

She giggled. "What is bull hockey?"

"Cuss words without cuss words," he laughed. "And your man loves you. He's just afraid."

"And you know this because?"

"I've seen the same expression when I look in my mirror," Tyler admitted.

"I'm good," Elsa murmured, but then silently added, *for now.* She missed Liam. Missed what they had, and wasn't sure about the next step.

"Friends?" Tyler offered hesitantly.

She could admit there were benefits to having a male friend. Especially one who expected nothing from her.

"Friends," she agreed.

"Good."

He stood and pulled her up with him. As soon as the thought, *Liam has a few inches on him* appeared, Elsa realized she was truly over Tyler James.

"Let me walk you out."

Tyler opened the door and gave her a crooked smile. "Think Paula's peering through her curtains across the street?"

"I'd bet on it." Elsa laughed. "Take care, Tyler."

He ran down the steps and waved and, just as she'd anticipated, her phone buzzed before he'd even started his car.

> Emma: How did it go?

※

New York City
Queen's Court Medical Center
September 1
11:30 p.m.

Liam tossed his dirty uniform shirt in his locker and pulled on a clean t-shirt. He'd reached for his duffle, when Tim, the new rookie firefighter/paramedic he worked with, yelled, "Liam, line 1."

"Who is it?" Liam snapped. "I'm on my way out."

"Doctor White, from the Emergency Department."

"And you couldn't help him?"

"Didn't want me," Tim shrugged. "Asked for you."

"Alright," Liam grabbed the phone and hit one with a little more force than needed. "Yeah!"

"Know Joe Stevens?" Randy White asked with no preamble.

"No," Liam denied. "Should I?"

"You sure? Officer Joe Stevens?"

"Did you just say Officer Joe Stevens?"

"Yes." Liam could hear someone shouting for Randy's attention and he quickly yelled 'hold him,' before returning to the line. "He's in my ED. GSW to the chest. Pneumothorax, but won't allow my team to treat him until he talks to you. Can you come?"

"On my way!"

Liam hung up, slammed his locker, and took off running.

Officer Stevens.

With the locker room on the second floor, Liam sprinted down the stairs, raced down the hall and through the lobby.

Officer Stevens, of the *'Can you think of any reason someone might want to cause you harm?'*

He used his identification card to get through a set of electronic doors and then took a shortcut through the billing office.

Gunshot wound to the chest.

Another set of electronic doors took him through the volunteer's office.

Pneumothorax. A collapsed lung.

Liam burst through the doors into the Emergency Department. "White?" he barked when someone stepped in his way.

"Bay four," they responded.

Randy White was waiting for him just outside the room.

"Get the information he has for you and get out of our way. He should already be in surgery."

"Sorry, Doc," Liam murmured, trying to see into the room. "I've no idea what he wants to tell me. What about his partner? Officer Brody."

"Already in surgery. You've got five."

Liam stepped into the space where Joe Stevens lay. There were bloody towels on his chest, an oxygen mask covered his face, and a nearby monitor tracked his vitals.

"Joe," he whispered. "It's Liam. What do you need to tell me?"

Joe's eyes fluttered. "You," it sounded like he said.

"Yes, me. It's Liam," he repeated. "What is it?"

"Know."

Was I right?

"Know what? Or is it who?"

"In. Watch Joe."

Before he could say more, an alarm sounded, and the blood pressure cuff automatically inflated.

"Pressure's dropping," Liam replied when Doctor White rushed into the room.

"Sorry, Reade. He's done for now. I'll page you when he wakes up."

"Thanks, Doc."

Liam stood out of the way as they rushed past him, pushing the injured man toward the operating rooms.

What was Joe trying to tell him? Know. In, and watch Joe.

Did Joe know more? Or did his partner know anything?

His steps were much slower on his return to the locker room. He grabbed his duffle and walked outside. It had been over seventeen hours since he'd arrived in the ambulance with Daria. Somehow, though, it seemed much longer.

Liam left the hospital grounds, crossed Broadway and started toward 86th Street. With every step, events from the day replayed in his head. It wasn't until he started toward 79th Street he heard footsteps.

His sixth sense shouted *run*, but if he were imagining things ....

He quickened his pace, and crossed 79th, walking toward 72nd. When he did so, the footsteps grew louder, more measured.

"Screw the lovely walk." Liam veered left, and headed toward the subway on 72nd and Central Park West.

He ran down the stairs, landing on the platform just as the announcement for the doors to close began. With a quick glance over his shoulder, Liam dove onto the train and ducked below the window. As the last signal was heard and they started moving, he peered out again to see a male, dressed in an over-sized coat, staring at the moving vehicle.

Damn!

The faster the train moved, the more his adrenaline flowed. But the years of being the brother of an undercover officer woke up enough for him to decide his next move.

Off one line, back on another. Liam spent several minutes taking a round-about way to the 86th station where he could jump off. But then he found himself out in the open while he jogged the rest of the way to his apartment building.

However, once there, he didn't completely feel safe until he reached his apartment and saw the piece of white thread in the door. It had become habit while Killian worked undercover, but he hadn't thought about it in years. Was his sixth sense working on overdrive even before the incident with Daria? Had that been why he'd made a point of adding it before leaving for work earlier in the day?

Liam entered his apartment, glad Barbi and Justin were back in their own place. He was still worried, though.

Elsa.

Of course. However, but he was also worried about Killian, Emma, and his father.

Stop! You know Killian will take care of Emma, but you want to take care of Elsa.

How? She's in Swan Harbor ....

Go to her.

Could he?

Don't you want to?

If he went to Swan Harbor, was he bringing the danger with him?

You know how to prevent that. Killian taught you well. Go to her.

He could admit he missed her. It was the next step he wasn't willing to take.

Face it, you won't rest until ....

Liam sent a quick text to alert Killian.

Liam: We need to talk. I'm heading your way.

Or should he wait? Would the morning allow a fresh perspective?

Swan Harbor
Elsa's Cottage
September 2
2:30 a.m.

Elsa groaned and turned over, trying to fall back to sleep. The shadows grew darker, swirling around her. But no matter what she did, the fog was still there.

She couldn't see or hear anything specific, just knew something or someone threatened. *That*, she could feel.

It took time, but slowly, the fog faded, and she could focus on the figure. The person became clearer—sharper, until finally, she could see that it wasn't a woman but a man. Who was he? Why was he running? More importantly, why was he in her dream?

Come, she tried to tell him. *Maybe I can help.*

His fear was palpable, yet he never stopped. Was he running toward something, or away?

Hurry, hurry. Let me help.

The fog continued to disburse, allowing her to see his face. If she tried, she could touch him.

You came.

You knew I would. Didn't you?

I hoped you would.

I'm ....

Just as their fingers touched, a car rushed toward him, and he disappeared.

"LIAM!"

Elsa sat straight up, her face wet from tears and her heart racing. "Just a dream. It was only a dream."

Her phone said it was just after 2:30 a.m., but she knew she wouldn't be able to go back to sleep. Instead of tossing and turning, Elsa untangled the blanket and slipped from bed.

The cold floor had her grabbing the afghan her mother made and going to the kitchen.

While she waited for her hot chocolate to heat, parts of the dream played over and over. What had it meant? Was Liam in trouble? Or had her talk with Tyler brought thoughts she'd pushed away back to the forefront of her mind?

She poured her hot chocolate into a travel mug, wrapped the afghan around her, and settled in a papasan chair on the veranda. Her little cottage sat on a slight incline, with the back giving a partial view of the sea and the town, and she could usually choose what to watch.

Except tonight. There were too many thoughts cluttering her mind.

Did you doubt?

Tyler said Liam had feelings for her. So did Emma. That was something she could agree on. He felt something. What, though, was anyone's guess. Were his feelings for her the same as for his other women friends? Or was it something deeper as she'd begun to suspect? Was it he refused to allow himself to love?

But she wanted more. She wanted ....

A twig snapped, causing her heart to jump, and goosebumps skated across her skin. Then a shadow moved, and Elsa's pulse raced.

It's just a wild animal, she tried to convince herself.

When her pulse refused to slow down, Elsa grabbed her mug, slipped into the house, and locked the door behind her.

She peered around the curtain, and the hairs on the back of her neck stood up. While the shadows didn't seem as wide, she couldn't be sure. The quiet quickly gave way to a nearby dog barking, cause her goosebumps to spread. Then another dog barked, and another, each one just a little farther away.

She needed ....

Liam.

An alarm. That's what she needed ... just an alarm.

FIVE

Swan Harbor
Veterinarian Clinic
September 2
7:00 a.m.

Emma opened her eyes to find Millicent standing on her chest.

"It's too early," she groaned, rolling over to go back to sleep.

Not surprisingly, Millicent pushed her head against Emma several more times as if to say, *Get up. Get up now.*

"You're not going to let me go back to sleep, are you?"

Millicent's stare had Emma rolling out of bed. As soon as she did, the cat burrowed under the covers and closed her eyes.

"Aren't you hungry?" she tried once more.

The cat opened an eye, then promptly closed it again. Her message came through loud and clear. It said, *Go away.*

"Spoilsport."

Since her pet didn't need anything right then, Emma went looking for Killian. She found him sitting at the kitchen table, with a pastry and cup of coffee from Paula's in front of him. He was on the phone, and his fingers were in constant motion.

"Not sure," he said to whomever was on the other end.

But their answer wasn't to his liking, as the longer he listened, the more he frowned.

"Maybe ten minutes or so. Could have been longer."

There was a tenseness in his voice that woke her worry meter. She started toward him, hoping he'd pull her down onto his lap.

"Killian? Is everything okay?"

"Hold on," he said into the phone. "Morning, Doc. You're up early." Killian smoothly slid out of the chair and seated her before she realized what was happening. Then he gave her a cinnamon bun and murmured, "I'll be right back," and disappeared down the stairs.

"What the heck was that?"

Emma couldn't remember him ever leaving the room when he'd been on the phone for work. Unless she was doing something that required concentration. Never just to let her eat.

She couldn't be sure it didn't have to do with a new case. After all, it was the end of summer and the tourists hadn't all gone home. Except something told her if it were a case, she would know. He talked about work all the time.

Or at least he talked about the people at the office. Dylan's complaints about work still being done to their house. Amy's budding romance with Shawn. Rusty's comments about Roland learning to ride or something about Rene's position as the mayor.

Emma tore into her roll a little more and decided she'd push her *'Let's share our burdens boyfriend'* harder. Perhaps if she used a different tactic, the outcome might be more to her liking. She'd been saving a few items from the *Rebecca's Fantasy* catalog that might distract him.

"Sometimes a girl has to take things into her own hands."

Emma tossed out the wrappings and grabbed a piece of paper.

Thank you for the pastry. Follow the clothing to find me, and be prepared to 'bare all your burdens.'

Your loving Fiancée

Emma left the note in the center of the table, along with her sleep shorts. She dropped her shirt in the bedroom doorway, and ....

❧⚮❧

Swan Harbor General
September 2
2:00 p.m.

ELSA RUSHED INTO THE EMERGENCY DEPARTMENT OF SWAN Harbor General and scanned the room. After the panicked call she'd received from Rene Langley, she wasn't sure what to expect, but wanted to be there for both mother and son. Which was how she'd always imagined practicing in a small town would be like. Why didn't Liam understand that?

Perhaps it's because you've never told him.

Hush!

You just want everything to be his fault.

"Roland Langley," she murmured to the volunteer sitting at the desk, ignoring her inner voice's last comment.

The perky brunette grinned. "He's in bay 3."

"Thanks."

Elsa found seven-year-old Roland sitting on a stretcher with an ice pack wrapped around his left wrist.

"Doctor Elsa!" Roland exclaimed. "Look what I did!"

He winced when he attempted to lift his arm to show her, and his big, brown eyes filled with tears.

"That looks like it hurts," Elsa murmured softly.

"Yeah, it does. Especially if I do this." Once again, he tried to move it.

"Hmm, maybe you shouldn't move it then." Rene gently ruffled his black curls before turning her attention to Elsa. "Thanks for coming. I hope you didn't have to rearrange too many things."

"No, I'm good." Elsa smiled. "I'm trying to keep Fridays flexible. Who's going to tell me how this happened?"

Rene sent Roland a pointed look. "Would you like to share?"

"I was just trying to put Ruari's headstall on like Maggie does." He shrugged his bony shoulders. "But the horse got mad."

"Ruari is your horse?"

"Well, technically, he's Maggie's." Rene went on to explain that the horse's previous owner had abused him.

"Ruari didn't like it when you tried to do what Maggie does, huh?"

"No." Roland quirked one corner of his mouth, causing his deep dimples to pop. "I didn't mean to make him mad, mama."

"I know." Rene tugged him close for a hug. "But sometimes, especially with animals, we have to be patient and wait until they trust us."

"Yeah," he mumbled. "That's what Maggie said when I asked her if I could put Ruari's headstall on yesterday."

"Oh, she did, did she?"

"Yes, mama," Roland replied just as Doctor Pearl Houston pushed back the curtain.

"Elsa." Pearl's twinkling blue eyes met hers across the top of Roland's head. "What brings you to my neck of the woods?"

"She came to check on me," Roland offered.

"He's right," laughed Elsa. "Rene called, so I came to lend moral support. Are those the X-rays?"

"They are." Pearl pulled the film from the envelope. "And just as I suspected—"

"I broke it," Roland mumbled.

"You did," Pearl confirmed. "But the good news is, it's a clean break of one bone in your wrist. We'll put a cast on your arm, and before you know it, you'll be good as new."

"I guess." Roland dropped his eyes, disgust written all over his face.

"What's wrong, Ro?" Rene asked him. "I thought you'd be excited to show off your cast when school starts next week."

Roland sighed. "It's not as cool as when Ethan broke his. He broke two bones."

"True," Pearl agreed. "He did. But when that happened, I didn't have glow in the dark casts."

"Really?" His eyes sparkled. "I'm ready then."

Pearl helped Roland transfer to the wheelchair and told Rene where they would be. "We won't be long."

"And that's my cue to call Rusty," Rene winced. "I'm surprised he hasn't shown up already."

Elsa bit her lip. "I'm sorry, but that's my fault."

"Your fault?" Rene frowned. "How?"

"I had a weird dream early this morning and then thought I saw someone watching my house. It freaked me out."

"I can imagine." Rene shuddered. "So Rusty and Killian were at your place?"

"They were. I asked Killian for the name of an alarm company, and he and Rusty came by to check things out."

"Let me know what happens. The idea of being watched is scary."

"Tell me about it." Elsa shivered. "I still haven't gotten rid of the goosebumps."

They separated, with Rene heading outside to call Rusty and Elsa in the opposite direction. She stepped through a set of double doors and looked up just as Liam entered the lobby.

Crap!

Elsa scooted behind a giant pillar and peeked around. Yes. It was Liam.

Why is he here?

Maybe for you?

Why didn't he call?

Ask.

Before she could do anything, she needed help and called Emma.

"Elsa?"

"Liam's here."

"Liam's where?" Emma asked. "And why are you whispering?"

Elsa peered around the pillar again. "I'm at the hospital."

"Okay." She could picture Emma nodding along. "And you called me because?"

"What should I say to him?"

In the background, she could hear Emma asking Sadie for advice.

"Tell him hi and ask him why he's in town," Emma repeated Sadie's words.

"That's it? After not seeing or talking to him for a month, I just say hi?"

"Sure."

"I could have come up with *that* on my own."

"Sorry." Except the apology didn't sound too apologetic. "You're still meeting us at Sally's for dinner, right?"

"Yes."

"Good." Emma giggled. "Invite Liam."

"Wait, what—?"

The line went dead before she could finish her question.

You've run into him in a hospital before. You can do this.

Had she ever hidden from him?

No. In fact, just the opposite. Even more so when she knew what might happen once they were alone.

New York City
Queen's Court General Hospital
Eight Months Earlier
January 10

IT'S HER, LIAM REALIZED, WHEN ELSA STEPPED FROM A ROOM AND turned toward him. While he hadn't seen her since New Year's Day, he hadn't stopped thinking about her. The way she'd looked that night lingered in his mind. Just as the memory of how right it felt to hold her in his arms did.

As they drew closer to each other, he worried about what to say. It wasn't until they met in the center of the hallway, and her bright blue eyes met his, he knew to say.

"Have a few, Doctor Winters?"

Elsa tilted her head, and a sexy little smile played along her lips.

"A few what, Lieutenant Reade?"

"Minutes."

He tugged her down a corridor until he located an empty room.

"I might have a few. Do you need something?"

A million suggestive thoughts flew in and out of his head, but none seemed appropriate just then.

Liam took her hand and tugged her against him.

"Just this."

He kissed her lightly, then hovered just above her mouth, waiting to see if she'd meet him halfway. Her pupils widened in the shadowy room and their breaths mingled. They stood there longer than a second as he counted heartbeats, wanting nothing more than her kiss. Finally, just before he'd given up, she took the extra step and their mouths met.

Elsa tangled her fingers in his uniform shirt, working to get closer and let him in.

Time ceased to matter as their mouths mated in a way that said, 'I've been waiting for this.'

Liam tightened his arms, pulling her thin frame closer, so close her stethoscope dug into his chest. Except he didn't care. Her lips were soft and sweet, and he wanted to go on tasting them forever.

Swan Harbor General
September 2
Present Day
2:30 p.m.

When Elsa skirted back around the pillar as if she didn't want to be seen, it brought Liam back to the present.

It's your fault if she doesn't want to see you.

He knew that to be true, but things were different.

Were they really?

Maybe …a little. The question was, would she talk to him?

Several moments later, she walked back around the pillar, and Liam was waiting for her.

"I've always loved you in the color blue." He fell into step next to her, taking advantage of her surprise to direct her toward the exit. "It makes your eyes look so pretty."

"Liam," Elsa whispered breathlessly.

"That's my name." He grinned down at her. His mouth went dry, and the bravado coursing through his system disappeared. "I …"

"You what, Liam?"

I missed you.

"How are you?"

"I'm good."

Except those weren't the words he'd wanted to say. Those were stuck inside. If she walked next to him a little longer, then perhaps the words would break free.

"Liam, why are you here?" Elsa stopped to ask.

Now what?

He glanced away from her blue-eyed stare, and what he saw captured his attention. There were no skyscrapers nor crowded streets. Instead, mountains and more trees than he'd seen in years lay before him. It gave him peace—a feeling he'd not expected.

"Luis said hello." Liam steered her away from the building and toward the parking lot. "He wanted to know what I did to run you off."

"Oh?"

There it was again. That one word that said so much, yet to him, its meaning remained elusive.

"Yeah. He noticed you hadn't been around."

"And you told him I moved?"

"Yeah. Made me promise I'd give you something when I saw you again."

"Oh?"

The way her sexy mouth sassed that one word created a maelstrom of emotions he wasn't sure how to handle. All he knew was with the daydream he'd had earlier, he needed ....

"Damn, El."

They passed a tree that wasn't large, but big enough for what he had in mind. He spun her around and pressed her against the trunk, covering her body with his.

"Lia ..."

He swallowed the rest when he sealed their mouths. Once their lips touched, there was nothing soft about the kiss. It was one of desperation.

Their lips clung to each other, giving voice to words hidden deep within his soul. Words he'd never thought or felt, and ones he'd shied so far away from, he wasn't sure what they meant. Words he'd not even considered when Debi Monroe had been a part of his life.

Words he ....

Liam slowly lifted his head and took a step back, intending to apologize. Then he glanced down at her upturned face.

Her eyes were glazed over, and her pupils were blown wide. There was a red ribbon of blush highlighting her high cheekbones. And her kiss-swollen lips begged him to jump back in.

Laughter and a slamming car door gave Liam the distraction he needed to step away.

"I suppose—"

"There you are. We've been wondering what was taking so long."

A few choice words ran through his head when his brother's voice provided the cold slap of water he'd needed.

"Here I am." Liam turned to greet Killian and his partner, Rusty. "What are you two doing here?"

"Rusty's little boy broke his wrist." Elsa stepped closer, her voice much more controlled than he was feeling.

"Bugger that! How'd that happen?"

"He was trying to put the halter on Ruari," Rusty sighed. "And since the horse has been abused, well ..."

"Now Roland has a nice glow-in-the dark cast to show his friends," Elsa added with a laugh. "Would you like me to take you to him?"

Liam sent his brother a dirty look, and saw something in Killian's eyes that said, *We need to talk, now!*

He took a deep breath and looked at Elsa. "Can we talk ... later?"

Their eyes met and the messages hers were sending were coming hard and fast. None of them said, '*Go, I don't want to see you again,*' though.

She glanced from him to Killian and back. "I have plans for later ..."

"Oh?"

Was it with the infamous Tyler?

"Bloody hell, Liam," Killian snapped. "She's having dinner with Emma and me. You can talk to her there."

"Alright." He grinned. "If that's okay with you."

"It's fine. I'll see you later."

Liam watched her until she was out of hearing distance and turned on his brother. "What's so bloody important you had to step in and muck things up?"

"What are you talking about?" Killian frowned. "You're having dinner with her tonight, aren't you?"

"Yeah, but ..." He shrugged, wishing he had some idea of what she'd thought of the kiss. "Never mind. What is it?"

"Let me fill you in on my day, and you can let me know if you remembered everything."

Liam gave him another dirty look. "I'm not completely daft."

"Sure about that, brother?"

Was he? Some days, he wondered.

THE FARTHER THEY WERE FROM LIAM, THE SLOWER HER HEART and the easier she could breathe. He confused her ... and that kiss ....

"Gray was supervising the installation when Killian and I left your house," Rusty filled her in on her new alarm system. "He'll be there when you get home to show you how it works."

"That's nice of him."

"It's part of what he does," Rusty reminded her. "And since you're on county land, if it's triggered, it will ring right into the sheriff's department."

"That's good."

Now that she knew the alarm would be there tonight, she hoped some of the creepy feelings she'd been having disappeared. She loved her little cottage and didn't want the good vibes to be ruined. While some people might say, *'This is Swan Harbor, nothing happens here,'* she was used to big cities. You locked your door and installed alarms. Especially if you were seeing people in the shadows.

It had taken only a call to Killian earlier in the day. He'd recommended she hire Sadie's husband, Gray Hunter, and his business, HCI. And based on what she was being told, that had been a wise decision.

Unlike that kiss. That hadn't been such a wise move.

She could still taste him. Still feel the imprint of his lips on hers. Feel his hardness pressed into her much softer parts. How was she going to sit beside him during dinner and carry on a normal conversation?

Then how was she going to say goodbye to him all over again? That was the real question.

SIX

Elsa's Cottage
September 2
4:00 p.m.

Elsa followed Gray from room to room as he explained her new alarm system. There were contact points on each of the windows and doors, as well as automatic lights around the house. However, as he showed her how the system worked, she had a hard time keeping her focus on him. Especially once they reached the backyard. Then her attention went to the why she'd needed one.

"See that clump of trees?" Elsa pointed to the back of her property.

"Yes."

The hesitation in his voice had her giving him a second look. Had she missed something?

"You said the lights are on motion sensors, right?"

"Yes."

"So, if someone or something ran along there, would it trigger those lights?"

"Yes." He grinned when she squinted at him and added, "The lights reach 70 feet and a person or blowing leaves can trigger them. They're very sensitive."

"Then what?"

"They come on."

"But when the lights come on, do they call the sheriff's department?"

He took her inside to the control panel, then pointed to her phone. "There's a panic button on the panel. And once you set up the phone app, you can hit it from there too."

"Okay. Thanks." Elsa took the packet of information and walked him to the door.

"Let me know if you have any questions."

"I will, thanks. Tell Sadie hello."

He waved goodbye, and for the first time since early morning, she was alone. The goosebumps were still there, but not as prevalent. When the feeling they gave her didn't supersede her feelings from Liam's kiss, she let it go and called the vet clinic.

"I need help," Elsa stated as soon as Emma answered the phone.

"Here, talk to Sadie for a minute while I take another call."

"What's up?" Sadie asked.

Elsa began to explain everything, but her thoughts scattered.

"Your husband just left," she started with. "I now have a fully functional security system."

"Fully functional," Sadie laughed. "Is that doctor speak for you have no idea what he said?"

"Something like that," Elsa agreed.

"He does like those big words, but I hear there's another man in town making you nervous. Tell Auntie Sadie about it."

Elsa surprised herself by sharing everything.

"You know," Sadie's sigh was melancholy, "there was a time several years ago when my best friend Jessie and her now husband, Cameron, were having trouble communicating."

"I'm sure you offered words of wisdom," Elsa replied tongue-in-cheek.

"Well, of course," Sadie chuckled. "I told her the same thing my mama always told me."

"You listened to your mama?"

"Sometimes," Sadie hummed. "Anyway, she told me boys were just as scared about what to say and do around us as we are. That if you like a boy to take back the power."

"Take back the power?" Elsa repeated. "What the heck does that mean?"

"It means turn the tables on him."

"But?"

"I'm back." Emma had taken the phone from Sadie. "Captain Jack is worried about Jonesy. I didn't have the heart to tell him I'd never treated a swan before. Anyway," then because she'd been friends with Emma forever, Elsa could imagine her shaking her head as if to push her thoughts away until later. "How did it go with Liam?"

Her lips still tingled, but she didn't want to say that.

"Okay." Elsa grinned at the memory of the disgruntled look on Liam's face when his brother had arrived. "Killian showed up, so I took Rusty to find Roland and Rene."

"Killian needed to talk to Liam?" Emma asked. "He didn't tell me Liam was coming to Swan Harbor."

"Really?" Elsa remembered asking Liam that very question, but he'd not answered.

He kissed the living daylights out of you.

"What happened? I can hear something in your voice."

"Nothing," Elsa blurted, feeling like the little girl who got caught cheating on a test.

Emma laughed. "Sorry, but I don't believe you."

"He kissed me, okay?" Elsa huffed. "There, I said it. He kissed me, and my mind turned to mush. Now, what do I need to do?"

"He kissed you?"

"That's what I said," Elsa mumbled. "Now what do I do?"

"You know, El," Emma drew out the words as if she were trying to gather her thoughts. "You need to decide what you want. You said you played the con, hoping Liam would either ask you to stay or ... come here. Well ..."

"He's here."

"He is. Now, what do you want? I'll see you in an hour."

Elsa hung up and went to shower. She had a lot to sort through. There had been a time when she'd thought maybe something with Tyler was possible. But no longer. Besides, it didn't matter that Swan Harbor had other single men. Sadie was right. Her heart already knew.

The Beachside Inn
September 2
6:00 p.m.

LIAM STEPPED INTO THE SHOWER, HIS CONVERSATION WITH Killian still fresh in his mind.

Liam gave Killian a dirty look. "I'm not completely daft."

"Sure about that, brother?"

"Bloody hell, Killian," Liam ran his hands through his hair in frustration. "Just spit it out, will you? Did you hear more about Santora?"

Killian heaved a sigh and sauntered toward the front of the car, settling on the hood. "Nothing concrete. The request is still making its way through the system, but he's not without support."

"Which means, if that person I saw on the subway platform really was following me—"

"—It could be an associate of Santora's," Killian agreed. "Did you remember—?"

"—All the precautions we'd created when you were undercover? Yes." Liam ticked them off on his hand. "Took several trains in a circuitous manner. Left the thread in the door. Made sure there was nothing in my apartment that could connect either of us to Ian Jones. Drove my car, exchanged it for one of dad's, and signed back into our shared account so you can track me."

"I'm sorry, Liam." Killian shook his head with disgust. "I really thought I'd put everything dark in my life behind me and now—"

"It's not your fault, Killian," Liam tried to assure his brother. "You didn't make Santora evil. Hell, you're not even the one who blew the case out of the water."

"Bloody hell, Liam!" Killian snapped. "I know that. But it's killing me to think Emma and Swan Harbor could be in danger."

"Wait," Liam frowned. "Swan Harbor? Do you have reason to believe Santora or his goons will come here?"

"Gut. Six sense. Hairs on the back of my neck," Killian grimaced. "Plus..."

Liam whipped his head toward Killian, and his brother's expression said something else was going on. "Spill it."

"Did Elsa tell you anything that happened last night?"

The thought they'd not done much talking popped into his mind. Instead of saying anything crass, Liam shook his head and waited.

"She called me this morning and asked for a recommendation."

"For?"

"A home alarm," Killian admitted.

Liam's brows went up, as that was the last thing he'd expected to hear. "In Swan Harbor? That doesn't sound right."

"It's not," Killian agreed. "But I guess sometime in the early morning hours, she thought she saw someone in the shadows."

"Thought, or knows?"

"As far as Elsa knows, thought," Killian admitted. "Rusty and I spent a little time digging today, and while I have nothing concrete—"

"—There's a possibility someone was watching her."

"Yeah."

"And you don't think she needs to know that someone 'might' have been there?"

Killian winced. "I was trying to protect her and Emma."

"Emma doesn't know about Santora, does she?"

"Bloody hell, of course she knows about him," Killian grumbled. "I told her everything before we got engaged."

"That's not what I meant." Liam sent his brother a pointed look. "She doesn't know Santora could get out of prison and—"

"—Come after me." Killian pushed up and walked several feet away. "No, but put yourself in my place."

Liam studied his brother for several seconds, trying to decide what to say to diffuse the tension. "I don't know, Killian. Emma seems a little high maintenance for me."

"Ha!" Killian barked. "You don't think Elsa is high maintenance?"

"We're just friends," was out of his mouth before he could stop it.

Killian pinned him with that steely-eyed gaze he'd used when on the force. "You and I both know you're lying to yourself, but until you're ready to hear a few truths, carry on. I suggest you be Elsa's friend. Seems someone suggested the same thing to me a while ago, and it was good advice."

"Be her friend." Liam flipped the shower off and grabbed a towel.

Does that involve kissing?

Once dressed, he left his hotel room and took the stairs to the lobby.

"Hey, Liam," Tia Patterson, the owner and manager of The Beachside

Inn, greeted him. "Eating in tonight?"

"No, I'm meeting Killian and Emma at Sally's."

"Oh, I might see you then. I *think* I'm meeting Nic there. It just depends on his work."

"Have a good evening," he called.

"You too."

A tone in her voice had him glancing back over his shoulder as he left the inn. Killian had mentioned that, at one time, Tia hoped for something to develop between her and the infamous Tyler. Liam could admit the possibility of Elsa moving to Swan Harbor for Tyler had crossed his mind. But after Elsa's kiss, he wasn't sure her move to the small town had been for someone else. However, it didn't mean he wouldn't like to hear it from her. If he did, maybe he could work out the real reason.

But as her friend, you can find out.

It was a nice enough place to live, he supposed. Mountains, the sea, open spaces, and good friends. Close enough to Portland to get away now and then, but offering a slower pace of life not possible in the city.

But she's going to grow bored and want to leave.

How do you know? Did you ask her?

No, he hadn't. Except that's what happened when people moved places they didn't belong, wasn't it?

Who says she doesn't belong here? Did you ask her what she wanted?

Had he?

It was something for him to think about as he made the drive to the diner. By the time he'd parked and walked through the door, the only conclusion he'd come to was he didn't know. What did that say about him, as a date or as a friend? More importantly, though, what did that say about him as a man?

Especially when Elsa was standing between two men, and they were all laughing at something, making him feel like the proverbial third wheel.

Sally's Diner
September 2
6:30 p.m.

Elsa knew the minute Liam walked into Sally's. The air grew more electric, more alive, and that invisible connection between them ignited.

Take back the power.

In the past, when they were *dating,* and he'd met her somewhere, she'd always gone to him. Right then, something had her waiting for him.

Emma's eyes met hers and she raised a brow, as if to say, *Well?*

I'm taking back the power.

For some reason, the statement made her want to giggle. Especially when she chanced a peek toward the door and Liam stood frozen, as if he couldn't decide which direction to go—backward or forward.

"Liam, over here." Killian waved his brother back. "You remember Ben and Tyler from the engagement party, right?"

"Right." Liam glanced from one to the other. "Ben?"

"Ben Matthews."

"Ben's my attorney," Emma offered with a grin. "It's thanks to him I own my vet clinic."

"And Tyler?"

A little devil inside of Elsa pushed her hand on Tyler's arm. "This is Tyler James. He's an old friend."

Tyler's dark eyes met hers and the sparkle in them said, *Really? That's where you want to go?*

"Hey there, darlin," he teased in an exaggerated drawl. "Who are you calling old?"

"Elsa and Tyler met at summer camp when they were sixteen," Emma explained with an impish grin.

"Sixteen?" Liam's gaze met Elsa's. "Did you go to the same high school?"

"Oh, no." Tyler grinned. "Elsa went to a high-falutin school, and I just went to a lowly public one."

"We met at summer camp." Elsa took pity on Liam, but then added a little dig, "Tyler wrote me a song. Do you remember that?" She elbowed Tyler teasingly.

"Oh my gosh, Elsa," Tyler groaned. "Don't even go there."

"How did it go, again?"

"I've slept since then, but I remember ..."

He hummed a few bars and crooned, *"Hey baby, when you smile at me.*

You make me as happy as a bumblebee. It makes my heart go bump, bump, bump. Until all I want to do is jump, jump, jump."

"Oh my, that's awful." Elsa laughed. "I can't believe I told you it was the most beautiful song anyone had ever written for me."

"It's probably the only song anyone has written for you," Tyler replied.

"True," Elsa agreed, then added for Liam's benefit, "Believe it or not, he can sing. He owns Siren's Song."

"Oh?"

Elsa's lips twitched at Liam's succinct response.

"It's down on the pier."

"You'll have to stop by sometime," Tyler suggested.

"That's a good idea." Killian agreed. "Liam will be here at least through the weekend."

At least? Elsa wondered about the unspecified time frame. But Liam didn't provide the answer she wanted. Instead, his response was noncommittal.

Tyler glanced at his watch. "It was nice to see everyone. However, I need to run and relieve Lois and Rupert. They're wonderful with Bethany as long as they don't have to put her to bed."

"She wants her daddy to put her to bed?" Elsa guessed. Then a melancholy sliver zipped through her, and she had to fight to maintain her smile.

"She does," Tyler agreed. "I'll see y'all later."

He glanced down at her and the twinkle in his eyes said, *Watch this* as he leaned toward her. With the feel of Liam's kiss still lingering on her lips, she turned enough, so the kiss landed on her cheek. His chuckle said, *I see what you did.*

Once Tyler and Ben were gone, Sally led them to a booth. Elsa slid across the seat and waited with bated breath while Liam scooted next to her.

Keep the power, she reminded herself.

Except Liam was sitting beside her, wearing her favorite cologne. That meant, every time he moves, she got a whiff. It was a fight not to lean against him and press her face against his chest.

"What's good here?"

"Everything," she murmured, fighting the pull of his blue eyes. "I think I'll get the stuffed shrimp, or maybe the lobster pie. But the clam chowder looks good too."

Emma rolled her eyes. "Just decide, Liam. El can never make up her mind and will want a taste of whatever you're having."

Elsa's eyes met Liam's, and the way they darkened told her he was thinking about the same thing she was … the kiss.

"Be nice." Elsa forcibly took back the power and pointed at Emma. "I still know some of your secrets."

"Speaking of." Emma turned to Liam. "Did El tell you she thought someone was watching her house last night?"

"Emma!"

LIAM EXCHANGED LOOKS WITH HIS BROTHER. "KILLIAN FILLED me in."

"He did?"

"Yes." Liam squeezed Elsa's fingers. "Told me they spoke to your neighbors."

"That while they heard the dogs barking, that was it," Killian picked up the story. "And you know how active your neighborhood spy line is."

"A spy line?" Liam grinned, hoping to draw the conversation to something lighter.

"Just you wait, honey." Sally, the diner's owner, set their plates on the table and joined the conversation. "For instance, I know you're staying at the Beachside, and you made a stop by the hospital today. If you give me a chance, I bet I can find out more." Then, with a wink, she left, leaving Liam feeling like a fly under a microscope.

"Wow."

"Oh, Liam," Killian chuckled. "You've not seen anything yet."

"And it doesn't bother you?" Liam asked, his question encompassing the entire table.

"You get used to it." Killian wrinkled his forehead. "It gives the word informant a whole new meaning."

"I can see that."

He was quiet for a few seconds, watching Elsa help herself to a taste of the shrimp on his plate.

"And it doesn't bother you?" he asked when her laughing eyes met his. "The lack of privacy?"

Elsa tilted her head, and when the tip of her pink tongue swept along her bottom lip, he had to look away.

"It's different and took time to get used to. But something about living in Swan Harbor feels right."

It wasn't what he'd expected her to say. However, it added to his thoughts about figuring out why she'd moved. Perhaps he'd been wrong about her getting bored in a small town.

He tuned back into the conversation to hear Emma say, "When we were sophomores, we took a road trip to Disney World."

"Oh Emma!" Elsa laughed. "Don't tell that story."

"Why not?" Emma giggled. "We had so much fun."

"Well, yeah. We did, but …"

Elsa's pink cheeks were charming, and it wasn't long before Liam pushed his plate away just to watch her. She sparkled, and the tinkling of her laughter caused his heart to race. Had that ever happened in New York City?

Did you allow it to happen in New York City?

Did he really have that much control over his feelings?

You tell me.

He heard Killian say, "Eight lovely ladies on the prowl," and realized he'd lost track of the conversation.

"I've heard stories about spring breaks in Florida." Liam side-eyed Elsa. "Tell me you were legal, at least."

The guilty look on Elsa's face made him even more curious. "Well, well, I'd never have guessed."

"It was just that one time," Elsa explained. "And it was all Aurélia's fault."

"Oh?"

Her eyes grew wide, but he refused to look away, forcing her to maintain eye contact.

"Yes," she huffed.

"And who is this Aurélia?" Liam questioned. "Let me guess, she's from France."

"Well, duh," Elsa giggled. "It really was all her fault."

"The infamous Aurélia strikes again," Killian murmured.

"What?"

"Nothing!" Emma sent his brother a warning look, causing Elsa's cheeks to pinken even more.

"I feel left out," he pouted.

"And that's how it's going to stay." Elsa sent him a stern look.

"Yes ma'am."

Her lips twitched, and he had to physically hold on to the seat to keep from kissing her. What was happening to him? Was it the town, Elsa, or both?

"I hope you saved room for pie." Sally gathered up their plates as efficiently as if she'd been doing it for years. "It's apple."

Liam's taste buds watered. "With ice cream?"

"Of course." Sally nodded. "Homemade."

"That sounds wonderful," Elsa groaned. "But I'm too—"

"I'll take one," Liam decided. "And bring two forks."

"You got it."

"That wasn't necessary."

"We'll eat and then I'll walk you home."

She side-eyed him. "How do you know I didn't drive?"

"Swan Harbor's spy network." He pushed the pie toward her. "Now, dig in."

SEVEN

Sally's Diner
September 2
8:00 p.m.

Liam casually took her hand as they walked. It caused her heart to tick up a handful of beats, scattering her thoughts.

Decide what you want.

Did she want Liam?

Is your heart beating?

It was racing.

Do you love him?

Did she? Was what she felt for him love?

She thought so, but was he willing to love her back? Was it possible for her to have a relationship like her parents?

You promised not to compare.

They walked several stores down Main Street, not saying anything. She wanted this forever. The question was, how did she go about getting it?

"Do you need to go directly home?" Liam asked, squeezing her fingers.

"What did you have in mind?"

The banked heat in his eyes when he looked down at her sent her thoughts straight to the gutter.

"A walk along the pier?"

"I'd like that." She directed him to a side street, then took that proverbial leap. "Is what Killian said true? You're at least staying through the weekend."

"Yes."

"What does that mean? You hadn't said anything about taking a vacation before I moved."

"Spur of the moment."

"Oh?"

She thought he growled in a predatory manner. Except that wasn't Liam.

"So, Tyler," he tossed out in what she assumed was to be offhanded. Yet the tension in his voice belied his purpose.

"What about Tyler?"

"You've known him a long time."

"Yes."

"And?"

Elsa had to fight not to giggle because the less she said, the more frustrated Liam grew. Which wasn't like him either. He'd never asked about any males they saw when they were out.

"Damn, El." Liam pulled her back into the shadows. "Did you move to Swan Harbor to be with Tyler?"

Oh, Liam.

Her heart melted, and she wanted nothing more than to walk into his arms.

Remember the power.

"That would be the easy answer, wouldn't it?"

"What do you mean?"

He frowned down at her and Elsa forced herself to take a step backward. "I mean, if I said yes, I moved here for Tyler, then you would have your answer. You wouldn't have to dig into things that might not be comfortable, right?"

"Well, did you?"

A part of her wanted to keep pulling that thread and see where it went. The other part of her wouldn't allow it. Hurting him was not her goal.

Except, do you know what your goal is?

For him to want me, which reiterated her answer.

She needed to touch him and, almost against her will, placed her palm flat on his chest. "No, Liam. I didn't move to Swan Harbor for Tyler."

"No?"

His heat reached out and drew her in, just like when they were sitting side by side in the diner.

"No. It's like I told you. Tate offered me a really, really good opportunity and …"

"And?"

Elsa linked her arm through his and continued walking.

"This is going to sound weird, but it's almost like I was being led here."

He barked out a laugh.

"I never pictured you as a person who believed in the mystical. How did I read you so completely wrong?"

"Did you read me at all?" Liam reared back as if she'd slapped him, causing Elsa to curse her slippery tongue. "I'm sorry. I shouldn't have said that."

Liam covered the hand she'd hooked through his arm. "No, El. I want you to say what's on your mind. In this, you might be right. Maybe I didn't take the time to get to know you. The time to get to know your wants, desires, and needs."

The huskiness in his voice brought tears she had to blink away. She couldn't have the power *and* cry.

"So, tell me more," he prompted. "About being drawn to Swan Harbor."

Could she trust him with her dreams?

But if you don't, is there any chance of getting what you want?

"What do you know about my upbringing?"

"Not much," Liam admitted. "I'm sorry."

Did she know much about his past? Only what she'd heard from Emma. "Perhaps you're not the only guilty one."

"You might be right. Would you tell me about young Elsa?"

She laughed, suddenly unbelievably happy.

"My father was a professor at Georgetown, and my mother is a doctor. A pediatrician, just like her father and like me."

"Was? Your parents aren't living?" Then he murmured under his breath, "How could I have not known that?"

"My father passed when I was in med school," Elsa sighed. "I was a daddy's girl, and miss him every day."

"And your mom?"

"Mom still lives in Georgetown," Elsa continued. "She retired several years ago but still guest lectures periodically."

"So, you grew up in a big city, and according to your friend Tyler, went to a 'high-falutin' school. Private?"

"Yes," she admitted. "And while there are advantages to being in a big city, I always felt something was missing."

"What makes you think it's a place you're missing, and not ..." his voice dropped an octave, "something or someone?"

She shrugged. "I don't really know. My grandpa was a doctor in Newport, and when I pictured my future, that was what I saw."

"How do you know it's supposed to be in Swan Harbor?"

"Remember when we came for Emma and Killian's engagement?"

"Of course."

"There was just a feeling when we arrived. Like I had walked the streets, stood on the cliffs, and looked out at the sea. It felt like home, but I didn't realize that was what I was feeling until later."

"Then you were offered the opportunity to have what you'd always dreamed of having—"

"And I thought it was fate."

❧

The conviction in her voice was something he'd never heard before, unless she was talking about her work. But again, he wondered if that was because he hadn't been paying attention or because it wasn't there.

"Killian says the same thing about Swan Harbor," Liam murmured. "That as soon as he arrived, he knew it was where he was meant to be."

"Emma too," Elsa murmured. "Which is interesting, as when we met in college, I'd never expected her to end up in a small place. Captain Jack would say it's because the heart knows."

"Captain Jack?"

She pointed toward one end of the pier, where a seventeenth century Spanish galleon rested.

"Yes, Captain Jack. That's his restaurant, Captain Jack's Fine Dining."

"Original."

"Hush," she giggled. "I agree Captain Jack is a bit of an eccentric man, but I think he's very kind and means well."

There was something in her voice he couldn't put his finger on that said she had more thoughts on this older fellow than she was saying.

"You think?"

"Oh, nothing nefarious, I'm sure. Emma says he gives her funny looks, like he's trying to place her."

"And you? What do you say?"

"Remember when I walked out of Sally's in June?"

"Yes."

They'd been at Emma and Killian's engagement party, and the entire evening he'd felt a constant push and pull toward her. When he'd heard her say she'd been offered jobs outside of New York City, a feeling he couldn't label began churning around inside.

"Emma told me Killian kept you from coming after me."

Here it is, he thought. The moment he'd expected. Except now that he was in the middle of it, he wasn't sure how to explain.

"That's right."

"Why?"

"It was dark out and I didn't like you wandering around alone."

He could feel her studying him periodically as they continued walking toward the big ship.

"There's more," she tossed at him, not in an accusing way, but more in an *I'm calling you on your bull* way.

"Are you sure?" he threw right back, rather than look inside to give her the answer she wanted.

"I am," she murmured. "And for now, I'm going to allow you to keep the secret."

"Only for now?"

"Yes."

Liam looked down at her and her eyes were sending messages he'd never been willing to read before.

I'm here.

Talk to me.

Should I be patient?

Give me time, he wanted to say. *Something is happening inside.*

"What are you doing to me?" he whispered.

"I don't know, Liam. What am I doing to you?"

"You're making me "...

He couldn't go on because he'd sound daft if he said she was confusing him. It had him thinking about things he'd never thought about before.

"Hmm, well, you think about it. But now, allow me to introduce you to Jonesy."

"Jonesy?"

Elsa pointed toward the water, where he could just make out white feathers.

"A swan?" He stepped closer to peer into the dark water. "I didn't think they were up this far north."

"Emma said they usually aren't, but I gather Jonesy has been coming to Swan Harbor every summer for as long as people can remember."

"Alone?"

"Yes. I don't think he likes me much. Gives me the side-eye stare when I come down here."

Liam laughed. "There you go again, being fanciful. He's a swan. I'm sure he loves anyone who'll toss him a bit of seed."

"Maybe so. Captain Jack is worried about Jonesy. Called Emma today to tell her."

"So, Emma's researching swan issues."

"Yes."

"You can never stop learning," he murmured, thinking about his job back in New York. There was always something new and yet, there was also a sameness to what he did.

"Tell me about your new job."

As they walked back to town and took the road up toward her little cottage, she talked and possibly, for the first time, he listened.

"In New York, when you spoke about work, I knew it was important to you, but this you ... is different."

"How so?" Elsa pulled out her keys and took the first step to where she was level with him. "Am I really different here?" She let that hang in the air for several seconds. "Or is it you?"

He'd been trying to figure that out for hours. "Maybe both."

Their eyes locked and damn if he didn't want to kiss her. "Think your spy line is watching us?"

Elsa giggled, temporarily breaking the spell.

"Possibly." She unlocked the door and stepped inside to turn off her alarm. When she turned back around, she grinned. "Okay, probably."

"I thought so." Liam thumbed over his shoulder. "The curtains on that front window fluttered when we walked by."

"Paula, as in Paula's Pastries, lives there. I wouldn't mess with her."

"I'll remember that. Elsa, I ..."

She surprised him by placing her finger over his lips. "I know."

"You know?" He frowned. "What do you know?"

"I know this." Elsa kissed him—only a brief meeting of their lips. Yet one of the most powerful kisses they'd ever shared. "I know," she repeated. "I'll see you tomorrow."

"Goodnight, Sweet Elsa."

On his way back to his car, Liam felt like he was floating.

Now, who's being fanciful?

He could admit the town was affecting him in a way he'd not expected—especially his thought processes.

Liam had been gone ten minutes, yet Elsa could still feel the imprint of his kiss. Something was different about it. *Something* was different about him.

Could she trust what she *thought* she saw?

Do you have a choice?

Not if she wanted everything.

Elsa considered sitting on her porch and think about Liam. But the feeling of being watched had her running a bath. Just before she stepped in, her phone buzzed.

She considered ignoring it, but habit had her grabbing her robe and running for it.

She missed the call, but seeing the area code caused her heart to race. When she tried to playback the message, her hands shook so much, it took several tries to hit the button.

"Elsa, it's Doris Harden, your mom's neighbor. I hate to bother you, but thought you'd want to know. I stopped by to check on Patty and she'd burned herself. Since I don't drive after dark, I called the ambulance. Three nice young men took your mother to the hospital. Call me if you have questions. I'll be at home, 202-555-7890."

Elsa pressed the number to return the call.

"Doris, it's Elsa. How's my mom?"

"Well, now, honey," Doris began, making Elsa grit her teeth to keep from pushing the other woman. "Patty was in pain when those young men put her on the stretcher."

Elsa frowned, trying to connect the accident with her no-nonsense mother.

"How did this happen? Mom is always so careful. And she loves to cook."

"Well ..."

Elsa's breath caught while waiting for Doris to go on.

"Patty told me not to worry you, but your mama isn't quite the same woman she used to be."

"What are you not telling me, Doris?"

"Her memory isn't very good these days. She's even gotten lost on walks, and the police had to bring her home."

"Has she seen a doctor?"

"You know your mama."

"Which means no, because doctors are the worst patients."

"That would be my guess. What would you like me to do?"

"I need to take care of a few things, but I'll try to get a flight out tonight. I'll call once I know when I'm landing."

"Okay, honey. You be careful."

When Elsa hung up, her thoughts were going in multiple direction. Years of practice had her lining them up in order of importance.

Airport.

Pack.

Tate.

Audrey.

While she packed, she called Emma.

"Elsa, is everything okay?"

"No ... yes." Elsa took a breath and tried again. "I'm sorry to call so late, but my mother's neighbor just called."

"What happened?

"My mother burned herself and is in the hospital."

"What can I do? Did you call Liam?"

Crap.

"Not yet and I have to leave, or I'll miss my flight."

"Where are you flying from?"

"Portland."

"Okay, take care. I'll tell Liam."

If she would have been in her right mind, those words might have scared her. That her focus was on the rest of her list had her moving on. She'd deal with everything else later.

Veterinarian Clinic
September 2
10:00 p.m.

Emma worried that calling Liam would make her feel guilty. However, the opposite proved to be the case. Elsa shouldn't be alone and someday she'd appreciate her friend's meddling. At least she hoped so.

"Was that Liam, Doc?" Killian asked.

"Yeah." At her single word answer, he turned off the television.

"What's going on, Doc?"

Her ploy earlier in the day to get Killian to talk had been a royal failure. He'd flipped off the water, kissed her, and left. It had annoyed her, but she'd understood. Even more so when she learned he was meeting Rusty at Elsa's. She knew him well enough to know there was more going on, and something told her Liam was involved.

"Elsa called to say her mother was in the hospital."

"Is everything alright?"

"Elsa doesn't know much, but she's flying to DC tonight. I told Liam he should accompany her."

Emma settled in the corner of the sofa next to Killian, her cat Millicent, and his kittens, Trudi and Nina.

"That's probably a good idea," Killian hummed. "He needs to get out of town ..." Then he clamped his jaw shut.

"I thought we promised we wouldn't keep things from each other."

"Bloody hell, Emma!" Killian jumped up and stalked across the room. "I'm trying to protect you."

"Killian." She hesitated until he looked at her. "I love you."

"And I love you, Doc."

"But protecting me by not telling me there's potential danger could put me in harm's way, right?"

The muscle in the side of his jaw pulsed for a handful of seconds. Finally, he relaxed, seemingly at peace with what he was going to say.

"I didn't want my darkness to touch you ... to touch this place."

"What place? My clinic? Or is it Swan Harbor you're worried about?"

Killian returned to the sofa and pulled her onto his lap. "It's about Santora," he murmured, never once looking at her.

Emma cupped his jaw, forcing him to maintain eye contact. "He's in prison, right?"

"As far as I know, he's still in prison. But Liam told me in June his lawyers were trying to get the case thrown out."

"Can that happen?"

"I hope not."

"It's a possibility, though?"

"Aye."

Her thoughts were racing, but she refused to fly off the handle.

"And?"

"On Liam's way to work on Thursday, a car almost ran him down."

Emma tightened her hand on Killian's shoulder. "Who? Why?"

"We don't know. Once the police came by, their questions set Liam on edge. And then ..."

"There's more?"

"Later that day, both cops were admitted to the hospital. They'd been shot. Then on his way home, Liam thinks someone followed him."

"You said your captain made it appear as if Ian Jones died, right?"

"Aye."

"Then why go after Liam?" However, the look on his face answered her question. "Somehow they figured out who Ian Jones was, and know who Liam is."

"Maybe. I spoke to Captain Weaver, and he's doing some digging. Rusty and Dylan are helping me look into things."

"Which is why Liam had to get out of town?"

"Aye."

The events from earlier in the day flashed by, and a few dots connected.

"Were you lying about someone watching Elsa's?"

He dropped his head against her shoulder and sighed. "Doc, there isn't anything concrete, but—"

"—You can't rule it out."

"I'm sorry, Doc. If I could go back ..."

Emma kissed him, just a quick brush across his mouth.

"Elsa and I talked about this, and I wouldn't want you to change anything."

He side-eyed her. "Nothing?"

She knew he was referring to a situation with the floozies he'd dated before she came to town.

"Nothing. If you change the past, it changes who you are. I love you just the way you are."

"I really am sorry, Doc. But I'm happy Liam is away from New York for a few days and Elsa isn't alone. If it's any consolation, when I worked undercover, I set up some safety systems. One of them is that I always know where he is ... that is, as long as he has his phone."

"Tracking?"

"Aye, let me show you." Killian opened the app on his phone and signed in. It spun for a few minutes, then a map with four blips on it opened.

"There's you." Emma touched one dot before moving to the one next to it. "And me? Are you checking up on me?"

"Not because I don't trust you, Doc."

"Oh, I know." She pushed his thumb away and located Liam's ping, just outside of Swan Harbor. Then she touched the fourth. "Does that belong to some floozy from your past?"

"That's Beatrice Morgan, Violet's grandmother. It's my way of making sure she's safe."

"You're a good man, Killian Reade," Emma murmured against his mouth.

He toyed with her lips for several minutes, never settling for long. "Doc?"

"Hmm." Emma carded her fingers through his hair, wanting to hold him in place.

"Didn't you say you'd saved some *Rebecca's Catalog* purchases to show me?"

"Maybe."

"Then what are you waiting for?" In one smooth motion, he pushed her off his lap, stood, and tossed her over his shoulder.

"Killian!"

"Hush, Love!" He clamped his hand on her butt, and slammed the bedroom door behind him, leaving their three felines on the outside.

EIGHT

Portland International
September 2
11:00 p.m.

Liam glanced sideways at Elsa as he took the exit for the Portland International Jetport and followed the signs to long-term parking. When he'd arrived to pick her up, instead of an argument as he'd expected, she'd given him a sweet smile. Once more, he was seeing a new side of her. It had him floundering and unsure what to say or how to act.

He parked, and when he rounded the front of the car, caught her eye. She was watching him, an expression on her face he couldn't decipher. One that had him pulling open her door and reaching for her. "Come here." As if it were the most natural thing in the world, she slid into his arms.

"I'm sorry," she murmured against his collarbone. "I feel like my brain is sluggish."

"That's normal, you know that."

"I know. But I'm a doctor—"

"Who are horrible patients."

She laughed as he'd intended and took a couple of deep breaths before stepping back.

"I'm ready."

"Expected nothing less."

Her smile was sweet, and as they walked toward the terminal, she slipped her hand inside his. His heart soared, as he'd been given a gift.

Since they didn't plan on checking their bags, ticketing was relatively painless to everything but his credit card. They breezed through security, and it was a simple walk to the gate.

"Are our seats together?" she whispered, the first words she'd said since the parking garage.

Liam gave her a crooked grin. "No, but I'll see if I can charm the attendant at the gate."

She arched an elegant blonde brow. "And if the attendant is male?"

"I can still be charming."

"Yes, you can."

When she laughed, he was yet again confused. On one hand, it lightened his worry about her, but on the other, he got the feeling there was a message he was missing.

Once they arrived at the gate, a female attendant was standing behind the desk. Before he could step forward and try his charm, Elsa took over.

"Give me your ticket and I'll see if she'll put us together."

"You don't think I can charm her into doing it?"

"I know you can," she grinned. "That's why I'm going to do it."

"Oh!" he smirked, pleased with her territorial behavior. She'd never done that before. Had he wanted her to, though?

In all the time they'd known each other, jealousy hadn't been a part of their relationship. Then he'd walked into Sally's, and she'd been standing between two men he didn't know. A feeling he hadn't recognized washed over him that hadn't gone away immediately. It wasn't until she'd told him she hadn't moved to Swan Harbor for Tyler he'd relaxed. Except, did he have rights to feel what he was feeling? Better yet, did he even want those rights?

"Here you go." Elsa gave him his ticket. "We're good to go."

"That was lucky."

"I'm just good." She tugged him along behind her.

"What did you say to her?"

"Are you sure you want to know?"

"Definitely need to know now." Liam shoulder bumped her. "That look on your face has me very curious."

While the attendant scanned Elsa's ticket, a secretive smile passed between them. It made him more determined to find out the truth.

"What did you say?" he whispered, noting the pretty blush dotting her cheekbones.

"What do you think I said?"

Her grin was pure devil, and he wasn't sure how to handle that side of her.

Are you sure about that?

Yes! If they went in that direction, he'd have to explain his behavior after they'd made love the night of Killian and Emma's engagement party. Instead of pulling her closer, he'd run like a tosser.

"Liam?" She turned toward him, close enough her shoulders brushed against his chest.

He glanced into her upturned face and his heart rate skyrocketed. "Yes, love?"

"Why are your cheeks turning pink?"

She was so close he could smell her shampoo, making him fight not to lean in and bury his face against her soft neck.

"It's a little warm in here," he offered.

"Really?" The disbelief in that one word said she wasn't buying it. "I thought it was a little drafty."

Liam's good luck came when the line moved, and she didn't say more until they found their seats.

"Now." She buckled her seatbelt. "What were you thinking back there?"

What could he say? That a part of him wanted her to tell the attendant they were planning to become members of the mile-high club. Or would he settle for her admitting she wanted to be with him?

"That you needed my shoulder to lean on," he tossed at her, realizing he wanted *that* to be the truth.

ELSA SMILED. "THAT WASN'T WHAT YOU THOUGHT I'D TOLD HER.

"How can you be so sure?"

"I just know. It's no big secret. I just told her the truth."

"The truth?"

"Yes. That my mother is in the hospital and I needed your support."

"Really?"

"Yes." He didn't have to know she'd mentioned the possibility of a proposal.

"No." Liam leaned close enough she could see the flecks of grey in his eyes. "That's not all."

"How can you be sure?"

He brushed his fingertip across her right cheekbone. "You wouldn't have blushed if that had been all."

"Oh."

When his eyes flared, she knew she'd been lying to herself. He was giving her what she'd wanted from the beginning. What she'd always wanted.

"Watch it."

"Threats, Liam?"

Her heart raced. Yet she couldn't stop pushing to see how far he'd let her go before ....

Before what?

"Promises." He leaned toward her and planted a firm, possessive kiss on her lips.

Wow!

Her brain short-circuited, and before she could come up with a comeback, they announced the doors were closing. Then the reality of why they were in the plane came crashing down around her.

"I'm sorry I didn't call you," Elsa whispered. "But I'm very glad you're here with me."

"Oh, El." Liam pushed up the armrest between them and put his arm around her. "I'm glad I'm here too. Things between us have been different, and I wasn't sure ..."

It was too scary to breathe while he talked. Having him so close, holding her and saying things she'd longed to hear was heaven. Why was he, though? What had changed? Was it as he'd suggested, and they were both different away from New York?

"You weren't sure about what? If I wanted to be with you?"

"That. Plus, I've realized I need to think about a few things. I promise we'll talk later. But El, tell me about your mom. What's going on?"

Inside, it was a struggle not to squeal like a kid who'd just gotten a treat. With the need for an explanation, though, she forced herself to sit up and move his arm so she could link their fingers.

"My mom's neighbor left me a message," she began, feeling the phone call had been days ago and not hours. "Doris stopped by to check on her, and she'd burned herself."

"That's all she said? Nothing about how?"

"Cooking." Elsa shrugged. "Which is not like my mom at all. She's usually so competent in the kitchen, but ..."

Doris's comment about her mother being forgetful and getting lost played heavy on her mind.

"But what, El?"

Elsa nibbled on her lip while she filtered through exchanges she'd had with her mother the past year.

"My mom has been forgetting things. I was just asking myself how I could have missed that."

"When was the last time you saw her?"

"Last summer," Elsa groaned, annoyed she'd not pushed a little harder. "I was supposed to go to DC for Christmas."

"Let me guess," Liam retorted. "Marshall canceled your vacation at the last minute and took one of his own."

Elsa knew there was no love lost between her old boss and Liam, but his comments had her wondering if there was more.

"Something like that," she acknowledged. "I think wife number three decided she would rather spend Christmas in Paris instead of New York."

"Lazy sod," Liam muttered.

"I'll agree with that." Her lips twitched, happy he was on her side. "Anyway, when I told mom, she said she'd come to me, but she canceled, and Emma came instead."

However, she talked to her mother at least once a week and had noticed nothing different.

Are you sure about that?

Crap!

"Oh, man." Elsa pieced together a few conversations she'd had with her mom. "How did I not recognize what was happening?"

"Talk to me."

"I just realized she's been forgetting things for a while. Little things, like where I lived, or the name of where I worked. The name of her favorite store, or an ingredient she put in a casserole she used to make."

"When we land, are we going straight to the hospital?"

"I think so. Mom's neighbor said she'd leave a message if they send mom home."

"It's good she has neighbors who care."

A tone in his voice had her glancing up quickly to catch an expression on his face she'd never seen.

"You have a good neighbor, but," she let it hang several beats, "you weren't talking about now, were you?"

✽

Liam cursed whatever had come over him since leaving New York. There'd been too many times when he'd thought something only to have the words fall out of his mouth. That wasn't like him. He didn't talk and rarely allowed feelings to seep through. With Elsa, though ....

He sent her a crooked smile. "No, Luis is a great neighbor. But growing up, we weren't always so lucky."

What are you doing? You never talk about those times?

Then, without stopping to second guess, he barreled on and tossed the same question she'd asked him. "What do you know about my upbringing?"

"From you?" Elsa nudged his shoulder. "I know nothing. From Emma, I know you've been in the states a little over twenty years. Your mother went back to England about fifteen years ago, and your father sells real estate."

"More than most people."

"Sorry?"

Liam glanced down and noticed how different their hands were. Hers dainty to his larger, soft to his rough, manicured to his often bitten.

"Don't be sorry, El. But why didn't you ask me?"

"I did."

"No—"

"Yes, Liam." Several expressions worked their way across her face. "Are you sure you want to get into this now?"

"No," he admitted, feeling more nervous than when he'd thought he was being followed. "But maybe I need to hear it."

"Oh, Liam."

Elsa dropped her head on his shoulder, and the fine blonde strands brushed against his face.

"I'm tough, Sweet Elsa."

She shook her head slightly, and the smell of her shampoo wrapped around him. "No, you aren't. You just think you are."

"That doesn't sound very manly," he mumbled, not at all sure he was okay with the conversation any longer.

"Okay, let's see. I think the first time I asked about your childhood, you made a joke and said you'd never been a child."

Liam winced, recognizing that deflection as he'd used it before.

"The next time I asked, you said you'd 'skipped straight from being an infant to being an adult and touched nothing between.'"

"Bugger," he muttered. "I was a right knob head, wasn't I? You didn't ask again, did you?"

"Maybe once more," she admitted. "You said, 'we'll talk about it later. Liverpool's playing.'"

Liam blew out his breath with disgust. "Why didn't you kick my arse?"

"Would it have done any good?"

"Maybe not." Then he saw the look on her face and ducked his head. "No. I'm sorry."

"Is that your way of telling me you really were a child at one time?"

"I deserved that." Several thoughts circled inside until, finally, he returned to the comment about neighbors. "We lived in Blyth, which is a small town in Northumberland, England. However, we moved around a lot, never settling in one home for long."

"Did your father sell real estate in England?"

A laugh burst forth before he could control it. "Hardly. My father worked in the shipyards. But it never seemed like there was enough money. And mum let him know it too. She was never happy."

"Did your mom work?"

"She focused on her hair, her nails, and making sure Killian and I behaved. At a job, though, no. Mum was from money and used to people doing for her. I often wondered why dad stayed with her."

"He loved her."

Her quiet response stirred him, settling something deep inside he'd tamped down so long ago, he'd forgotten it was there.

"So, he did." Liam thought back to before they'd left England. "We had nothing, and dad disappeared for a few days and when he returned, suddenly it seemed every day there was something new. Clothes, furniture, jewelry."

"Did your dad get a different job?"

He'd asked himself that same question many times, but had never asked his father.

"I don't know," he sighed. "That went on for six months or a year. Then one day, Killian and I came home from school and our father was loading the car with suitcases."

"What did he say?"

"That we were moving to America."

"How did you feel?"

He'd felt upset about leaving his friends, angry because he hadn't been told, but oddly excited.

"Annoyed, because there was a cricket game I wanted to play in, but happy to be leaving school. I didn't care for my teacher, Mrs. Fisher. A daft cow, she was."

"Typical boy."

"What can I say? Dad said we'd go to Disney World, and I was alright with that."

"There weren't friends or neighbors you were going to miss?"

"Not really," he replied, knowing it made his childhood seem lonely. "There was one old couple that used to yell if we played too loudly in front of their home, but other than that ..."

"And once you moved to the states?"

"We settled in New York. Dad changed his name, became a realtor and, for a few years, things were fine. Killian and I were pain-in-the-arse teens with smart mouths, and then mum left and I grew up pretty fast."

"Why did your dad change his name?"

"Said Flynn sounded like a peasant. That Finley sounded much more aristocratic."

The pilot announced their descent into Washington D.C. and Liam glanced at Elsa. She'd gone quiet. Thinking about his story? Or about her mother?

He rubbed the back of her hand across his lips. "See, it's not that exciting."

"It's exciting because it's your story, that's all. Thank you for sharing."

Again, she'd given him a gift. What else had he missed?

Georgetown
September 3
1:00 a.m.

AS THEY DEPLANED, ELSA KEPT TRYING TO WRAP HER HEAD around the fact Liam had shared. He hadn't shared just one small thing, but more than she'd expected. She had so many questions, but worried once the moment was over, it would be over.

Remember the power.

Initially, Sadie's suggestion made little sense, but it seemed as if a door was being opened and he was meeting her halfway. Once they reached the door, then what?

Take what you want.

But what's that?

Everything.

"I need." She thumbed toward the ladies' room and ducked inside.

Away from him, she could breathe, think, and remember why she was here —her mother. Once again, she was centered.

"You can do this." When she walked out of the bathroom, Liam was on the phone. It reminded her she hadn't checked hers.

"Elsa, honey," Doris's tired sounding voice came across the line. *"Patty is in room 321 at Georgetown General. Jerry will wait to speak to you. If you'd rather talk to him tomorrow, call him."*

"What is it?" Liam asked.

Her eyes met his and while there was concern, there was something else. "Is everything okay?" she asked him instead.

He tilted his head. "Fine, love. Why?"

"You were on the phone, and ..." she shrugged, unable to give voice to her thoughts without sounding like a dweeb.

"Oh, just an update about a patient, that's all."

"Are you sure?"

"We're here to take care of your mother."

He took her hand, and they resumed walking toward the exit. Something told her he was not giving her the entire truth.

"Do we need to rent a car?" He pointed toward the signs, directing them to another area.

"I thought we'd take the subway to my mom's and just use her car. Is that okay?"

"It's fine, love."

A little thrill shot through her every time the word love rolled off his tongue. She knew he didn't mean it literally, because she'd heard him use it when speaking to others. But the way his voice grew huskier and his tongue slid around the L, seeming to caress it, ratcheted up her heart rate.

"Was there any more news about your mom?"

"Just that she's in the hospital and Jerry is waiting for us," she replied tiredly.

"Jerry is her doctor?"

"He was always Uncle Jerry to me." Elsa smiled fondly. "He was the best man when my parents got married. His wife Charlotte and my mom are childhood friends. That he's waiting for me worries me."

Once they were on the train, Liam tucked her a little closer to his side. "Why? Maybe your mother just doesn't want to be left alone."

"Maybe," Elsa conceded. "It's just a feeling."

"I'm here."

"I'm glad."

"Me too, Sweet Elsa. Me too."

She wanted to focus on her mother, but the way his husky words were sending little thrills through her body had her wanting to scream.

Where's the power?

NINE

Georgetown
September 3
1:30 a.m.

AS THE ELEVATOR SLOWLY ROSE TO THE THIRD FLOOR, ELSA'S insides clenched tighter and tighter. She kept thinking about the last time she'd spoken to her mother.

"And you really enjoy living in that place? Where did you move again, honey?"

"Swan Harbor, mom," Elsa answered impatiently, thinking about the boxes that needed unpacking. *"Remember, you told me you'd heard about it from grandpa?"*

"I did? That's right, I did." Patty laughed, but it sounded distracted, as if she too were thinking of other things. *"But you really enjoy it?"*

"Yes, mom," Elsa sighed again, having answered the same question several times. *"How's Doris and Bill?"*

"Who?"

"Doris and Bill," Elsa repeated. *"Your neighbors."*

"Oh her," Patty's voice lowered as if she were afraid of being overheard. *"I think she's spying on me."*

"Spying on you? Mom, why would Doris spy on you?"

"Well, honey," Patty continued in an exasperated voice. "You know why. Remember, she stole my prize roses years ago and said they were hers? And now, she wants my cupcake recipe."

Elsa frowned, as she couldn't remember her mother ever working in the garden. It was Doris that had flowers of every color dotting her back patio.

"Mom, I didn't know you gardened."

"How can you say that?" Patty's voice turned frosty. "I've gardened your entire life."

Not really caring one way or the other, Elsa gave a noncommittal response and asked about the cupcakes.

"I'm making your favorite," Patty chirped.

"Chocolate?"

"No, honey," Patty corrected. "Strawberry. Don't you remember for your fifteenth birthday ...."

Liam squeezed her fingers, bringing her back into the present.

Elsa glanced up at him and the tender look on his face had her fighting not to walk into his arms. "I'm okay."

"There you are." Doctor Jerry Wallace stepped away from the wall he'd been leaning against and hugged her. "How was your trip?"

Elsa wanted to stay strong and not lean on anyone, but he smelled exactly like he had when she was a kid. *Just for a little,* she thought, relaxing against him.

She stepped back and noticed him watching Liam and had to smile. It was the same look she'd seen on her father's face when a date had picked her up.

"Uncle Jerry, this is Liam Reade. He's a," she let the word hang in the air for a few seconds, then added, "friend."

Liam arched a brow, but held out his hand. "It's nice to meet you, sir."

"How's mom?"

Jerry ran his hand through his hair, and his expression was pensive, sad, resigned. "Your mom has second-degree burns on her right hand. She was lucky this time."

"There's more, isn't there?"

"I'm afraid so." He glanced at Liam, then back at her. "We should talk before you see Patty."

"Okay."

"Let's go sit."

Elsa latched onto Liam's hand as they followed Jerry down the hall and into a small waiting room. Because of the lateness of the hour, they had the room to themselves.

They sat, and Jerry glanced at Liam again. She assumed that was his way of asking for permission to speak freely.

"It's okay," she murmured. "Liam's a paramedic, so he'll understand what you're saying."

"Okay." Jerry nodded once, took a deep breath, and uttered the words she'd been expecting but had hoped not to hear. "Your mother has Alzheimer's."

Cognitive Decline.
Losing things.
Difficulty communicating.
Unable to live alone.
Forgetting me.

She reached for Liam's hand. "When was she diagnosed?"

"Last November."

"About the time she canceled her trip to New York," she murmured.

"Patty told me about that." Jerry leaned forward to rest his elbows on his knees. "You know how much she hates depending on others, but looking back, she'd hidden it for quite some time before speaking to me."

"How long?"

"A year," he sighed. "Maybe more."

Elsa could feel everything rising inside but forced it back down, determined not to fall apart yet. While this might not be her hospital now, she'd volunteered here as a teen, and everyone knew her.

"Is she on medication?"

"That, I don't know," he admitted.

"Wait a minute," she snapped. "How can you not know? You're her doctor, her neurologist, for heaven's sake." Then she got a look at his face and the light went on. "Mom's part of a research study, isn't she?"

"She is," he acknowledged. "I'll give you all the information you need. After this incident, though, I'm not sure—"

"—If she can live independently," Elsa finished.

"Right."

Except would her mother allow someone to live with her? Jerry hadn't been wrong in stating her mother didn't like depending on others. She'd often pushed her family away, instead of pulling them closer. Would this be any different?

"I'm sure you're going to have more questions, but let me take you to see her."

"Okay."

When she stood and glanced at Liam, he was watching her with intense blue eyes. A part of her wanted to push him away. To tell him she didn't want him seeing her weak and vulnerable, but she couldn't find the strength.

"I'll wait here for you, if you want me to ..." he offered, almost as if he'd read her mind.

"Do you want to wait out here?"

"I want what you want," he whispered.

"You do?"

Did he? Did he, really?

LIAM KNEW ELSA WAS FIERCELY INDEPENDENT, A TRAIT SHE'D inherited from her mother. He'd been pleased when she'd admitted he was there. They'd been on the plane, though, away from the reality of confronting a parent who was ill and facing a debilitating disease.

Would she continue to let him stand with her? Or would she push him away, preferring to standalone?

Elsa opened her mouth, and a part of him expected her to turn down his offer. Then she uttered, "Come with me," and it felt like his heart took flight. He wanted to scoff at his fanciful thoughts, but he couldn't come up with any other way to describe them.

"Really?" he repeated.

"Please."

Liam took her hand, and they followed Jerry down the hall toward room 321.

Once they reached her mother's room, Elsa hesitated before entering.

Patty Winters was lying on the bed, her right arm wrapped in gauze, watching the door. She was older than he'd expected, upper sixties, he'd guess, meaning Elsa was a later-in-life child.

Elsa let go of his hand and rushed forward to hug the older woman. "Mama. Oh, mama. What have you done?"

Patty's eyes met his over Elsa's shoulder, and he could have sworn for a second she didn't know her daughter.

Could she have hidden the disease longer than Jerry suggested? Had she allowed the early stages to slip by instead of helping Elsa make the tough decisions? Would she expect her daughter to move back to Georgetown? He couldn't see that happening, but if she did, what about him?

This isn't about you. But why are you wondering? When Elsa told you she was moving, did you try to change her mind?

"Who's your friend, honey?" Patty's gaze never left his.

"Liam Reade, Mrs. Winters." Liam stepped forward to take her outstretched hand.

Her smile grew, and she pushed up a little straighter in the bed.

"Aren't you just the cutest thing? Please call me Patty. Mrs. Winters sounds so old."

"Mother!" Elsa exclaimed, her face turning red. "Don't say that."

"Why not?" Patty glanced at Elsa briefly, then back at Liam. "It's true, and he has a sexy accent too. You didn't tell me you were dating anyone new."

"I didn't?" Elsa squeaked.

"No." Patty playfully wagged her finger. "Who was it you were dating the last time you were home? Was it Mike, Mickey, or something like that? You remember him, Jerry? Max just loved him."

Elsa's face lost all color, and if he hadn't caught her, she would have fallen.

"I've got you," he whispered, gluing her to his side and sending Jerry a '*Help me out here*' look.

Jerry stepped in front of Elsa. "Are you talking about Mitchell?"

"Mitchell!" Patty nodded. "That's his name. Darling boy. What happened to him, anyway?"

"She saw me." Liam took the initiative.

"Is that so?" Patty glanced at Elsa. "I don't see a ring on her finger yet."

Elsa sent him an '*I'm sorry*' look. "Mother!"

A corner of his mind thought he should panic at hearing those words with his name. Except, just because he'd never imagined it as part of his future didn't mean it wasn't a nice thought.

"We've not been dating long." He winked at the older woman. "You wouldn't want me to rush her now, would you?"

"No." She frowned. "But don't wait too long because you never know."

Liam glanced at Elsa and had to agree. You never know, and with what he'd learned today, he had more questions.

"When can I go home?" Patty asked Jerry. "These sheets are just so rough, and those nurses keep waking me."

"It won't be long, Patty. Maybe tomorrow afternoon."

"That's fine." She turned to Elsa. "Will you stay and see me tomorrow?"

"I'd planned to stay for a couple of days, at least, if that's okay." Elsa had regained some of her equilibrium and was once again conversing with her mother in a semi-normal manner.

"Good." Patty crooked her finger toward Liam, forcing him to let go of Elsa. "Are you staying at the house tonight?"

His eyes met Elsa's, and hers went wide with panic.

"I believe so," he answered hesitantly.

"Okay, just do me a favor. Take the blue room, as the bed is more comfortable. Also, don't drink all the scotch."

Elsa sagged against him, and he fought not to chuckle.

"I'll keep that in mind."

"I'll be back tomorrow to take you home, mom." Elsa kissed her mother on the cheek. "Don't give the nurses too hard a time, okay?"

"Okay, dear." Patty's voice dropped to a whisper. "I like your young man. He's a keeper."

"He has his moments."

They exchanged a few more words with Jerry and then made their way back to the elevator.

"When did you date Mitchell, El?"

Her sigh was one of utter sadness, as if the entire world were resting on her shoulders.

"When I was an undergraduate."

Liam wanted to take her in his arms and hold her, but something told him this wasn't the time. In the elevator and on the way to the car, she clung to his hand. Almost as if she were afraid holding it was the only thing keeping her grounded.

"Do you want me to drive?" he asked once they'd reached the car, and she'd still not said anything.

"No, I need ..." her voice faded, and he understood. She needed something to focus on besides what she'd just learned inside the building behind them.

"Alright, love, I'm here." Liam opened the driver's side door and helped her inside. "Don't you leave until I'm seated," he teased.

Her chin quivered just a little before she caught herself. "Quit being a lazy knob and get in."

Liam chuckled. "It's either knob head or lazy sod, El."

"I know. Now," she motioned with her head, "get in."

He jogged around the front of the car and climbed inside, wondering if she was going to allow herself to fall apart. If she did, would she let him comfort her?

Georgetown
Patty Winter's Townhome
September 3
2:30 a.m.

By the time they'd arrived at her mother's townhouse, Elsa was feeling proud of herself. There'd been a few times when the scary thoughts had appeared, but she'd successfully pushed them away. The logical part of her knew there'd come a time she wouldn't be able to do so. The emotional side wanted to put that off as long as possible.

"Nice place," Liam murmured when they walked inside.

Elsa glanced around with a critical eye. "It was where we lived, but it never really felt warm, like I'd always imagined a home should."

"Your mom didn't let you build blanket forts and leave your clothes laying on the floor?"

"Blanket forts? What are those?"

"Come on, El, tell me you're not serious."

She stopped on the third-floor landing and looked down.

"About knowing what a blanket fort is? No. The only forts I know about are in backyards in trees."

"And I thought I had a deprived my childhood." Liam quipped.

A sliver of something twisted inside and she must have made a sound because the next thing she knew, Liam yanked her against his chest.

"Bloody hell, El." He tightened his arms around her, pressing her against his hard body. "What did I say?"

Was she ready to dig into her relationship with her mother? To admit thoughts she'd carried with her a lot of years but had never given voice to?

Or did she need to hold on and make plans for what came next?

Liam's heat wrapped around her, and a part of her wanted to climb inside. She wished he would take ....

"Liam." Elsa tugged his shirt from his pants and slid her hands underneath to touch his smooth skin. "I need ..."

You.

Their eyes met in the shadowy hallway. He was watching her, waiting for what—she wasn't sure. Then his lips were on hers and all that mattered was what he made her feel.

His lips plundered, all-consuming, pulling her along in the rush. *So right*, she thought when he trailed kisses down one side of her neck and a red-hot line of fire followed in its wake.

Her breath caught when his hands skimmed up her side, pulled her shirt up and over her head.

"Yes." Elsa moved his shirt aside and whispered kisses across his hard chest.

"More," she mumbled when his thumb brushed across her nipple and a spark shot straight to her core.

"Elsa." Liam's eyes delved into hers, but she didn't want to talk.

"Kiss me." She tugged his head back and captured his lips.

The world swirled around them, the only sounds the desperation of their kisses. He pushed her leggings down and when she stepped out of them, lifted her and carried her into the nearest room.

"So pretty..." He tracked hot kisses along her stomach. "Soft ..."

Elsa's thoughts scattered, and all she could do was feel. She needed him to take away the pain racing around the fringes of her consciousness, threatening to overwhelm her.

"I need ..."

The more his lips and hands touched, the bigger the feeling inside. It built and her only thought was for it to hurry, to push away the pain. Higher and higher it rose, sweeping her along in its wake.

"It's okay, El." Liam's warm breath brushed across her sensitive areas and the rolling wave inside grew.

Churning ....

Climbing ....

She was helpless as it pulled her along faster and faster.

Consuming ....

She didn't want to let go. It felt too good and what was on the other side wasn't where she wanted to be.

"I've got you," his velvety soft voice promised.

But who's got you? Except the assault from his mouth was too delicious, too perfect. Before she was ready, giant waves slammed into her, carrying her over the crest.

She was weightless, floating along, and then Liam pushed her over once more. Her heart raced, her body liquified, and in her mind's eye, she kept thinking she should do, say, or think.

"Come here."

Liam wrapped a satin spread around them and, with her cheek pillowed on his lightly furred chest, Elsa listened to his rapid heartbeat.

Who has the power now?

Except the answer was elusive, fluttering out of reach.

"Thank you," she murmured. His arms tightened around her, and giving herself permission, she let go.

TEN

Georgetown
Patty Winter's Townhome
September 3
7:30 a.m.

LIAM SLOWLY OPENED HIS EYES, WONDERING IF HE WAS GOING TO see last night had been a dream. He was lying on top of a blue comforter in his jeans with his shirt tossed onto the end of the bed. Elsa's smell surrounded him, telling him he hadn't dreamed of having her come apart in his arms. That had happened.

What about you, though?

Did he regret giving her pleasure? He'd given her the escape she'd needed.

That wasn't the question. Why are you still holding back?

Later, he pushed the thoughts away, just as he'd done for the past month.

It was her feelings that mattered now. Where had she gone?

For a split second, a zip of panic flew through him that she left. Then the rattle of pipes registered. "Shower," he murmured, wishing he had the balls to join her.

Since he didn't, he grabbed his bag and rushed through his morning routine. They needed to talk about more things than just last night, but he'd settle for one thing at a time.

After he dressed and stepped into the hallway, he could still hear the shower running.

Was she hurt?

Or was she washing off his smell?

"Bugger that." Liam padded barefoot through the house, the sounds leading him down a hall and into a plush room, the mirror of his but yellow.

"Elsa," he called, not wanting to startle her.

When she didn't respond, he pushed open the bathroom door. He could see her through the frosted glass.

"Oh, El."

Liam grabbed a large towel and opened the shower door.

She'd crumpled to the floor and buried her head in her crossed arms. The sight of her shoulders shaking almost undid him.

"Come here, love." Liam turned off the water.

Elsa glanced up and somehow he knew he would remember the look on her face forever. Another one of those times her eyes were saying things that, in the past, he'd left unread.

"I've got you." Liam helped her stand and wrapped the towel around her, before swinging her into his arms.

Elsa held onto his shoulders, and again it left him feeling like he was her lifeline. A title he would have run from a month ago, but after seeing her in Swan Harbor, it felt like a gift.

He sank onto the commode and propped her on his lap.

"I should ..." Elsa squirmed in his arms.

Liam tightened his hold. "Hey, you know how much I've always wanted to rescue a wet damsel, don't you?"

"Really? You never told me that."

"Well, I can't share all my secrets, now can I?"

"Liam, I ..."

Elsa lifted her head for him to see her red-rimmed eyes and puffy lower lip. His heart flipped, and the only thing he could think was to say, "You're beautiful."

"Right." She rolled her eyes. "Like red and puffy is so attractive.

Liam cupped her jaw. "Beautiful, but," he gently ran his thumb over her full bottom lip, "did I do this?"

Elsa dropped her gaze, and a gentle blush covered her cheeks. "I was trying to be quiet."

"So, you bit it." He hugged her a little tighter. "Please don't hide from me."

"'Kay." It was just the barest of sounds, but it sent goosebumps rushing through him.

After everything he'd done, she trusted him.

"I'm sorry," Elsa muttered, side-tracking his thoughts.

"About the tears?"

"Well, those too." She glanced up briefly, and the blush still covered her cheekbones.

"What are you sorry for, love?"

Elsa sat up a little straighter and held on to the towel with both hands. "I'm sorry about ... you know ...?"

Then he got it. She was sorry about leaning on him last night.

"Are you regretting it?" he asked, unsure of how he'd feel if she said yes.

"Are you?"

"Uh uh uh," Liam playfully scolded. "You brought it up."

"But ..."

Their eyes locked and once again, hers were saying so much, it was a struggle to keep up.

"I just. You didn't. It's just." Then her voice faded, and she leaned against him.

Liam lifted her chin with his finger. "Elsa, love, you gave me a gift last night."

She raised a brow. "That's not quite the way I remember it."

He grinned, because he couldn't deny his body had wanted, and after she'd fallen asleep in his arms, it had taken time for him to relax.

"You gave me your trust." Liam gently kissed her, lingering a little longer than he'd intended.

"Is that what I gave you?" Several expressions crossed her face, but instead of continuing to argue, she simply said, "Thank you."

"Any time. Are you ready to talk about what you learned? That has to be pretty earth shattering."

Elsa looked down, her hands busy, constantly pleating and un-pleating the towel.

"How about this?" he offered her another out. "Why don't you get dressed, and I'll start coffee. Once you're downstairs, it's your call."

"Okay." She moved out of his way.

Liam took several steps toward the door, and, just before he walked through, looked back. When their eyes met in the mirror, he winked and left her alone.

She was standing in a pool of light shining through the window, and the way it highlighted the lighter gold strands in her hair ignited a need deep inside.

What could he do about it?

ONCE HE SHUT THE DOOR, ELSA SAGGED AGAINST THE COUNTER. There were so many thoughts and emotions running through her, she didn't know which to focus on first.

There was Liam and the way she'd wantonly thrown herself at him. She'd needed to forget, even if only for a moment. To feel pleasure, instead of the pain Jerry's announcement had wrought. Surprisingly, she didn't feel embarrassed, which was something she didn't understand. His words and actions were evolving, and she wanted nothing more than to hold on and see where it went.

Right then, though, she was in Georgetown because her mother was in the hospital after burning herself. Something that happened because Patty had the diagnosis of Alzheimer's. A disease that would take her memories, her self-reliance, and her very independence. Based on Jerry's timeline, her mother had relied on herself for a while. But Elsa wasn't sure how *she* should deal with it.

You learn to lean.

Which wasn't a trait she often did. Emma hadn't either before she'd moved to Swan Harbor and met Killian. Slowly, he'd wormed his way into her heart, and her friend was learning to share her burdens. Could the same be said for Liam? Should she trust he would be there for her?

Please don't hide from me.

Did that mean what she wanted it to mean? She wasn't sure, but she had to make some decisions. The sheer number made her stomach clench. Except there weren't other options, meaning it was time for her to face the day.

She made it downstairs to find Doris scrambling eggs and Liam at the table with a cup of coffee.

"Good morning, Doris. What brings you by this early?"

"I wanted to check on your mama." The other woman smiled. Then, in one smooth motion, she turned off the stove, set a fresh cup of coffee on the table, and slipped two pieces of bread into the toaster. "When I arrived, your young man was looking for the coffee grounds, so ... here I am."

"But ..." Elsa frowned, still feeling a bit lost. "How did you get from helping Liam find the coffee to cooking us breakfast?"

"Oh, that's easy." Doris opened the refrigerator to show it was practically empty. "I was looking for the creamer and saw you had no food."

"So, you went home and got some eggs and bread?" Elsa poured sugar and cream into her coffee. Instead of drinking it, she enjoyed its warmth. "You didn't have to do that."

"Oh, I just brought eggs." Doris scooped them onto plates and set them on the table. "Liam found the bread. Besides, it's nice to cook for young people again."

Elsa met Liam's gaze over the top of her cup. He was watching her, and she wondered if he was waiting for her to fall apart again. Or could it be because he enjoyed looking at her? If she had a choice ...

"Thank you." She remembered her manners.

"Now, don't bother getting up." Doris patted Liam on the shoulder. "I'll see myself out."

When the door shut, Elsa picked up her fork and toyed with the food on her plate. The thought of taking a bite, though, turned her stomach.

"I'm sorry. I should have checked the refrigerator."

Liam took her hand. "Stop. Not everything is your fault. Anyway, the actual story is a little different from Doris's."

The way he'd consistently tried to soften a few blows and made light of serious wasn't a side she'd expected to see. His comment had her fighting a smile, because Doris's busybody behavior was normal.

"Oh?"

Liam's eyes flared, reminding both of their kiss in Swan Harbor.

"I *was* looking for coffee and had decided to run to the nearest coffee shop when—"

"—You opened the door to find Doris."

"Yes."

It was quiet while he ate, giving her a chance to glance around the kitchen. Her mother had always been a creature of habit about some things. One of those had to do with her morning caffeine fix. Just like always, the coffee pot was in the same place, as were the canisters.

"Liam, you've made coffee at my apartment before. How come you couldn't find the coffee at my mom's? Wasn't it in the third canister, like at my apartment?"

"Not quite."

"The small canister?"

He shook his head, and the look in his eyes propelled her across the room. She found several sticky pads of paper in the smallest one cannister. Pencils in the next. The second was empty. When she opened the largest one and saw evidence of her mother's disease, tears flooded her eyes.

"Oh, mama," she cried, her knees giving out.

Liam caught her and pulled her against him. "It's going to be okay."

"No!" Elsa denied. "It's never going to be okay."

She blinked away the tears and pulled multiple notes from the jar. *Oven. Sink. Pantry. Door.* Steps to make coffee ... a reminder to turn off the stove.

The canister was full of reminder notes Patty had written. Except they weren't the typical note a person might write, such as an appointment date and time, or a grocery list. These were reminders of what something was called, or steps for completing tasks most people could do in their sleep.

"Do you know what this means?"

"Your mother's been compensating for a while."

"That's exactly what it means!" Elsa snapped, anger raging inside, threatening to overwhelm her if she didn't let it out. "She's suspected this for a long time! Then, when she got the actual diagnosis—over ten months ago— she still didn't tell me."

"Maybe she didn't want to tell you over the phone." Liam soothed his hand down her arm.

Elsa shook off his hand. "That's not it. It's because she's still trying to fix things she can't control. The same thing she's been doing my entire life.

Someone's hungry, make them a sandwich. Someone's cold, here's a blanket. Someone's sick, give them a pill. Someone has cancer, let's do chemotherapy. Someone has leukemia, let's …"

Her voice faded and for several seconds, her anger swirled and churned.

"She couldn't control things then," Elsa continued. "Olivia died, and I lived. While she might wish she had the cure, there isn't one. Sometimes bad things happen, and we don't know why, but isn't that when you turn to your family?"

❧

ELSA VIBRATED WITH ANGER, BUT SOMEHOW, HE PREFERRED THIS Elsa over the one with tears.

"Isn't that natural for some people?" Liam murmured. "To not want to lean on others?"

It was what happened in his family after his mum left. His father had turned to the bottle. Killian had turned to women. He'd become everyone's friend. If you didn't allow them close, they couldn't hurt you.

"Maybe," she sighed. "But I'm her daughter. Once she found out, she knew there was a small window to make the hard decisions together. She's never trusted me with anything important."

Liam felt like he was wading into a minefield and wasn't sure how to proceed. "You're referring to something specific, aren't you?"

"When I was sixteen and away at camp—"

"Would this be when you met Tyler?"

Her lips twitched. "Yes, and stop it."

"Stop what?"

"Trying to play peacemaker." She gave him a look, wanting to say more, but after a slight hesitation, continued, "My grandfather died, and she didn't tell me. Then, when I was in medical school and my father had a heart attack, she didn't tell me. It wasn't until the second one happened, and it was too late that I learned about the first."

"She's protecting you."

"Is she?" Elsa whirled around and took off down a small hallway. "Or is she protecting herself?"

He followed her, the question hanging in the air.

She pulled a photo album from a shelf and flipped through it. When she glanced up, the sadness was back, but he thought she'd turned a corner.

"My parents were married right after my dad graduated from college, and he took a position at Oxford. Two years later, they had Olivia."

Liam looked at the proffered album showing a little girl who could have been Elsa's twin.

"They were the perfect little family. Dad taught, and mom stayed at home. She cooked, cleaned, and took care of Olivia. Then Olivia got sick."

While she was talking, Liam had been flipping through the pages and landed on a photo of a frail teenager. Bald, as if she were going through chemotherapy.

"Acute Myeloid Leukemia," Elsa sighed. "Chemo wasn't enough, and then my mother found out she was pregnant with me. Was I planned? There was a time when I thought so. When I asked my father, he said I was 'a gift.'"

"You didn't believe him?"

"No, I believed him, but I always wondered if my mom felt the same way."

"You didn't ask her?"

"Hardly," Elsa scoffed. "Olivia wasn't something mother talked about. I often wondered if it was because it hurt too much, or because she saw it as a failure on her part."

"What happened to Olivia?"

When Liam went back to the photos, the next one showed the teen sitting in a hospital bed holding cupcakes.

"That was Olivia's fifteenth birthday," Elsa explained. "She was recovering from pneumonia, and my mom made her strawberry cupcakes. Except my mom was thirty-two weeks pregnant with me and not feeling well. After they celebrated, my dad took her home to rest."

Liam reached for Elsa's hand, needing to hold on to her as what was coming had to be bad.

"That night, everything went horribly wrong. My mom went into labor. I was born two months early, and my sister died in her sleep."

"Ah bloody hell, El." Liam pulled her into his arms. "How?"

"A compromised immune system that led to pneumonia causing a pulmonary embolism."

They leaned against the sofa, and Liam could see how a child would think she'd been born to save another child. But why hadn't she asked her mom?

"You said your mother didn't talk about Olivia …"

"No. In fact, I only found out about Olivia by accident."

"Bugger that, El. They didn't tell you? Show you pictures?"

"No," she sighed. "I found a photo at my dad's office and asked questions. That was when he called me a gift, but it was a painful time for my mother. He said once she was strong enough, she would tell me."

"Did she?"

"Not in so many words." Elsa's smile was a melancholy. "My mom went to med school and began researching leukemia. However, she started leaving the photo albums on the shelf. I'd always hoped we'd reach a stage where she would tell me about Olivia. But now …"

She let that hang, and he knew what she was thinking. That with Alzheimer's, she'd be lucky if her mother remembered much of her life's stories.

"They say individuals with Alzheimer's go through stages."

"That as the stages progress," Elsa picked up. "They basically go back in time memory-wise."

"Which explains the confusion about Mitchell."

"Wasn't the first time." Elsa repeated the cupcake conversation with her mother right after she'd moved to Swan Harbor. "Makes me wonder if she was making strawberry cupcakes when she burned herself."

Liam ducked his head as the remnants of the cooking fiasco were in the trashcan under the sink.

"She was. Doris must have cleaned up and tossed them out after the ambulance arrived.

"I thought so." Elsa put the photo album back on the shelf. "Right now, I need to figure out what's what."

He didn't have experience in doing what she needed to do, but he still wished to take some of her pain.

"I've heard sharing your burdens helps," he repeated, what he'd told Killian. "I'm here."

Elsa walked into his arms and muttered what he thought sounded like, "But for how long?" The words caused his heart to ache, and for the first time in his life, he wanted to promise her forever.

ELEVEN

Swan Harbor
Sally's Diner
September 3
10:30 a.m.

Killian read Liam's text again.

> Liam: Message this morning from Randy White, the E.D. doctor who treated the officers. Brody died last night from his wounds. Stevens is in critical care and on a ventilator.

"Bad news?" Hayden, Sally's nephew, set down a cup and filled it with coffee.

"What?" Killian glanced up at the younger man, his mind still filtering through the message.

"Bad news?" Hayden pointed at the phone. "You were frowning."

"Oh." *Bloody hell awful news.* "Aye. News from New York," Killian replied noncommittally, not really wanting to get into things. "But shouldn't you already be back at school? I thought classes started this week."

"They do." Hayden slid into the booth. "I transferred to Swan Harbor U this year."

"Really?"

"Yeah. I lost my scholarship. I'll live upstairs and work at the diner."

"But ..." Killian studied the younger man that reminded him of himself. "I thought your grades were good."

"They are."

"Then how does one lose a scholarship?"

"I got caught hacking into the school's computer system, okay?" Hayden spit out disgustedly.

"And?"

"I was trying to impress a girl."

"Alright, now we're getting somewhere," Killian laughed. "What were you going to do for her?"

"Change her grade," Hayden admitted. "She made a C in physics and wanted an A."

"And they caught you? That's it?"

Hayden's face turned red. "They turned me over to Uncle Danny. Said it won't show up on my school record, so I can get into Swan Harbor U, but I have to do community service. Three hundred hours of it."

"Three hundred hours for what?" Emma arrived, her ponytail droopy, but looking beautiful.

"Community service," Hayden replied.

"Oh, well, Maggie always needs help at her sanctuary."

"Scooping poop?" Hayden wrinkled his nose. "That sounds disgusting."

"It's just a thought," laughed Emma.

"Okay, thanks." Hayden stood and let Emma slide into the booth. "Hot chocolate or coffee?"

"Hot chocolate, thanks."

Killian watched him amble toward the counter. "Did you know he was transferring to SHU?"

"I think so," Emma frowned. "Sadie heard Sally complaining to Mary and filled me in."

Killian filed his unsettled feelings away and focused on his fiancée. "How was the visit at the Langley's? Problems?"

"Dental issues," Emma chuckled. "I had to float Ruari's teeth, as they were a little rough. I filed them and before I left, he was already eating. Something tells me he's quite the drama queen."

"I'm glad it was an easy fix. One less thing for Rusty to worry about."

"It was. But I can tell you're worried about something else." She interlocked their fingers. "Share your burdens?"

Killian sighed, wondering what happened to his inability to hide what he was thinking from others.

"Is it Liam?" Her voice lowered. "Or something with Santora?"

"Liam and Elsa are fine," he assured her. "They're on their way to the airport right now. But ..."

"But?" Emma squeaked.

"One cop died, and the other is on a ventilator," he admitted. "I wish Liam didn't have to go back to the City yet."

"He can't take time off?"

"Not without notice."

"He works for Queen's Court, right?"

"Aye." Killian leaned over the table and lowered his voice. "I know what you're thinking, and I love you for it, but no, this isn't your fight."

"What do you mean, 'no, it's not my fight'?" Emma's green eyes flashed. "He's your brother, right?"

"You know the answer, Doc."

"So that means someday he'll be my family. I thought ..."

"Doc." Killian closed her hands between his. "I love you'd even think about doing something like talking to your mom about this, but no."

"But my family owns ..."

He knew she'd worked for years to put distance between her and her family's wealth. Even her mother, Ava King, had stepped away from King Industries, and was spending time on her not-for-profit organization.

"They do, Doc. And I love you offered to help Liam ... and me. But we will get through this, I promise."

"When's Liam going back? Tonight?"

"No." Killian ran his hand through his hair. "Liam's working nights this week, so he's heading back in the morning. But still ..."

"You'll worry."

"Aye."

"Like he used to worry about you when you worked undercover," she finished with a satisfied smile.

"I see what you did there."

"Good." Emma giggled. "Now feed me. I'm starved."

"Liam was right," Killian grinned. "You are high maintenance."

When she giggled and glanced down at the menu, Killian once again thanked the fates that brought her to him. He just hoped good fortune continued to smile on him.

I-295 to Swan Harbor
September 3
2:30 p.m.

Elsa leaned back against the plush leather interior and sighed. "How come you brought your dad's car instead of your prized convertible again?"

Liam gave her a side-eyed glance. "A funny sound," he offered in an off-handed manner. "Decided I didn't want to chance it."

"So, you traded for your dad's plush ride?"

"Only the best for my girl," he tossed out.

Elsa's breath caught at his words, but when she looked at him, he was singing along with the radio. Had he misspoken, or was something truly changing between them?

"When do you have to go back?"

"Are you trying to get rid of me?" Liam teased.

"No, it's just ..."

I'll miss you.

He reached across the console and took her fingers.

"I know."

Do you?

She glanced his direction and there was something about the way he looked that took her breath away. Thick, caramel-colored hair that curled when it was too long. A strong jaw, he'd left scruffy, and bright blue eyes that could go from navy to glacial in a split-second. Plus, he was nice. Not just the pretend kind, but friendly to everyone. Which made it even more difficult to know where she stood with him.

Because usually, he didn't allow people close, preferring to keep them at an arm's distance. Was that changing?

She could only hope so, especially after ....

"What are you thinking?" His twinkling blue eyes locked on her.

"Nothing." She cleared her throat when her voice cracked and felt the heat climbing up her neck toward her cheeks.

Liam chuckled, the sound sending a spark straight to her core.

"You're lying. And by the look on your face, it's quite a delicious thought."

Take back the power, she reminded herself.

Elsa lifted a brow and offered in a prissy voice, "Maybe it is, maybe it isn't."

When his response was a growl, she had to wonder if he could hear her heart galloping like a herd of *Equus caballus,* as Emma would say.

"You can have your secrets," he purred, "for now. But just wait ..."

The way he left it hanging sent her mind spinning into ways she'd like him to get her to talk.

"Threats again, Liam?"

"You know better than that, El," he chuckled. "Promises.

Help!

Are you sure you want it?

"You didn't tell me when you were leaving?" She opted for a safer topic.

"Tomorrow morning. I'm on nights this week. I wish ..."

When his voice faded, she didn't know if it was because he wasn't sure what to say, or because he knew it wouldn't make a difference.

"Me too." She forced her thoughts away from their impending separation.

"What was that sigh for?" Liam smiled. "Let me guess. Was it because you had to lie to your mother, or because the lie worked?"

"Same thing."

When they'd arrived at the hospital to pick up Patty, she'd been yelling at the nurses. She was obstinate and unsafe, unaware of her inabilities. Jerry and Elsa had tried to reason with her, but how do you reason with someone who isn't cognitively intact?

You can't, they'd decided, finally choosing to tap into her awareness level.

Patty refused to believe she was ill. While she understood she was no longer seeing patients, she believed she was still involved in research.

Enter Mindy Grant, Patty's long-time assistant. She was certified as a nurse's aide and willing to put up with her mother's moods. At least Elsa hoped so, as it allowed for her mom to be at home with a caretaker. A win for everyone. For the time being, anyway.

"El," Liam's butter-soft voice pulled her attention back to the here and now. "Will you promise me something?"

"What?"

"You're supposed to say, 'yes', or 'I promise'," he prompted.

He rubbed her fingertips over his jaw and the whiskers both tickled and turned her on.

"Oh, I am, huh?" Elsa gave a long-suffering sigh. "I promise."

"Promise me that if you need me, you'll call me."

It wouldn't be the same as having him there to hold her, but she didn't think she could go back to not having him in her life.

"Okay."

The rhythmic shushing sound of the tires on the pavement lulled her into a dreamy state. Before she was ready, they exited I-295 onto Cove Highway. Its four lanes stretched for several miles before dividing around a copse of trees, to join once again on the other side. Just before Swan Harbor, the road split a second time, with one vein running through the center of town and the other circling along county lines.

A deer in the distance captured her attention. She was watching it run gracefully into the trees, when Liam shouted, shattering the peacefulness.

She turned back in time to see a bright red sports car from the other direction fly across the median.

"Hold on," Liam barked.

Elsa grabbed hold of the armrest with one hand and the console with the other. Her heart climbed into her throat and fear zipped up her spine.

In front of them, almost as if in slow motion, the red car barreled into the front of a black sedan, sending it spinning out of control.

"Liam!" she screamed in horror as the red car crumpled against the guardrail.

They careened toward the crash and Elsa tensed, bracing for impact. Somehow, at the last minute, Liam steered them safely onto the shoulder.

"Are you okay?"

"I'm fine," Elsa told him, fighting to keep her voice from shaking.

"Call 911, love." He squeezed her hands, jumped from the car, and took off running.

Elsa made the call and had just tossed the phone back onto the console when Liam yanked open her door.

"There's a small first aid kit in the glove compartment," he shouted, already on his way toward the trunk. "I've got another one back here."

Her training kicked in and, surprisingly, as she stepped onto the road, her nerves evaporated.

The dark car had spun around, ending up facing the wrong way. Even with the sun bouncing off the windshield, she could tell the airbag had deployed. But the sound of a crying baby pulled her to the back-passenger door.

No!

The locked door and tinted windows had her pressing her face close to peer inside. Except, she could only see the edge of a rear-facing car seat and a waving little arm.

I'm here.

Her thoughts scattered, but unable to reach the child, she ran around to the front and knocked on the driver's side window. "Hey," she shouted. "Can you open the door?"

The ambulance and firetruck's sirens grew louder, but they weren't coming fast enough. Every few minutes, she rattled the door handle and knocked on the window, hoping ... praying the woman would open the door. The longer the door remained closed, the louder the baby's screams, ripping away little pieces of her heart.

Not again. Not again.

"El, are you okay?" Liam jogged back toward where the ambulance had parked.

"There's a baby, Liam." She fought to remain focused. "And the doors are locked."

"Hold on, love."

He took off again, and she heard him yell, "Liam Reade, NYC Paramedic ..."

It wasn't long before two of the Swan Harbor firefighters started toward the sports car, and Liam ran back to the ambulance with the third.

A feeling of helplessness rushed through her, not unlike the one she'd gotten when Jerry had given voice to Patty's diagnosis. Physicians searched for answers and took care of patients, rarely taking the time to stand around.

Just like when ….

Except she couldn't cure her mother. Her only option was to plan for what came next and lean on Liam.

The helplessness she was feeling standing next to a hurt woman and crying baby was different. She couldn't do anything ... yet. However, she could make plans for what needed to be done. As well as what *not* to do.

"This is Rod." Liam thumbed over his shoulder at the young EMT he'd arrived with. "Has the woman moved at all?"

"A little, but I don't think they were purposeful."

"Okay, here, hold this." He handed her a bag and went to work with a tool that would help open the door.

Elsa turned her attention to the baby, whose cries had grown louder. Seconds later, Liam had the door open.

"Go!" Liam took the bag from her and dropped it on the ground. "Help the child, love."

She squeezed Liam's arm in support and ran around to the other side of the car. Rod had pulled out the car seat and when his eyes met hers, she saw fear.

He's young and new at this, she thought, or he would have been masking his emotions.

"What is it?"

"It's Julianna," he whispered in a trembling voice. "My cousin's baby."

Crap!

"Put her there." Elsa pointed to an even spot on the ground and hurried forward. Then grabbed some gloves, a light, and a stethoscope. "The driver is your cousin?"

"Yeah." He swallowed. "That's Tracey Gibson, she's ..."

"Sally's daughter." Elsa remembered meeting her briefly right after she'd moved to town. "Her father is Doctor Patterson."

"Yeah."

His face was red, and he was sweating, behaviors she wasn't used to seeing in the EMTs she encountered. Liam's motions were smooth, fluid, natural. But he'd been doing the job for years. Rod's actions were those of someone who hadn't been involved in many rescues.

Trembling voice, shaking hands. Nervous.

"How long have you been working for Swan Harbor Fire?"

"Today's my first day," he admitted.

Crap! Poor guy!

"Oh, wow, trial by fire, huh?"

Another ambulance arrived, drowning out his response and her initial thought was, *I hope they're more experienced.* Then she felt guilty because these men worked for her new hometown.

"Rod, come help me transfer," Liam's shout had the younger man tossing the notepad he'd been writing in towards her and running to help.

Next step ... save the child.

"Okay, Julianna," Elsa murmured. "Let's get you to the hospital." While the little girl appeared to be fine, she'd just been involved in a severe car wreck, and experience had taught her you never know.

LIAM WATCHED THE AMBULANCE CARRYING THE MOTHER AND child leave, heading back to Swan Harbor General. While he knew Elsa was where she needed to be, he was worried about her.

It hadn't escaped his attention that the situation wasn't that different from another accident they'd been involved with not so long ago. One that left its mark on Elsa, and if something similar happened this time, he wanted to be there for her. Besides, he missed her.

You miss her? Already? What are you going to do when you're ...?

He slammed the brakes on those thoughts, because nothing had changed.

Bugger that! If you'd just face the ....

"Liam?"

It was almost a relief when his brother called his name, and he could push off the thoughts yet again.

"Killian." Liam let out a tired breath and went back to watching the paramedics and firefighters who were working to remove the driver from the red sports car. "What are you doing here?"

"Heard about the wreck and when I checked your location, I saw you were in the center. What happened?"

"Kid in the sports car was going too fast and lost control."

"Looks like Simon Coleman's car," Killian grunted.

Liam frowned. "I'm assuming you've encountered young Simon before?"

"You could say that." Killian shook his head. "He wrapped his first car around a tree while texting. Performed community service, but it doesn't seem like it made an impression."

"I have a feeling things might be different this time," Liam confided. "Legs are crushed under the dash, and I heard one guy mention a fractured pelvis."

"Ouch."

"You could say that again. Anyway, thanks for checking on me. I need to go check on my gi—" then he caught himself and amended it to, "Elsa. She rode with the baby and mother from the sedan."

Killian winced. "Did you get a name?"

"Tracey," Liam frowned, "didn't hear a last name." But the look he'd seen in Elsa's eyes told him she'd been thinking the same thing he was.

"You're still driving back tomorrow?" Killian asked, and Liam could hear the underlying worry in his brother's voice.

"Yeah. Any news from your sources?"

"No. But I trust Captain Weaver."

"Okay." Several half-scenes began in Liam's head, but where any of them were going, he wasn't sure. "You need a ride? I'm going to the hospital."

"No, I drove." Killian waved toward where he'd left his car. "Let me know if you need anything else."

Wearily, Liam climbed into the car and the scent of Elsa's perfume immediately surrounded him. Since picking her up Friday evening, he'd encountered his share of emotions. But because of where they were and what had happened, he'd continued to shove them aside, needing to get through the moment.

Except they hadn't gone away. Instead, they were sitting there ... hanging out on the edges of his consciousness. Waiting for him to acknowledge them.

Their kiss in the hospital parking lot.

Dinner at Sally's.

Walking her home.

An all-powerful goodnight kiss.

The feel of having her come apart in his arms.

His heart squeezing when he found her crying in the shower.

Stop! This isn't you!

Could it be, though? Did he have the strength to face the past in order to have a future?

He wasn't sure, but every time he thought about leaving Elsa behind in Swan Harbor, the burning in the center of his gut churned.

How was he to fight that?

TWELVE

Swan Harbor General
September 3
3:00 p.m.

As soon as they arrived at the hospital, Elsa followed
Julianna into the Emergency Department. The memories of another time
when a baby had arrived after a car crash threatened to overwhelm her, but she
refused to give them air.

The problem was she felt she was banging her head against some invisible
wall, and she didn't know how to get around it.

"Julianna's crying. Shouldn't we take her out of the car seat?" Rod asked
as they'd climbed into the ambulance.

"Let me take her out of this car seat," he offered again as soon as they'd
arrived, and the baby was still crying.

"Not yet." Elsa took a deep breath. "I don't want her moved yet."

"But why?" he pushed a little harder. "She's fine, and Tracey is awake and
asking for her daughter."

He's young. You were once too.

"Do you want me to talk to Tracey?"

The look of relief on his face answered her questions about the family dynamics.

"That would be good," he mumbled, never taking his eyes off the baby.

"Okay. Stay with Julianna and talk to her. Just don't take her out of that car seat."

Elsa left him with the baby and went looking for Tracey Gibson. She found her awake, holding a bloody towel on her head and arguing with the nurse.

"I'm fine, Allison," Tracey was saying. "Just put a bandage on my head and let me go check on Julianna."

"Tracey." Elsa walked into the room and flipped the curtain closed.

"You!" Tracey's angry eyes shot sparks. "Rod said Julianna was fine. Bring her to me."

"I will just as soon as I give her a thorough checkup," Elsa promised. "In the meantime, let Allison take care of your head."

"But Rod said," Tracey's voice quivered.

"I just want to make sure she's really okay," Elsa repeated.

Tracey's blue eyes clashed with hers for several seconds until finally, the young mother wilted. "You'll let me know?"

"As soon as I know something," Elsa promised.

With that taken care of, she changed into scrubs and followed Julianna's cries. When she stepped into the room, the baby's movements sucked her back into the memory she'd been trying to fight.

"Winters, Garcia, come with me," Doctor Marshall Lucas snapped. "Multiple MVA on the Parkway."

Elsa glanced at Carmen Garcia, a new intern at Queen's, and they took off after Doctor Lucas.

"What do we know?" Elsa asked when she finally caught up with him.

The way he looked at her always made her feel like an idiot, as if she should have known the answer before she asked.

"Four cars, we're getting five victims. I believe three are peds."

They rushed into the Emergency Department just as several sets of paramedics flew through the doors, the last one carrying a car seat.

"Winters." Doctor Lucas barked. "Bay 5."

Elsa stepped into bay 5, coming face to face with the gorgeous blue-eyed paramedic she'd seen several times. Lieutenant Reade, she noted, reading the tag on his uniform shirt.

"What do we have?" Elsa snapped.

His lips twitched, making her want to roll her eyes at how prissy she sounded.

"Jordan, age eight. Alert, vitals good, but complaining his chest hurts. Breath sounds normal."

"Okay, thanks." She smiled and stepped around him. Dark, solemn eyes greeted her. "Hi Jordan, I'm Doctor Winters. Can you tell me if anything hurts?"

"Here." He rubbed his hand over his chest. "Where's my mom?"

"I'm not sure. Let's get you taken care of and we can go find her, okay?"

"'Kay." A single tear slid down his cheek, and her heart twisted a little.

Elsa tightened her jaw, wanting to stay neutral. Empathetic and professional were her goal, but it wasn't always the easiest. Plus, don't let them see you cry.

"I just want to take some pictures of these ribs." She gently touched his bony chest. "Then we'll go find your mom."

As soon as transport arrived to take him for X-rays, Elsa went looking for the mother. In bay 4, she found Doctor Lucas working on a toddler. Bay 3 was an adult male, she assumed, was the father. And in bay 1, the car seat was on the floor, as if forgotten.

"Hey there." Elsa squatted in front of the car seat and screamed, "Code White!"

"I said not yet!" Elsa snapped, jumping back to the present.

Swan Harbor General
September 3
5:30 p.m.

Liam found her in the small chapel, just like he'd found her the last time. Then, even as her shoulders shook, he couldn't comfort her and tell her it wasn't her fault. That time there'd been grief because of death.

He started towards her, his steps hushed by the plush carpeting. Before he could say anything, she fell into his arms.

This is where she belongs, floated through his head before he could stop it.

"Elsa, love." Liam soothed his hands down her slender back and tightened his hold on her. "Tough memories?"

She nodded and took a deep breath before stepping back. "I kept pushing them away but ..."

"They kept showing up?"

"Yes."

He knew the story as well as Elsa. He'd been involved in transporting the family to Queen's Court Medical. When they'd arrived on the scene of the accident, the child had appeared to be fine. Some thirty minutes later, when Elsa found the infant, her pupils were fixed and dilated. Cause of death—a brain bleed, secondary to being stuck by flying debris.

"And Julianna? What happened?"

"The baby is in a medically induced coma." Elsa wiped the tears from her face.

"Oh, El." Liam led her to a pew and settled her in the curve of his arm. Then he waited.

Examining the emotions running around inside wasn't what he'd intended when he'd stepped into the quiet of the chapel. With his arms around her and knowing she willingly turned to him for comfort, he felt like he had little choice. The thought of something happening and him not being there for her unsettled him. Could he live with himself *if* the baby died, and he hadn't been here for her?

"Did you know today was Rod's first day with Swan Harbor Fire Department?"

He hadn't expected that question, and it took him several minutes to catch up.

"I thought he looked young."

"Twenty." She scooted back and angled toward him. "EMT training, passed his exams and minimum number of hours."

"And his first trauma accident was family."

"Not only family." She laced their fingers together and the word complete zipped by. "The kid in the sports car was a high school friend."

"Ouch."

Too much too soon, he thought, filing it away to investigate at another time.

"But how does Rod's training factor into Julianna's situation?"

Elsa sent him a side-eyed look he interpreted to be '*I knew you'd make me talk*'.

"When I stepped around the car at the accident and Rod turned with the car seat, there was fear in his eyes," she began. "Then, while I examined the baby, he followed directions with no problem."

"But that changed?"

"Yes. When we arrived, I followed the baby, and he disappeared. Minutes later, he was back, hovering, wanting to take Julianna out of her seat," she continued. "I think he was getting an earful from his cousin, so I offered to go talk to her. But when I returned ..."

"He was trying to take her out again?"

"No. There was another man in there who was, and I lost it. Told Rod I was going to report him to his captain and asked the other man who the hell he thought he was."

Liam brushed his knuckles across her cheek. "Let me guess. It was Julianna's father."

"Yes," she winced. "When he stepped away, and I got a look at Julianna's movements, I freaked. Extension and flexion, but of her left arm only."

Liam whistled. "Posturing?"

"Yes. I grabbed a collar and started tossing out instructions. Once I sent her up for a CAT scan, I kept thinking about that little girl in New York. That if we wouldn't have left her there, all alone, then maybe ..."

Her chin trembled and tears pooled in her eyes, and Liam's heart broke.

"Oh, love. You can't think like that." He kissed her on the forehead and just the touch of his lips to her soft skin ignited a spark deep inside.

"We do the best we can do and learn from mistakes. Isn't that what you did? Took your experiences from New York and worked to make sure they didn't happen here?"

"That's why I wanted the baby to stay in her car seat." Elsa frowned. "I don't know why that was such a big deal."

Liam had watched Elsa more often than she knew, interacting with patients and their families. For them not to respect her medical opinion was unusual.

"Did you tell Rod you were a pediatrician?" She raised a brow in question, making him prod a little more. "Did you tell them why you didn't want to take her out of the car seat?"

She gasped and her eyes went wide. "I ..."

"Not about the little girl in New York." He hurried to correct any misconception. "But why you didn't want her moved, medically?"

There were several expressions that crossed her face, and something told him she wasn't done beating herself up.

CRAP!

"I, I ..."

She had, hadn't she? Or had she been so focused on trying to push the memory away and concentrate on Julianna, she'd forgotten basic stuff. *Explain what you're doing, and people will cooperate more.*

"How could I have forgotten something so simple?"

"It happens." Liam squeezed her fingers and scooted closer. "In this case, did getting angry at the adults help the child?"

Had it? Had she handled the case correctly?

"Why did you push for a CAT scan?" he asked without waiting for an answer.

"With the way the baby was moving, especially only on one side, I worried about a brain injury or something else neurological."

"Just like the baby in New York?"

"Yes."

"Then what happened?"

"I was watching the CT being done and Doctor Patterson walked in." Elsa sent Liam a crooked smile. "He's a tall man, and the head of the neurology department, *and* Julianna's grandfather."

"Oh?"

She smirked and wanted to say, '*Isn't that my word?*' Instead, she tried to explain, "I thought maybe ..."

"He would belittle your abilities like Marshall?"

Her first thought was, *How did you know that?* "Something like that."

"Marshall has that reputation, does Doctor Patterson?"

Elsa thought back to her first meeting with Julianna's grandfather and grinned. "He's soft spoken and has a reputation for pushing for answers. But he's so ... tall, you expect him to be different."

"A fighter for his patients." Liam tilted his head and his blue eyes twinkled. "Sounds like someone else I know."

His compliment sent a feeling of pride zipping through her, as that was how she wanted to be known. A fighter for her patients.

Like you're fighting for what you want with Liam?

"Was it the doctor who stood next to you during the CAT scan or the grandfather?" His question sent her thoughts away from the personal and back into the medical.

As the images of Julianna's head, neck and back flashed by on the monitor, the door opened and the man she knew as Doctor Patterson rushed in.

Elsa met his stare, prepared to defend her stance. Except the man looking back at her wasn't what she'd expected. His eyes were a deep chocolate brown and in them she saw just how worried he was about his granddaughter.

"Doctor Patterson, I'm—" she began.

"—Duh-Duh-Doctor Winters," he interrupted. "Your reputation precedes you."

Her breath caught, as that statement could mean several things.

"My, my reputation?"

She glanced up, and there was a twinkle in his dark eyes she hadn't expected.

"Puh-Puh-Pearl Houston says you are an excellent addition to the Swan Harbor General's staff. Marshall Lucas and I go way back."

Wait, what?

"Doctor Lucas and you ..."

"Went to medical school together," Danny Patterson admitted. "He's an asshat personally, and I can't imagine working for the man, but he knows talent when he sees it. And he said you were a very gifted physician."

She had to fight not to show her surprise.

"That was kind of him."

"Ha!" Danny barked. "Kind and Marshall Lucas don't belong in the same sentence. Now tell me what's going on with my granddaughter."

"He listened." Elsa's eyes met Liam's. "Then discussed Julianna's care with me as if he respected my opinion."

She didn't know why, but Doctor Patterson's praise only reiterated her feelings of belonging in Swan Harbor. If only ....

"Did the scan show anything?" Liam asked quietly, making her realize she'd left out a few pieces of her story.

Elsa reorganized her thoughts and explained, "Nothing overt showed up, which is good news. However, because Julianna's neurological system isn't fully developed, we may not yet be able to detect it. We're keeping her asleep for a few days, as it's the only way to make sure she stays still."

"Which allows any bruising around her spinal cord to heal, right?"

"That's right. We'll wake her up tomorrow and go from there. I'm hopeful though."

She blinked rapidly, fighting not to fall back into the constant questioning of her abilities.

Liam tugged her into his arms. "Your plan is good. Not only did you get the approval of the child's grandfather, but also one from the head of the neurology department. You did a good job."

The emotion in his voice had Elsa leaning back enough to look into his eyes. He had shuttered his emotions from her more often than not in New York. Since he'd come to Swan Harbor, she'd imagined him saying things to her she'd only dreamed of before. Could she trust what she was seeing?

Fight for me.

Trust me.

Be patient.

He kissed her lightly and pulled her up. "Are you hungry?"

"Maybe a little," she admitted. "But I don't want to leave."

"Hospital cafeteria?"

"You don't have to ..."

Liam stopped her words with another kiss. "I'm where I want to be, alright?"

A little corner of her mind kept thinking he was leaving tomorrow and how much it was going to hurt. The rest of her head ... and heart, couldn't be happier.

"Okay." She kissed him again. "Thank you."

"Anytime, love." He slung his arm around her and directed her from the chapel. "Anytime."

Oh, Liam, she thought, as her heart expanded and spilled over.

Love ....

The Beachside Inn
September 3
9:30 p.m.

It was late by the time Liam kissed Elsa on the steps of her cottage and drove back to the Beachside Inn. Except, as he stepped into the homey lobby of the old inn, it wasn't relief he was feeling, but loneliness. Not an emotion he'd experienced much, nor knew how to handle.

"Hey, Liam." Tia unfolded from the sofa where she'd been sitting in front of the fire. "How's Julianna, Tracey and Scott? It's lucky you and Elsa were there when the crash happened."

Liam frowned, as the speed at which news traveled in the small town still caused his head to spin.

"And you know about the accident because of the gossip chain? Or is that the spy network?"

She laughed. "A bit of both in this case. Tracey is my cousin."

A light went on in Liam's head at her last name. "Patterson, that's right. As in Doctor Patterson?"

"Yeah, that's my uncle. My father is Danny's brother, Troy. He's a lobsterman."

"Fresh seafood at Sally's." Liam grinned. "Handy."

"That's one way to look at it," she agreed with a laugh. "Elsa okay? Uncle Danny said she was wonderful with Julianna, but he was worried about her."

Tia's statement had several emotions coursing through him. Pride that Elsa's skills were being noticed, and a sliver of what felt suspiciously like jealousy that another man was worried about his woman.

See, that wasn't so hard to admit, was it?

And frustration, he added silently, almost as an afterthought, he wouldn't be around for her.

"El is fine," he rushed to defend. "She's worried about Julianna, but she's a bloody fine doctor and will take care of the baby as if she were family."

Tia smirked. "Does she know?"

"That she's a good doctor?" He shrugged. "I'm sure she does."

"Nice evade." She shook her head. "Quite like your brother ... or at least your brother before Emma."

Liam frowned. "Evade?" He was fairly sure he'd missed something along the way, but was too tired to pull it out and examine it. "You're up late." He switched subjects, hoping she'd take the bait.

Another smirk crossed Tia's face. "Maybe not like Killian." With a shrug, she changed topics. "Nic and I took a walk, and were enjoying a drink by the fire. He went up just before you arrived."

"A walk," Liam repeated. "That sounds like a good idea. Maybe I'll ..."

"Go for it. Head toward the pier, though. It's pretty rocky in the other direction."

"Will do, thanks."

In deference to the wind blowing off the water, he grabbed his leather jacket and stepped onto the hard-packed sand. It was quiet. Almost too quiet, as he was used to noise at all hours of the day and night back home. Was that part of what was troubling him? The differences in the small town versus those in the City?

There was just a feeling when we arrived. Like I had walked the streets, stood on the cliffs, and looked out at the sea. It felt like home.

Elsa's words rattled around inside and he could admit they unsettled him. Except was it because he could see the truth behind her statement of feeling as if she'd always belonged? Or was it because the place she considered her home wasn't a place he belonged?

Are you sure of that?

Bloody hell, no! He wasn't sure of anything, except ....

You're lonely.

"Bugger that."

He'd come to Swan Harbor to tell Killian about the man on the subway platform and about the officers. It hadn't been for Elsa.

Are you sure?

No. That had been established. He wasn't sure about anything.

A flutter drew his attention to the water, where he could just make out the white feathers of the swan.

"Looking for company tonight, mate?" Liam asked Jonesy.

When the swan swam closer to shore, he had to wonder at his sanity.

"I don't think he likes me," Elsa said. "Gives me the side-eye stare when I come down here."

The swan met *his* gaze head on, and Liam decided he was going daft when he imagined he could understand what was being said.

I'm alone because my mate died too soon. What's your excuse?
What had Barbi said the day Elsa told him she was moving?
Sometimes we have to let go of the past in order to move toward the future.
Did he want to be alone? He didn't think so, but if he were to face his past, he needed help.

Liam: Driving back tomorrow morning. When will you be around?

He was halfway back to the Beachside when his phone buzzed.

Finn: Friday, soon enough?

Liam: Fine.

Once he talked to his father, what then? Elsa would still be in Swan Harbor and Santora would still be a threat.

THIRTEEN

Swan Harbor
Sheriff's Department
September 7
12:30 p.m.

Even though the week had been surprisingly uneventful, Killian hadn't stopped worrying about all the 'what ifs.'

He worried about Liam.

He worried Santora was going to be released.

He worried he'd been found and everything he loved was in jeopardy.

He worried Emma was in danger.

But even though he worried, the six sense he'd relied on for years to stay alive was unusually silent.

Which was why, when he was waiting at Sally's for his order and the hairs on the back of his neck tingled, he took notice. This differed from what he'd come to expect since his move. Not the typical dirty looks from an old date or someone he'd ticketed. The churning in his gut told him it was real. Someone was watching him.

Killian stepped back and glanced at the mirror behind the bar, casually surveying the diner.

Sydney was at his usual table and kept glancing up every few seconds. He was most likely looking for something newsworthy.

Nic Nucci, the man seeing Tia, was at a corner table and kept glancing in his direction. What was his deal?

Morgan and Chloe, women he'd once dated, kept trying to catch his eye. Was his eerie feeling because of them? Or was he just getting soft after eighteen months in his new home?

"Ladies." He tipped his head in their direction on the way out, expecting the feeling to disappear. Once outside, though, it persisted, pushing him to listen ... to look.

Slowly, he perused the sidewalks, searching for the unfamiliar. Something out of place, or someone who stood out.

A movement to his right heightened his senses. Killian nonchalantly glanced in that direction, just as someone darted across the street and disappeared.

Forget about it. Go eat.

Was he looking for something that wasn't there?

After Violet and with what was happening in New York ....

Killian skirted around the people on the sidewalk and hurried in the direction he'd seen the figure disappear. By the time he made it to the cross street, he didn't see anyone.

An abandoned apartment building took up the entire block. An old gas station stood on the other side of the street and the road gave way to an alley, leading to the beach. On the way back to work, though, the feeling persisted.

"Lunch." He held the bag aloft as he passed Dylan and Rusty on the way to the conference room.

"Why are you ...?" Rusty began when he arrived. Then quickly asked, "What happened?"

Killian tossed Rusty his lunch. "Start eating. We'll talk when Dylan gets in here."

While they waited for Dylan, Killian kept going through his feelings ... his steps. The sense of being watched had persisted until he'd walked into the sheriff's department.

"What's up?" Dylan sauntered in, spit out a succinct response, and pushed the door closed. "Santora?"

"I don't know," Killian admitted. "But my gut started churning while I was at Sally's."

"What did Emma feed you for breakfast?" Rusty quipped.

"Wanker," Killian shot back.

Rusty snickered and tossed out, "Plonker."

"Boys." Dylan tiredly ran his hand through his hair. "Can we get back to the problem?"

Killian exchanged looks with Rusty. *What's up with him?*

Rusty shrugged, leaving both in the dark.

"Now," Dylan continued. "Your gut churned."

"Aye." Killian threw his wrapper in the trash. "I know this is Swan Harbor, but my years undercover helped me develop a pretty good sense of my surroundings. Someone was watching me today."

"Who was at Sally's?" Dylan snapped, once more in full sheriff mode.

"Sydney."

"Looking for a story," Rusty stated.

"My thoughts too," agreed Killian. "Nic Nucci was there."

"The one dating Tia?" Dylan frowned.

"Aye." Killian glanced at Rusty, then back at Dylan. "What does he do, again?"

"Technology," Dylan offered. "He's teaching at Swan Harbor High this year."

"Why?"

While he didn't know many of the teachers at the high school level, Killian hadn't been aware there were holes in the curriculum.

"Apparently, the other teacher was teaching them skills that aren't considered basic computer science," Rusty smirked.

"Must be who taught Hayden to hack into his university's computers." Killian shook his head, still surprised by the young Patterson's downfall.

"Could be," Dylan agreed. "Who else was in Sally's?"

"Chloe and Morgan," Killian admitted.

"Hell hath no fury," Rusty reminded him of how angry the women had been when he'd started dating Emma.

"I thought of that," Killian snapped. "But bloody hell, that was eight or nine months ago."

"Anyone else?" Dylan asked.

"There was a guy, or at least I think it was male." Killian concentrated, trying to remember more about the elusive figure. "Turned onto First street. By the time I got there, they were gone."

"First street?" Dylan perked up.

"Aye." Killian nodded. "An old apartment building takes up most of the block. On the other side is an old gas station."

"My parents lived in that building before they were married," Dylan grinned. "I think HCI is trying to buy it. Maybe it was someone working for Gray."

"Could be." While Killian thought there was a possibility, it didn't explain his feeling of danger. "Rusty and I will check it out."

"Sounds good," Dylan responded absently. "Let me know."

Once he left, Killian frowned. "I've never seen him that distracted at work."

"Nor look that disheveled," Rusty added. "Something's going on."

"Think it's the coke selling guy?" Killian quipped.

"Don't be such a dick," Rusty grumbled, still annoyed over the incident.

❧

Swan Harbor General
September 7
2:00 p.m.

ELSA WALKED INTO THE ROOM WHERE JULIANNA AND HER parents, Tracey and Scott, had stayed since Monday. Each day, they'd turned off the medications that kept the baby unconscious and watched her movements. While there had been steady progress, they were still watching. Something inside, though, told her, 'today's the day.'

Hope.

"Come on, Juli," Tracey cooed. "Open your eyes for mama."

The more her mother spoke to her, the stronger Julianna's eyelids fluttered.

"That's a big girl," Tracey continued. "Let me see those pretty blue eyes."

Elsa held her breath as the baby's eyes slowly opened and she waved around her left arm.

Tracey stroked the bottom of Julianna's left foot, and when a normal Babinski was present, cried, "Look, she's moving."

"Try the other side," Elsa suggested. "Start with her hands."

"Can you grab mama's hand?" Tracey whispered, stroking Julianna's right palm.

When the baby turned her hand toward her mother's, Elsa had to force down tears. "And now her foot."

Tracey took a deep breath, glanced at her husband, and stroked the baby's foot.

Elsa's breath caught and as the little toes flared, her knees almost gave out.

"That's good." Elsa smiled at the happy parents. "She's ready for the next step. I'll get that set up."

"Thank you, Elsa," Tracey sniffed.

"You're very welcome." Elsa grinned, relieved it was almost over and the outcome hadn't been a repeat of the incident in New York. "I'll be back later."

When she left the room, millions of emotions coursed through her, threatening to spill.

Liam. She ducked into an empty room and hit dial.

"'Lo," Liam's sleep rough voice came across the line.

I miss you.

Crap!

"Oh, Liam," she sighed. "I forgot the time. Call me later."

Before she hung up, she heard, "Elsa, love. What is it?" and her heart flipped.

"It's Julianna," Elsa breathed. "She's awake and everything looks good."

"Of course she is." Liam's husky baritone caressed the words. "She had you fighting for her."

"Thank you, Liam," Elsa's voice broke. "I wish ..." *You were holding me. I was holding you. You loved me.*

"Me too, El," Liam whispered. "Me too."

Do you?

"I'm sorry I woke you—"

"I'm not," he interrupted. "These moments matter to me. *You* matter to me."

Her heart tripped, but since she couldn't come up with anything else to say, murmured, "Go back to sleep. I'll call you later."

"I'll be waiting. Goodbye, love."

Before she was ready, the call ended.

"Elsa?"

"Doctor Patterson." Elsa turned from the window with a smile. "You've seen Julianna?"

"I told you to call me Dan." He came completely into the room. "And yes, I've seen my granddaughter. She's perfect. Thank you."

Elsa fought her natural inclination to push off the work she'd done to help the baby.

"I'm glad–"

"You're supposed to say, 'thank you.'" He laughed. "At least that's what my wife would say."

"Thank you," Elsa murmured huskily. "Did you decide which rehabilitation center would be best?"

"Wuh-Wuh-We're going to do that now," he promised. "I'll let you know as soon as we decide."

Elsa watched him leave and tried to remember if she'd ever felt this much a part of something before. It was everything she'd hoped for, except ....

Keep the power, she reminded herself. How did one do that, though, when you weren't living in the same place?

The question remained for the next several hours while she made notes in Julianna's chart and prepared for the little girl to be transferred.

It stayed with her when she stopped by her office to assure all was in order for her pediatrics board exam.

Then remained when she stopped at the A&P to find something for dinner. While she wandered around the store randomly throwing stuff into her basket, she realized shopping wouldn't solve her problem.

The Swan Harbor 'gossip chain' had been busy, and everyone had questions and congratulations about Julianna and her recovery. It was a struggle to maintain patient confidentiality, yet not come across as a stuck-up snob.

"Elsa, are you okay?"

"I'm fine, why?"

"You were frowning." Molly gave her a look of concern. "I thought you'd be celebrating. After all, you saved Julianna."

"That's why I was frowning," Elsa admitted. "Patient confidentiality and Swan Harbor don't really go hand in hand."

"Tell me about it." A crooked smile crossed Molly's face. "It's hard to keep anything secret in this town."

Something in the other woman's tone had Elsa glancing down. "Oh!" she exclaimed when she noticed what Molly was holding. "Are you?"

Instead of happiness and excitement she would have expected, Molly's chin quivered.

"Do you want to talk?" Elsa hesitated a second and added, "After all, you've been listening to my Liam woes for weeks now."

Several expressions came and went on Molly's face, before she replied, "I heard he went with you to see your mother."

The way Molly changed subjects had Elsa wondering if she'd stepped too close to some friend line. After all, she was the *new girl* in town, and maybe being a '*Share your burdens*' person had to be earned.

"He did," Elsa grinned. Then she tried to backpedal her offer so Molly wouldn't feel pressured. "Hey, I didn't mean to put you on the spot. It's okay–"

"Actually," Molly interrupted with a relieved smile. "I'd like to talk. Thanks."

Her words calmed something inside. "Okay, good. Let me grab a few more things and I'll meet you by the front door, okay?"

Molly nodded and dropped the pregnancy kit into her basket. "Thanks. I'll see you in a minute.

Elsa watched the other woman walk away and wondered what was going on in Molly's head. How would it feel if ...? She slammed that door shut, as she wasn't there yet.

But you didn't know you wanted forever with Liam until ....

Shut up! This is different.

Is it?

By the time she met Molly, her thoughts weren't any more settled than her friend's. How was she supposed to offer sage advice about the possibility of impending motherhood when her own emotions were all over the place?

"I'm terrified," Molly blurted.

"You sound normal so far," Elsa pointed out. "Do you want a baby?"

"Yes!" Molly exclaimed. "But I'm terrified I'm not. I know, it makes no sense, but we've been trying for a while and ..."

"You're afraid to get your hopes up?" Elsa suggested.

Molly laughed, albeit a humorless one. "Maybe. I keep thinking if I don't take the test, I can pretend I am. Dylan's lost so much in his life, and I really want to have a baby with him."

Elsa knew Dylan's parents and twin brother had died in a car accident when he was younger. But with her mother's life-altering diagnosis still fresh in her mind, she stepped back from the idea of loss and into her professional mode.

"Isn't it better to know early? Then you can see your doctor and get started on vitamins and ..." When she saw Molly's expression, Elsa mentally face-palmed. "I'm sorry, that wasn't what you wanted to hear."

"No, but maybe it's what I needed to hear. Burying my head in 'what ifs' won't do anyone any good, especially if I'm ..." She let the sentence hang and placed her hand over her stomach. "It would certainly explain a few things."

"Morning sickness?"

"More like all-day sickness," Molly groaned. "But let's talk about something less scary for a while. Tell me about you and Liam. Did you guys work things out?"

"I thought you said less scary," laughed Elsa.

"Come on," Molly prodded. "I've been dying to know what happened while you were away.

Since returning from her trip, Elsa had tried not to define her time with Liam.

"Things were everything I've wanted but scared to hope for," she settled on.

Molly smiled. "See, in Swan Harbor, the heart knows. And I'm going to say the same thing to you I said to Emma. When your heart speaks, it's best to listen."

"I'm trying," Elsa admitted. "And trying not to bury my head in those 'what ifs' you mentioned. I'm trying to be hopeful."

"Hope and hearts," Molly offered. "What more is there?"

"Seems like a statement that could fit both of us right now."

"Agreed." Whatever else she was going to say faded when Elsa's phone chirped. "Go ahead and get that. We'll talk later."

Elsa's heart raced, as she knew that sound. "Hi," she answered breathlessly.

New York
To Tarrytown
September 7
5:30 p.m.

HER SEXY VOICE SENT A ZIP OF ELECTRICITY FROM LIAM'S HEART to his balls, causing his jeans to tighten. "Hello to you too."

"Liam," she giggled. "I didn't expect to hear from you so quickly."

"I'll let you go if you're busy," he offered, when he couldn't decipher his feelings.

"Liam?"

"Yes?"

"I, I just meant ..."

Her hesitation had Liam slamming the brakes on whatever was going on inside to focus on her.

"Elsa, love, forgive me. I didn't mean to come across as a jealous shrew."

"Jealous? You? But ..."

"You don't think I'm capable of jealousy?" he asked, not sure he wanted to hear her answer.

She was quiet for so long he thought about pulling the question back.

"No. Yes. But that would mean," she huffed. "I don't know."

"You don't know what?" he pushed again, because surely, she knew how he felt.

But do you?

Do I what?

Know how you feel?

Yes. No. Yes.

See? You need to stop being a ponce. You're just confusing her.

Her? Bloody hell, she'd been confusing him since the night of Killian and Emma's engagement party. It started when she'd turned her sassy mouth in his direction and then gone for a walk. Once she'd returned ....

Yes?

You know what happened. For the first time, they'd made love, and the experience tore him apart.

It was that bad?

Bloody hell, no! It was that good. It was everything he'd feared but hoped for. Everything he'd wished for but knew would never be his.

Why?

Because ....

"Liam? Are you still there?"

Focus on her!

"I'm sorry again, Sweet Elsa." He tightened his hold on the steering wheel and jumped a little closer to that line. "I'm on my way to see my father."

"Oh?"

"Damn, El." He adjusted in the seat. "Do you know how hard it is?"

"It?"

Liam chuckled. "That came out all wrong. I was talking about how hard it is to say certain things."

Nice save.

"What are you finding it so hard to say, Liam?"

Tell her.

"That," sweat beads popped out on his forehead and his heart expanded, "I, I miss you."

See, that wasn't so hard.

Once the words were out, he realized how true they were. He missed her and didn't want to end up alone like Jonesy.

Comparing yourself to a swan again?

"Oh, Liam," Elsa whispered. "I miss you too."

With her words, his heart expanded even more. "Yeah?"

"Yes."

"Good."

"Wait, what?" she giggled. "You think it's good that I miss you?"

"I do. That way, you won't forget me."

"I thought that was what you wanted when you didn't ask me to stay in New York," she replied. "When you walked into the hospital, I was—"

"Happy? Excited? Upset?" He tossed out several adjectives, hoping she would agree with any or all.

"Shocked," she offered, one he'd not considered.

"Shocked? But shocked in a good way, right?"

"What do you think?"

Her voice grew husky, and it took all his willpower not to forgo the trip to his father's and head for Swan Harbor.

"It felt good to me, too." He opted for a direction he might have shied away from at any other time.

"You're going to talk about our kiss?" She met him in a place he hadn't expected.

"Of course, the damn kiss," he growled.

"Wow! This is a new side of you," Elsa observed. "I've just never pictured you as a growler before."

Her focus on how he'd said something and not *what* had him running to catch up.

"No?"

"No." He imagined her nibbling on her bottom lip, trying to decide how much to say. "In movies, television, or books, growling is a sign of passion."

"And I'm not allowed to be passionate?" he asked, confused as he thought that's what she wanted.

"It's not that you can't feel passion, Liam," she went on. "It's that you won't let yourself. Or at least you've not let yourself feel it ... or love before with me."

Liam's heart raced. Was it from fear because of what he thought she might be saying? Or was it because of what he wanted her to say?

It was quiet on the other end of the phone, then he heard, "Doctor Elsa. Look at Lila. She hurt her paw."

"Beth, honey, she's on the phone," a deeper voice followed.

When Elsa returned, she sounded distracted. Was it because she was upset by what she'd said? Or was she getting off the phone for other reasons?

"I'll let you go." Liam took the initiative, assuming she was going to hang-up. "I'm almost at my dad's place. We'll talk soon. Bye."

Then, because he felt like he'd completely lost the plot, he hung up.

"Arsehole." He slammed his fist on the steering wheel in disgust.

It doesn't have to be this way, you know?

Prove it.

Give me a chance.

Okay. You've got the weekend.

FOURTEEN

Swan Harbor
A&P Grocery
September 7
6:00 p.m.

He hung up! But with Tyler and Bethany watching her expectantly, Elsa couldn't crumple to the ground like she wanted.

She knelt down at Bethany's level. "Did you start school this week?"

"I did," Bethany exclaimed. "I've decided I'll stay."

"Was that in question?"

Tyler exchanged looks with Bethany before answering. "I told her if she didn't like it, she could go straight to work. I need kitchen help at the club."

"Ahh." Elsa grinned at Beth. "I don't blame you then. Kitchen work is not fun."

"'Specially the trash, and washing the dishes." Beth pinched her nose, so the rest of her speech sounded like she had a cold. "It's smelly."

"Wise decision." Elsa booped Beth on the nose with her finger. Then stood, ready to face the father. "Guess you'll have to look elsewhere for kitchen help."

"Yeah, guess so." His voice faded, and he tucked his fingers into his back pockets. "Uhm, Elsa."

Almost as if he was unsure what to say, he hesitated, making her fight to stand still under his scrutiny.

"Yes," she prodded when she couldn't stand the quiet any longer.

"We're friends, right?"

"Yes."

"Listen, I'm just going to put this out there," he spit out so quickly her head spun. "Lois and Rupert's fiftieth anniversary party is in a couple of weeks, and I was wondering if you would go with me?"

Elsa frowned, remembering his 'I need to focus on Beth and don't have time to date speech.' Plus, there was Liam.

"You're asking me out?" she repeated, making sure she'd heard him correctly. "Like on a date?"

His expression was both comical and confusing.

"No, no, no," he backpedaled. "Not on a date date."

"Oh, just as friends?"

"Yeah." He let out a relieved breath. "When I go to events, you wouldn't believe—"

"—How many single women throw themselves at you?" Elsa was finally beginning to get the picture. "You want me to protect you, don't you?"

His face turned red. "Please. Unless, Liam ...?"

"Is coming to town?"

"Well, yeah."

"He's not."

"So? Will you?" Tyler asked again. His expression reminding her of a puppy wanting a treat.

Elsa snickered. "I'll protect you from the wild women of Swan Harbor."

"Thanks, Elsa. I'll catch you later."

Once they were gone, Elsa could no longer push her difficulties with Liam away. She felt much like the ball in a tennis match. From the kiss that had left scorch marks on her heart to their kiss when he'd dropped her off Monday night, she'd thought they were working toward something. What was going on with him on the phone?

He'd been flirty, then jealous. Sexy, then distant.

And he'd been giving you what you've dreamed of, a hint of jealousy and that growl you find so sexy.

True, but what did that mean?

The urge to call Emma was strong. But how could she expect someone else to explain it to her, when she didn't understand it herself?

Back home, she caught herself checking her phone every few seconds. It annoyed her so much she changed into an old comfortable pair of jeans, one of Liam's old sweatshirts and boots. Then, leaving her phone behind, Elsa headed toward the water.

Liam and his behavior followed her, though.

After she'd moved, she hadn't heard from him for the first month. Then, just minutes after he'd walked into the hospital, he'd kissed her like there was no tomorrow. Not only that, he'd gone with her to Georgetown and supported her in ways she'd never expected.

Their talks were intimate, and he'd shared a story about his past.

Had she imagined him saying he missed her? Or the touch of jealousy she'd thought she heard in his voice?

When she spotted Emma squatting near the edge of the pier, watching the swan, she pushed her thoughts aside.

"What brings you to town? Did you come to check on Jonesy?"

Emma brushed her hands off and stepped away from the edge. "Originally, no. I came to drop off something at the jewelry store, but Captain Jack waylaid me."

"To check on the swan?" Elsa glanced out at the majestic bird. Just like every other time when she was close, it felt like he was giving her the side-eye.

"Yeah, I wanted to check on Jonesy myself."

"Did you come up with any conclusions?"

Emma laughed, but there was an underlying vulnerability to it Elsa wasn't used to hearing.

"*Cygnus olar,* close to 63 inches long, and a wingspan of close to 94 inches. Jonesy is a male and has been coming to Swan Harbor every summer for years. Depending on the weather, he disappears in September or early October."

"Most of those facts, I could have looked up," Elsa pointed out.

Emma blew out her breath. "I know. Initially, I didn't believe Captain Jack, but seeing Jonesy now, he looks—"

"—Like he's losing his hope," Elsa murmured absently.

"What?" Emma tugged Elsa down onto a bench. "Did you just say something about the swan losing his hope?"

Elsa shrugged. "I don't know. I ran into Molly at the A&P—"

"And Tyler and Bethany too," Emma added.

"Spy network?"

"Gossip chain," laughed Emma. "But tell me about Jonesy."

"You're the vet." Elsa waved toward the swan. "Look at him, though. He spends all day swimming alone and has been that way for a long time. Isn't Swan Harbor," she made quotes with her fingers, "the haven of hope for lost hearts?"

"Yeah." Emma glanced back at the swan. "You think he's losing hope? Or are you talking about you?"

"Me?"

"El, what's going on with Liam?"

"How do you know it has something to do with Liam?"

"I've known you for a long time," Emma reminded her. "Spill."

"I've no idea," she finally admitted.

"Well, I've a little experience with a Reade man." Emma grinned. "Let's get ice cream, you share, and we'll figure out how you can take back the power."

"And not lose hope."

"This is Swan Harbor," Emma reminded her. "There's always hope."

Tarrytown, NY
Finn's Home
September 7
6:30 p.m.

LIAM HAD DRIVEN PAST HIS FATHER'S HOME IN TARRYTOWN twice, but hadn't worked up the nerve to stop. He'd been too busy replaying every moment of his phone call with Elsa and trying to figure out where he'd gone wrong.

A part of him was saying he'd been a fool for not telling her how he felt. Yet, the other side said it was because he'd gotten too close to that emotional line he'd created for himself when his mother had left. Could he change thought patterns he'd carried with him for over fifteen years?

Do you want to be alone?

I want Elsa. The thought of confronting his ghosts, though, caused his gut to churn.

The next time he drove by, his father was waiting on his front lawn. As much as he wished it weren't true, he'd run out of excuses and turned into the driveway.

"It's nice of you to drop by." Finn Reade glanced at the shiny gold watch on his wrist. "Thought you were going to be here an hour ago."

He could make excuses. However, since it was his father ....

"Sorry, I'm late. I hope you didn't wait for me to eat."

"No, I'm fine." Finn led the way into the house. "Are you hungry?"

"I'll just ..." Liam held up his overnight bag and nodded toward the stairs.

"You know where your room is."

"Thanks."

On his way upstairs, Liam could feel his father's dark eyes boring a hole in the center of his back. He dropped his bag on the king size bed and, with his running days over, started back down the stairs.

Liam found Finn sitting on the terrace, staring into the woods that boarded the back of his property.

"Can I get you anything to drink?" Finn, the always gracious host, asked as soon as Liam settled.

"No, I'm good."

Finn propped his elbows on the arms of his chair and steepled his fingers in front of him. His dark hair was brushed back off his forehead and even on a Friday evening, he was still wearing tailored slacks and a dress shirt.

"Tell me why you borrowed my car again," Finn began in an off-handed manner.

"I told you, dad. Mine was making a funny noise." He used the same excuse as with Elsa.

Finn raised a brow in disbelief. "Too funny of a noise to drive to Maine. Just not funny enough you had to worry about driving it out here."

"Well, yeah." Liam winced. "It didn't start until—"

"Liam, are you in danger?"

"Why would you ask me that?" Liam frowned. "Killian's the ... cop."

"Who spent many years undercover, and his last case involved Santora Callandra."

Liam glanced up, curiosity and fear warring with each other inside. Somehow, his father was leading him into a trap.

"You know?"

"About Violet? Yes. Killian told me in January."

"What do you know about Callandra?"

"I know he's trying to get the charges brought against him dropped." Finn's voice hardened. "I know when Killian was undercover, somehow you kept track of him."

"What makes you think that?" Liam shot back.

"Please." Finn cocked his head. "You've kept watch over your little brother since he was born."

"So, I have," Liam sighed. "Killian and I developed a system to keep track of each other."

"A code?" Finn asked. "Sounds elaborate."

"Maybe." Liam shrugged. "Different color threads on the apartment door, never taking a direct route home, a tracking system on our phones—"

"—And driving a car that's not yours when taking trips," Finn surmised. "Especially ones to Swan Harbor."

Liam glanced at his father and felt like he was ten and getting into trouble.

"What happened?" Finn prodded.

"Nothing much," Liam downplayed the situation as he was wont to do.

"Liam." Finn hesitated, and Liam slowly lifted his chin to meet his father's dark gaze. "Your entire life, you've taken care of others. Killian, your mother," his voice dropped, "and me."

"I was the oldest." Liam offered the same reasoning he'd always lived by. "It was my job."

"To defend your little brother from bullies," Finn conceded. "But not to coddle your mother's whims or to tuck me into bed after she left."

"You were sick," Liam began.

"I was bladdered," Finn interrupted. "Stop with the excuses."

"Sorry."

"Stop being sorry," Finn demanded. "For years, Killian hid behind his looks, but you hide too, Liam."

"Killian hid behind his looks so he could see how many women he could screw," Liam snapped. "I'm not like that."

"Oh, I didn't say you were like that," Finn pointed out.

"But you accused me of hiding."

"And you do," Finn hummed. "But it's your affability you hide behind. You're everyone's friend."

"And that's a bad thing?" Liam frowned. "How can having friends be a bad thing?"

"It's not, son." Finn's voice softened. "The bad thing is, you won't allow yourself to get close enough to see what's next."

Elsa's words echoed inside his head.

"It's not that you can't feel passion, Liam," she went on. "It's that you won't let yourself. Or at least you've not let yourself feel it … or love with me."

"You know I'm right." Finn leaned forward. "Does your visit have anything to do with Elsa?"

"What makes you say that?"

"I saw the way you two were together at Killian's engagement party. You feel something for her."

"Of course." Liam bit his tongue to keep from finishing the comment with his usual 'friends.'

"You want more?"

"I don't know," Liam murmured. Then his eyes met his father's and amended, "I think so. Killian seems so happy. I'm just not sure there's such a thing as forever."

"People aren't meant to be alone, Liam," Finn's quiet voice held a tone that was new … different.

Like the swan.

"I could say the same about you."

"This isn't about me."

There it was again, Liam noted. A tenor in his father's voice he'd not heard before.

"Have you met someone?"

"Why do you ask?"

Liam studied his father and, while Finn had become very adept at hiding his thoughts, the ruddy spots on his high cheekbones were a tell.

"Just a feeling," Liam offered.

"You've always wanted everyone paired up," Finn revealed. "Except yourself. And when someone got too close, you pushed them away. Elsa's the first person you've let close since that girl in college. What was her name?"

"Debi Monroe," Liam muttered. "What I feel for Elsa is nothing like my feelings for Debi, though."

"Of course not," Finn replied. "You're a different person than you were then. And Elsa is not Debi."

"No," Liam scoffed. "Debi tried to badger, cry, and yell, to get me to bend to her will."

"And Elsa?"

"She left me."

"And moved to Swan Harbor?"

"Yeah." Then he jumped in with both feet. "I've been told by several people in the last month, I need to face the past before I can move forward."

"Conquer your ghosts?"

"Yeah. You did it. Killian did it. But I can't do it alone."

"We all need help now and then, Liam. What can I do for you?"

"I," Liam shoved down the sick feeling he'd carried around for years and said words he'd never thought to say, "I want to talk to mum. Do you know where she is?"

Finn jumped up to lean back on the balcony's railing. "That wasn't what I thought you were going to say."

"So, do you?" Liam pushed. "Do you know where mum is?"

Finn brushed his hands through his hair and sighed, but Liam wasn't sure why. Was it because his father knew something or because he didn't?

"I had an investigator tracking your mother for a few years after she left," Finn admitted. "That was ten years ago or more."

"Will you ask the investigator to find her?"

Finn took a deep breath, and a conversation with Killian floated by.

"Do you think Father is still in love with Mum?"

"What?" Liam quickly glanced in Killian's direction.

"I was just thinking about my conversation with dad. He never said he no longer loved mum. Do you think if she returned, he'd take her back?"

"I don't know." Liam shrugged, his voice a tad frostier than before. "You didn't ask?"

Asked? No, his father somehow had anticipated what he'd wanted to know, but there had been holes in his confession. "He admitted he'd finally laid his ghosts to rest. And, I admit, he looks good."

"I say it's about time," Liam snapped. "Claire Reade didn't care to be a mum, and I say good riddance."

He hated she still had the power to make him so angry. If he could let go of the anger, then maybe he had a chance with Elsa.

Of course, that's assuming she's still talking to you.

"If it means that much to you," Fin replied quietly. "I'll reach out to the private investigator first thing on Monday."

"Thanks." Liam felt like weight lifted from his shoulders.

"I'm happy to help." Finn glanced at his watch again. "You'd better get dressed. We have reservations at my club, and when we return, we're going to call your brother and talk about Callandra."

"But ..." Liam frowned at the tenseness in his father's voice.

Just before Finn stepped into the house, he turned around.

"No one messes with what's mine. If he does, he's a dead man."

Liam's jaw dropped as, without another word, Finn disappeared inside. That wasn't the polished Finley Reade he'd become after moving to the states. That man was the shipyard worker from Blyth, Flynn Reide.

Swan Harbor
Veterinarian Clinic
September 7
7:00 p.m.

EMMA WIPED OFF THE TABLE AND TOSSED THE TOWEL IN THE general direction of the counter. It hit the edge and slithered to the floor.

"Killian, the towel fell."

"I see that, Doc. What do you want me to do about it?"

"Pick it up," she retorted.

"You're closer," he tossed back.

She thought about pushing but decided it wasn't worth it and regrouped.

"Killian," Emma tried again. "What's going on with Liam?"

The tic in his jaw when he was trying not to say too much started pulsing.

"Nothing that I'm aware of." Killian closed the dishwasher door, dried his hands, and leaned against the cabinet. "What are you trying to find out?"

She nibbled on her bottom lip for a few seconds before offering, "I ran into Elsa today."

"And then went to Sally's," he smirked.

"Well, yeah. But Liam was on his way to see your dad."

Killian shrugged. "Probably taking dad's car back. Or ..."

"Or?" Emma took a step toward him, hoping he would meet her halfway. "Has there been any news about Santora?"

Killian took a step closer, and the sexy grin on his face caused her heart to race.

"No, Doc. Nothing new on that end."

"But something happened, didn't it?" She tilted her head, and the way he wouldn't maintain eye contact told her she was on the right track. "Open book, Reade."

"I thought I was being watched today, that's all."

"Were you at Sally's?" Emma took a half step closer to him, so about two feet still separated them.

"You know I was." He took another step. "So I'm sure you know more than I do."

"I do. For instance, I heard Chloe thought your butt looked nice in those black jeans you were wearing."

"She does have a good eye," he quipped. "Anything else?"

"Morgan thinks you need a haircut." Emma glanced at his hair and her fingers itched to run through the black strands. "It is a little on the shaggy side. Maybe ask Helen to trim it, but just a little."

He held his thumb and index finger about an inch apart. "This much?"

"No," huffed Emma, pushing his fingers closer together. "This much."

Killian tugged her against his chest. "What took you so long?" He tightened his arms around her waist and placed a quick kiss on her mouth. "Now, why all the questions about Liam?"

Emma laid her cheek against his chest and closed her eyes.

"Doc, don't go to sleep on me."

"Sorry, I was just trying to figure out how to explain." She leaned back so she could watch his eyes. "Apparently, he and Elsa got pretty close while they were away."

"Oh?" Killian raised that brow of his that turned her on. "Isn't that a good thing?"

"Yeah," Emma frowned. "But then today he called, acted jealous and practically hung up on her."

"Really?"

"That's all you have to say?"

"What do you want me to say?

He kissed her and a corner of her mind realized he was trying to distract her. And the more his lips toyed with hers, the more she wanted to let him.

"Come here." Killian lifted her onto the counter and stepped between her legs. "Now, where was I?"

"Here." Emma tugged him close until their mouths met.

His heat beckoned and the idea of moving to the sofa had just formed when his phone buzzed.

"Bloody hell!" Killian reached for his phone. "It's Liam."

"Answer it and ask him why he's being so pissy to my friend." Emma hopped off the counter. "Then invite him to the anniversary party. I'll be waiting for answers."

Emma left him alone to go find her phone.

> Emma: Killian is talking to Liam. I told him to invite his brother to the party.

> Elsa: You did what?

> Emma: Told Killian to invite Liam to the party.

> Elsa: You know I'm going with Tyler, right?

Emma snickered.

> Emma: Yes. I'm betting Lieutenant Liam Reade isn't going to be crazy about that.

> Elsa: I hope you know what you're doing.

"Me too, El. Me too," Emma murmured.

FIFTEEN

New York City
Queen's Court Hospital
September 13
2:00 p.m.

Liam stood outside Joe Stevens's ICU cubicle and waited for the nurse to give him the go ahead. Two weeks had passed since the officer had tried to tell him something. Surgery and a ventilator waylaid any further conversation. Would today be the day he finally found out what the message was?

"You can have five minutes," the nurse whispered when she came out of the room. "Just don't upset him."

There was a voice inside Liam saying maybe he should follow up on that comment. He shelved it, though, and stepped closer to the bed.

Joe's dark eyes followed him, the sensation not unlike the feeling of being observed by others. The man's eyes flared with recognition. Yet, he was quiet ... waiting.

There were tubes and monitors connected to the officer, but a quick glance at the man's vitals assured Liam he was stable.

"Do you remember me?" Liam noted the steady beep of Joe's heart. "My name's Liam Reade."

"I remember." Joe's voice was hoarse from the tubing he'd only just gotten rid of.

"Good." Liam took a breath and plunged forward. "Do you remember coming to see me a couple of weeks ago?"

"Yes. Little girl hit."

Liam's subconscious picked up on the fact that the beep tracking Joe's heartbeat ticked up a notch.

"That's right." Liam fought an internal battle for several seconds. When Joe's heart rate increased, he backed away. "Her name is Daria. She has a broken arm but is going to be fine."

Joe's heart rate decreased ....

"Good to hear."

"I agree." Then Liam pushed a little more. "That's the day you were shot, right?"

Joe's heart rate increased, and a look of distress crossed his face.

"I'm sorry about Officer Brody."

"Me too," Joe mumbled. "Good partner."

His heart rate ticked up another few beats per minute.

"That night when you were in the Emergency Department, I got a call from your doctor. Said you wanted to tell me something."

Liam watched several expressions fly across the officer's face, and the beep from the heart monitor sped up.

"Did I say anything?"

The question hadn't been what he'd expected. "Not much that I could understand. Sounded like you said, know, in, watch and your name, Joe. Can you tell me what it meant?"

Joe closed his eyes and Liam realized he was tiring, and his heart rate continued to speed up.

Was he nervous?

In pain?

Scared?

"Can you tell me why you needed to talk to me?" Liam tried again.

The heart monitor grew louder, and the beeps came closer together.

Suddenly, Joe's eyes flew open, and he grabbed Liam's hand. "Watch Joe," he got out before sagging back onto the bed.

The heart monitor grew even louder.

"You need to leave." The nurse hustled Liam out of Joe's room. "I told you not to upset him."

"Does he get upset easily?" Liam asked, curious if it was a common thing.

"Not sure," the nurse admitted. "But yesterday afternoon, he was very upset."

"Who was visiting?"

"Not sure." The nurse repeated and pointed toward the desk. "You can check the log on your way out."

Liam smiled his thanks and copied the names of the visitors. They meant nothing to him, but he hit speed dial to run them by Killian.

"What happened?" Killian barked without even offering a greeting.

"I talked to Stevens." Liam got right to the point. "I'm not a cop, but if I was, I'd say he was nervous."

"What makes you say that?" Killian asked.

"He was hooked up to a heart monitor," Liam explained. "By the end, his heart was racing. The nurse told me it happened when he had visitors before."

Killian was quiet for a few seconds, and Liam had to assume he was taking notes or reading, as he could hear crinkling papers.

"Did he say anything?" Killian followed up.

"That was the odd part." Liam still felt a bit creeped out by the experience. "He grabbed my hand and told me to watch Joe. I assumed that meant to watch him. Then his heart rate spiked, and they kicked me out."

"Bloody hell," Killian muttered. "I wish there was a way to know who visited him yesterday."

"And the big brother comes through again," Liam boasted. "I wrote the names down. I'll send you a picture."

"Guess you're not a total muppet," Killian quipped. "By the way, have you talked to Elsa?"

Liam sighed, knowing he was being a complete prat. Until he'd let go of the past, was it fair to give her hope?

Swan Harbor

Sheriff's Department
September 7
4:00 p.m.

KILLIAN SHOOK HIS HEAD AT HIS BROTHER'S STUBBORNNESS. "Stop being a wanker, Liam. Send her a text or some flowers. No matter what, I thought you were her friend."

"I am, but ..." Liam was quiet for a minute and Killian could hear his radio come to life. "I've got to go. I'll send the list."

"Knob head," Killian mumbled, waiting for the picture to appear.

"Liam still hasn't contacted Elsa?" Dylan flipped a chair around and straddled it.

"No." Killian studied his boss, who still appeared more distracted than normal.

"Do I need to talk to him?" Dylan offered. "My sage advice worked with you and Emma."

Killian laughed. "Should I call you Doctor Prince?"

"It has a nice ring, doesn't it?" Dylan preened a little, then with a smirk, tossed the most recent incident report on the desk. "While you're waiting, here are a few things to take care of."

Killian glanced at Rusty. "By the look on your face, I gather you've read them?"

"Just wait," Rusty snickered. "It's Swan Harbor at its finest."

"Let me see." Killian flipped through the pages, immediately noticing several calls that were atypical. "Are these real?"

Dylan ran his hands through his blond hair, leaving it standing on end. "Very real."

Killian sent another look to Rusty for support. "Dylan, mate, is everything alright?"

"Fine." Dylan frowned. "Why?"

Killian waved his hand in front of Dylan. "You're disheveled."

"And tired," Rusty added.

"Everything okay with you and Molly?" Killian tossed out, wondering if he'd missed something.

Dylan was quiet for several minutes, forcing Killian to steal another look at Rusty. But his partner was just as much in the dark.

"I can't believe the gossip chain hasn't gotten hold of this," Dylan muttered.

"If it's that big, I can't either," Rusty concurred. "Usually, the chain is spot on.

"So?" Killian waited expectantly.

Before he said more, Dylan shut the office door.

"Come on, mate," Killian pushed again.

"We think we're pregnant," Dylan spit out in a rush.

"Congratulations, Dylan." Rusty grinned. "Until you're a father, there's no way to describe the feeling."

"Thanks." Dylan sat there for a minute. "To be honest, I'm not sure how I feel. Excited. Scared. Happy. Stupid, huh?"

"I've not had the privilege of being anyone's father yet, Dylan," Killian told him quietly. "But Jessie turned out just fine."

Dylan smiled. "Yeah, and she's going to be excited. We want to wait until the ultrasound before telling everyone."

"Guess that explains why you've been so tired lately," Rusty quipped.

"Aye," Killian added. "From what I gather, it takes practice to procreate."

"Boys," Dylan muttered. "Back to work."

"Hope once the babe's here, you lose your grouchiness," Killian grumbled.

"No, he'll sleep less," Rusty replied. "He'll just be grouchier."

"You're a bunch of old women." Dylan nodded to the report. "I gave you entertainment."

"That's right." Killian glanced at the first one. "Mr. Stu Hagger called at 7:55 a.m. to report his bacon was missing. I'd wager it was Leroy."

Rusty snickered. "No. It was the wife."

Killian read on. "At 10:00 p.m. last night, a call came in because they kept hearing someone yelling for help."

"He was yelling for his cat, whose name is Help," Dylan explained with a laugh.

"Help?" Killian scoffed. "What kind of name is that? Poor thing."

"Exactly," Rusty offered, tongue-in-cheek. "It's not nearly as regal as Trudi or Nina."

"Or Millicent," Killian reminded them, adding Emma's cat to the mix.

Rusty grabbed a piece of paper and cleared his throat as if preparing to give a brilliant speech.

"Lance, from Haven House, called to report that someone broke into several of the apartments and all that's missing are … drum roll, please."

Dylan began drumming on the desk with his fingers.

"Their brassieres," Rusty finished.

"Really?" Killian grinned at Dylan. "Think it's the panty bandit from last Christmas?"

"I'd bet on it."

"And no ideas?" Killian frowned. "That's cocked up."

"It's definitely different," Dylan conceded, just as Killian's phone buzzed with the text from his brother.

Liam: Sorry. Here's the list.

Killian opened the picture. "Prue Stevens and Linc Stevens. I'm guessing the parents."

Dylan agreed. "Who else?"

"Darrel Jarvis, Howard McCain, and," Killian hesitated a beat, "Dennis Weaver and John Jokowitz."

"*That's* cocked up," Rusty intoned.

"You said it," Killian groused, ready for the entire situation to be behind them. "I guess I need to call Weaver again."

"After you do, why don't you two take a drive to Swan Harbor U." Dylan pointed to the bottom of the page. "The alarm to the research lab has been triggered a few times lately, but nothing seems amiss."

"Any idea what would be in a research lab someone would want?"

"Drugs?" Rusty shrugged. "Guess it depends on what they're researching."

"True," Killian acknowledged. "I gather we're investigating the bra theft first?"

"We are." Rusty chuckled. "Should be an uplifting experience."

"That was bloody awful." Killian clucked.

"You're welcome."

A loud pop had Killian and Rusty ducking back inside.

A second shot quickly followed.

"Bloody hell," Killian barked. "What's going on?"

Rusty opened the door enough to peer out. "Smoke in the distance." He motioned toward the cliffs.

"Help! They're doing it!" someone yelled. "They're doing it!"

"That's Leroy," Killian growled.

He and Rusty stepped outside to see Emma's assistant running down the main street toward them.

"They're doing it!" Leroy yelled again.

"Bloody hell, Leroy," Killian snapped. "What's going on?"

"The junkyard's exploding!" Leroy waved toward the smoke.

"Recycling?" Rusty suggested.

Leroy's look said '*Are-you-crazy?*' "No. It's those young hooligans."

"Alright." Killian side-eyed Rusty. "Looks like our plans just exploded."

"Talk about bloody awful," Rusty retorted.

"You work with what you've got."

Swan Harbor
Elsa's Medical Office
September 7
4:45 p.m.

ELSA PIERCED THE SKIN ON THE BACK OF HER PATIENT'S ARM ONCE more and pulled the stitch tight. She tied a knot and then another before clipping off the excess.

There, she thought, studying her handiwork. Sufficient, considering the anger flowing through her, threatened her usually steady hand.

She grabbed the antibiotic cream and covered the wound before placing a clean gauze pad over it.

"Come to the office in ten days so we can remove them."

"It hurts," fifteen-year-old Harrison whined when she taped off the gauze bandage.

"If eight stitches in the fatty part of your arm hurts, imagine how Gavin feels," Elsa pointed out. "Or Caleb, Nate, Matt or Alex."

"Yeah," Harrison mumbled, his eyes downcast. "We screwed up."

"That you did," Elsa agreed. "Can you put your shirt back on, or do you need help?"

"I can do it," he grumbled, and she had to fight to keep from grinning.

"Are you sure? If you don't want my help, I can get your mom."

"No!" Harrison's eyes widened. "I can do it."

"Well, if you're sure," Elsa hummed. "I'll give your medication and the instructions to your parents."

"Okay."

She left him struggling with his shirt and took the supplies to his parents.

Once she dealt with the parents of the six boys, and left instructions with the nurses for Caleb and Gavin's care, though, her anger hadn't subsided. A part of her knew it didn't completely stem from the situation at the junkyard. However, this was something she could work to fix. For the moment, the Liam situation seemed to be beyond her control.

Which is why she stormed into the mayor's office just before 5:00 p.m.

As she'd expected, Rene's secretary, Agnes Marston, was parked behind her desk, her nose buried in the latest romance novel.

"Is Rene available?" Elsa asked in what she considered her physician's voice.

Agnes slowly lowered her book and looked over her horn-rimmed glasses.

"Can I help you, Miss?" she asked in a frosty voice.

Pit bull somehow lodged in Elsa's mind.

"It's Doctor Winters," Elsa replied in a clipped voice. "I'd like to speak to Rene ... please."

"I'm sorry, Doctor Winters." Agnes set her book aside. "The Mayor asked not to be disturbed. Can I take a message?"

Elsa's fingernails dug into her palms when she clenched her fists. For a heartbeat, and then two, she weighed her words.

"No, you may not take a message. I need to speak to Madame Mayor, now."

Rene's office door suddenly opened. "Elsa? Is something wrong?"

"Yes, Rene, it is," Elsa snapped. "May we talk ... now?"

"Sure." Rene swung the door open wider. "Come on in."

"Thank you." Elsa tossed a smirk over her shoulder at Agnes and flounced through the door.

Rene's office was large and more homey than opulent, surprising her for some reason.

"Have a seat." Rene pointed to an oversized sofa.

The other woman's elegance and graciousness threw Elsa for a few seconds. "I'm sorry to just barge—"

"Stop," Rene interrupted. "It's okay. Besides, I owe you one. You made a special trip to check on Roland when he broke his arm."

"How is he?"

Rene laughed. "He's fine. Loves his new teacher, Miss Fowler, and already has a ton of signatures on the cast. But," she grinned, "in typical male fashion, he won't let me forget how much he's suffering."

"I'm glad to hear that."

"Tell me what's got you so riled up," Rene prompted in her direct manner.

Elsa looked away from Rene's dark eyes for a second, and then back. "Did you hear about what happened today?"

"I heard someone found dynamite," Rene replied. "But surely that can't be true."

"It's true," Elsa answered. "In some tunnels over by the bridge."

"There's a whole maze of tunnels under Swan Harbor," Rene murmured. "I thought they were blocked off, though."

"Apparently not," Elsa asserted. "Last I heard, Dylan, Killian, Rusty and several others were trying to decide what to do with the dynamite."

Rene hummed, a concerned pucker forming between her brows.

"I'm sure I'll hear all about it from Rusty. But something tells me that's not the problem."

"I wish," Elsa sighed.

"What happened after they found the dynamite?" Rene prompted.

"The six boys took a few sticks and had some fun," Elsa made air quotes, "exploding things."

"They didn't ..."

"I'm afraid they did."

"Were they hurt?"

"Cuts, scrapes, a few stitches for all but two of the boys."

"Something in your voice tells me that's why you're here," Rene observed.

"Good catch," Elsa noted. "Look, I realize this isn't New York—"

"Gee, you think?"

"But some changes need to be made with the EMTs and their training, or I'm afraid someone is going to die."

"What happened?"

Elsa briefly told her about the situation with Rod and Julianna. Then she jumped into the situation with the boys.

"I was in my office when I heard the explosion," she began. "After living in New York for so long, I ignored it. I'm not sure how much time passed before I got a 911 text from Killian to bring my medical kit and drive to the junkyard."

"Why didn't they call for an ambulance?"

"They tried," Elsa sighed. "But an accident on the highway required both ambulances. Killian called me because the boys were minors."

"Had to have been more than that," Rene guessed.

Elsa winced. "Potential TBI, traumatic brain injury," she clarified. "The boys were blowing up appliances. The first one was a stove and when all went as planned, they moved up to a refrigerator."

"Which didn't go as planned?"

"Not hardly. The boys were too close, and the debris flew. Mostly cuts and scrapes. Except, one boy was hit in the face, barely missing his eye. The second boy was hit in the head and knocked out."

"Is he going to be okay?"

"I think so," Elsa assured her. "We created a make-shift gurney and transported him in my car. Swan Harbor needs another ambulance or two, and the EMTs—are so young. Why?

Rene's brows rose. "Why are they so young?"

"Yes."

"I'm not sure when it started, but when I became mayor, the SH Fire Department was barely functioning. It was nothing more than a volunteer service. Just when I thought we were making progress, the chief paramedic moved to Bangor."

"Why not promote one of the other guys?"

"Not enough experience." Rene's dark eyes sparked. "Know someone who might want to move to Swan Harbor?"

Elsa sucked in. "You've been talking to Emma."

"Actually, this time I heard about it from Rusty." Rene smiled indulgently. "Said Liam is being a right knob head."

"That sounds like Killian," Elsa smiled wistfully. "I just ..."

"Give it time," Rene told her. "Remember in Swan Harbor, it's best to—"

"—Listen to your heart," Elsa murmured. "Because the heart always knows."

"Very good." Rene grinned. "Now, back to your dilemma. There's money for a chief paramedic. However, money to buy another ambulance is another story."

"Thanks for listening, Rene. I'll see myself out."

She'd done what needed to be done and fought for her patients. Once home, she slipped onto the veranda and watched the sun slowly disappear.

Know a paramedic?

"Oh, Liam," she murmured. "What's going on with you?"

Just like every other time she'd asked, no one answered. It left her wondering why the pieces weren't connecting, and if there was still hope for a future with Liam.

SIXTEEN

New York City
O'Toole's
September 14
8:30 p.m.

Liam leaned back in the booth and stared moodily at the Guinness in front of him. It was a Friday night, and he had the entire weekend ahead. Yet he was miserable.

It's your own fault.

Bugger that. He knew it was his fault and was working on it. So far, though, the private investigator hadn't located his mother. Until that happened, he wasn't sure what to say to Elsa.

You could give her hope.

Meaning?

Tell her about the search.

How does that help?

She'll know you care.

He cared, but wasn't sure he believed in forever. That wasn't something he'd observed in action.

Forever starts one day at a time.

Nice thought but ....

"Here." Kim tossed a folded piece of paper on the table and slid into the opposite side of the booth.

"What's this?"

She thumbed over her shoulder toward the door. "Some guy gave it to me when I stopped by the bar. Said to be sure you got it."

That hyper sense his brother always talked about kicked in, and the hairs on the back of his neck stood at attention.

"What guy?" he barked, scanning the area in front of the bar and next to the door.

"I don't know," Kim groused. "Just some guy."

Liam picked up the piece of paper, trying to hold on to the edges. But with Kim watching, he didn't want to call attention to what he was trying *not* to do.

Bloody hell, he thought, finally opening it enough to see the words printed in capital letters.

SANTORA GETTING OUT. WATCH JO. HE KNOWS.

"What is it, Liam?" Kim's concerned voice cut through the fear rising inside. "You look like it's bad news."

"You could say that again," Liam muttered. "I need to go. Catch you later."

Kim grabbed his shirtsleeve. "I'm worried about you, Liam."

He studied her for several seconds. "Thanks, Kim. I'm going to be fine. Tell Ross I said hey."

"I will," she sighed. "But ..."

"Gotta go," Liam repeated. "Later."

As he walked away, he could feel her stare. He wanted to tell her he was happy for her and Ross. He wanted to tell her not to give up hope for him and Elsa. That could wait. What he had to do couldn't.

Liam stepped outside and perused the area, looking for what, he wasn't sure. With all appearing as usual, he took off toward the subway, where he hopped on and off trains. When he made it home, his neighbor, Luis, was standing in front of his apartment door.

"Luis? What's going on?"

"Liam, amigo." Luis met him in the middle of the hallway, holding an envelope. "I was going to leave this for you."

"Where did you get this?"

Luis grinned, his black eyes sparkling. "I found it in my box. No biggie."

The envelope was lightweight and flat, but stiffer than a piece of paper. His name and address were typed on a label and attached.

"Thanks, Luis."

"No problem." Luis waved and turned back toward his apartment. Just before he opened his door, he looked back. "Did you ever pass on my message to Elsa?"

The message he'd exchanged with Elsa wasn't quite the same one Luis had been referring to.

"Would that be the one about your niece or nephew?"

Luis rolled his eyes. "My sister. She got into medical school. Tell Elsa thanks for helping her out."

"Will do."

When Luis disappeared into his apartment, Liam checked for the white thread.

Had it moved?

No, it was there. Lower than he'd thought, causing him to sag against the door.

Once inside, he dropped the envelope on the table and studied it.

It was a 9"x12" brown clasp envelope, mailed two days previously with a Manhattan postmark.

Liam used a knife to slit the end. When he peered inside, he could tell its contents were pictures. Several, in fact, but why was he receiving them?

His heart raced and sweat beads covered his forehead as the photos slid onto the table.

"Oh, bloody hell!"

❧

Swan Harbor
Elsa's Cottage
September 14
9:00 p.m.

When her phone buzzed, Elsa opened one eye and sent the offending device a dirty look. It would wait. She closed her eye and sank further into the hot water.

She'd just allowed her muscles to relax when her phone buzzed again. Should she answer it? Her motto, if it's important, only worked if it was the same person. As soon as it stopped ringing, Elsa closed her eyes again. She had some heavy decisions to make and unlike last time, these she would make alone.

Elsa stepped inside her cottage and dropped everything she was carrying, trying to find her phone.

Crap, she thought when she saw who was calling. What now?

"Jerry," Elsa answered breathlessly.

"Did I get you at a bad time?" The tone of his voice alerted her the call wasn't just social.

"No," Elsa sighed. "I just got home. You're calling about mom, aren't you?"

"I'm sorry, Elsa," Jerry replied, and she could imagine him leaning back in his office chair, phone in one hand, pipe in the other. "Patty is giving Mindy a hard time. She keeps sneaking out of the house."

Elsa sucked in her breath and a sick feeling in the pit of her stomach swirled.

"But she's still wearing her tracking bracelet, isn't she? Is she getting lost?"

"Not lost, really," Jerry denied. "So far, Mindy has tracked her, and the neighbors are really helpful, but—"

"—The streets are busy and Mindy's getting up in age too."

"I'm sorry, kiddo," Jerry apologized again. "I hate putting this off on you."

"She's my mother, Jerry. How much time do I have to decide?"

"You know how Alzheimer's is, El," Jerry murmured. "But I wouldn't wait too long."

"So, you're telling me she's already changed from when I was there? I was hoping the memory medication would help."

"So was I, but you know it works differently for every person." Jerry repeated what he'd said when she was in Georgetown. "There are others we can try if this one doesn't work."

"I know. Let me think about things." Elsa's thoughts were already whirling with all the plans that needed to be made. "I'll call you in a few days."

"Okay." He hesitated, then came back with, "Remember Elsa, you didn't hear any of this from me?"

"You're secret's safe."

"That's a good girl. I'll talk to you soon."

But what should she do for her mom? Move her into a memory care facility, find another caretaker, or move her to Swan Harbor? Was that selfish? Should it be the daughter who moves back to Georgetown to be closer to her mother?

Before she could second guess her decision, Elsa climbed out of the tub. She slipped on sleep pants and a long sleeve T, grabbed her phone, and hit dial.

"Hello."

"Giennie, I'm sorry to bother you," Elsa began. "But I have a problem."

"You're not bothering me," Giennie assured her. "What's up?"

In as few words as possible, Elsa explained her mother's situation and what she was hoping to find.

"You'd like an older two-bedroom home, one floor that would be easy to safety proof, right?" Giennie clarified.

"I think so," Elsa sighed. "Maybe putting her in a smaller place will be less confusing."

"Let me check the listings and I'll get back to you," Giennie promised.

"Thanks. How's Harrison?"

Giennie chuckled. "Physically, he's fine. He lost his technology, except for schoolwork, and Paddy put him, Matt, Nate, and Alex to work in the gym."

"I'm glad all is well," Elsa told the other woman. "Let me know about the house."

"Will do," Giennie assured her, before disconnecting the phone.

With that taken care of, Elsa checked the message left earlier.

"Elsa, it's your mother," Patty whispered. *"Please call me right away. Mindy keeps trying to tell me she's living with me while we do our work. That can't be right, because I do not remember inviting her into my house."*

"Oh, mama," Elsa murmured, fighting off the rush of tears.

But the memory of Liam holding her and whispering, *Please, don't hide from me,* brought on a fresh rush of pity.

"Don't hide from you?" Elsa muttered. "However, it's okay for you to hide from me?"

Would he show at the anniversary party tomorrow night? If he did, what would he say? Would he explain his disappearing act? If he did, should she forgive and forget?

Take back the power.

Right. Except, how to do that eluded her as she hit the button to call her mother.

"Hello."

"Hi, mom. How are you feeling?"

"Elsa, honey," Patty gushed. "I'm feeling fine, just fine. I was just looking at those pictures you sent me."

"Which pictures?"

"Oh, you know," Patty explained. "The ones of you and your roommate at that fancy party."

"Are you talking about Emma?"

"Yes, that's her," Patty chuckled. "I still can't believe who her dad is ... Peter Foster. I never would have imagined."

It took Elsa several minutes to figure out what and when her mother was talking about. Then it clicked. She'd sent pictures of her and Emma to her mother in January and told her the news about Peter.

"Remember we used to watch that movie he was in, **A Sun and Sand Romance**?" Patty sighed. "He was quite dishy."

"Sure mom," she agreed, although it had been Charlotte, Jerry's wife, watching the movie.

"The dress you wore that night was so pretty," Patty jumped back to the pictures. "Did your young man like it?"

"My young man?" Elsa asked hesitantly.

"Yes." Patty's giggle was almost girlish. "That young man you were with last week. He was so charming. And that accent reminded me of when your father and I lived in England. I always found it so sexy."

She remembered Liam?

"You remember Liam?"

"Was that his name?" Patty hummed. "Nice name. Of course, I remember him. He told me about seeing you across the ballroom. How you took his breath away."

"He said that?"

"Oh, yes," Patty gushed. "He's quite smitten. I believe he's a keeper."

What would she say if Elsa told her what had happened recently? Would she tell her to fight or to kick him to the curb?

"Tell me about the dance, honey," Patty pleaded. "Where was it held?"

"The Four Seasons Midtown," Elsa murmured. "The Christmas decorations were beautiful, and Emma and I had a lovely time."

Well, until the end, she amended, remembering what had happened.

"Tell me about it," Patty encouraged.

Elsa remembered stepping out of the car with Emma and how excited she'd felt. Before then, she'd only seen Liam periodically, mostly when he brought patients to the hospital. Somehow, she knew when she saw him walking toward her, life would never be the same.

"There he is." Elsa grabbed hold of Emma's elbow. "My heart's racing. How do I look?"

"Beautiful," Emma replied absently. "Go get him."

As he drew closer, Elsa found she had to fight not to step into his arms.

"Hi," Elsa replied breathlessly.

New York City
Liam's Apartment
September 14
10:00 p.m.

"Good evening," Liam murmured, hoping he didn't sound too much like a twit. "You look lovely."

"Thank you." A shy smile crossed Elsa's face. "You look very handsome."

She glanced at Killian, making Liam feel like a ponce.

"This is my brother." Since he couldn't introduce him by his real name, Killian became, "Zorro."

Then, when he couldn't wait any longer to hold her, Liam asked, "Would you care to dance?"

She didn't hesitate, but quietly took his hand and followed him to the center of the dance floor.

"Your friend's safe with Zorro," he murmured, more for her benefit than for her friend's.

"I know."

Liam tucked her a little tighter against his chest. "Oh, you do, do you? Are you psychic?"

"Hardly." She looked around his shoulder to where Killian was pulling her friend into his arms. "If my friend hadn't trusted him, I would have known."

He spun her around a few times and couldn't help but think how right she felt in his arms.

"Really? My brother looks smitten. Enough about them, though. I want to know about you."

Elsa's blue eyes twinkled. "What happened to secret identities?"

"I could ask you the same thing," he chuckled. "Wasn't it you who slipped a note in my pocket that said, 'I'll be wearing peach'?"

"Who, moi?"

"I hope so," he murmured huskily. "You're the one I've been wanting to meet, Elsa."

She dropped her head against his chest, and he felt her take a deep breath before once again glancing up.

"That's good to hear, Liam. Because I've been wanting the same thing."

His body hardened. His heart pounded. And staying focused became difficult when all he could think about was dragging her into a corner.

What was she doing to him? He'd been holding her for less than an hour, and she'd sent his well-ordered thoughts into chaos.

"How do you like working for Marshall?" Liam moved the conversation to a safer topic.

"He's a good doctor."

Liam chuckled. "Very diplomatic."

"I can be ... most of the time."

"You don't lose your cool?"

The music changed into a slow, dreamy song, and Elsa's gaze once again met his.

"Only when something is really important. Usually, no."

"It's almost like you're offering a challenge."

"Oh?"

The way her lips rounded into a perfect O scattered his thoughts even more.

"You're not?"

"How about you?" Elsa tossed back. "You have a reputation as someone who is friendly and never loses his cool."

"Oh?" He smirked when her eyes flared.

She inhaled quickly, and he heard her mumble, "Oh, Emma," and take a step away to dig into her little handbag. "I need to take this picture."

The persistent buzzing of his phone brought Liam back to the present.

"It's about time you got back to me," he snapped. "Where have you been?"

"Sorry," Killian's tired voice came across the line. "I've been dealing with a few things."

That Killian didn't retaliate with a snarky comeback had his thoughts going straight to Elsa.

"What happened?"

"Kids found dynamite," Killian sighed.

Kids! Elsa!

"Is everyone alright?

"They are now," Killian confirmed. "Two of the teens are spending the night in the hospital."

"And the dynamite?" Liam frowned. "I'm guessing Swan Harbor doesn't regularly have to deal with dynamite."

"You could say that again," Killian grumbled. "No one knew who had jurisdiction, knew where or how to store it. Even now, I'm not convinced it's in the best place possible."

"That sounds ominous."

"Let's hope not," Killian sighed. "It's out of the way in an empty building, and only four of us know where it is."

"Is El alright?"

The succinct response Killian spit out was exactly what he deserved.

"Physically, she's fine," Killian shared. "Emma said something was going on with Elsa's mother, but that's all I know. Why don't you come and check on her yourself?"

"Stop pushing me," Liam snapped. "Look. I'm happy you found Emma. But what does happily ever after mean, anyway?"

"Come to Lois and Rupert Duncan's fiftieth anniversary party tomorrow night." Killian replied. "You can see for yourself. Besides, after what you got in the mail ..."

"And you haven't even seen the pictures," Liam cringed. "Sickening."

"I need to see them."

"I know," Liam acknowledged. "I'll send the pictures in the order I received them."

"Alright." Killian hesitated a beat. "Come to the party, Liam. Elsa needs you." Then the line went dead.

"Bugger that," Liam grumbled, organizing the pictures to send to his brother.

Swan Harbor
Veterinarian Clinic
September 14
11:00 p.m.

KILLIAN RUBBED HIS HAND THROUGH HIS HAIR AND WAITED FOR the pictures to arrive. Was he ready to see them?

Do you have a choice?

Not if he wanted to stay ahead of the danger, he didn't.

The first picture was one of him as Ian Jones, meeting with Tino Ricci, a member of Santora's gang.

The second was a picture of Tino's tortured body spread out on the street.

A picture of Violet's body.

A picture of the article depicting the fiery crash that ended Ian Jones's life.

"Bloody hell," Killian murmured when the next photo appeared.

It showed him walking into Bea Morris's apartment.

Another of him and Liam going into the Four Seasons Midtown the night of the New Year's Ball.

It was the last two that twisted his gut, though.

A picture of him, his father, and Liam having dinner that last night before he'd come back to Swan Harbor.

Lastly, an image of Liam and Elsa standing next to a car talking. Across the photo was a note written in black marker.

Pretty Woman. I'd hate it if something happened to her.

A note accompanied the pictures.

Are you sure you should trust the ones you trust?

> Killian: When was that picture of you and Elsa taken?

> Liam: The day she moved to Swan Harbor.

Killian's gut twisted with that last bit of news. Was she followed?

> Liam: Forgot about this note. It was passed to me at O'Toole's.

And then another picture arrived.

SANTORA GETTING OUT. WATCH JO. HE KNOWS.

Killian had to fight not to wake Dylan and Rusty, but he needed to rethink a few things. Namely, could he really trust Captain Weaver? If he could, then who the bloody hell had found out he was Ian Jones and not dead?

SEVENTEEN

Swan Harbor
Veterinarian Clinic
September 15
4:00 p.m.

Liam turned onto the drive leading to the Swan Harbor Veterinary Hospital. He'd known about the party for two weeks and knew Elsa was attending with Tyler. Killian had pushed him to come, as had Emma. And he'd stubbornly refused until ....

Until he'd received an envelope full of pictures.

Until he'd had a dream that turned into a nightmare.

Until he'd faced a reality without Elsa in it.

He'd packed his bag, grabbed his tux, and jumped in the car for the long drive. When he'd passed the Swan Harbor sign, a feeling he couldn't name washed over him.

Was it as Elsa said, and he was also being led here? Or was it because he wanted what Killian found with Emma? A sense of belonging, and a chance to be a part of something bigger than being alone in New York.

Someone knocked on his window, pulling him back to the present.

"Liam?"

Emma was standing outside his window, staring at him expectantly. It had him wondering how long he'd been woolgathering. When he climbed out of his car, he was tongue-tied.

"Killian said you weren't coming," she murmured.

"I wasn't."

"What brought you to your senses?"

A laugh escaped before he could stop it. "You don't pull punches, do you?"

Emma shrugged. "Did it have anything to do with the pictures?"

"Killian showed those to you?"

She smiled and nodded for him to follow her inside. "We're trying to share our burdens."

"I'm glad he listened."

"You don't take your own advice?"

"I just—"

"Think you don't need anyone?" she jumped in.

"No, that's not—"

"Think you don't deserve a happily ever after?"

Their eyes met and her steady green gaze had him feeling like he was a kid all over again.

"It's a bit more complicated than that," he finally offered.

"Oh, I know all about complex families," Emma tossed back at him. "But hey, I'll stop pestering you to share with me if—"

"—I'll share with Elsa," he guessed.

Emma's smile grew. "You said it. And now," she hesitated when Killian came inside, "I'll leave you two to talk while I go get ready."

"I'll be up in a minute, Doc."

When Killian kissed Emma and watched her as she walked out of the room, Liam had to turn away. His brother trusted. Why was it so hard for him?

You know why.

He did. Words said by his eighteen-year-old self weren't the ones that lingered. Those were the ones tossed back by his mother that kept him from crossing that line he'd set.

"Liam?"

He glanced back at his brother, who was sitting on the sofa surrounded by three cats.

"Sorry to drop in like this."

"What happened?"

"What do you mean?"

Killian lifted a brow. "You're not bloody daft."

"Nightmare." Liam shrugged, not sure if he wanted to offer more.

He could feel Killian staring and defiantly stared back.

"I'm not some perp you can intimidate into spilling their guts."

A corner of Killian's mouth kicked up in a semblance of a smile.

"I'm the one who's in law enforcement here. This is my fight."

"Not any longer, Killian," Liam snapped. "Whoever took those pictures, tried to run over me, followed me and then mailed the envelope to my apartment, made sure I was involved."

"You need to tell Elsa what's going on."

"Which parts of it?" Liam asked. "The parts that involve Santora or the parts about mum?"

"Mum?" Killian repeated. "What does mum have to do with any of this?"

Liam wanted to bite his tongue for opening his mouth, but he'd assumed his brother knew.

"I asked dad to find her," Liam finally relented. "You made peace with your ghosts, and I thought—"

"So mum is one of your ghosts too?"

"Seems so," Liam admitted. "Her words still haunt me. I'm not sure what I'll say to her when dad finds her, but I—"

"—Thought if you confronted the ghosts, they'd go away."

"Worked for you," Liam shrugged.

"So, it did," Killian agreed. "I'm here if you need me."

"I know. Now, I'll let you get dressed, and I'd better go see if Tia has a room available."

"Want us to pick you up tonight?"

Liam started to say no thanks but then remembered the woman he was here to see was going with another man. Reinforcements might be in order.

"I'd like that, thanks. See you then."

ELSA PULLED THE PEACH DRESS OUT OF HER CLOSET AND STOOD IN front of the mirror to study her reflection. She hadn't planned to wear it, but that was before Emma's text.

> Emma: Guess who showed up? Liam. Wear the peach dress.

> Elsa: The peach dress? Why?

> Emma: Remind Liam of that magical night and take back the power.

Elsa slipped the dress over her head and thought, *Here goes nothing*.

Once dressed, the anger she'd carried all week faded. It left behind sadness, making her need to rush out to confront him. She'd grabbed her keys to do so when her phone rang.

"Hi Giennie. Is Harrison, okay?"

"He's fine." Giennie's breathless voice came across the line. "Listen, I found a house, but do you think you can meet me in the next twenty minutes?"

"But–"

"I know you're going to the party with Tyler, but just trust me."

"Okay, sure." At least it would keep her from making a fool of herself. She made note of the directions and sent Tyler a text.

> Elsa: Giennie wants me to look at a house for my mother on the way to the party. I'll see you there.

> Tyler: Do you want me to go with you?

> Elsa: No, that's okay. Stay with Beth until the sitter comes. I'll see you later.

It wasn't until she climbed into her car, she remembered what she'd forgotten to do.

"Crap!"

Her gas gauge was sitting at just above empty. However, since the house wasn't that far from the hospital, she went with it. Until she stopped for the light at the bottom of her street and her car coughed.

"I don't have time for this."

She hit the gas and as her car picked up speed, she let out the breath she was holding.

"It's okay. I'm okay," she silently chanted, glancing at the directions for her next turn.

"Pass The Beachside Inn," she mumbled, fighting the need to see if Liam's car was in the parking lot.

"Then left at The Beach Shack."

As she approached the last landmark, she pressed a little harder on the gas and reached to turn up the radio.

Pop!

What was that?

Her first thought was a passing car kicked up a rock. But then her car lurched, telling it was more than that.

Crap!

Elsa grabbed the wheel, and with her heart in her throat, drove onto the side of the road. It took several seconds for her to stop shaking enough for her brain to process what had happened. When she climbed out and saw her flat tire, her anger returned full force.

This was all Liam's fault. If he hadn't done his little disappearing act, he would be attending the party with her. He had, though, and she was going to have fun with Tyler.

She'd reached for her phone to call for help when a car pulled up behind her.

"You!" she snapped, when Liam climbed from his car. He looked so sexy her knees almost buckled.

Crap!

"Elsa?" Liam's long legs covered the distance between them. "What happened?"

Elsa stood slowly and fought to bring her temper back under control. She still had to meet with Giennie, after all.

"What does it look like?" she retorted. "I have a flat."

He glanced down at his tux and sighed. "Let me change it for you."

Take back the power.

"No." Elsa grabbed her small handbag and the directions. She slammed the door with a little more force than, then gave Liam a directive. "You may give me a ride. I'll call for help."

Without waiting for any further comments, she marched to his car and slid inside. Her heart was pounding, her breathing was erratic, but she'd never felt more alive.

Liam glanced in her direction. The look in his blue eyes would make Sadie and Emma proud. Or at least, she assumed so.

"Where are we going?"

"Take a left at the next corner," Elsa instructed without answering the question directly.

He sighed, so softly she wouldn't have heard it if she hadn't been listening. While the sound had her heart flipping, she refused to be detoured.

Liam drove effortlessly and in less than ten minutes, he'd pulled up in front of a small wood frame house with a single detached garage.

"I'll not be long." Elsa climbed out to meet Giennie on the walk.

"Elsa, I'm glad you could make it."

Giennie gave her a look that said, *'That's not Tyler,'* when Liam quickly followed her. It prompted her to add, "My car had a flat, and Liam gave me a ride."

She could tell Giennie wanted to say more, but with Liam within earshot, she waved toward the house.

"Officially, this isn't on the market yet," she hesitated and then explained why she'd wanted to meet so quickly, "but the owner recently passed, and had Alzheimer's."

"So, all the safety precautions have been done?"

"Yes," Giennie nodded. "The owner's son was planning to undo all of them, but ..."

Could it be as easy as that?

"Lead the way." Elsa followed the other woman toward the small home.

The Lighthouse Inn
September 15
7:00 p.m.

Emma reread the text from Elsa.

> Elsa: Liam is waiting with me while my car is taken care of. I took back the power and will explain at the party.

"I thought you said Liam was riding with us?" Emma asked, trying to figure out the sequence of events between Elsa and Liam.

Killian gave her a side-eyed look. "He forgot black socks and said he'd meet us there. Why?" He brushed a kiss across the hand he was holding. "You afraid to be alone with me?"

Emma rolled her eyes. "You know that's not the case. Something happened to Elsa's car, and he's with her."

"Isn't that what you wanted?"

"For Liam and Elsa to be together?"

"Aye."

"Well, yes, but ..."

"They'll get there, Doc," Killian tried to assure her. "Maybe he's taking my advice and telling her what's going on."

"About everything?"

"That, I don't know," he replied softly, as the valet opened her door.

It was quiet while they made their way into the hotel and congratulated the anniversary couple. They sparkled, she thought, as a fleeting image of her and Killian in fifty years floated by.

You need to set a date first.

She would, she promised herself. Just as soon as everything was settled.

Promises, promises.

Before Emma could look for her fiancé, Captain Jack appeared. Almost as if he'd been on the lookout.

"Doctor Foster ..." Jack's voice faded.

It took her a minute to realize why he'd stopped talking. He was staring at her grandmother's old charm bracelet.

"Isn't it pretty?" She held up her arm, the heavy silver chain shiny after being cleaned.

"Very." He gently touched the piece of jewelry. "Just like its owner. Now, about Jonesy."

"I told you, Captain Jack," Emma repeated the same thing she'd tried to tell him before. "Jonesy won't let me close enough to do a thorough check."

"Oh dear," he sighed. "I was afraid of that. I'll have a talk with him."

She had to fight not to scoff, but nodded as if it was the most obvious solution. "My friend Elsa says he looks like he's losing hope."

Captain Jack gasped, and his eyes went wide. "Oh, don't say that. Swan Harbor can't lose its hope." As quietly as he'd appeared, he disappeared into the crowd.

"Was that Captain Jack?" Elsa murmured.

Emma nodded. "How did you know?"

"After you've talked to him, you always have a glazed look on your face." Elsa laughed.

"Especially if he's talking about Jonesy and not Bandit." Sadie directed them into a corner where Molly was sitting.

"What have I missed?" Emma looked at each of the women, her gaze finally landing on Molly. Instead of the perky brunette's usual effervescent self, there was something off. "What's wrong? You don't look so great."

Molly glanced up and Emma could have sworn there was a green cast to her fair complexion.

"I'm," then Molly blanched, covered her mouth, and rushed off.

"She's pregnant," Elsa whispered as they followed Molly into the ladies' room.

"Pregnant?" Emma glanced at Sadie. "Did you know?"

"Didn't I tell you?" Sadie frowned. "I could have sworn I told you."

"I'm surprised Killian didn't tell you," Molly groaned, coming out of the stall and rinsing off her mouth and hands. "Dylan spilled the beans."

"He never said," Emma grumbled. "And you." She pointed at Elsa. "You're new in town. How did you find out first?"

Elsa shrugged, "Right place ... like today, I guess."

"Tell us." Molly turned away from the sink. "I need something else to think about besides my spinning stomach."

"Are you sure?" Emma asked, still not liking how pale Molly looked. "Do you want us to go get Dylan?"

"No." Molly grabbed Emma's hand to stop her from leaving. "I'm fine. Just pregnant."

A toilet flushing had Molly clamping her lips shut, and everyone peered around the corner to see who was now privy to their secret.

"Congratulations, Molly." Sally exited the stall with a huge smile on her face. "And don't worry, your secret's safe with me."

"Thanks, Sally." Molly smiled. "Got any magic potions for pregnancy sickness?"

"Oh, you poor thing." Sally wrinkled her nose. "I had that something fierce with Tracey. Try lemon drops."

"Lemon drops?" Molly repeated.

"Lemon drops," confirmed Sally. "Not sure why, but they settled my stomach. Haven't touched them since."

"Thanks, Sally." Molly looked at Elsa expectantly. "I'm waiting."

"Me too." Emma nudged Elsa. "Start talking."

LIAM STOOD IN THE SHADOWS AND WATCHED AS THE PEOPLE danced around the large room. The Lighthouse Inn was the grandest Swan Harbor had to offer. Yet he couldn't help but compare it to the last dance he'd attended.

The room wasn't as big, the decorations not as polished, and everyone knew everyone. But the word to describe what was going on around him eluded him. Was it a celebration? Support? Recognition? Community? Or was there a word that combined a little of all those feelings?

"You look troubled."

Liam met the gaze of the man he'd seen talking to Emma earlier. Older, possibly mid-seventies, dressed well, and held himself as if he was ex-military.

"What makes you say that?"

The man gave him a look that said, *Are you sure you want to go there?* Instead of answering, he glanced back at the dance floor.

"Ever imagined spending fifty years with someone?"

Liam's gaze automatically searched for Elsa, but when he saw her across the room, he couldn't stop the words, "Me? I'm not sure it's in the cards."

As he said them, though, he realized it wasn't the thought of spending fifty years with her that scared him. It was the thought of not having those years that caused the burning in the center of his chest.

"Your future is what you make it," the man stated cryptically. He tapped his head. "The decision isn't made here." His hand moved to his chest. "It's made with your heart. Listen to it."

"Listen to my heart?"

The man nodded. "It always knows."

Before Liam could think of a response, Emma walked up, and the older gentleman tipped his head and disappeared into the crowd.

"I see you met Captain Jack."

"Was that his name?" When she nodded, he went on, "He didn't say, just told me to listen to my heart."

Emma laughed, a light-hearted sound reminding him of Elsa.

"You didn't tell her," she threw at him.

Liam turned his attention back to Emma instead of focusing on the way Tyler was holding Elsa as they danced.

"When was I supposed to do that?" he snapped. "Should I have said something while we followed a realtor around? Or while waiting on the mechanic?"

"What about on your way here?"

Liam brushed his hand through his hair. "It's more than a ten-minute conversation, Emma."

Killian pulled Emma close to his side. "Doc, come dance and leave Liam alone for now."

Emma sent a pointed look toward the dance floor, and then back his direction as if to say, *Ball's in your court.*

Liam got the message loud and clear. While Killian might enjoy a bit of frottage on the dance floor, that wasn't the card he'd drawn yet. As soon as the music switched to a new song, he took a step and didn't stop until he was standing next to the couple he'd been watching.

"May I have this dance?"

For a second, he wasn't sure Rupert was going to allow his wife to dance with another man. Then they looked at each other and Liam observed *silent communication* at its finest.

Lois Duncan playfully shoved her husband aside.

"Get me a drink, sexy. This young man needs some advice."

"Just remember whom you belong to," Rupert teased. "And you." He pointed his finger at Liam. "Watch your hands."

"Yes, sir," Liam promised, unsure if the other man was seriously warning him away or not. "I'll treat her like glass."

"See that you do."

Lois stepped into his arms and Liam had thought *What the bloody hell am I doing?* right before she smiled up at him.

"What has you so troubled?" Lois surprised him with her blunt manner.

"Should I ask how you know that?"

"Psychic."

Her succinct response took him aback for a minute until he got a good look at the twinkle in her eyes. "Gotcha!"

"You did." Liam laughed. "Had me going there too."

"Now," Lois patted him on the cheek, "what would you like to know?"

"What's the secret to forever?"

He'd posed the question, expecting to be laughed at, but then a dreamy expression crossed Lois's face.

"Forever isn't a guarantee, you know. To build a foundation, you start with a little hope and toss in a lot of love. Once your ground is solid, you work together to build your future, brick by brick."

"But what if the bricks topple?"

"You fight together to rebuild."

Her impassioned speech ignited the embers inside he'd fought to keep at bay.

"How do you know it won't fall again?"

She grinned up at him. "You want a guarantee?"

"Doesn't everyone?"

"There are no guarantees in love, Liam. But if you don't allow yourself to try, you will definitely fail."

Which was his problem. He didn't allow himself to move toward the next step because he didn't want to fail.

EIGHTEEN

Swan Harbor
The Lighthouse Inn
September 15
10:00 p.m.

Elsa peered around Tyler's shoulder, trying to see whom Liam was dancing with. Except there were too many couples in the way.

"Here." Tyler laughingly manipulated them into a different place. "Is that better?"

"I'm sorry," Elsa huffed.

"Don't be," Tyler assured her. "We're friends, and I know where your heart lies ... and his."

"Okay," Elsa sighed. "But if you know so much about him, explain why he's acting like such a jerk."

"He's a man."

"That's the best you can come up with?"

When Liam had gotten out of his car on the side of the road, she'd had the strangest feeling he'd been relieved to see her. He'd been caring and solicitous, both with giving her a ride to look at the house and waiting for her car to be towed. She'd pushed, hoping he cared enough to push back.

"Elsa, Liam's scared."

"How do you know?"

Tyler shrugged. "Not sure. Maybe I recognize the look on his face. Did you talk?"

"Not much," she admitted. "He stayed with me until Shawn picked up my car and brought me here."

"Did he say anything when you arrived, knowing you were meeting me?"

"He asked me if I would save him a dance."

"Yet you haven't danced with him."

"He hasn't asked." And she'd surreptitiously been watching him all evening.

"Maybe he's waiting until close to the end of the party. Maybe he wants to take you home."

"You think?" She heard the hopeful tone in her voice and wanted to scold herself for being tempted to make it too easy. "I'm sorry. That didn't come out right. Aren't I supposed to be protecting you from the single girls?"

"That's true." He grinned. "You did promise to protect me. But you need to do what you need to do."

"When the heart speaks, it's best to listen," Elsa murmured.

"Something like that."

"You're a nice man, Tyler."

"I know." He laughed. "Now, let's see if I can get Liam to come and ask you to dance."

He manipulated them until Elsa had a clear shot of Liam and the woman he was holding in his arms. "He's dancing with Lois."

"Lois, really?" Tyler glanced around. "I didn't think Rupert was sharing tonight."

Elsa shrugged. "Whatever Lois is saying to Liam, he's listening carefully."

Tyler chuckled. "She's giving him relationship advice, offering to share a pie or cake recipe, or regaling him with stories from her days as a spy."

"Spoken like someone who's been on the receiving end."

"More than once."

Elsa's laughter caught when she saw Lois slump in Liam's arms.

"What is it?"

"It's Lois." She pushed Tyler away and ran across the room.

Elsa reached Liam just as he lowered Lois to the floor and immediately began checking for a pulse and breath sounds. Friends surrounded them and time stood still, each second precious.

Rupert pushed his way closer, and the agony on his face twisted the knot in her gut a little tighter.

"Lois!" Rupert's voice broke, and Elsa had to clench her jaw to keep the tears at bay.

At the older man's agonized cry, Liam looked up and, in his eyes, Elsa saw what he wasn't saying out loud.

No pulse.

"Call 911," he shouted at someone standing behind her. "Possible Cardiac arrest."

Elsa moved close to Lois's head, working in tandem with Liam as he started chest compressions. Time was of the essence, to both decrease the damage and increase the older woman's survival chances.

One, two, three, four, five ….

Elsa waited for that fifteenth compression, ready for her two breaths.

She was a professional and could perform the life-saving technique in her sleep, but the more times they went through the rotation, the harder it was to distance herself. Images of Lois, the person, kept floating inside her head, threatening to push aside her objectivity.

Lois and Rupert walking along the pier holding hands.

Lois and Glynnis in the park with Bethany.

Lois and Liam dancing and laughing.

Her knees hurt from the hard floor, and as soon as the paramedic placed an oxygen bag over Lois's mouth and nose, Elsa moved aside.

"What happened?" Jeremy, one of the paramedics, asked.

"Lois was dancing and then sagged against Liam. When he couldn't find a pulse, we started CPR."

"I've got a pulse," Liam murmured before stepping aside.

"Lois, I'm here. Lois, honey, I'm here," Rupert repeated multiple times.

Elsa's eyes locked with Liam's, and in them she saw the same emotions she'd been feeling. The fight to remain detached at war with the caring person who'd just been laughing with the victim.

I'm here. I know what you're feeling. You're not alone.

Liam reached for Elsa's hand, realizing this time it was him holding on to her as if she were his lifeline. He'd done what needed to be done to save Lois's life, but with every chest compression he kept hearing her last words.

I learned a long time ago to live each day as if it's my last, because you never know.

How would he have felt if her last words were to him and not to the man she'd loved for over fifty years?

He watched the EMTs transfer Lois onto a stretcher and had to fight not to correct their technique.

What I could teach you ....

"Thank you." Rupert shook Liam's hand, then followed the stretcher.

Once the stretcher disappeared, everyone started talking at once. Liam glanced into Elsa's upturned face, and what he saw had him catching his breath. He wanted to take her in his arms and say so many things, except a part of him had gone out that door with his dance partner.

"Are you okay?"

"I'm fine." She blinked rapidly and pushed away the tears he could see in her glassy gaze. "You did a good job."

Liam ducked his head, uncomfortable with her praise after the way he'd shut her out.

"*We* did a good job," he whispered.

"Yes, we did."

"You've got a ride home, right?"

"Liam?"

Her question had him second guessing his decision until he remembered the agony on Rupert's face.

"We'll talk, I promise." He cupped her jaw and placed a tender kiss on her lips. "I've got to go."

"Go?" she called before he'd gotten too far.

"To the hospital," he tossed over his shoulder on his way out.

While he stood waiting for the valet to get his car, she grabbed his elbow and her flashing blue eyes met his. "I'm coming with you."

"You don't have—"

"Shut up!" Elsa snapped. "I'm sick and tired of you thinking *for* me. You don't have the monopoly on being allowed to be there for someone. I'm coming."

"You forgot your coat." He draped his tux jacket around her shoulders.

"Emma can get it."

The valet drove up, and without waiting for him, she opened the door and climbed in.

"Bugger that," he murmured, confusion washing over him.

On the way to the hospital, Elsa appeared to be lost in her thoughts. Why hadn't he told her where he was going? Why hadn't he invited her? Was he afraid she'd say no? And what about her comments before she'd gotten into his car? Was she right?

I'm sick and tired of you thinking for me.

Was that what he was doing?

You're not that bloody daft, are you?

Alright, he was trying to take care of her, like he tried to take care of everyone. When you cared, wasn't that what you were supposed to do?

You don't have the monopoly on being allowed to be there for someone.

Had anyone been there for him before?

The better question is, have you allowed yourself to need anyone before?

No, because if you don't need them, they can't hurt you.

As soon as they arrived at the hospital, Liam followed Elsa through the halls to a small waiting room.

"I'm going to change into scrubs." She barely got out before handing him his jacket and walking away.

Liam wanted to tug her into his arms and hold on tight. His nightmare still lived in his memory—vivid and real. But he couldn't quiet the word *Wait!* inside.

The burning in the center of his chest grew hotter, wilder, stealing his breath. Liam dropped into a chair and tried to fight. Yet the nightmare washed over him, bringing back feelings of fear and helplessness.

Liam turned over, his sleep haunted by the images that had spilled from the envelope onto his table. Killian, a dead man, him and Killian, them with their father, and finally the image that haunted him. A photo of him and Elsa the night before she left New York. That was bad, but the words written across the image threatened to tear him apart.

Pretty woman. It would be a shame if something happened to her.

She was safe, he repeated, hoping to fall into a deeper sleep. His phone rang, and without checking to see who'd called, he answered.

"'Lo."

"Liam." The timber of Killian's voice vanquished all thoughts of sleep.

"Killian, what happened?"

"There's been an accident, Liam," Killian sighed. "I'm sorry. I didn't know they'd go after her."

Liam couldn't breathe, and what felt like a knife twisted in his chest.

"Emma?"

"No."

"Don't tell me," Liam shoved the lump in his throat aside to whisper, "Elsa?"

"Aye. I'm sorry, Liam."

"What happened?" he barked, barely holding onto his sanity.

Killian groaned. "Elsa, Sadie, Molly, and Emma were having one of their female solidarity sessions. After it was over, they all walked to their cars and when Elsa started hers, it blew."

"It blew?"

"Aye," Killian confirmed. "She's gone, Liam."

"No!"

His cry had awakened him from the nightmare and propelled him to make the drive to Swan Harbor. He needed to tell her everything. Except he didn't know where to start.

Did he tell her about the danger or about the search for his mother?

"Liam?"

Elsa's perfume surrounded him and when he opened his eyes and saw her, tears of relief filled them.

"Elsa, love."

LIAM'S ENDEARMENT HAD ELSA'S HEART FLIPPING SEVERAL TIMES. Then it sank into the pit of her stomach.

She rubbed her thumb across his cheekbone, surprised when she encountered wetness.

"Are you okay?"

He leaned into her hand and nodded. "I'm alright."

Elsa showed him her wet finger. "Then what's this?"

"Leftover from a nightmare," Liam sighed and enclosed her hand between both of his.

His cryptic reply had her studying him a little more closely.

"Do you want to share your burdens?"

"Not here, love." A semblance of a smile crawled across his mouth. "But we *will* talk."

Elsa tilted her head, thinking if she could read the messages in his eyes, she'd know if he was serious. Except the longer she looked, the more she saw what she'd hoped.

"You mean that, don't you?"

"That we'll talk?"

"Yes."

"I do, El."

"And I get to ask questions?"

He side-eyed her. "If you must."

Would he tell her what was going on? Or would he tell her what he wanted her to hear?

"I'll trust you, for now."

He ducked his head and a look of regret crossed his face.

"I deserved that."

"Liam, I ..." Before she could say more, he placed his finger over her lips.

"Stop. We'll work it out."

"You think so?"

"I know so. But now, let's find Rupert. Is that alright?"

The words '*I love you*' almost escaped, but she wasn't planning to be the first one to say them. Their last conversation on the phone when she'd told him he didn't let himself feel passion or love had made her wary.

"They were taking Lois for an Angiogram," she told him. "Maybe Rupert is with her."

"Lead the way, and I will follow."

Oh man. If only that were true.

They found Rupert pacing just outside the Emergency Department.

"Elsa ... Liam .... They took my Lois, and I don't know where they went."

Elsa exchanged a look with Liam. She hooked her arm through Rupert's and directed him to one of the waiting rooms.

"Do you want coffee?" Liam asked the older man.

"Bah," the older man retorted. "Whiskey is what I'd like, young man."

Liam chuckled. "I doubt they serve that in the vending machines."

"How about some juice?" Elsa offered. "Or maybe just a bottle of water?"

"I guess," Rupert sighed.

Liam's gaze met hers. "Would you like one too?"

"I'd like that, thanks."

He walked away, his loose-legged stroll in his tux making her think of a model on a runway.

"I'm glad your young man was the one dancing with my Lois when she ..." Rupert's voice broke, and Elsa had to fight the tears that wanted to spill. "I've known CPR for more years than I can count. When it's your wife, though, ..."

Elsa related, in that she'd had to fight thoughts of Lois, the friend, while trying to save the woman's life.

"Liam's a paramedic in New York City," Elsa replied. "We worked together at Queen's Court."

"Are you talking about me, El?" Liam returned, handing each of them bottles of water.

"Who me?"

"Don't believe everything she tells you, Rupert," Liam told the older man. "Elsa likes to elaborate."

The more Liam teased, the more color returned to Rupert's cheeks, which was a good sign.

"Go, El," Liam encouraged.

Elsa gave Liam a wide-eyed stare.

"What?"

"You're getting antsy." Liam pointed to the way she was jiggling the bottle of water. "Go get answers."

He was more observant than she'd thought, but she didn't have to be told twice.

Rupert's faded blue eyes studied him, making Liam fight to remain still.

"What's holding you back?" the older man asked nonchalantly.

"Who said I'm holding back?"

Rupert relaxed in the chair and crossed one leg over the other.

"There was a time when I wouldn't allow myself to get close to anyone."

Liam thought about refuting the statement, but if his running days were over, he needed to face the tough questions. Especially since Elsa had said something similar.

"You've been married for fifty years," Liam responded wryly. "What caused you to change?"

"Lois."

If it were only that easy.

"That's it? Meet Lois and," Liam snapped his fingers, "old habits disappear?"

"Hardly," Rupert let go of a dry laugh. "But I realized it was better to have loved, even if it didn't last, than to never love at all. Consider that," he concluded, just as Elsa returned with an older woman who introduced herself as Shayla Blackburn.

"How's Lois?" Rupert pressed the doctor for an answer.

"Lois is resting comfortably," Doctor Blackburn explained. "If it's okay with you, I'd like to schedule Angioplasty first thing in the morning."

"Angioplasty?" Rupert's frightened gaze met Liam's. "That doesn't sound good."

"Angioplasty isn't without risks," Doctor Blackburn conceded. "But Lois has a blockage in two arteries, and that alone can be more dangerous than using the balloon."

"She's right," Elsa added her support to the cardiologist's. "Blockage can lead to strokes or another heart attack."

Rupert nodded. "Okay. Can I see her?"

"I think she would like that. Are you ready to go now?" Doctor Blackburn asked.

"Do you want us to come with you?" Liam wasn't sure if wanted Rupert to say yes or no.

"No, thank you, Liam," Rupert answered. "I'm going to take care of Lois and call our daughter. It's time for you to do what you need to do."

"Let us know if you need anything," Elsa told the older man quietly.

Once Rupert and the doctor disappeared, Elsa pinned him with one of her blue-eyed stares.

"What did he mean by that?"

"He told me he was going to kick my arse if I didn't treat you right."

Elsa studied him for a second and a corner of her mouth curved.

"No he didn't."

"Close enough." Liam took her hand and led her back the way they'd come. "Can I take you home?"

"And then what?"

He still wasn't sure where to start, but tugged her into an alcove and wrapped her in his arms.

"Then we talk."

"You sound scared."

"I've just never been good at sharing," he whispered.

Elsa's steady gaze bore into his, her eyes once again throwing messages at him he'd never been willing to read.

She kissed him softly, and then continued, "Liam, in our professions, we face life and death situations all the time. But when we were working together to save Lois's life, it was a fight to maintain my objectivity."

"Me too," confessed Liam.

"Then there's my mother's illness, which just in the last few days has taken another turn. I don't want to go through life wondering 'what if.'"

"If you don't allow yourself to try, you will definitely fail," Liam murmured against her mouth.

"Something like that." Elsa kissed him, but before he could take it deeper, she stepped back. "So, where do we go from here?"

"Elsa love." He dropped little kisses on her mouth, never staying in one place long. "We start with a little hope and go from there." The words were barely out before she tugged him closer and he could finally partake in what she was offering.

NINETEEN

Elsa's Cottage
September 15
11:45 p.m.

On the drive across town, Elsa's thoughts were all over the place. Her heart still raced from being held. Her lips still tingled from being kissed. Yet, her fear still lingered.

What if he told her they had no future?

Come on. After those kisses, do you really think that's a possibility?

She didn't, but she also wanted to be prepared.

Remember what he said. We start with a little hope ....

She still had that, didn't she? If not, would he have the power to hurt her?

No.

Then Liam pulled into her driveway and his headlights bounced off her car. The sight temporarily waylaid her thoughts.

"That's weird."

"What?"

"My car's back. I didn't expect it to be back until Monday when everything opened."

When opened his car door, the security lights allowed her to get a good look at his expression.

"You had something to do with it," she stated when he pulled open her door.

"What?" he asked absently.

Remember the power.

Elsa climbed from the car, and the wind blew straight through her scrubs.

"Come here." Liam tugged her up and into his arms.

She wanted to be strong, to play coy, but she'd meant what she'd said at the hospital. The week had been an emotional roller coaster and after everything, she didn't want to live her life leaving behind any 'what ifs.'

His heat surrounded her, and the way he touched her confused her.

"Are you coming inside?"

The security light clicked off, plunging them into darkness. While she waited for Liam's answer, the beat of her heart synced with their breaths.

"Do you want me to?"

The vulnerable tone in his voice was one she'd never heard. It strengthened her thoughts about Liam and his capability versus his willingness to feel love, passion, or jealousy.

Before their trip to see her mother, he'd asked what she was doing to him and acknowledged that they were both changing. Could that mean what she thought, and he *wanted* to change?

We start with a little hope ....

"What do you think?"

"Tell me," he whispered.

The vulnerability remained, and she couldn't help but think he was asking for more than he was saying.

Elsa cupped Liam's jaw and tugged his mouth closer to hers. "I want you," his breath hitched, and a thrill rushed through her, "to come inside."

He exhaled forcefully, and she had to wonder what he'd been thinking. Had he been worried she'd not wanted him?

"I want that too," he whispered against her lips, saying things with his kiss he'd never verbalized before.

The heat from the kiss mixed with the cooler air had a shiver running through her. Liam immediately tucked her closer against his side and directed them toward the porch.

"Are you cold?"

"Maybe, a little."

"See." He nuzzled her temple and his hot breath had other parts standing up and taking notice. "I told you to get your coat."

"You were going to leave me," she pouted.

"I didn't know if I had rights," Liam murmured.

Oh, Liam. "No?"

"No."

"But you had rights to take care of my car and make sure it was back tonight."

The sheepish look on his face confirmed her suspicions. He'd spoken to the mechanic.

"Thank you, but why?"

"Why did I arrange for your car to be waiting?" he asked once they were inside.

"Yes."

"I don't know. Maybe I was worried about an emergency. If you were called in, you would have been stuck."

Elsa's breath caught, and her heart felt like it had melted.

"Oh Liam."

Elsa dropped her things on a small table and laid her hand on his chest. The temptation to get distracted was so strong, she took a step backward.

"Thank you, Liam. Sometimes you ..."

She left it hanging, as she was unsure how to go on. Did he want her to put him on the spot? Or was he planning on explaining the whole push-pull thing between them?

"Sometimes I what?" he prompted in a way he'd not done before.

But she wasn't ready to put those thoughts into words yet. Instead, she brushed off the questions, led him into the back room, and turned on the gas fireplace.

"Make yourself comfortable. I'm going to put on warmer clothes."

When Liam looked back at her from where he was studying the photos on her wall, she couldn't interpret his expression. Was it fear? Or was it relief?

"I'll be right back."

"Alright."

Liam's silence was unsettling and instead of the calm she'd been feeling earlier, her anger threatened to erupt.

It wasn't until she was halfway to her bedroom he said, "I'll be waiting."

Rather than continuing forward, his quiet response had her retracing her steps and stopping a foot in front of him.

"You'd better be waiting when I finish changing, buster! If you aren't, I'm coming after you. I'm tired of this up and down crap, and I want answers. Understood?"

His lips twitched, but whatever she'd seen in his eyes was gone.

"Aye, Aye, love," he teased, once again back to the man she was used to. "Hurry back."

"I'll be back when I'm back." Then she flounced into her bedroom and sagged against the door.

Now what? Was it too late to reach out to Emma or Sadie?

LIAM HUNG HIS JACKET ON THE BACK OF A CHAIR, THEN unhooked his bowtie and crammed it into his pocket. His heart was racing, his palms were sweating, and he felt much like he was swimming in mud. Nothing made sense, and he still wasn't sure what to say or where to begin.

The ever-present awareness he felt whenever she was near alerted him she'd returned just before she pulled him onto the sofa.

Was he ready?

Too bloody bad if you aren't, that quiet voice snapped.

"You look lovely," he whispered, noting she had on one of his NYFD sweatshirts.

"Stop that."

Liam frowned. "Stop telling you how lovely you are?"

"Stop being charming."

"You think I'm charming?" he asked, his grin growing.

"You know damn well you're charming," Elsa snapped. "Just about every female who worked at Queen's thought you were charming and considered you a friend."

A part of him wanted to continue teasing her about her play on words, but ....

"My father said I hide behind my affability," Liam murmured, the admission surprising him.

"What?"

It wasn't until he remembered his father's words,

... you won't allow yourself to get close enough ...

and they bounced against Elsa's words of a similar vein he knew where to start.

... it's not that you can't feel ... but you won't allow yourself ...

"You were right. When you said I wouldn't allow myself to feel passion or jealousy or—"

"—Love?"

"Yeah." Liam rubbed his hand over the burning in the center of his chest.

"I wondered if it was me," she whispered. "If you just couldn't feel those things for me."

Liam took her hand, feeling once again as if it were a lifeline holding him steady. "It's really just the opposite. I never realized how much control I had over my feelings ... until you left me."

Elsa tilted her head and a look of confusion crossed her face. "Left you?"

"When you moved to Swan Harbor. Were you trying to get me to wake up?"

The reasoning hadn't been something he'd given much thought to until he'd said the words. Then, he got a good look at her face, and had to wonder if there was some truth behind them.

"You told me you moved because of a good job. Right?"

Elsa winced. "Tate offered me a good job, but ..." she let that word hang for several heartbeats, before admitting, "I was hoping you would ask me to stay or—"

"—Come with you?"

"Yes."

Her voice was so soft, he only caught what she said because he was watching her. He thought maybe he should be angry because, like Debi Monroe, she'd tried to manipulate him.

Did she really?

Yes!

Really? Seems she left, and it wasn't until you arrived in Swan Harbor your thoughts changed.

You want me to believe it was Swan Harbor that manipulated me?

If you want to get technical, it was after you imagined Jonesy asking why you were lonely.

"I can't decide if I should be angry or thank you."

"What do you want to do?"

"I want ..." Their eyes met and before he'd consciously figured out what he wanted, he'd tugged her across his lap. "I want this, Sweet Elsa," he murmured, taking the opportunity to get lost in her embrace.

She was soft, warm, and tasted like heaven. How had he spent so long in her company and kept her at arm's length?

Practice.

Stupidity.

He was a fool to have pushed her away, and no matter how much he tried, he couldn't get close enough.

"Oh, El ..."

Liam kissed her, then trailed butterfly kisses across her petal-soft cheek. He slid his hand under her oversize sweatshirt and the heat of her silky skin called to him, reminding him of their night in Georgetown. Would she give him that gift again?

He covered her breast and slid his thumb across her nipple, causing it to pebble.

Elsa hissed, and the sound reverberated in his head.

Loser.

Stop!

Not a man.

Stop!

Real men don't cry.

The words echoed inside until he froze, his mind once again controlling the actions of his body.

"Liam." Elsa cupped his jaw and gently stroked his cheeks. "Liam, look at me."

"I'm sorry." Liam slowly opened his eyes to meet hers. "I didn't mean for that to get so heated. Forgive me?"

He dropped his head against her shoulder for a heartbeat or two. Then, in one smooth motion, he sat up and tucked her against his side.

"Talk to me," she pleaded.

While the memories had been like a slap in the face, Liam's body still throbbed. His thoughts scattered, working to come up with an explanation.

"Remember when you came to the apartment and told me you were moving and Barbi was there?"

"Yes. I wanted to scratch her eyes out and cry at the same time."

His laugh sounded hollow, but his thoughts had been similar regarding Tyler.

"Barbi and I have known each other forever. And not like that," he clarified before she'd asked.

"Never?"

Liam rolled his eyes. "David was my best friend in high school and Barbi is his older sister. After mum left, dad turned to the bottle and Killian was seeing how many girls he could catch. I needed ..."

"A friend."

"Maybe. Anyway, Barbi suggested I needed to let go of my past so I could move into the future."

"Is that what you want?"

❧

THE ENTIRE TIME SHE WAITED FOR HIM TO ANSWER, ELSA'S HEART raced, almost taking her breath.

We start with hope ....

"At the time, I didn't believe so," Liam admitted. "But when I walked into Swan Harbor General and you ducked around the pillar, the memory of our first kiss was suddenly there, in the front of my mind."

"In Swan Harbor?" she frowned. "What about at Queen's Court after I left? Did you think of me?"

"Oh, El," Liam groaned. "I was a stubborn fool. Everywhere I turned, you were there. Yet I refused to allow my thoughts to bloom into full-fledged memories. It hurt too much."

Her heart squeezed at his admission, and she pinched her thigh to make sure she wasn't dreaming.

"What made you think about our first kiss?"

"The scrubs you were wearing."

"My scrubs?"

"Yeah." He wiggled his eyebrows comically. "They were bright blue with that little snowman on them. Your eyes look so pretty when you're wearing them and when I saw you, it sucked me back into that room in Queen's."

"That was a pretty good first kiss, wasn't it?"

"The best," he agreed. "And the more time I spent with you, I had to wonder if your fanciful thoughts about being led here were true for me as well."

"Believing in the mystical, Liam?" Elsa teased. "That doesn't sound like you."

"You don't know the half of it."

"That sounds curious."

"Let's just say," he muttered tongue-in-cheek. "This town has a way of making you think about things you've never thought about."

"Really? How do you feel about that?"

"Confused."

"About?"

Liam stared over her head and appeared lost in thought.

"Have you ever believed something and then suddenly you find out maybe that's not the truth at all?"

"Hello," she reminded him, "Olivia."

"Right. You were an only child and suddenly, you weren't."

"Yes."

"For years, I've never considered the future. Just assumed I deserved only what I had."

"Why?"

"Let's just say," Liam sighed. "Ghosts from the past have a way of shaping our present ... and our future."

"Have you confronted your ghosts?"

"I'm trying."

"Why?"

A little pucker developed between his brows. "Rupert and Lois showed me forever is possible and I want that ..."

Tears filled Elsa's eyes, and she held her breath, trying to stop them from overflowing.

"—With you," he breathed the words she'd longed to hear.

"Oh, Liam. I want that too."

He cupped her face and brushed away her tears just as she'd done for him earlier.

"Be patient." He kissed her softly, but she could feel his restraint not to let it burn out of control.

"Wait," Elsa pushed him away slightly so she could think clearly. "I can be patient, but …"

"But?" Liam's side-eyed look said he was waiting for her to say something bad.

"No more of this back and forth crap."

"Back and forth crap?" Liam blinked a few times. "Elsa, honey, I still live in New York, so back and forth—"

"Not that type of back and forth," she interrupted. "I meant back and forth as in, you're there one day and ignoring me the next. *Talk* to me. And please, *don't* keep things from me."

He winced, and a sliver of fear shot through her.

"What?"

"About that."

"There's more?"

"Yes, but to be honest, I'm surprised Emma has said nothing."

Elsa jumped off the sofa and stepped out of Liam's reach. "Wait! There's more and Emma knows?"

The guilty look on his face answered her question, and she had to think over her conversations with Emma. Had she felt like there was something being kept from her?

The answer was no, making Elsa wonder why. Had Emma gotten good at hiding things from her? Or was it on her, because she hadn't been looking?

"Emma has said nothing, but I will deal with her later. Tell me!"

"What do you know about Killian's undercover work when he worked in New York?"

Elsa shrugged. "Just what you told me. He worked undercover for around ten years. Why?"

"Let's just say I'm very happy you're not living in New York right now."

He was keeping things from her, and she couldn't decide what the best course of action was. They'd talked a long time, and he'd opened up in ways she'd never expected.

"Why are you glad I'm not in New York?"

"It's just safer in Swan Harbor." The words were barely out of his mouth before he stalked toward her, his intent obvious. "Come here."

"Wait!" Elsa pushed back and continued with the question that had her stomach spinning. "If I were in New York, would I be in danger?"

His answer was in the way he dropped his eyes. It was in the way his nostrils flared and his jaw tightened.

"So," her voice trembled, "since I'm *not* in New York and you are. Does that mean *you*'re in danger?"

Liam stared at the woman in his arms who meant more to him than he'd realized was possible. Could he lie?

"I don't know." He opted for a partial truth.

"You don't know?" Her voice rose with each word, and he could hear both the fear and anger in them.

"I can say this," he tried again. "Killian taught me well when he was undercover, and I'm taking all the precautions."

"Liam ..."

"Come here." He tugged her fully into his arms. "I'm being careful, but you have to promise you'll be careful too. I'm glad you have a security system."

"You don't think ..."

"What?"

Please don't have her ask me about the person she thought she saw.

"Nothing."

She tightened her arms, hugging him as if she never wanted to let him go. It felt right, so right that he never wanted to let her go.

"It's late, love." Liam kissed her again. "I'd better go or the gossip chain and the spy network will burn up the lines."

Elsa chuckled. "Let them."

When their lips met, he wished the ghosts in his head would quieten, so he could grab hold of the heaven only Elsa could offer.

TWENTY

Swan Harbor
Veterinarian Clinic
September 17
6:20 a.m.

Elsa turned into Emma's driveway just as the sun peeked over the horizon and parked next to the yellow bug. With the windows still dark, the occupants were in for a shock, but that was too damn bad.

She slammed her car door with just a little more force than was necessary and stomped up the steps to knock.

Three quick knocks were followed by three lighter ones.

It wasn't long before she heard heavy footsteps, and the door opened.

"Bloody hell, Elsa," Killian barked. "Do you know what bloody time it is?"

"I know what bloody time it is," she shot back. "Where the bloody hell did your brother run off to this time?"

"I'm not Liam's keeper," Killian snapped. "He's a grown man."

"Who's caught in the middle of something because of you." She jabbed her finger into his chest and pushed him aside. "Can you promise me he's going to be safe?"

"Killian?" Emma called from the top of the stairs. "What's going on?"

"Elsa's paying a visit," Killian grumbled. "Go back to sleep, Doc."

"Don't you go back to sleep." Elsa pointed at her long-time best friend. "I also have a bone to pick with you."

Emma exchanged looks with Killian and continued the rest of the way down.

"El, it's early, and you know I don't function well before caffeine. Why don't you come upstairs and explain what's going on?"

Elsa glanced at Killian, who indicated she proceed him up the stairs. "Fine. Then I want answers."

She heard Killian mutter, "By all means," but ignored him until they sat down.

Killian set three cups on the table, filled each with coffee and put the pot away.

"Start from the beginning."

"Liam told me about Santora," Elsa admitted. "Why didn't you tell me?"

"I ..."

Emma linked her fingers with Killian's. "He was trying to protect us and Swan Harbor."

"Is Swan Harbor in danger?" Elsa looked between Emma and Killian, wondering which would give her the answers she needed.

"I don't know," Killian finally admitted. "If he told you about this, why are you waking us so bloody early?"

"Killian." Emma quieted him, and, for the first time, Elsa's anger wilted a little.

"Okay, fine," Elsa huffed. "I'm sorry. But he was supposed to spend the morning with me, and I woke to this." She pressed play on Liam's message.

"Elsa, love. I'm sorry to cut our time short, but my dad just sent a text and needs to see me right away. Maybe when we talk again, I'll have laid those ghosts to rest. I'll call you as soon as I can.

"Bloody hell." Killian reached for his phone and spent several minutes texting with someone.

When Elsa looked at Emma and she shrugged, it forced her to wait—something she was tiring of. It wasn't long before Killian laid his phone on the table and pointed to a dot.

"That's Liam. He's safe, and just getting on I-295."

"Why are you tracking him?" Elsa asked first, even though she had dozens of questions.

Killian sighed and briefly explained his reasoning. Elsa understood, but she wasn't sure how knowing where his brother was when they were so far apart helped.

"Where's he going?"

"To my father's."

Elsa clasped her hands together and leaned forward. "While Liam didn't tell me specifically who the ghost was, something tells me he's going to need me when he confronts them. Can you give me directions to your father's house?"

Killian was quiet for a few seconds, and then turned to Emma, almost as if asking what he should do.

"Liam shared his burdens," she reminded him. "He's on his way to do what he has to do. If that were you, would you want me there?"

He tipped his chin. "Aye."

"Thank you," Elsa mouthed.

"Let me have your phone." When she handed it to him, he continued, "I'll put my dad's info on your GPS."

"And is Liam going to be safe?"

"I'm doing everything I can from this end," Killian replied. "Until someone makes a move, that's all I can do."

Elsa took her phone, her heart heavy. "I hope that's good enough."

But as she started her car and headed out of town, she couldn't keep her tears at bay. It felt as if she'd just found him again, and it wasn't fair. Like Rupert and Lois, she wanted to make a lifetime of memories with Liam.

You were with him yesterday.

That's not enough. She wanted more times together.

More lazy mornings.

"It's too early," she murmured, answering the morning knock.

"Tsk tsk." Liam kissed her, his lips sugary from the bite of pastry he'd just taken. "I brought you some sugar."

More times spent with friends.

When they stepped into Lois's hospital room, holding hands, the older woman's eyes twinkled.

"Hey there, handsome. Looks like you had a better time last night than I did."

"Lois!" Rupert scolded his wife. "Don't tease these young kids."

"Oh, hush." She winked at Elsa. "I know what I'm doing."

"She's fine, Rupert," Liam assured the older man. "Her advice was invaluable.

"See," Lois preened. "He appreciated my advice."

"Your advice?" Elsa looked from Lois to Liam.

Liam lifted their clasped hands and kissed her fingertips. "It was her idea to start with a little hope."

"He's right." Lois smiled. "It's the first ingredient to forever."

Elsa blinked, and her heart flipped.

"Come here, El," Liam whispered against the side of her head. And just being in his arms made her feel complete.

The rest of the day, they'd laid in front of the fireplace, kissed, and talked about those little things Liam had always run from. When he'd left to drive back to the Beachside, she'd found it harder to say goodbye than the night before. It forced her to think about how it would feel when he left to drive back to the City. Except this time, he'd not left her with a proper goodbye kiss and hug.

She wanted to be angrier, except every time she felt her temper rising, her inner voice reminded her.

Calm down! He's dealing with the ghosts.

Were the ghosts the reason he'd called a halt to their lovemaking? Somehow that made sense, especially considering what had happened after they'd made love in June. He'd stepped back, creating a wall between them she'd not been able to scale.

Maybe when we talk again, I'll have laid those ghosts to rest.

He'd been there when she'd first heard of her mother's diagnosis. While her behavior had certainly not been what she'd expected, she couldn't regret anything. She wanted to be there for him, no matter what or who his ghost was.

And if it's a woman from his past?

Then she'd deal with that, too. He'd told her he wanted a future with her, and those were not words Liam Reade took lightly.

We'll start with a little hope.

Elsa had plenty of hope, and just like she'd been guided to Swan Harbor, her heart was trying to tell her something. This time, she was going to listen and fight for what she wanted.

Then, when it was all over, she would decide her next course of action. It didn't stop her from worrying about how Liam would respond once she arrived. Would he accept her support or would he push her away as he'd don so many times?

Tarrytown, NY
Finn Reade's Home
September 17
1:00 p.m.

"Son," Finn murmured, "pacing back and forth in front of the door won't get him here any faster."

Liam sent his father a dirty look. "I'm aware of that. But what's taking so long?"

"Same reasons as before," Finn sighed. "His flight was delayed, and it took him longer than usual to get through customs."

"He told you nothing?"

"Obviously, you don't know Sanders," Finn retorted. "He's a man of few words."

"Did he tell you if he was bringing mum with him at least?"

"He didn't. But he didn't say he wasn't either."

Meaning there was a fifty-fifty chance when his father's investigator walked in, Claire Reade would be with him. Liam wasn't sure how he was supposed to feel about that. His gut churned, his heart raced and a part of him wanted to run. But he'd meant what he'd said to Elsa. Rupert and Lois had shown him forever was possible, and he wanted that.

You start with a little hope ....

"Are you ready, Liam?" Finn asked quietly when the doorbell chimed.

"No," Liam muttered. "But do I have a choice?"

Finn's dark eyes met Liam's as if to say, *'This was your idea'*, as he pulled open the front door. "Sanders." His father shook the investigator's hand and waved him inside.

Liam waited, listening to his father's voice and for the voice of another.

"Well, hello," Finn continued. "I didn't see you standing there."

This is it, Liam thought, turning to face the door. Except it wasn't his mother standing next to his father.

"Elsa? What—?"

Liam wanted to say he didn't need her to hold his hand, but then he remembered how he'd felt after saving Lois.

"—Am I doing here?"

"Well, yes ..."

Don't question it! Accept her support just like she accepted yours when you showed up to take her to the airport.

"I'm glad you're here." It was then he realized how stupid he'd been for not asking her to come with him.

She gave him that sweet smile he loved so much and slipped her hand into his.

I'm here. Thank you for not pushing me away.

"Sanders, this is my son, Liam, and his friend Elsa," Finn made introductions. "Why don't we sit, and you can explain what you've found?"

A look crossed Sanders's face that had Liam tightening his hold around Elsa's hand, as if his life depended on it.

"Did you find Claire?"

"Claire?" Elsa murmured.

"My mum."

Sanders exchanged looks with his father, making Liam wonder if Finn knew what was coming next.

"When your father hired me to locate Claire Reade fifteen years ago," Sanders began. "It took a while for me to track her down. Her movements were erratic. She'd show up in one place, disappear for a while, only to show up somewhere else. Then she settled in Dunbar."

"It's close to Edinburgh," Finn added, "where Claire lived as a child."

Had she found what she'd been searching for?

"Since it took a few days to locate her, I'm assuming she wasn't in the same place when you went back this time."

Sanders gave a quick shake of his head, then pulled a book from his briefcase, causing the churning in Liam's gut to grow. "I'm sorry to have to tell you, but your mother is deceased."

"Deceased?" Liam whispered.

Sanders nodded. "She'd dropped her married name and was once again Claire Jones. It made it a little more difficult to locate her trail this time."

"When? Where?" Liam asked, trying to process the facts being handed to him.

"About a year ago." Sanders handed a book to Liam. "The where, a mental hospital in Liverpool."

A mental hospital?

Liam flipped through the pages of the book, thinking maybe there would be answers for him. Blank pages, partial pictures, rudimentary drawings, half sentences. Nothing that in any way said the book had belonged to his mother.

"Where did this come from?"

"I got it from the nurse who took care of her," Sanders replied.

"Did you know?" Liam asked his father.

"That your mother was dead?"

"Yes."

"Not definitively," Finn admitted. "But I wondered."

"Why would you wonder that?" Liam heard the disbelief in his voice.

Finn gazed out the window and several expressions crossed his face. Liam knew that while Claire Jones Reade had made life difficult for her oldest son, she'd been even harder on his father.

"For years, I tried to tell myself your mother's difficulties were my fault," Finn replied. "But when I was confronting my ghosts, I finally realized they weren't mine, but hers. While we were married, I did everything in my power to make her happy, even ..."

"Even change your name?" Liam hazarded a guess.

Finn tipped his chin. "Even that. But Claire wouldn't allow herself to be happy. She reveled in controlling other people's happiness and making them feel small when they didn't get what they wanted."

"Or do what she said," Liam added. "Do you think she killed herself?"

"She didn't." Sanders corrected the assumption.

"No?" Finn asked, obviously surprised.

"No," Sanders assured them. "Complications following a surgery."

That's something, at least, Liam thought, once again picking up the book.

Some pages were full—words bunched together in such a way he could only make out one or two of them. Others had a picture, or a picture and a few words.

He made out the name Flynn and the old spelling of their name Reide. It was crossed out with the new spelling Reade written next to it. There were drawings that looked like children and faces with different emotions. Pages filled with angry pictures, and pages filled with happy ones.

Then he turned the page and the words and pictures roared through him.

The acid in his stomach churned, and a knot rose in throat.

Loser.

Stop!

Not a man.

Stop!

Real men don't cry.

Liam's control over his emotions had been one of his traits that both frustrated and fascinated Elsa. But as she watched surprise, anger, and sadness cross his face, she had to wonder what he saw. Then, as if a curtain came down, he set the book on the table and sauntered across the room.

What had he seen?

Finn sent his son a concerned look and stood to see Sanders out, leaving them alone.

Liam's body posture said, don't-touch-me and I-don't-need-you, but as she got closer, his eyes said something completely different.

She hurt me, but she was my mother.

I don't want to care, but I do.

"Liam." Elsa stopped an arm's length away. "Why didn't you tell me your mother was your ghost?"

A harsh laugh escaped. "Right! Poor little Liam has mommy issues."

"Stop it," she snapped. "You heard your father. Your mother had issues that were *her* issues. They weren't your father's, and they certainly weren't yours. You were a boy."

"I was eighteen when she decided she'd tired of being a mum," he cried. "I both hated and loved her."

"And she loved you, Liam," Finn replied. "Claire just had a funny way of showing her love."

"That's an understatement," Liam murmured. "She was the woman of mercurial moods. Happy if I behaved exactly as she wanted and mean if I didn't."

Elsa handed him the book. "Show me the picture you were looking at."

Liam sent her a look she interpreted as, *How did you know?* But took the book and flipped it open. "Happy now?"

Elsa glanced at the visible pages, and a lump climbed into her throat.

Claire had written *sorry Liam* over and over on one page. On the other side, she'd drawn a circle with eyes and a frown that appeared to be crying. The words were smeared, making Elsa think tears had dripped onto them.

"Oh, Liam." Her heart broke for the boys whose mother hadn't given them the unconditional love they'd needed. But knowing the men they'd become caused her tears to fall.

"Don't cry for me, El." Liam cupped her face, sweeping the wetness away. "I survived."

When their eyes met, the love and tenderness she saw looking back had her fighting not to respond.

"You did much more than survive, Liam," Elsa whispered. "You thrived and became the amazing man who's standing in front of me."

"The man who's terrified of getting too close to people, because he doesn't want to be hurt," he replied wryly. "That doesn't sound like thriving."

"It takes more courage to face what we can't do," she pointed out. "And just like Lois said, forever begins with a little hope."

"Plus, listening to your heart."

"You've been talking to Captain Jack, I see," Elsa quipped.

"Is it that easy?"

"No, but Sadie would say, *Take back the power.* If you do that, things aren't as scary."

"Take back the power?"

"Yes." Elsa hugged him and pulled him down onto the sofa. "Tell me."

LIAM WATCHED HIS FATHER LEAVE THE ROOM, SO HE WAS ALONE with Elsa. Could he share the story that had served to shape his future?

"I was eighteen, a senior in high school, and full of myself," he grinned.

"You?"

"Behave." Elsa stuck her tongue out and he had to fight to stay focused. "My mother had lofty goals for me. She wanted me to go to a fancy university in England. If that couldn't happen, I had to attend the finest one in the states."

"And that wasn't what you wanted," Elsa guessed.

"You could say that again," Liam admitted. "I wanted to attend a small state college with my friend David and my high school girlfriend."

"Oh, so the real story comes out."

"What can I say?"

Her lips twitched. "What was her name?"

"Teresa." He held his hands in front of him in a crude manner and wiggled his eyebrows. "She was stacked."

Elsa looked down at her own chest and her face pinked. "You're out of luck if that's still what matters."

"It's not the size that matters," he winked, "but the response."

Her face grew redder, and he couldn't keep from leaning in for a firm, but way too brief kiss.

"To appease my mother, I'd applied to the schools she'd approved of, but every time an acceptance letter arrived, I tossed it in a pile."

"Because it wasn't Teresa's school."

"It wasn't David's school," he clarified. "We had big plans."

"I bet," she murmured tongue-in-cheek.

Liam raced into the house, dropped his backpack on the floor, and reached for the mail.

"That doesn't belong there, Liam." Claire snapped.

"Sorry." He quickly flipped through the college envelopes. "I'll get to it."

"See that you do."

He gave her a disgruntled look and tossed the mail back onto the table. "I didn't get one."

"You didn't get what?"

"My acceptance letter to the state college," Liam grumbled. "I told you that's where I'm going."

"No, you aren't."

The finality in her voice had the knot in Liam's stomach rolling. "What did you do?"

Claire looked up at him with her patented 'Who me,' expression. "I don't know what you're talking about."

"Yes, you do!" Liam pressed.

"Oh, alright." She gave him a quick glance before returning to study her fingernails. "I threw your application in the trash."

Anger rushed up inside. "You did what?"

"Threw it away," she repeated. "That state school isn't good enough for you."

"I don't care," Liam barked.

Claire's eyes flashed, and she stalked toward him. "What did you say?"

"That I don't care," he yelled. "This is my life."

"No, it isn't." She pointed her finger at him. "You will do as I say."

"Or what?"

"Do you want to be a loser, like your friend David and his insipid parents, John and Marianne?"

"How are they losers?" Liam screamed. "Marianne is a much better mother than you."

Claire slapped him so hard tears sprang to his eyes. "You don't know what you're talking about. I only want the best for you, and instead of being grateful and thanking me, you behave like a sniveling brat."

She'd taken a few steps, then turned and looked back over her shoulder. "Oh, and Liam, real men don't cry. Remember that."

Liam rubbed his hand across his mouth, and it came away bloody from where his teeth had cut his lip. "I hate you."

Claire whipped around, and her eyes were cold. "Well, seems we have something in common, because I hate you too. I don't know how I ever could have given birth to someone who will never amount to anything. Now cleanup for dinner."

A shiver ran through Liam. "I didn't eat that night, and when I got back from school the next day, she was gone. I never knew why."

"I can fill in a few of those missing pieces," Finn offered, returning to the room. "When I got home that night, I asked Claire why you weren't joining us for dinner. She told me you were trying to decide which college you wanted to attend."

"But you knew I wanted to attend the small state college."

"I did." Finn nodded. "One thing led to another, and she confessed to throwing out your application."

"What did you say to her?"

"I told her if you wanted to go to the state college, that's where you were going, and if she was so unhappy, she knew where the door was."

Liam sucked in his breath. "And she left?"

"She left," Finn confirmed. "Son, I'm sorry your mother said such horrible things to you, but her problems were not yours. I told Killian this in January, and I'll repeat it. Claire and I weren't right, but she gave me you and your brother, and that I can't regret. As I said before, people aren't meant to be alone. Emma and Killian have found something special, and I want that for you."

Liam's eyes met Elsa's, and Lois's statement echoed in his head.

You start with a little hope and toss in a lot of love. Once your ground is solid, you work together to build your future brick by brick.

"We start with a little hope—"

"—And see where it goes," Elsa whispered.

He wanted to kiss her, but didn't think she'd approve of it in front of his father. "Would you like to take a walk?"

Again, a sweet smile crossed her face, melting a little piece of his heart. "I'd like that."

"Good, come on." Liam swept her out onto the patio and the door was barely closed before he tugged her into his arms.

She felt perfect, and as he sunk into her, he had to wonder if they were ready for what came next.

TWENTY-ONE

Swan Harbor
Sally's Diner
October 1
2:00 p.m.

"Look at her." Killian waved across the room to where Sally was weaving in between tables. "She has to be what, in her sixties?"

"Probably," agreed Rusty.

"Then how does she do it?" Killian sat back against the booth and had to hold in a groan. After a week of re-certifying sessions, his muscles were complaining.

"Good genes," Rusty smirked. "She really kicked your arse, didn't she?"

"Aye," Killian grumbled, still unsure how he'd ended up in a martial arts standoff with the owner of the diner. "Why didn't you have to take her on?"

Rusty laughed. "I'm not a git. Besides, I've seen her in action. Sally has some moves."

"Why thank you, Rusty," Sally preened. "Need anything else, boys?"

Killian's phone chirped. When he reached for it, his back muscles screamed.

"Would you like me to get it for you?" Sally's twinkling eyes met his.

"Bloody hell, no," Killian groused. "I'll get it later."

"If you say so." Sally pulled a small packet from her pocket and tossed it on the table. "Those might help the aches. Lunch is on me."

She picked up their dirty plates and shot Killian a mischievous grin. "Any time you want a work-out, let me know. Just because I'm in my sixties doesn't mean I don't have moves." Then, with a wink, she sashayed across the diner and stopped to talk to Sydney.

"Bet I'm going to be featured in Sydney's next article."

"Probably so," laughed Rusty. "Maybe even on the front page."

Killian glanced at the packet Sally had left and, shoving aside his pride, dumped the tablets into his hand. "Rum would work better."

"Agreed. But we have to work. Think that was who called?"

"It wasn't."

Rusty frowned. "You sure about that?"

"Aye," Killian lowered his voice, "It's Weaver's ring tone."

"Oh, think it's good or bad news?"

"I used to think no news is good news. But something tells me the last two weeks have lulled us into a sense of false security."

"I was afraid you were going to say that."

As Killian followed Rusty out of Sally's, he focused on putting one foot in front of the other without groaning.

"Hey Killian," Shawn Jackson, owner of Marine Auto, met them as they exited. "Heard Sally kicked your ass."

"Yes, she did," chuckled Rusty.

"Does the entire town know about my shame?"

"Probably," Shawn laughed. "Several who were watching posted videos. Last I saw, the video on Twitter had over a thousand views."

"Wonderful," Killian sighed. "Just what I didn't need. See you later."

A contemplative look crossed Shawn's face. "Did you get the envelope I left for you last week?"

"At the office?"

"Yeah. It was what I found when I repaired Elsa's tire."

Killian's senses heightened. "Why would you leave it for me?"

Shawn shrugged. "Your brother told me to let him know what happened, and since he's not around."

"You left it at the department."

"Yeah." Shawn's voice dropped to a whisper. "It was a bullet."

Killian exchanged concerned looks with Rusty and then glanced back at Shawn. "Have you mentioned this to anyone else?"

"No, I don't think so."

"Good. Can you keep it to yourself?"

"Sure. Not a problem."

It was quiet for several minutes while they walked down the sidewalk. Just before they crossed the street, Killian stopped. "Do you feel it?"

"You mean that little sensation in the back of my neck?"

"Aye."

"Yes," Rusty grumbled. "And if you're feeling it, I can't blame the buffalo shrimp I had for lunch."

"Told you to get the turkey," Killian quipped as they crossed the street and he casually glanced back over his shoulder.

"See anything?"

"Nothing. But I know they're there."

"Just who are they?" Rusty stopped just inside the sheriff's department and looked out the door.

"Wish I knew," Killian mumbled, listening to Weaver's message.

What he heard had his thoughts swirling with everything he needed to do to keep his family safe. Except, while he was in Swan Harbor, what about Liam and his father in New York? How could he make sure they weren't in more danger there than he was here?

"It's not good, is it?" Rusty murmured.

"No," Killian retorted. "Weaver is pretty sure someone was searching through my file."

"You suspected that, though, right?"

"Aye." Killian pulled the folder he'd started and jotted the date and a few notes. "But having it confirmed is still a punch in the gut."

"What else did he say?"

"Santora's out."

"Damn," grunted Rusty.

"My sentiments exactly," Killian agreed, sending Liam a quick text.

New York City
Queen's Court Hospital
October 1
3:30 p.m.

> Killian: Santora free. Be safe.

LIAM'S BREATH CAUGHT AND THE ONLY THING HE COULD THINK
of was talking to Elsa.

> Liam: Are you busy?

> Elsa: I have a few. Why?

As soon as he read that, Liam stepped outside and made the call.

"Liam." Elsa sounded breathless, but he could hear the smile in her voice. "Did you enjoy the video?"

"Poor Killian. Something tells me he's going to be sore."

"He was hobbling when it was over, and I heard Sally was teasing him at lunch." Her voice turned serious. "That's not why you called. Did something happen?"

"I can't call just to tell you I miss you?"

"Oh, Liam. That's getting easier to say, isn't it?"

She was right. It was getting easier to say. Just as it was getting easier to allow himself to step over the line he'd created years ago.

You start with a little hope ....

"I'm just double checking we're still on for tomorrow."

"We are," she giggled. "I can't wait. It's been a long two weeks."

"For me too, El, but that giggle has me nervous. What do you have planned for us?"

"You don't trust me?"

"Oh, honey, I trust you until ..."

"Until?"

"Until you giggle like that, and then I worry."

"I'm putting you to work."

"What do I need to fix?"

"Well, I was hoping you would help me with my mom's house," she explained hesitantly. "But if you—"

"Stop right there. I don't care what we do as long as we're together."

"Me too. Thank you."

"You can thank me when you see me." Liam took a deep breath and plunged forward, knowing she was going to worry. "Besides telling you I missed you and asking about tomorrow, I wanted ..." The words stuck, and he needed to be holding her, protecting her.

"Just spit it out, Liam."

"I just got word from Killian that Santora is out."

Elsa inhaled audibly. "Are you okay?"

"I'm fine. Until I get to hold you in my arms, I'm going to worry."

A feeling that was new for him to admit. So much so, he wasn't sure how he was supposed to behave.

"I'm fine," she assured him. "After work, I'll go home and set my alarm."

"Promise?" he barely got out before his radio burst to life.

"Yes. Call me later."

"I will, love. Bye."

Liam took off running and jumped into the ambulance. "Riverside and 91st," he shouted.

Tim powered up the truck and, as he roared out of the hospital's drive, Liam grabbed hold of the safety bar. Oh, the exuberance of the young, he couldn't help but think as they rounded the next corner.

His adrenaline kicked in as it always did when going out on a call, and he was already sorting through what they might encounter. Even with the normal rush coursing through his system, though, a part of him was still thinking about Elsa. Was his heart already in Swan Harbor?

Listen to your heart, it knows.

Was he ready to do just that?

They turned onto West 72nd and followed it to West End Avenue, where they turned north. With rush hour traffic in full force, Tim wove the truck in and out like a pro and once again, Swan Harbor popped into his head.

Less traffic.

Elsa!

His inner voice provided the real reason for the little town's appeal.

Once they reached 91st and parked alongside several police cruisers, Liam went searching for details.

"Hey Bret." He greeted an officer he'd known for a while. "What do we have?"

"He's one of ours," Bret barked. "Young couple found him under some trees in the Crabapple grove. Multiple gunshots. Last I heard, he was in and out of consciousness."

He's one of ours, reverberated in Liam's head. This shooting coming so close to Officers Brody and Stevens had to cause some nervousness.

"Who is it?" he asked, his stomach already preparing for a familiar name.

"A lieutenant from Brooklyn," Bret replied. "Jokowitz."

Liam's blood ran cold and as he went searching for his partners, he couldn't help thinking, '*The circle is getting smaller.*'

He reached the scene just as Wade and Tim were transferring Jokowitz onto the stretcher. Liam grabbed a pair of gloves and went to work.

"What do we have?"

Wade cut Jokowitz's pants leg open, then pointed toward the 4x4s stacked over a wound. "Gunshot to chest, possibly a 9 mm with no exit. One in the thigh and a graze to the right temple."

"Do we know what happened?"

Wade was quiet until they lifted the stretcher and were tightening the straps around the patient. "I overheard the officers talking. He thinks it was a meet gone bad. And get this... the head shot was taken after the lieutenant had already fallen."

That piece of information had Liam's thoughts scattering for a reason. "Making sure he was dead?"

"That's my guess," Wade agreed. "But how could someone miss that close?"

"Startled?"

"Maybe."

Was Jokowitz involved in the Santora case at the same time as Killian? And if so, was this his doing? Or was it random, and there was no connection between the cases at all?

With all the unanswered questions, Liam found he was constantly checking his surroundings. There were times he felt he was being watched.

However, New York City was a busy place, so he was never sure. As they pushed Jokowitz through the double doors of the Emergency Department, he looked over his shoulder. Not for the first time, the sight of a man had his blood running cold.

Was that the same person from the subway platform?

Bloody hell. What's next?

Swan Harbor
Elsa's Cottage
October 1
7:30 p.m.

Elsa arrived home much later than she'd anticipated, but was relieved on several counts. The house she'd looked at for her mother was officially hers, and she had a lead on a live-in caretaker.

The days ahead wouldn't be easy. Explaining change to dementia patients was hard in the best of times, and Patty had already proved to be argumentative. Plus, as she became more confused, the complications would grow. How was she to handle it alone?

You're not alone any longer, remember?

Which she did—most of the time. Those were the times she could close her eyes and still feel Liam's arms around her and hear him whisper,

... don't hide from me ....

Could she do that? Lean on him even with the physical distance between them? Was it possible the daunting task wouldn't seem so daunting with him supporting her?

We start with a little hope.

Elsa grabbed her mail and climbed the steps to her home, and not for the first time, wished Liam lived in Swan Harbor. That he was working as Swan Harbor's Chief Paramedic, and they were ....

Stop rushing things, Elsa.

Once inside, the lonely feeling persisted, and instead of studying for her pediatric boards, she sent a quick text to her friends.

Elsa: Any sage advice on what to say to my
mother about moving to Swan Harbor?

Molly: Don't ask, just tell.

"Spoken like someone who works with six-year-olds," Elsa murmured, waiting for the others to respond.

Emma: You know I'm better with Animalia.

Sadie: Don't.

Elsa: A lot of help you guys are.

Sadie: True. But we were spot on with Liam.
When's he coming again?

Elsa: Tomorrow.

Emma: What are your plans?

Elsa: He's helping me paint my mom's house.

Sadie: That creates a lot of interesting
opportunities.

Elsa: With painting?

Sadie: Oh, yes. In fact, when Gray and I ….

Emma: Don't scare her Sadie.

Molly: Afterward, we should meet at Sally's. It will
give Liam the push to stay.

Emma: Shouldn't he want to stay because of
Elsa?

> Sadie: Well, sure. But it doesn't hurt for us to help give him a little push.

> Molly: So, Sally's?

> Emma: You must be feeling better.

> Molly: I am and want to eat everything in sight.

> Elsa: Sally's sounds fun. I'll tell Liam.

> Sadie: Sounds good.

Elsa laid her phone on the table, and a large brown envelope mixed with the day's mail caught her attention.

Something had her carefully reaching for it and flipping it over to see who'd sent it. Instead of a return address, the only thing on the front was her name printed in capital letters. Who had put it in her mailbox? Was it the mailman or someone else?

The envelope reminded her of a conversation with Liam.

"I need to tell you something," Liam began in a voice that scared her.

"About?"

"Killian is pretty sure it has something to do with Santora," he replied without actually explaining anything.

"Okay," she responded hesitantly. *"What happened?"*

"Last Thursday, when I arrived home, Luis was getting ready to leave an envelope outside my apartment."

"The mailman put it in Luis's box by mistake?"

"Yeah, that's what he said."

Elsa shrugged. *"People get other people's mail all the time."*

"True," Liam conceded. *"But it was what was in the envelope that's worrisome."*

He looked down at their clasped hands and was quiet for so long, Elsa almost prodded.

"The envelope was a brown 9"x12" one," he explained, *"and inside there were pictures."*

Her heart raced and she couldn't help but feel they were watching a mystery show on television. One where you waited for the bad guys to make their moves and were left wondering if the good guys would win.

"The first few were of Killian and some guy he knew undercover, but it was the last one that still haunts me."

"What was it?"

"Us. You and I," he clarified. "That last night you were in New York before moving."

Elsa's stomach churned. "Someone was watching us?"

"Yes, Sweet Elsa." He pulled her into his arms. "Please be careful. I don't know what I would do if anything happened to you."

She'd assured him she would be careful. But as she stared at the envelope, she couldn't stop the shiver that shot up her spine.

Don't open it.

Right, she thought. That so wasn't her. But it didn't stop her from making sure she'd set her alarm. Nor did it keep her from closing the curtains. Even with the precautions, she couldn't stop the feeling of being watched.

Are you sure about this? She picked up the envelope to study it.

It was just like the one Liam had described. A 9"x12" brown envelope with a clasp that was taped shut.

Call Liam!

What can he do? He's in New York City.

Call Killian!

But what if it's papers Giennie forgot to give me for the house?

She would have written a note.

What if the note is inside?

Fine, look! Just don't say I didn't try to warn you.

Except as she slit the flap and peered inside, she couldn't stop the sick feeling in the pit of her stomach.

When she tipped the envelope and allowed the pictures to slide onto the table, the cold spread outward.

There were five and before she'd even pushed aside the fourth to look at the fifth, her phone was in her hand.

"Elsa." Killian answered and his voice sounded so much like Liam's, the tears she'd been keeping at bay spilled over. "What is it?"

"Pictures," she whispered. "I got pictures."

"I'll be right there."

⁂

New York City
Queen's Court Medical Center
October 1
8:30 p.m.

Liam had been staring out the breakroom window for the past twenty minutes. He'd decided either his eyes were playing tricks on him or the man from the subway knew where he worked.

"Bugger that," he murmured, dialing Killian's phone.

"Liam," Killian answered tersely, sending Liam's worry meter off the charts. "Before you say anything, she's alright. Just a little scared."

Liam frowned. "What are you talking about?

"She didn't tell you?"

Liam wanted to razz his brother about the martial arts fall of shame, but his gut said there was more going on.

"Tell me."

"Elsa received some pictures."

"Damn, Killian." Liam pushed the fear inside back down. "She's alright?"

"Yes. She's fine. But if that's not why you called, then what is?"

Liam mentally rearranged his thoughts and started with the first thing that had occurred.

"There was another police shooting."

"Bloody hell," Killian snapped. "Who was it this time?"

"Jokowitz."

"What?"

"You heard me," Liam acknowledged the unspoken fear in his brother's voice. "Found in Riverside Park, shot three times around 5:00 p.m."

"Is he alright?"

"No." Liam shook his head, even knowing his brother couldn't see him. "Talk about things going pear shaped."

"Tell me." Killian repeated the very words Liam had just uttered.

"We pushed him into the Emergency Department, and as soon as we wheeled him into bay 4, he opened his eyes."

"Calm down, Lieutenant Jokowitz," Liam murmured, hoping to keep the other man still. "You're at Queen's Court. Let them take care of you."

Jokowitz kept thrashing his head back and forth, finally displacing the oxygen mask so Liam could see his lips move.

"What's he saying?" he asked Wade, who'd been ready to help transfer the lieutenant onto a bed.

Wade leaned closer and frowned with concentration. "I'm not sure but sounds like he's saying, 'ry n didn't no.'"

"Then Jokowitz crashed and they couldn't save him. The doctor said he suspected the bullet had lodged, and the thrashing caused it to nick his heart."

"Bloody hell," Killian grumbled. "I wonder what he was trying to say and who shot him. Were there any leads?"

Liam filled him in on what Wade overheard and then took a breath and muttered, "But there's more."

"Don't tell me you're being followed.

"Well, not yet." "Liam peered back out the window to see if he could find Mr. Trench coat. "Remember the man from the subway?"

"Aye. What about him?"

"I think he was hanging around outside the hospital when we drove up with Jokowitz."

"Bloody hell, Liam. When do you get off?"

"I'm off," Liam admitted. "Been trying to figure out what to do."

"Go out a back door and take a completely different route," Killian told him. "You're coming tomorrow with Elsa's gift, right?"

"Assuming dad's contact came through," Liam confirmed. "Elsa's pediatric boards are next week and I'm riding back with her."

"Good. Drop by your apartment, pack, and take the train to dad's tonight. Drive up tomorrow. Make sure no one follows you."

"Alright." Liam took a deep breath. "Now, tell me about the pictures."

"Are you sure you want to know?"

"Honestly?" Liam barked out a dry laugh. "no. But she's my ..." The words lodged in his throat and he couldn't go on.

"I know, Liam," Killian whispered. "We'll take care of her until you get here."

"Thank you." Liam cleared his throat. "Now, the photos."

"There were five," Killian began. "Several of you and her in New York, taken between June and July. One of her taken the night she thought someone was watching her."

"Damn," Liam snapped. "So, you can no longer claim no concrete proof."

Killian grunted. "No. There's one of Elsa and Emma on the pier with Jonesy, and the last one is you walking into Queen's."

"Is she being watched, or am I?"

"I don't know."

"What now?"

"I'm going to ask her to come stay with us, but ..."

"She doesn't want to leave her home."

"No. She says she needs to study."

"Do you want me to talk to her?"

"Would you?"

"Now? Or once I'm at dad's?"

"Now," Killian pushed. "Then I can stash her someplace safe and only have to worry about one of you."

"Thanks, little brother," Liam quipped. "I'll try."

As soon as the line disconnected, Liam scrolled to Elsa's name and his thumb hovered, while he tried to stem its trembling.

Elsa answered, almost before it had completed one ring. "Oh, honey. I'm so sorry I wasn't there with you."

"Me too."

She sounded too calm, and that added another layer to his fear.

"Killian told me about the pictures. Will you please let him take you someplace else tonight?"

"But, Liam," she whispered. "It's my house."

"I know, honey." He clenched his jaw, trying to come up with the words to convince her. "But do you really think you'll feel safe there alone tonight?"

"No."

Which was a big admission for her.

"I know you want to study tonight, right?"

"Yes."

"Then please go with Killian and Emma. I'm going to my dad's so I can get there earlier tomorrow. I have a surprise for you."

"A surprise for me?" she asked, and her voice had lost some of its distance.

"Yes, love. For you. I'll call you when I get to my dad's. But please, El, don't make me worry about you anymore than I am."

"That goes both ways, Liam."

"I'll be okay."

"You'd better. I'll go with them, but call me or else …"

"Promise, love. I'll talk to you later."

As soon as the line went dead, he went searching for a back door.

TWENTY-TWO

Swan Harbor
Elsa's Pediatric Practice
October 5
11:00 a.m.

Elsa had come into the office with plans of rearranging her schedule for the following week, but her thoughts were sluggish. Sleep had been elusive, as the worry she was carrying around weighed her down, and she needed to see Liam. His arms were the cure to what currently ailed her.

We start with hope ....

"Elsa?" Audrey tapped on the office door. "Are you ready?"

"Sure. What do I need to do?"

"Are you sure you want to do this now?" Audrey sent her a concerned look. "You seem distracted. Is everything okay?"

Elsa dug inside for a few of her emotional reserves. "It's just going to be a big week and—"

"—You're feeling overwhelmed because of everything that needs to be done."

"Something like that."

"If you're sure."

"I am. Thanks." Elsa smiled. "Show me what you need."

Audrey pointed at the computer screen. "This is for next week. Which of these can I reschedule?"

Elsa glanced at the schedule. Before she could make any suggestions, though, an approaching siren distracted her.

"That doesn't sound good."

"It's getting louder too." Audrey frowned. "Let's go see." Then, without waiting for a response, she disappeared out the front door.

Elsa followed, but her pace was much more sedate. Once outside, she couldn't stop looking around to see if she was being watched.

Take back the power, she reminded herself, hoping Sadie's words of wisdom would make her feel stronger.

And it did, as she straightened her spine and focused on the ambulance as it zipped past.

"That's odd." Elsa watched the truck make a U-turn at the end of the block and head back in her direction.

"What?"

Before she could respond, the vehicle slid to a stop in front of her and the driver's window slid down.

"Liam?"

"Hey, pretty lady." He opened the door and climbed from the truck. "What are you doing all the way over there?"

"What are you waiting for?" Audrey whispered, giving her a little shove.

Liam hadn't moved, but she could see the worry in his eyes, even with him standing fifty feet away. What was she waiting for, indeed?

He's here!

Hurry, hurry!

Five feet.

Four feet.

Three feet.

When she was close enough, Elsa launched herself into Liam's arms.

"I've got you," he murmured against her mouth.

Elsa's heart raced and while she wanted to sink in, she tempered her response.

"Wow."

He kissed her again, a firm, steamy kiss causing her knees to weaken, so he was taking more of her weight.

"How? What?" Elsa took a step away so she could think straight.

"How? What?" Liam slanted a look in her direction. "You need to do a better job than that, Doctor Winters."

Her thoughts were still pinging all over the place, but she latched onto the most obvious question. "Why are you driving an ambulance that says 'King's Castle-Boston'?"

"I needed a ride," he teased.

"Liam."

"Oh, alright," he capitulated. "I told you I was bringing you a gift."

"You did."

"This is it." He thumbed over his shoulder at the truck.

"An ambulance." She forced down the tears that threatened. "How did you know?"

He gave her a crooked grin. "I heard you were advocating for Swan Harbor to have a new ambulance."

"So, you brought me one?"

Liam chuckled. "I had a little help. Made a comment to my dad, who made a comment to a friend, and ..."

"Eventually you made it happen."

Elsa couldn't think of the right words to tell him what she was thinking. This was one time where he said and did things that had her fighting not to say the words in her heart.

"I ..." She let it hang, wanting to give it voice but not wanting to scare him.

"You?"

"I'll have to come up with some way to thank you."

"Oh, honey," he whispered for her ears only. "I have a few ideas if you need them."

"I bet you do."

He swallowed and the way his Adam's apple bobbed had her wanting to lean forward and lick it.

"Now, Doctor Winters," he murmured huskily. "Where would you like me to leave your new wheels?"

"You're serious, aren't you?

"Swan Harbor needs a stronger fire department."

"And more paramedics." she added, wondering how he'd respond.

His eyes flared, but whether it was because the idea appealed or terrified him, she wasn't sure.

"I'm here, El," he replied, not answering her question directly.

"So you are." She kissed him once more. "Ready to paint?"

"Lead the way—"

"—And you will follow."

"Is that alright?"

"What do you think?"

He glanced around, and a corner of his mouth lifted. "I think we shouldn't give your friends any more fodder for gossip."

Elsa giggled. "Good luck with that."

"It will take some getting used to ..."

When he hesitated, Elsa's heart sped up, wondering if he was saying what she thought.

"But I'll get there," he finished.

"I hope so."

"I will," he assured her. "And now, the truck?"

Should she sic Rene on him or send him to the station?

"Would you mind dropping it at the fire station while I finish up a few things? Then we'll meet for lunch."

"Alright. Send me a text when you're ready to meet."

"I will." Her heart soared, and the weight she'd been carrying felt lighter. "I'm glad you're here."

"Me too." He kissed her, causing her knees to buckle.

Elsa's heart skyrocketed, and she had to fight not to dive back in for more. "Be still my beating heart."

He winked, then climbed into the ambulance. "If you liked that, you'll love what's next."

The spit in Elsa's mouth dried, and she mentally took a step backward.

"See you later." Liam waved, and with the sirens blaring, took off toward the fire station.

Oh man, how was she going to remain focused on what needed to be done?

Swan Harbor
Elsa Mother's Home
October 5
3:30 p.m.

THE RHYTHMIC BACK-AND-FORTH MOTION OF THE PAINT ROLLER had Liam's thoughts bouncing from one topic to another.

Was his heart already in Swan Harbor?

Was he being led here?

Fanciful thoughts for a man who had never believed in fairytales, and who thought happy endings were for other people. But somehow, since Elsa had moved here, he found he wanted things he'd never wanted before.

When he'd left the ambulance at the fire station, multiple people asked *when* he was starting work and not *if*. Could he move from New York City, where he'd worked his way through the ranks, to a smaller town and paramedic unit?

Elsa's here.

His gaze unerringly went across the room to where she was painting around the trim.

She was wearing leggings, a paint spattered shirt, her hair was in a messy ponytail, and she'd never looked happier.

"You're supposed to be painting, not staring at me," she teased.

Liam placed the roller in the pan and stalked toward her. "I'm a talented guy, and can do both."

"Oh?"

He narrowed his eyes. "You doubt me?"

She giggled, waving her brush around. "I don't see any evidence of your talent."

"You want evidence?"

Liam closed his hand around her wrist and tugged her against his chest. "Alright, Doctor Winters, you want a sample of my talent?"

Elsa's eyes dropped to his lips before popping back up. In them, he saw promises of dreams and wishes he'd never imagined.

"You're happy, aren't you?"

"Very."

"Is it me?"

One of her blonde brows arched and her face grew serious. "Liam, you're a part of my happiness. But so is living in Swan Harbor, and my practice, and my friends."

What was she trying to tell him? That she didn't need him to be happy?

He stepped back and thought about her words. Did he need her to be happy? In New York, he had friends, a job, and he was happy, but ....

"What are you thinking?" Elsa slid her hands around his waist and rested her cheek against his shoulder.

"About happiness," he admitted.

"Oh?"

"You do that on purpose, don't you?" he growled.

She giggled, and before she could say anything more, there was a knock on the door and Killian, Gray, Dylan, and Rusty spilled in.

"I thought you said you were painting." Killian set the cans he'd been carrying on the floor.

Liam pointed at the wall he'd just finished. "I was just telling El how talented I was."

Killian's eyes twinkled. "Is that what you were telling her?"

"It is." Elsa linked her fingers with Liam's. "I was waiting for proof."

"What are you all doing here?" Liam asked, effectively changing the subject.

Dylan grinned. "We heard there's a painting party."

"A painting party?"

"Sure." Gray dropped his supplies in a corner. "This is Swan Harbor, where friends help friends."

A sense of belonging, and being part of something, instead of alone in New York.

His eyes met Killian's, and Liam could see just how much his brother had changed. Swan Harbor and Emma had helped Killian become the man who cared for others. He was no longer the person who only cared about himself and adding names to his black books.

But that's not you. You care about others.

Was Killian's journey to care about others, whereas his was to care more for himself? With Elsa, he found he wanted that fairytale ending he'd never believed possible.

"Where do you want us?" Rusty pointed to the cans they'd carried in. "We stopped by the hardware store and picked up the rest of the paint."

"And brought the music." Dylan set up his Bluetooth speaker and phone.

"We even have drinks." Gray flipped open the lid of a cooler.

"Emma wanted to help," Killian explained. "But with Molly pregnant—"

"—She needed to stay away from the fumes," Elsa murmured.

"Molly, Emma, Sadie, and Rene are at the apartment," Dylan replied. "We're supposed to send Elsa to them."

There went his opportunities to steal kisses. One look at Elsa's emotions and his heart flipped.

"Is that alright with you, El?" Liam murmured. "I know you wanted me to do all the work."

"Is that okay?" Elsa's voice broke. "What do you think?"

"I think you say thank you and point them in the right direction."

"Give them orders?" she laughed. "I can do that, and then you can walk me out."

"My pleasure."

He squeezed her fingers and when she walked away, he realized every time he saw her, she held a little more of his heart.

"Does she know?" Killian asked softly.

Liam almost said, '*Know what*?' then decided it was a waste of time.

"Not yet. I'm just figuring it out myself."

"Who would have thought?" Killian shook his head in disbelief. "But I have to say, life has never been better."

"Even with Santora breathing down our necks?"

"Even then," Killian sighed. "I hate like hell that madman isn't behind bars. However, I refuse to allow him to take away what I've found. I *will* defeat him."

"You're not in this alone, Killian."

"A part of me gets that," Killian confessed. "The other part can't help but feel it's my responsibility because of what went down in New York."

Liam understood Killian's feelings. "Just promise me you won't go after Santora alone. Remember what happened to Brody, Stevens and Jokowitz."

"I'm aware," Killian began, only to leave the words hanging when Elsa returned.

"Are you ready for your assignment?"

"Your woman's a taskmaster," Killian tossed over his shoulder as he followed Elsa from the room.

"That wasn't a promise," Liam murmured. Killian might want to protect others, but who was going to protect him?

Swan Harbor
Sally's Diner
October 5
8:30 p.m.

Elsa leaned back in the booth and watched everyone milling around her. She still had a hard time believing everything that had transpired in the last few hours. But as she'd told Liam, she wouldn't look a gift horse in the mouth.

"You look happy." Emma slid into the booth across from her.

"Liam said the same thing. He wanted to know if it was because of him."

"He doesn't think you can be happy without him?"

"I don't think that's it completely." Elsa frowned, his words still bouncing around inside. "What Claire said to him still haunts him. He still needs to learn he's not the loser his mother said he would be."

"Words can wound," Emma murmured. "But they can also heal."

"True. You worked things out with Ava," Elsa responded. "Anything new with your father?"

Emma winced, giving Elsa her answer. "I take that as a no."

"He's coming east next month, and I invited him to Swan Harbor," Emma shared. "I'm nervous."

"Oh, Emma," Elsa exclaimed. "I think it's wonderful. You might have both parents at your wedding."

"That whole concept just feels so," Emma waved her hand around as if searching for the right word, "odd."

"I can see that." Elsa grinned. "Marriage wasn't something we talked much about."

"Forever wasn't on my list yet," Emma agreed.

"It's Swan Harbor and its hope."

"Don't joke about Swan Harbor's hope," Emma warned. "Especially around Captain Jack."

"I'll try to remember that," Elsa promised. "But look, the painting crew has returned."

Liam sauntered toward her, and Elsa had to fight not to let her mouth drop open.

"This doesn't look like Molly's and Dylan's." He stopped shy of their table, his expression expectant.

"That's where we started." Emma slid out of the booth and into Killian's arms. "Then word got around and somehow we ended up at Sally's."

While Emma was talking, Elsa slid from the booth. She just didn't immediately step into Liam's arms.

"I was wondering about that. We could have used more sets of hands."

"My brother groaned about being sore the entire time," Liam snickered. "He's quite the whiner."

"Wanker," Killian tossed out. "Let me see you take on Sally, and then we'll talk."

Emma laughed. "Poor baby. How about a massage?"

"Now you're talking." Killian wrapped his arm around her. "I'm hungry. Is there any food left?"

"Come on, let's feed you. You guys coming?"

"We'll be there in a minute," Liam responded before Elsa could decide what to say.

"I'm surprised you're not starved," she murmured. "You were painting for hours."

"Oh, I'm hungry." He led her into the back hallway and pressed her against the wall. "I'm hungry for this."

Before she was ready, his lips were on hers. It was one of those open mouth kisses that caused her heart rate to skyrocket and had her knees threatening to give out.

Teeth and tongues dueled as bodies fought to be closer. Elsa tangled her hands in Liam's shirt and held on as he stole her breath and threatened her sanity.

One of them groaned, reminding her where they were. She wrenched her mouth free and buried her head against Liam's shoulder.

"Not that I'm complaining, but what was that for?"

He cupped her jaw and the look in his eyes had her waiting, hoping to hear
....

"I understand what you meant earlier ..."

"Earlier?" she asked, as he'd jumped back to a conversation and not taken her with him.

"When you said about me being a part of your happiness," he explained.

"I—"

Liam quieted her with his kiss. "I now understand happiness comes from inside." He kissed her again. "Everything else is just a bonus."

"And?"

"Our future is ours to build. So ..."

"We start with hope ..."

"And listen to our hearts."

"Captain Jack would be pleased."

"Bugger that." Liam pulled her closer. "I just care what you think."

"Oh, I'm happy."

Liam slipped his arm around her waist and led her toward the front room. "You can show me how much when we're alone."

Elsa's thoughts scattered, and her imagination took flight.

TWENTY-THREE

Swan Harbor
Sheriff's Department
October 8
3:30 p.m.

With Liam and Elsa in New York City, Killian's worry had ratcheted up a notch. There'd been no new information from Weaver, and nothing seemed out of place in Swan Harbor. Yet that sixth sense of his kept knocking, telling him he was missing something.

Intending to go through the evidence one more time, he opened his bottom drawer. The sight that greeted him had him pushing back from his desk as if he thought it would explode.

"Rusty," he snapped. "Have you been in my bottom drawer?"

"No, why?" Rusty responded absently.

"Look."

The tenor of his voice must have relayed the importance, because Rusty immediately pushed his chair closer.

"There's an envelope in your drawer," Rusty shrugged. "What's the big deal?"

"Rusty." Killian's voice came out a bit more clipped. "Look at the bloody envelope."

"Alright fine." Rusty looked closer. "It's brown, 9"x12" and says Killian R–" He glanced up. "That's not the envelope Liam received. Is it?"

"No."

"Elsa?" he asked hopefully.

"No."

"So, what you're saying is—"

"—Someone put this in my bloody bottom drawer."

"Amy?"

Killian took several deep breaths before going to ask the office clerk.

"Amy." He fought to maintain a neutral voice. "Did you leave an envelope in my bottom drawer?"

"The only one I've seen lately was the one from Shawn. Maybe Walt?"

She was referring to Walt Manning, the evening desk sergeant, who'd been part of the sheriff's department for forty years.

"When he gets in, will you ask him for me?"

"Sure Killian."

He'd taken several steps and thought of something else. "Has anyone been through here lately that doesn't belong?"

Amy gave him a look, as if to say, *Really?* Then she grabbed a notepad, wrote a minute, and handed it back to him.

"If I can think of anyone else, I'll let you know."

"Thanks."

Once back in the office, Killian tossed the paper onto Rusty's desk.

"We need to talk to Dylan about the security in this place."

"I take it Amy didn't put the envelope in your drawer?"

"That's the list of people who've been through here in the last couple of days."

Rusty read, "Sydney, Sally, Lance, Leroy, Patti, Nic, Shawn, Rupert, Hayden, Peyton, Judge Coleman, Liam, Elsa, Emma, Danny, Rene, Sadie, and Gray. Quite the list."

Killian laid the envelope on his desk. His name was written across the front in capital letters. He slit the end and peered inside. "Pictures."

There were three, and before he spread them out, he grabbed the folder and asked Rusty to follow him to the conference room.

Once there, Killian pinned each picture to an evidence board.

"It seems as if the person sending the pictures is trying to tell me something."

Rusty leaned on the table to study the photos.

"Are they pinned in the order received?"

"Aye." Killian pointed to the first eight. "Liam received these, and these five went to Elsa. The last three were left for me."

"What about lining them up in order of the day they were taken?" suggested Rusty.

Killian studied the photos and rearranged several of them. "This is Tino Ricci." He laid out the pictures as such—Tino and the girl. Tino and 'Ian.' Tino being questioned, and Tino dead. "He joined Santora's gang when he was sixteen. Started as a petty thief, and as long as Santora fed his habit, he remained loyal. Tino and Margherita were an item and 'for some reason,' he decided 'Ian' was poaching."

"Were you?"

Killian shrugged. "She was part of the case. As far as they knew, Ian was a playboy, but I spent no more time talking to her than any other female inside the organization."

"So Tino warned you off and ended up dead?"

"Aye. It was Tino who killed Violet. So, these pictures raise the question, was he trying to kill me because of Margherita, and not because he knew I was a cop?"

"Maybe," Rusty conceded. "And the explosion?"

"That happened after 'Ian' disappeared, and at the same time Santora was arrested. It was last year in March."

"And the other pictures?"

Killian switched around the rest of the photos, leaving him with the following. Him going to Bea Morris's. Him and Liam. Him, Liam, and their father at dinner. Liam and Elsa at O'Toole's, walking into Queen's, walking into Liam's apartment complex, and in Elsa's parking lot. Elsa being watched, and Elsa and Emma on the pier. The only one he was unsure of was the photo of Liam alone.

"When were those of you taken?" asked Rusty.

"December and early January." Killian stepped back and looked again. "They thought I was dead." He pointed to the clipping about Ian's accident.

"But someone saw me going into Bea's apartment in December and followed me."

"Was it you they followed to Swan Harbor? Or was it Elsa?"

"If it was me," Killian added. "Why were there no pictures from January to June?"

"What was going on with Santora?"

"Prison." Killian thought back to what he'd heard during that time. "And no talk of him getting out."

"Meaning, there was a catalyst," Rusty stated.

"What?"

Rusty shrugged. "Not sure. Right now, though, I need to finish my report for Judge Coleman."

When he left, Killian took pictures of the photos, typed a quick note, and sent them to Weaver.

He heard Rusty greet Dylan minutes before his boss entered the room and dropped into a chair.

Killian noted Dylan's slightly unfocused, bloodshot eyes and ragged beard.

"Is something going on, mate? With Molly? The baby?"

"Babies," Dylan corrected absently. "As in ... two ... babies, that is."

The realization his boss sounded scared had Killian sitting back and looking for ways to help.

"Are you saying you're having twins?"

"No!" Dylan corrected. "I'm not having twins. Molly is." He held up the right number of fingers. "Two babies ... at once. What do I know about babies? Much less two at a time?"

Dylan's pale face and the faraway look in his eyes had Killian taking the conversation in another direction.

"I wouldn't think it would be much harder than one." He shrugged, as if it was no big deal. "Summer," Killian named a dog from Emma's clinic, "had six and she didn't seem to have much of a problem."

"Summer?" Dylan looked at him as if he had two heads, but his coloring seemed a little better. "The *dog*?"

"Aye." Killian nodded, keeping a straight face. "She was a really good mother. With her six ... puppies, that is. And Daisy," he hesitated, allowing the father-to-be to catch up with the conversation.

"Daisy?" Dylan's tone seemed more 'with-it,' a little less shocked than when he'd walked in.

"Remember?" Killian went on. "The dog Rusty and I discovered in that old farmhouse. She had eight puppies and is a wonderful mother. Perhaps Molly could learn something by watching her with her litter."

Dylan barked out a laugh. "You want me to tell my wife," his laughter grew, "to observe a *dog* for mothering ideas?"

"Couldn't hurt," Killian deadpanned.

"I ..." Dylan couldn't get the words out before he doubled over, clutching his stomach.

Killian fought to maintain a straight face, but it wasn't long before he couldn't hold back his laughter.

"I'm sorry." Dylan finally regained his wherewithal and wiped the tears from his face. "Thank you for the laugh. I've been a little ... distracted, I guess."

"Just a little?" Killian groused. "You've been slightly bonkers. I'm happy I could make you feel better, but ... just so you know." He winked. "The offer still stands."

Dylan's lips twitched. "I'll keep that in mind. And now, how about a drink?"

"A drink?" Killian glanced at the clock. "It's a bit earlier than I've had a drink in a while. However, for the person who pushed me to find the man Violet wanted him to be, I can make exceptions."

"Damn straight." Dylan grinned.

"Thank you for that, by the way." Killian held out his hand. "Congratulations, Dad. I have a feeling you'll be just fine."

Dylan clasped Killian's hand, but instead of shaking it, he hugged him.

"Thank you, and you're very welcome. Now, about that drink?"

"Sure. Let me just put these away."Killian quickly took the pictures off the board.

"Sounds good," Dylan murmured. "Invite Rusty, and I'll text Gray to meet us."

When Killian locked the folder and envelopes in his bottom drawer, a chill slithered up his spine. It was followed by a sick feeling that settled in the pit of his stomach.

New York City
Liam's Apartment
October 8
6:30 p.m.

LIAM COULDN'T STOP THE GOOFY SMILE THAT CROSSED HIS FACE
when he read Elsa's text.

> Elsa: One more section and then I'm heading to
> your apartment. I have the key you gave me.

> Liam: I'll meet you there.

You gave her a key!

Words that three months ago, bloody hell, a month ago, would have freaked
him out. While he realized it wasn't the same as if they were cohabitating, it still felt
like a step toward something. Plus, when he'd offered, there had been no hesitation.

*"Why is it you're staying at a hotel again?" Liam asked, as they stepped into
the elevator at the Hilton-Midtown.*

"Because I don't have an apartment."

"But you could stay with me." Liam nuzzled her temple.

"Like you stayed with me in Swan Harbor?"

*"Touché." A corner of his mouth ticked up. "But in New York City, there's no
gossip chain."*

*"You're worried about what some little old ladies are going to say?" Elsa
wrapped her arms around his waist and laid her head on his chest. "Is it your
reputation you're worried about or mine?"*

*"Yours, of course." The doors opened, and he waited for her to get out. "I just
..." When she stopped in front of her room, he left it hanging.*

"You just what?"

*Elsa glanced back, and with just one look, invited him inside her hotel room.
As soon as she shut the door, she pushed him against it and slid her hands up his
chest and around his neck.*

"I find the fact you're worried about my reputation to be very charming."

Her nearness had his body immediately hardening. He palmed her butt, pressing her tighter against him.

"If you get any closer, I'm not sure how much longer my charm can last."

Elsa moaned, and the sound went straight to his crotch. He latched onto an earlobe and sucked it into his mouth before sliding his lips down the side of her neck.

"Liam, I have no doubt your charm will last just as long as it needs to last."

"Sweet El."

He brushed a kiss across her cheek and toyed with her lips, willing her to open and let him inside.

She wrapped herself around him until he could think of nothing but carrying her to the bed.

"I want you." He squeezed her ass and pushed her hips a little harder against his. "Can you feel how much?"

"Yes." But before he could dive in, she dropped her head against his shoulder. "Wait."

Liam's breath rushed out and he fought to regain control. Something he'd had more than his share of practice doing, especially around her.

"What is it, love?"

Elsa stepped back far enough for him to look into her upturned face.

"I want nothing more than to spend the night with you, but tomorrow…"

"Hold on El," he backpedaled. "I know you have a big day tomorrow. When do you fly to D.C. to pick up your mother?"

"Thursday." She nipped his chin. "Think you could switch up your schedule?"

"And spend all day Wednesday with you?"

"Yes. You wouldn't have to worry about the gossip chain or the spy network."

Liam ducked his head. "I'll see what I can do. When do you think you'll finish tomorrow?"

"6:30?"

His mind was already jumping ahead with plans. He'd make her dinner, then ….

"Here." He pulled out his keys and slid the house key off the ring. "Just in case you beat me home."

Elsa's hand trembled when she took the key. "Oh, Liam. You have no idea how much I…"

But he hadn't allowed her to finish whatever she was going to say. Instead, he'd kissed her. He'd wanted to tell her what was in his heart. Yet something held him back.

That was then, and when he stepped into his apartment building elevator, he was already making plans. He'd cook her dinner, and then he'd spend the next thirty-six hours telling and showing her exactly how he felt.

The elevator doors opened, and the first thing he saw was Elsa beat him home.

"Fancy seeing you here."

"Liam." Their eyes met, and instead of anticipation, he saw fear. "Luis was telling me you had another package."

"Thanks, Luis. You could have just left the package by my door."

"No, problem." Luis's dark eyes flashed. "I've got plans for tonight, so I'll leave it and let you say hello in privacy."

Liam laughed. "You're too kind."

"You know it, man."

Luis took a step toward Liam's apartment. When his foot caught on Elsa's briefcase, the box flew into the air.

"Get down!" someone shouted, and without thinking, Liam dove for Elsa, pulling her under him.

The box exploded, and as the sound bounced around and plaster rained down, Liam kept hold of Elsa, trying to get closer.

"Liam Reade."

His name being said in a hushed, clipped tone had him lifting his head.

"Bloody hell." He was staring into the eyes of the man who'd been standing outside the hospital.

"Who are you?" Liam snapped. "What do you want?"

"I'm a friend." The man stuck his hand in his coat pocket and Liam's blood froze. "Relax." He pulled out a business card and dropped it on the floor. "Get your lady out of town. Take care of your friend and then follow her. Have your brother ask Lance Diamond about me. He'll vouch for me. Hurry."

Liam glanced briefly at the business card. "What ...?" It was too late, though, as the man was gone.

"Elsa, love." Liam helped her up and, seeing Luis over her shoulder caused his insides to clench. "Are you alright?"

"I'm fine." Elsa brushed off the front of his shirt. "But ..."

"Listen to me," Liam replied, needing her to focus. "That wasn't an accident. I need you to go to my dad's. I'll meet you there."

He rushed her down the hall toward the stairway. "Get on the subway at 86th and take the 6 to 110th. Then run to Central Park North and take the 2 to 66th. Once there, backtrack to 72nd and take the D to 7th. Walk to 57th and then take the R to 63rd. Walk to 51st and take the 6 to Grand Central. When you get there, buy a ticket, and take the Hudson Line towards Croton-Harmon. Get off at Tarrytown and my dad will meet you."

Liam shoved her through the door, onto the landing. "I'll be there as soon as I can."

Elsa reached for him and tangled her fingers in his shirt. "But Liam ..."

He kissed her hard. "I love you. Now go."

New York City
October 8
6:45 p.m.

THE DOOR SLAMMED, ECHOING AROUND ELSA, AND EVERY PART OF her wanted to run back to Liam. If she did, though, he'd worry.

He loved her.

"Take the 86th," she breathed, starting down the stairs on shaking legs. Once she reached the first floor and could hear the sirens, something had her reversing and going through the door that would take her into the alley.

He loved her.

Elsa darted between two buildings and raced down the steps at 86th Street. The 6 was due in 2 minutes and while waiting, she hid behind a pillar and constantly watched the platform for anyone who might have followed her.

Come on. Come on.

When the train arrived, she waited until the last second, and then rushed inside. As soon as the doors slid shut, relief washed over her.

He loved her.

She wanted to sink into the seat and relive those moments in his arms. But the train raced to a stop at 110th and she had to jump out.

While she hurried from 110th to the station at Central Park North, Elsa felt like a sitting duck. Even more so when a car backfired, and it took every ounce of her strength to contain the scream, threatening to erupt.

Her next two stops flew by, but when she got off at 7th Ave, her mind went blank. Was she supposed to walk to 57th or 49th? By the time she made it to the next station, she'd wasted precious time and missed her train.

Hurry, hurry.

It was several minutes before the R arrived, and once she jumped on, she had to regroup. A part of her wanted to wallow. Whether it was about her mother or one of the many things that was happening because of Santora, it didn't matter. But who would that help?

No one, which was what propelled her from 63rd to 51st where she hopped on the 6 for her final subway ride to Grand Central Station.

Once Elsa arrived at the Grand Central Terminal, she stopped to get her bearings. The way the people rushed around her had her heart racing and her nerves feeling like they were pinging all over the place.

Take back the power, she reminded herself, skirting the crowds.

He loves you.

Words she'd been waiting to hear for months, and when she finally heard them, he'd shut a door in her face.

Take back the power.

"Croton-Harmon," she murmured, studying the schedule, while she stood in line for one of the ticket machines.

When it was her turn, her thought processes died, pushing her to remind herself again.

Take back the power.

She straightened her spine, pulled out her phone case, and, with fingers that were only slightly shaking, purchased her ticket.

Then, feeling much more in control, she walked through the terminal in search of her track. She wouldn't fall apart. Liam loved her, and just as soon as she saw him, she was going to tell him she loved him, too.

TWENTY-FOUR

Tarrytown, NY
Finn Reade's Home
October 8
10:30 p.m.

When Liam arrived in Tarrytown, his father was waiting in the parking lot.

"How's Elsa?" he asked before Finn could say anything.

"She's," Finn hesitated as if unsure what to say, then finally settled on, "strong. Elsa has questions. As do I. What happened?"

The knot inside Liam slowly relaxed. "My neighbor ended up with a package addressed to me," he began. "Which actually turned out to be lucky."

"Because?"

"It was a bomb," Liam explained. "One that was meant more to frighten than kill. When Luis tripped over Elsa's briefcase, and it flew out of his hands—"

"—The greatest danger was done to something and not someone," Finn guessed.

"Yeah. In this case, the walls. Luis had a few cuts and is being kept overnight for a possible concussion, but that's it."

"Very fortunate." Finn stared at him several seconds before continuing, "There's more."

Liam wasn't even going to ask how his father knew, but just accepted it. Finn Reade had always had the uncanny ability to read people. An excellent trait when you were trying to convince people to spend millions on property. Not so excellent if you were trying to keep something from your father.

"When the elevator arrived on my floor, I didn't realize anyone else was in the hall but Elsa and Luis, until someone screamed get down."

"Another neighbor?"

"The man who's been following me."

"From the subway?"

"Yeah." Liam pulled out the business card and handed it to Finn. "Special Agent Lee Simpson. Told me to have Killian check with Lance Diamond for verification."

"And what did Killian say?"

"Apparently, Lance Diamond was an agent at one time. Now he's semi-retired and is the caretaker at a boarding house in Swan Harbor. Killian's going to talk to him tomorrow."

"I'm glad you're alright." Finn surprised Liam by tugging him into his arms for a hug. "Here are my keys. I'm going to take the next train back to the city and stay at my apartment tonight."

"Dad, you don't need to do that," Liam protested.

Finn held up his hand to stop the argument. "I have an early morning appointment. And you and Elsa need to take care of each other."

A part of Liam wanted to argue. The rest of him, though, was pleased he and Elsa would be alone.

"Alright, if you're sure."

"Let me know what Killian finds out about the agent."

"Will do. Thanks."

On the drive to his father's, Liam wondered which Elsa was waiting for him. His father described her as strong. Was that the same woman who'd been strong when she heard about her mother's diagnosis and then leaned on him? Or would it be the one he'd spent time with in Swan Harbor after receiving the photos?

"Or someone new?"

The house was dark, and he'd decided she'd gone to bed when a movement in front of the French doors drew his attention.

"Elsa?"

"Liam."

He wasn't sure who moved first. Within seconds, though, she was in his arms.

"I've got you," he whispered, tightening his hold around her trembling body.

"Are you okay?" she mumbled.

"I'm alright. Are you? My dad said you were strong."

"I'm not sure I'd agree. I'm fine, though. How's Luis?"

Liam repeated what he'd told his father. "He should be back home tomorrow."

There was a part of him waiting ... wanting her to acknowledge the last words he'd said. Ones he'd never said before.

"I'm glad." The words hung for several seconds as she loosened her hands and peered around the room. "Where's your father?"

"Dad's staying at his apartment in the city," he finally offered, his mouth hovering barely a breath above hers.

Her hot breath blew across his lips, sending a shiver down his spine. "That means we're alone?"

"It does."

"Oh."

Liam's eyes flared, and he whispered a kiss across her mouth.

"You did that on purpose, didn't you?"

"Who me?"

"El."

"Yes."

Liam cupped her face, and their eyes met. "I meant what I said earlier. I love you. I'm sorry I've—"

"Stop." Elsa covered his mouth with her fingers. "Things happen when they're supposed to happen, Liam."

His heart raced when she exchanged her fingers with her soft mouth. Her kiss was brief, barely allowing a taste before her lips were gone and she continued, "I only have one regret about that moment."

Liam's racing heart sunk into the pit of his stomach and his mind searched for what he could have done differently.

"It wasn't romantic," he muttered, wishing he would have waited.

OH, LIAM.

Elsa's knees threatened to give out at his statement. She'd never expected him to be so vulnerable when he finally admitted how he felt about her.

"No."

"No?" A look of confusion crossed his face. "But, El, I thought—"

"Liam," she interrupted. "The only thing I regret is, you shut the door in my face—"

"But I—"

Elsa covered his mouth again, thinking she was going to just leave her hand there, until she'd said her piece.

"Are you listening?"

He nodded and the look in his eyes was so endearing, she fought not to jump on him and push their talk till later.

"If I move my hand, you'll wait until I've said everything?"

He nodded again, and the look in his eyes had her insides paying attention. "Promise?"

His hum caused her fingers to vibrate and anticipation rippled along her skin.

"I regret." She let the words hang a heartbeat and watched his eyes flare. "I regret I didn't tell you I ..."

"Bloody hell, El," Liam murmured. "You're killing me here."

She giggled. "I love you, Liam Reade."

"Really?" The look on his face said, '*Did I just hear you right?*' While underneath her fingers, his heart raced.

"Liam." Elsa kissed him slowly. "I love you."

Their lips met in a kiss that sent fiery sparks flying from where their mouths connected throughout her body. Her heart raced, her core softened, and her skin came alive.

He pushed her softness against the hard ridge behind his zipper. "Oh, El. What you do to me."

He tugged her shirt over her head and dropped it on the floor. She wanted to say something ... just didn't know what. Then he unhooked her bra, and her thoughts scattered.

It didn't take long before Elsa decided if he could touch, so could she. She pulled his shirt free and slid her hands underneath. His skin was soft—his muscles firm.

"More," she murmured when he cupped her breast.

Liam stopped, and she almost groaned until he went to work on his shirt buttons.

Yes!

"Need some help?" She spread his shirt apart and trailed butterfly kisses down the center of his chest. The soft hairs tickled her lips and his heat surrounded her. "Hurry."

A groan reverberated around the room, and she pressed her breasts against his chest.

Her nipples tightened, her breath lodged, and she wanted.

He loves me.

Those words were everything she'd ever wanted and no matter what he did, it wasn't enough.

"You feel amazing."

His fingers whispered across her skin, leaving behind nerve endings that tingled. They teased, taunted, drawing closer and closer to her most sensitive areas.

Elsa's heart raced, and she dug her fingers into his hips to keep from falling. His mouth was everywhere ... her lips, her cheeks ... before finally latching onto her earlobe.

She wanted to sink in and enjoy, but her thoughts were bouncing all over. If they made love, then what?

"Liam, look at me."

"Elsa," he groaned. "What is it, love?"

"I want you, but what's next?"

Liam slanted a look in her direction. "Don't tell me you've forgotten?"

His kiss was drugging, threatening to pull her into that place where her brain shut down and all she'd be able to do was feel.

He popped the button on her jeans, slipped his hands inside, and Elsa wanted to grab hold and let him carry her along.

"Don't run away afterward," she whispered.

Liam lifted his head, and she could feel him staring at her. He was breathing hard and a part of her regretted her words. Except the other side didn't think she could handle a repeat of the last time.

He leaned his forehead against hers. "Oh, El. I'm behaving like a cockwomble, aren't I?"

"A what?"

He didn't answer right away. Instead, he picked her up and sank into the closest chair, settling her on his lap.

Elsa's heart raced, and a part of her scolded herself. Her other part, though,

....

"A cockwomble," he repeated with a crooked grin. "A favorite word of Finn Reade's ... and means I'm a moronic idiot."

"No, you're—"

Liam's finger shut off the words as hers had done to him earlier. "Are you listening?"

She nodded, the cool air causing goosebumps to crawl across her skin.

"Elsa, love." Liam slid his hand down her torso, a line of heat following in its wake. "Here I am again, having to apologize to you." He expected she would try to stop him and slid his thumb across her lip. "We've not talked about what happened in Swan Harbor."

Do you want to hear this?

She really wished she could say it didn't matter, except she knew that would be a lie.

"After we made love in Swan Harbor," his voice dropped so low she had to focus to hear what he was saying. "In plain words, I was terrified. For fifteen years, I'd created this space around my heart where no one and nothing could touch it. A part of me always knew you were dangerous to my well-ordered life, but I refused to listen. There was something about you that pulled at me until I didn't just *want* to be around you. I *needed* it. Except every time I got too close, my heart contracted so I couldn't breathe, and I'd have to take several steps backward."

A light went off with his admission. "So that's where the push pull came in?"

"Yeah," he murmured against her bare shoulder. "Then you left me—"

"I left New York," she interjected.

"You left New York, and I felt like a part of me was missing. Even then, I was stubborn, and refused to acknowledge I needed you in my life."

"Until Santora gave you a push."

"No, love," he denied. "I was losing the fight, and it was only a matter of days before I would have ended up in Swan Harbor, anyway. Once I did—"

"—Your heart started talking."

"More like I started listening," he corrected. "Then I needed a knock on the head to be shown that happily ever after was a real thing."

"Lois and Rupert?"

He hummed in agreement. "I asked Lois what the recipe for forever was."

Elsa could hear the affection in his voice for the older woman.

"Tyler thought Lois was sharing a recipe, talking about her days as a spy, or giving relationship advice."

"He was right," Liam admitted. "She said you start with hope and toss in a lot of love."

The way his voice broke on the word love caused tears to spring to Elsa's eyes.

Oh Liam.

Liam cupped her jaw and angled her face toward his. "And now, to answer your question of what comes next. Lois said hope and love are the foundation for the future."

Her breath hitched at what she thought he was saying. "That's a nice way to describe forever."

"The best."

Liam kissed her, another one of those kisses that, even though they were only touching in a few places, consumed her.

"I want to build a future with you."

He gave her the words she'd longed to hear, without coming right out and asking the big question.

Have patience.

"I want that too." She wrapped her arms around his shoulders and nibbled on his neck, just below his earlobe. "Now, Lieutenant Reade. Take me to bed."

"My pleasure, Doctor Winters. I just hope I don't trip on my dad's stairs and fall on my arse."

Elsa slid her hand down his back and under the waistband of his pants. "And what a fine arse it is."

His growl was low and sexy, and with every step he took, her

Liam carried Elsa into the room he always slept in and elbowed the light switch, creating a warm glow.

"It's better to see you with." He wiggled his eyebrows teasingly.

"That goes both ways," she murmured against his lips.

"I aim to please."

He lowered her onto the side of the bed and slid his hands down her long legs.

"You're not doing too badly so far."

Her sultry smile and the way the light bounced off her bare torso had Liam's body screaming. *Touch me. Touch me!*

"So far?" He pulled off her shoe and tossed it over his shoulder. "Is this any better?" Her sock flew in another direction.

"Not bad."

Liam lifted her other foot, but the vixen once again showed him who was in control by stroking her bare foot down the front of his jeans.

"Easy, love," he hissed when she curled her toes and his body pulsed.

"You don't like?"

"Oh, I like." Liam forced a swallow. "But I don't want it to be over too soon."

"Oh?"

"That's it." He tugged her pants off and dropped them on the floor. "You won't need these for a while."

"I certainly hope not." Elsa grinned. "But one of us is overdressed."

Liam took a minute to just look at Elsa, her beauty taking his breath away. Had he ever felt as happy as he was at this very moment? She filled those empty spaces and gave him hope that forever was possible. How had he gotten so lucky?

"I'm getting there," he murmured, toeing off his shoes.

His heart raced, his body pulsed, and he wanted her now.

"You're too slow." She pushed his hands aside and reached for his zipper tab.

"Careful love."

"Oh, don't you worry," she teased. "I'm a doctor, and if there's a problem, I know just what to do."

His body went full staff, and he pushed his pants and boxers down and out of the way.

Elsa scooted back on the bed, moved the blankets aside, and crooked her finger.

"Come here."

"What do I get?"

Their eyes locked as he slowly crawled toward her.

"What do you want?"

"Everything, El." He placed a kiss on her flat stomach, just below her belly button, and her breath hitched. "Are we alright?"

"We're covered." She slowly lifted her left arm, where her implant was located, and sent him a sultry smile.

"I love you, El."

"I love you too."

As she flowed into his arms, Liam found he had to temper his actions. He wanted to touch and taste everywhere and everything. It had been so long since he'd had her beneath him, he didn't want to wait.

He whispered kisses across collarbone and down the center of her chest, latching onto her nipple.

"More," she groaned.

Liam didn't need to be told twice, for he was already on the move. With every kiss, stroke of his fingers, and brush from his lips, he told her how he felt. She was his heart.

"Oh, wow," she murmured.

Her body commanded, telling him where she wanted him to touch, to taste. Liam followed each direction, learning, listening, pushing her closer and closer to the top.

"Liam." Elsa grazed her fingers down his chest. "Let me."

"Next time, love," he promised, ratcheting up his assault, and working to bring her to the same place as he.

His body craved release, but he wasn't going over that ledge alone. He fought to contain the feelings inside. They were so much sweeter, so much more intense, and threatened to overwhelm and steal his sanity.

He tasted and teased, bringing her higher and higher, her moans guiding his every move.

"Hurry." She wrapped her legs around his, directing his movements, pulling him closer and closer to her heat.

Liam rolled over on his side and tugged her leg over his hip. "Oh, El," he groaned as a rush of emotions raced through him. "I can't."

"Then don't." With a little twist of her hips, her moist heat surrounded him.

He tensed, relying on his reserves, needing to stretch out the moment as long as possible.

"I said." Elsa tightened around him, threatening to blow the top of his head off. "Don't wait."

Her hips twisted, and all thought flew from his brain as his body screamed.

Move!

As that word rushed through his mind, he let go and could only feel. She surrounded him with love and when he was with her, he wanted to give her the world.

His focus was gone, but he still drove, willing her to tip over the top so he could follow.

"I love you." He punctuated each word with a thrust of his hips.

She groaned his name and with a twist and a few well-placed strokes, Liam caught her at the top and followed her over the edge.

He tightened his arms around her and as they floated in the aftermath, he could have sworn his heart was singing.

There you go again with your fanciful thoughts.

"Are we floating?"

He chuckled. "You feel it too?"

She hummed and pressed her cheek against his chest, and he couldn't believe how content he felt.

"We start with a little hope," he murmured, rolling her over.

She opened her eyes, and he drowned in their message. "Toss in a lot of love."

"And build the future one brick at a time."

"I like that." Elsa pushed him over onto his back. "Let me show you the first brick."

As her head lowered, Liam's thought processes scattered and all he could do was feel.

TWENTY-FIVE

Swan Harbor
Killian's Apartment
October 24
12:00 p.m.

WITH THE FIRST OF NOVEMBER RIGHT AROUND THE CORNER, Killian was running out of time to vacate his apartment. He'd known it was temporary when he'd agreed to sublet from Jessie and Cameron Hunter. But somehow, he'd thought he'd be in it until he and Emma were married and had picked out a place of their own. Instead, he was moving into her small apartment, above her business. On top of that, he'd not been able to get her to agree to a wedding date. At the rate things were going, it wouldn't surprise him if Liam didn't beat him to the altar.

"Bloody hell."

Killian ripped off a strip of tape and slapped it on the box he'd just finished packing. Intellectually, he knew he was angry about the Santora case. With the newest information from Weaver he'd received, it just added fuel. Emotionally, he hated it, as he felt like he was constantly performing a balancing act. One that could tip either way.

The door opened, startling him, and before he could react, Emma rushed inside, bringing the cold air with her.

"Yes, mom." She rolled her eyes, dropping a pile of books on the table. "I brought them with me."

Killian grinned at both Emma's exasperation with her mother, and at Ava's tenacity. Emma and her mother clashed—one wanted a date set, while the other ignored the hints.

"Here, Doc." Killian hopped up to help her remove her coat.

"Thank you." She kissed him quickly while her mother continued going non-stop on the other end.

"Sit." He pushed her into a chair. "Let me get your boots."

"That would be wonderful." Emma gave him her foot. "No, mom." She rolled her eyes. "I'm not saying it would be wonderful to move the wedding to Portland. Killian offered to take off my boot."

He dropped her boots by the door and hung up her jacket and could tell her patience was wearing thin.

"Yes, I know you do," she argued. "But Killian and I ... oh, hold on."

She pretended to get an emergency call and told Ava she would call her back.

"That wasn't very nice."

"I know," Emma sighed. "She won't stop pushing, though."

"Why won't you answer her?" He hadn't meant to say anything. Once it was out there, he realized he wanted an answer.

Emma was quiet while she carefully set the pile of magazines and her phone on the table.

"You know why." Her voice was cool, controlled, and a part of him still wanted to push it aside.

"I know why?" Killian brushed his hand through his hair and turned fiery eyes on her. "No, I bloody hell don't. We've been engaged since June. It's almost November and you still won't set a date. I'm wondering if you really don't want to get married. If maybe you're comfortable with how things are right now."

"How can you say that?" Emma grabbed his hand to tug him onto the sofa. "You know I love you."

"Then why won't you marry me?"

She sighed, and he thought she was trying to read his mind.

"What's this about?"

"Being upset because my fiancée doesn't want to marry me isn't enough?" he snapped, but he could tell she wasn't buying his response.

"Killian." Emma forced him to look at her. "You know how I was when I moved here, right?"

"Rigid. Persnickety. Prickly." A corner of his mouth ticked up. "Beautiful."

She shook her head, but there was little smile playing along her lips, "A lot has happened. You know that and I just feel—"

"—Pushed?"

"No," she assured him. "Overwhelmed. I still need to work things out with my dad, and now all this with Santora and not knowing ..."

Killian glanced away, hoping not to get into Weaver's call with her on top of everything else.

"That's it, isn't it?" she asked quietly. "Something happened. Is Liam okay? Did he meet with that agent?"

Not for the first time, he cursed her ability to ferret out his deepest thoughts.

"He's meeting with Simpson right now," he admitted. "Weaver called."

"And?"

"He found out who was digging through my file and discovered I'm Ian Jones and not dead."

"Who?"

"Jokowitz." He sent her a smile he knew didn't reach his eyes. "Isn't that bloody lovely?"

Before she could say anything more, his phone buzzed, and he saw Liam's picture flash across the screen.

"Excuse me. I need to get this." He took a deep breath and answered. "Liam. What happened?"

New York City
Liam's Apartment
October 24
1:00 p.m.

"Whoa!" Liam pulled the phone from his ear. "Who raised your ire?"

"Can it," Killian barked. "What the bloody hell did you learn from the agent?"

Once Killian spoke to Lance Diamond and heard Lee Simpson was trustworthy, Liam had agreed to a meeting.

"A couple of interesting pieces of information," Liam shared. "The first has to do with Jokowitz."

"Jokowitz?" Killian repeated. "Weaver just called me today about him. What did Simpson say?"

"Jokowitz was compromised."

Killian barked out a one-word response.

"My sentiments as well," Liam agreed. "I'm assuming he said something that upset Stevens."

"Is Simpson following up with Stevens?"

"Not sure."

"Maybe I'll reach out to him," Killian replied, almost as if he were talking to himself. "Apparently, Jokowitz was the one digging through my files."

"Think he was the one who sent the pictures?"

"It wasn't the agent?"

"No. Simpson said there's someone playing a game from within Santora's organization. They just don't know who it is."

"Now that's interesting," Killian murmured. "So, based on the pictures they've sent, I'm assuming it's someone who was there at the same time as 'Ian'"

"That makes sense," Liam agreed. "Who?"

"Not sure. But it gives me someplace to start."

"Okay. I'm leaving New York in the next hour and heading in that direction. How's the weather?"

"Snow's expected," Killian uttered the words Liam had feared. "Drive safely."

"Snow," Liam mumbled with disgust as he stepped onto the elevator of his apartment building. "What a welcome to Swan Harbor."

"Talking to yourself again, man." Luis slipped through the closing doors.

Liam grinned, embarrassed to be caught talking to himself. "Hey, Luis. How's the head?"

"It's good." Luis shrugged. "No big deal."

"Only you would say that. I'm glad you weren't really hurt."

Luis sobered, and his dark eyes flashed. "You and me both, amigo. Did the police ever figure out where it came from?"

An uncomfortable feeling zipped through Liam. For Luis's safety, he'd been told not to say much.

"No idea," Liam gave a partial answer. "But it gives me a good excuse to take a few weeks off."

"Going to visit Elsa?"

Liam's mouth curled and his heart raced with anticipation. "How'd you guess?"

"Come on, man." Luis unlocked his apartment door. "It wasn't hard."

"Well, it was a good guess." Liam's goofy smile grew bigger. "I'll tell her you said hey."

"Do that. Catch you later."

Liam waited until he heard the other door click before he checked for the white thread.

It was gone!

He counted to ten and looked again, but it still wasn't there. In his rush to meet with the agent, had he forgotten to leave it?

Bloody hell, what should he do?

It took him less than ten seconds to decide to open the door. If he called for help, and it was his mistake, he'd look like an idiot.

But what if someone is in there?

He'd already packed his bags, and they were waiting near the door. If he left it open ....

Liam slowly twisted the doorknob and pushed the door hard enough that it bounced against the wall.

No one was hiding behind it.

That knowledge propelled him through the opening, and while nothing appeared out of place, something was off. It took him a minute to realize there was a smell—part cologne and part sweat—that wasn't his. He grabbed his bags and took out his phone.

> Liam: You wanted me to tell you if I noticed something out of place. I think someone was in my apartment while we were meeting.

> Lee: I'll check it out. You leaving?

> Liam: Yes. Please check on Luis too.

> Lee: Will do. Safe trip.

Once he'd stepped into the hallway, Liam's heart rate slowed. He locked the door and started to his car.

Once on I-95, he activated his Bluetooth and called Elsa.

"Liam," she answered breathlessly after the third ring. "Are you on your way?"

"I am." His voice grew husky. "Why so breathless, love? You're only supposed to be that way with me."

Her chuckle rippled along his skin and he couldn't wait to hold her. It had been over two weeks since he'd said goodbye to her at the airport.

"We're still unpacking," she replied. "I didn't realize mom had so much stuff."

"Is Patty helping?"

"She's helping. It's just different."

They'd spoken little about how her mother was handling the move. While he wanted to kick his arse for not being there for Elsa, he'd followed her wishes. When they'd talked, she'd briefly mentioned her mother, and then the conversation had been about them. She'd asked questions he might have evaded in the past. This time, he'd paid attention to her answers.

"I should be there around seven. Do you want me to stop at Sally's and bring dinner?"

"You would do that?"

"Oh, El," he confessed. "Don't you know I would do anything for you?"

"You're a sweet talker," she murmured. "I've missed you."

"Me too, love. I have a surprise for you."

"Is it another ambulance?"

"It's not a car," he assured her. "But I think you'll like it."

"If it's from you, I'll definitely like it."

"Good. You can show me."

"Oh?"

"Minx."

"Drive carefully, Liam," Elsa whispered. "I'll see you when you get here."

"I love you. Text me your dinner order.

"Love you too, and I will."

Liam clicked off and shoved his phone in his pocket. His girl was waiting, and he couldn't wait to hold her in his arms.

Swan Harbor
Elsa's Mother's Home
October 24
5:00 p.m.

ELSA WATCHED HER MOTHER FLIT AROUND HER NEW HOME, arranging and then rearranging over and over. Being witness to her mother's decline regularly had been the most difficult thing she'd ever done. On the flip side, a few blessings came with the move.

Lilly Mason was the first blessing. She'd been the live-in caretaker for the previous home owner. With the family's recommendation, and Audrey vouching for her, the decision had been simple.

The second blessing was one of the more difficult parts of the disease. That was the transition from one stage to another. Patty had moved into stage 5 Alzheimer's and while she could recall some aspects of her personal life, her concept of time fluctuated. Some days, she understood Elsa was her daughter and other days she didn't. Those were the times Elsa went home and cried. However, the timing issue was a blessing in that Patty never asked to go 'home.' In her mind, she was once again living in Newport, the town of her childhood. That circled back to Lilly Mason, as she resembled the woman who'd cared for Patty when her mother passed.

"Grandma." Patty gave Elsa an expectant look. "Do you think these porcelain teapots look best on this shelf or over there?"

Right there was one of the hardest things about the disease. Having your mother call you by her grandmother's name—the woman she'd been named after.

"What do you think, Patty?" she asked, knowing if her mother didn't decide on her own, she'd argue.

Patty put her finger on her chin and studied the space. "I think over there." Then, for the next twenty minutes, she moved the teapots from one shelf to another.

Elsa carried a box of utensils into the kitchen and checked the clock for the dozenth time. Liam should arrive soon, making her wish she had Killian's app. If she could track him, she wouldn't worry as much.

You don't, though. You'll just have to wait.

"Grandma," Patty called from the other room. "Grandma, where are you?"

The slight hysteria in her mother's voice caused a pain in the center of Elsa's chest.

"I'm in here, Mo ... Patty."

Patty rushed into the kitchen, carrying a 9"x12" envelope.

A chill ran through Elsa when she saw what her mother was holding. "Where did you get that?"

Patty frowned, and a cloud passed over her face. "I, I, I found it. It has your name on it."

Elsa faced her mother and apologized for being so abrupt. "I'm sorry. You said the envelope has my name on it?"

Patty nodded, her mood flipping after the apology.

"May I see where you found it?"

"Sure," Patty agreed. "Come see."

She followed her mother into the living room, where Patty pointed to a box that still needed to be unpacked. When Elsa saw the envelope had come from the Georgetown home, and couldn't be from Santora, she let down her guard.

"What does it say again?" Elsa asked.

Patty glanced at the envelope and frowned. "Well, it says Elsa, but the last name is wrong."

"It's wrong?"

"Take a look." Patty flipped the envelope around. "It says Elsa Winters."

Elsa almost contradicted her mother—not the best option with a person who has Alzheimer's disease.

"What should it say?"

"Well, Elsa Fleming, silly," Patty scoffed. "Just like grandpa."

"Oh, okay." Elsa finally followed her mother's logic. "But Winters is my maiden name."

"Oh." Patty's face lit up. "Then here you go."

As soon as Patty gave her the envelope, she returned to dig through the other boxes, leaving Elsa free to fall apart.

Oh, mama.

On the front of the envelope, written in Patty's once elegant script was Elsa's name. It felt like a smaller envelope and a box were inside.

"Patty," Elsa forced out around the lump in her throat.

"Yes?"

"I'm going out for a little fresh air, okay?"

"Sure." Patty took out a photograph album and waved Elsa off.

Outside, Elsa sank onto the top step and slowly opened the clasp. As she'd suspected, inside was a smaller envelope with her name on it and a box she'd never seen.

Was this a list of her mother's wishes? The ones they should have made together when Patty was first diagnosed?

Elsa's hands were shaking when she removed several sheets of paper.

The date at the top of the page had tears springing to her eyes.

November 20

My Darling Elsa,

I've just come from seeing Jerry, and he's given me some news I've suspected for quite some time. He confirmed I have Alzheimer's disease, and I don't even know how I'm supposed to feel.

It's difficult facing one's mortality, especially when there's so much you want to accomplish. But with the nature of this disease, I understand eventually, my memory will fail. Before it's too late, I need to say a few things.

First, I want to talk about your sister Olivia. I was wrong not to share my memories of her with you. I can't give you the exact reason I didn't talk to you. The only thing I can say is I was protecting myself from pain, as well as keeping the darkness from you.

I know you were angry at me for doing just that, but a mother's job is to protect. If I couldn't keep Olivia safe, then what kind of mother was I?

As a physician, I realize that makes no sense rationally, but when I lost Olivia, a part of me died with her. While I had you and loved you with every fiber of my being, I was terrified and vowed to keep as much darkness out of your life as possible.

Olivia was born after several miscarriages. She was a frail child, and I doted, hoping to give her some of my strength.

She wasn't strong like you, and I. Olivia liked to garden, bake, read, and listen to music. After Max told me you knew about her, I spent hours laying out her life in photos to share with you. But I was too big of a coward to pull you down for a talk. And when you didn't ask, I told myself you didn't care.

But never doubt that your father's words weren't the truth. You were a gift. No! You ARE a gift. I'd hoped to have a houseful of children someday, but we'd tried for years to have more and had finally given up. And then you came along and brought us hope.

You were a tiny thing with a fighting spirit, and 'couldn't' wasn't in your vocabulary. You're beautiful, smart and when you followed in my and your grandfather Williams' footsteps, I'd never been happier.

However, besides my love of medicine, you inherited my

ability to compartmentalize. In our profession, the trait serves us well. However, it also makes it difficult for those who love us. Especially in uncomfortable situations because if they don't push, we're apt to let them slide.

If I could give you any advice, I ask that you learn from my mistakes. Talk to the people who are important to you. Tell them what you're feeling, thinking, and need. Don't expect them to read your mind.

Being a burden to you is not how I wanted to spend the last years of my life. That picture involved you married to a nice man with children for me to spoil. But based on the progression of my disease, I may not be fortunate to be here for those moments. Promise me you'll tell them about their grandma Patty and how I wished things had been different.

And before I forget (no pun intended), I'm including a locket that's been in our family for many generations. My father told me it held hope. And my hope for you is health, happiness, and love.

Thank you for letting me be your mom. I love you.

"Oh, mom," Elsa cried, brushing her tears aside and opening the box. Inside, she found a heart-shaped locket so tarnished she couldn't discern the design on the front.

"Elsa?"

"I'll be right there, mom."

Patty let the door slam and joined her on the step.

"You found the hope locket."

Elsa set the locket in her hand, its chain spilling over her palm while her mother's words bounced around in her head.

"The what?"

"The hope locket." Patty gently touched the chain. "My grandfather used to tell me it held enough hope to fill an entire town."

"We start with a little hope," Elsa murmured.

"I'm hungry." Patty quickly changed the topic. "Is it time to eat?"

Elsa checked her phone and saw the time for Liam to arrive had come and gone and there was no message. She called, hoping he'd answer. When it went straight to voice mail, her stomach began to churn.

Where was he? And why was he late?

TWENTY-SIX

Swan Harbor
October 24
8:00 p.m.

LIAM SLOWLY SWAM HIS WAY TOWARDS CONSCIOUSNESS. HIS head was pounding, his mouth felt like cotton, and his muscles weren't obeying his commands. *Ketamine injection,* he thought, beginning a simple assessment of his body parts.

He could feel his legs, but couldn't separate them, and they refused to work independently. Most likely, they were tied together.

His wrists were bound with rope, or something stronger, and he could wiggle his fingers. They felt numb, cold, and the circulation wasn't working like it should. The good news was, his bonds were in front, not behind him.

He was most concerned about was his head injury. It felt like marching bands from all fifty states had sent at least one bass drum to take up residence. His thoughts were slow, disjointed, and his memory was faulty.

Concussion? How? When? He hadn't been in an accident? Or had he?

While he might be confused about a few things, he knew he was in the back of a moving vehicle, and he hadn't gotten there on his own. *Who are these people?*

"How long do you think he'll be out of it?" the voice closest to his head asked.

"Not sure," the other voice answered. "What are we supposed to do with him?"

"Boss said someone would meet us in Swan Harbor," voice one responded. "Here's the address where we're supposed to keep him."

"What's the boss have against a paramedic?" voice two wondered aloud.

"It's not the paramedic that's the problem," voice one explained. "Boss wants the brother."

Santora Callandra!

Liam breathed in, but the pounding in his head grew louder, and he had to bite back a groan.

What had happened?

He remembered his tire blew just after he'd exited onto Cove Highway. When he'd popped the trunk to get the spare, then ....

Except, that was where his memories grew hazy, leaving him to assume it was then he'd been jumped, drugged, and tied up.

Bloody hell!

Liam tried to open his eyes, but the harder he tried, the more his head pounded. He needed to do something, but he was having a hard time organizing his thoughts.

"Is that it?" voice one asked.

"If it is, we park by the red door and stash the paramedic in the corner room," voice two replied.

Liam's heart raced, causing his head to throb even more.

"When's the boss supposed to arrive?" voice two went on.

"Tomorrow sometime." Liam thought he heard.

"... red door "

The car stopped, and cool air rushed over him as the door opened. He focused, trying to remain relaxed when they lifted him.

"How long ...?"

"... heavy ..."

Their words floated around him, and the temperature changed twice, then suddenly they were inside. The sounds echoed, making him wonder if the building they were in was empty.

"This it?"

A door opened, then he felt like he was falling and landed with a grunt.

"... untie him?"

"Nah ... car."

Six steps, a door closed, and it was quiet. Liam lay still and listened. He had a splitting headache, but he kept thinking there was something he needed to do.

Elsa!

Santora!

Killian could track him if....

His phone! He'd put it in his pocket, but was it still there?

They'd dropped him on his side and slowly, he stretched his fingers downward, trying to feel what he was lying on. A bed or a sofa?

Since his feet were tied together, he bent his knees, feeling to see if there was a back. His feet hit something, and it gave slightly, suggesting a cushion and not a wall.

Liam inched his fingers toward his pocket and could feel his phone was still in there.

The motion increased the pounding in his skull. While he knew the darkness would bring relief, he fought, knowing there was more he still needed to do.

Move the phone.

Liam took a breath and once more reached into his pocket, sliding his fingers on either side of his phone. But he couldn't get a tight enough grip and ended up pushing his hands deeper. Until finally, he tightened his middle fingers on the hard surface and inched the device out.

Just a little more, he thought, feeling the cooler air on his hand as it broke free from his pocket.

The thought, *I've got it* was just beginning to form, when the phone slid free. He moved his hands, planning to push the device between the cushions. Instead, it slipped and fell onto the floor.

Bloody hell!

The darkness was dragging.

Breathe!

After a few deep breaths, the dots faded, and Liam's thoughts came together enough to remember he wasn't done.

He tightened his abdominal muscles and rolled farther over onto his left side, reaching his arms toward the floor. His range of motion was short, but with a slow sweeping pattern, he searched for the fallen object.

A door slammed, and he heard footsteps.

Only one chance.

Liam used the last of his energy to sweep the phone back toward the sofa, hoping it would go underneath.

He could hear it sliding, but as the darkness overtook him, he didn't know if it was out of sight. If not, he was screwed.

Swan Harbor
Elsa's Mother's Home
October 24
9:00 p.m.

"HERE YOU GO, MOM." ELSA SET A PLATE ON THE TABLE IN FRONT of her mother. "I hope a sandwich is okay. I thought ..." Her throat closed, and tears threatened.

Where was Liam?

She tried to tell herself it was the traffic or the weather, but she knew him better than that. Knew if he could, he would call.

"Turkey?" Patty curled her lip. "Isn't there anything else?"

"No," Elsa snapped, immediately regretting her harsh tone. "Sorry. No, we need to go to the store, remember?"

"Okay." Patty lifted off the top piece of bread. "Do we have any cheese?"

Elsa sighed and bit her lip, fighting not to scream. "Let me check."

"Thank you, dear," Patty preened, happy to be getting her way.

"Swiss or Provolone?" Elsa asked, when she'd located both.

"Swiss."

As soon as she added cheese to Patty's sandwich, Elsa looked at her phone again. It was 9:00 p.m., two hours past the time Liam should have arrived.

"This sandwich is cold," Patty mumbled.

"It's a cold turkey and Swiss," Elsa spit through gritted teeth.

"Can you heat it for me, please?"

Patty held the plate and waited. Only the knowledge she would have attempted to do it on her own propelled Elsa to take care of it.

"Here you go." Elsa set it back on the table. "Toasted to perfection."

"Thank you."

She waited until Patty began eating in earnest before once again trying Liam. When he didn't answer, she sent a quick text.

But after fifteen minutes, her patience evaporated.

Elsa: Have you heard from Liam?

Unlike most other times, Emma didn't get right back to her.

Maybe his phone died.

He's in his car and can charge it.

What if he forgot his charger?

That's possible.

See, stop worrying.

When Lilly returned at 9:30 p.m. and Elsa hadn't heard from Liam or Emma, her worry meter sent her searching for answers. She spent ten minutes checking traffic and another twenty minutes driving around Swan Harbor, hoping maybe ....

"This is stupid, Elsa. You know what you need to do."

She drove straight to Killian's apartment and pounded on his door. When he didn't quickly answer, she knocked again.

"Killian." Elsa knocked a little louder.

"Bloody hell, Elsa. This is becoming a habit," Killian barked.

"Sorry." Elsa pushed her way inside. "Emma didn't respond to my text, so ..."

The rest of what she was going to say died when Emma strolled into the room wearing a *'cat that ate the canary'* look.

"I'm sorry." Elsa returned her attention to Killian. "I really hope I'm just being a hysterical girlfriend. Except with all this Santora crap, I'm a bit freaked."

Killian studied her for a heartbeat. He shoved the door shut and pointed to a chair.

"Too nervous," she told him, glancing at her phone to make sure a message hadn't arrived. "It's Liam ..."

"Who's on his way," Killian added.

"When did you talk to him?"

He shrugged. "A few hours ago, right after Doc got here."

Elsa snickered. "Do you know what time it is?"

He arched a brow, but said nothing until he'd located his phone.

"Bloody hell."

The look in his eyes sent a chill running up her spine.

"Liam said he would be in Swan Harbor by seven and he'd pick up dinner. I've tried calling and texting."

"No answer?"

"Straight to voice mail."

"Alright. Let me check."

While he opened his app and searched for Liam, Elsa felt Emma move close.

"What the hell?" Killian exclaimed, and his expression caused her heart to race.

"What is it?"

He slipped on his boots and had one arm in his leather jacket when someone knocked on the door.

"Maybe this is him."

"Detective Reade?" someone said when Killian opened the door.

Knowing it wasn't Liam caused Elsa's knees to give out, and she dropped into a chair.

"Who the bloody hell's asking?" Killian snapped at whomever was on the other side.

"I'm Special Agent Lee Simpson, and this is my partner, Special Agent Gabe—"

"—Ricci," Killian murmured. "Tino's brother?"

Elsa couldn't see the men, but recognized the name from the pictures.

"Have you heard from Liam?"

Before the question was complete, Elsa jumped up. "Where's Liam?"

"We were just wondering about Liam," Killian replied in an off-handed manner. But one glance at his profile and her fear climbed a little higher.

"Can you come with us, Detective? We found his car—"

"Where was it? Was there an accident?" Elsa interrupted. But then she got a look at the agents.

"You!" She advanced on the one with lighter hair. "You were there the night the bomb exploded."

He exchanged looks with his partner. "That's right, Doctor Winters. I'm glad everyone was okay. Now, Detective Reade, can you please come with us?"

"Killian, what's going on?"

Emma pulled Elsa away from the men.

"Hold on. Let Killian go see what's going on."

Elsa wanted to argue but stepped back and watched him grab his belt and kiss Emma goodbye.

"I'll let you know." He squeezed Elsa's hands and disappeared.

Elsa met Emma's concerned look with one of her own.

"When Killian looked at that app, he saw something he didn't like."

"You saw that too?" Emma huffed. "What, though?"

"You don't have the app?"

"Not on my phone. But ..." She put on her boots and grabbed her coat. "The app is on my computer. You coming?"

"What do you think?"

As Elsa followed Emma down the stairs, her sense of dread rose a little higher.

We start with a little hope and add a lot of love.

Where are you Liam?

Swan Harbor
October 24
10:30 p.m.

KILLIAN WAS FOLLOWING SIMPSON AND RICCI THROUGH SWAN Harbor toward where they'd found Liam's car. Except his brother wasn't there. Unless someone had taken his phone, he was in the First Avenue apartment building in the middle of town. And since Elsa was unaware of that, the only other reasons he could think of were not good news.

"Bloody hell, Liam. What's going on?" He parked behind his brother's car and climbed out to meet the two agents. "You just happened upon his car five plus hours from New York City," Killian barked. "How is that, and why the bloody hell were you following Liam?"

"Look." Simpson held up a hand to stop Killian's tirade. "We can get into that later. Can we just figure out what happened right now?"

"Fine." Killian stalked back to his car, grabbed a flashlight, and went searching for answers.

The car was parked in the softer soil on the side of the road with a flat right front tire. Its doors locked.

"You checked the trunk?" he asked, trying to determine if Liam had been attacked and his phone taken.

"Yes," Simpson confirmed. "Looks like he was getting the tire jack, and someone jumped him."

"Did you check inside?" Killian shone his light through the windows, and a piece of paper caught his attention.

"That note is why we brought you out here." Simpson added his light, highlighting the paper.

Killian's blood froze when he read the words.

Brother for brother. I'll be in touch. S

"Santora!"

"Yes," Ricci agreed. "He'll be here tomorrow. Do you know where they would have taken Liam? Do you have any idea who Santora's contact is here in Swan Harbor?"

Could he trust these men? Lance seemed to think so, but this was Liam.

"I don't know who the contact is in Swan Harbor," Killian opted for the simple question. "As for where he is, I have some idea."

"Where?" Simpson barked.

"Look!" Killian pointed at Simpson, pushing him back a step. "This is my brother, and my town—"

"We're Federal," Simpson interrupted.

"I don't bloody care," Killian roared. "Do you know who has him?"

"A couple of Santora's hired thugs," Simpson offered. Then he pushed for more information than Killian was willing to share. "Why are you holding back?"

"What makes you think I'm holding back?" Killian checked the time. "It's 10:30 p.m. Why don't I call the sheriff, and we can all meet at the office?"

Simpson and Ricci exchanged looks, and Killian knew they were thinking the same thing as he. Liam was 'safe' for a few hours, but what they didn't know was safety was a relative word.

"Fine," Simpson agreed. "Don't do anything rash."

"He's my brother!" Killian snapped. "It's not my stupidity I'm worried about."

Without waiting for a response, he stomped to his car and called the garage to have Liam's car towed. After that, he dialed Dylan.

"'Lo," Dylan whispered.

"Sorry to call so late," Killian began. "But we've got a situation."

"Hold on. Let me go to the other room."

While he waited, Killian's thoughts flew in multiple directions. He was worried about the building where they were keeping Liam.

"I'm here," Dylan returned. "What's up?"

In as few words as possible, Killian explained what had happened and told Dylan to meet him and the Special Agents at the department.

"Why are the Feds involved?" Dylan asked.

"One is the brother of the man featured in those pictures. I'm guessing they've been watching Santora and his gang for a while."

"Well, hell," Dylan grumbled. "Did you tell them why this could be a mess?"

"No. I didn't trust them not to go in guns blazing," Killian sighed. "Besides, I don't know how far things have gotten with the building."

"True." Dylan hesitated a beat. "Okay. Give me fifteen, and I'll meet you at the office. Want me to call Gray and Rusty?"

"Would you?" Killian mentally regrouped for the next call. "I need to update Emma and Elsa."

"Think that's a good idea?"

"No," Killian grunted. "If I don't, though, I'm not sure they'll sit back and wait. Emma knows more than the agents, and I'm not sure her and Elsa haven't already—"

"—Stuck their noses in," Dylan offered with a laugh.

"That's one way of looking at it," Killian agreed. "See you in a few."

He disconnected and dialed Emma.

"Killian," Emma answered before the first ring had even completed. "Why is Liam in that apartment building on First Street?"

Killian pinched the bridge of his nose. "Are you spying on me, Doc?" he tried to tease, hoping to sidetrack.

"Stop trying to sweet talk me," she grumbled. "What's going on?"

"Liam's been kidnapped," he snapped.

"Santora?"

"His goons," he admitted, even though it killed him.

"But Santora is involved," she pushed.

"Aye."

"What aren't you telling me?"

"Bloody hell, Doc," Killian bit out. "Can't I have a few secrets?"

When she didn't dignify his comment with a response, he amended, "Santora left a note. Brother for brother."

"Santora wants you and will let Liam go?" She laughed. "You know that's unrealistic."

"Look, Doc," Killian tried a different tactic. "I'm meeting with Dylan and Rusty and those agents. We'll figure it out, but I need you to keep Elsa away. I don't want to worry about you two on top of worrying about Liam."

"Okay," she agreed. "I'll try. But tell me something."

"I love you."

"I love you too, but that's not what I wanted you to tell me."

"What is it, Doc?"

"Killian," she lowered her voice, almost to a whisper. "Isn't that building where you hid the dynamite?"

"Aye."

"So, if there's shooting?"

"It could be over before it's begun."

"Be careful."

"I will, Doc."

And he would be careful. He just wasn't sure if what he was thinking was what she had in mind.

Swan Harbor

October 24
11:00 p.m.

Liam was floating, his brain trying to connect his thoughts. Except, every time they were within reach, they skittered away.

"Hey." Someone shook him roughly. "Wake up."

"Stop!" He shrank back from the rough voice. "Don't yell."

Who was yelling at him? Why did his head hurt?

"Let me help," another voice joined the first and hauled Liam into a sitting position.

"Wakey, wakey," voice one slapped his cheek.

Slowly, Liam opened his eyes half-mast, and it all came rushing back. He'd been kidnapped!

Santora!

Voice one slapped him again, this time a little harder, and he ended up tasting blood.

That smell. He recognized it. But from where?

"Did you give him too much ketamine?" another voice asked, this one farther away.

"No," voice two answered. "He hit his head when he fell."

Concussion floated through Liam's addled brain, and he struggled to keep his eyes open.

"Who 'r you?" he slurred, his tongue not obeying his brain.

"Not important," the third voice responded. "Your brother cooperates, and you can go your own way."

Liam was quiet, but something told him not to believe much of what they said.

"Ask him about his phone," the third voice directed, and something about the voice was familiar.

His phone! Where? Then he remembered. It had fallen on the ground, and he'd tried to shove it under the sofa. Since they were asking about it, did that mean he'd succeeded?

"Where's your phone?" voice two snapped.

Liam's thoughts were functioning in slow motion and when he didn't respond right away, someone slapped him again.

"Bloody hell!"

"He can talk. Now, where's your phone?" voice one repeated.

"Car."

"Check his jacket," the third voice instructed.

The guy on his right patted at Liam's pockets, jostling him so much, Liam could feel the bile rising.

Deep breaths through your nose, he reminded himself.

Swallow.

"It's not here. Must be in the car," voice one reported. "Want us to go look?"

"No, you imbecile," the third voice snapped. "Doesn't matter if it's there. Just as long as someone can't track him."

That voice, Liam knew he'd heard it some other time. But before he could grab onto anything concrete, it floated away.

"Okay." They pushed him down hard enough his head bounced against the back of the sofa.

"Bloody hell." When he tried to put his hand on his head, he realized they were still tied together. "Hey." Liam held his hands up.

"What do you think?" voice one asked.

"Undo the legs, leave the hands," the familiar voice retorted. "And lock the door.

"It's your lucky day." Voice two cut the ropes around Liam's ankles. "Can's through there. We'll be right outside."

"Doesn't feel like my lucky day," Liam murmured, the black spots once again threatening to pull him down.

TWENTY-SEVEN

Swan Harbor
Swan Harbor Sheriff's Department
October 25
Midnight

KILLIAN WAS STANDING NEXT TO RUSTY AND DYLAN IN THE conference room of the Sheriff's department, waiting for Gray to get off the phone.

"What's taking so long," Killian grumbled.

"Not sure," replied Rusty.

When Gray finally shoved his phone into his pocket, his expression had Killian's stomach twisting.

"Just spit it out."

"When we were trying to decide where to save or demolish the building, we scanned the blueprints and sent them to Cameron. The originals were returned to the library's archives. I can get Cam to send them, but I'm not sure what time zone he's in."

"Think Rene can let us in?" Killian asked Rusty hopefully.

"Let me call her," Rusty murmured, already taking out his phone.

"Gray, while we're waiting," Dylan suggested. "Walk us through the building again."

Gray grabbed a white board marker and drew a large rectangle on the board. "In one sense, you're lucky, as we've blocked everything off except the first floor."

"Lucky," Killian scoffed. "Blocked because the other floors have already been 'prepped' for demolition."

"Hey," Dylan reminded him, "little things."

"Right," Killian quipped. "Carry on."

"We're a go," Rusty replied, returning to the room. "Rene will bring us the keys."

"Good." Killian nodded to Gray. "Now, you can carry on."

"The first floor used to be a saloon, and a wide-open space. When it was converted in the early 1900s, they divided the first floor into an apartment in this area." Gray marked out the back half of the rectangle and one corner in the front. "There's a large sitting area, several small storage areas, and two offices. Initially, we put the dynamite in the storage rooms. As we've prepped, we've moved it throughout the building."

"So, it's not visible?" Killian questioned.

"Not unless they get into the storage areas, and we locked those," replied Gray.

"How many doors?" Simpson asked.

"Three," supplied Gray. "Front, one on each side. If Liam is in this corner room, which used to be an office, you can't get to him without being seen."

"Best bet on where Santora's guys parked?" Dylan asked. "Think they're in that back apartment?"

Gray pointed to where the division was removed. "We needed a load bearing column and ripped out the walls."

"So, they're in the storage rooms, which we doubt, in the sitting area, or in the other office?" Killian guessed.

"That's my bet," Gray confirmed.

Killian studied the picture Gray had drawn. "Windows? Basement?"

"We boarded up the bottom floor windows," Gray explained. "As for a basement ..." His eyes flared as if he'd just had an epiphany.

"What?" Killian frowned, ready to get moving.

"There's a space that was used for liquor storage." Gray suddenly became animated. "The only way into that room from above ground is from an office."

"Which office?" Killian paid closer attention.

Gray hummed. "The corner one, I think. But I'm not sure."

"You said above ground," Killian reminded them. "Is there another way to get into that room?"

"From the tunnels." Dylan exchanged smiles with Gray. "I bet those plans are in the library's archives with the building's blueprint."

"Well, bloody hell," Killian grumbled. "What are we waiting for?"

"The key," Rusty reminded him.

Swan Harbor
October 25
12:15 a.m.

ELSA PACED BACK AND FORTH IN FRONT OF EMMA'S DESK AND watched the dots on the computer screen.

"It's after midnight. Why haven't they moved?"

"I don't know," Emma replied. "Maybe the plan is taking longer to figure out."

"Plan?" Leroy, Emma's assistant, entered the office. "Plan for what? How to keep Pickles happy?"

"Give Pickles a treat." Emma pointed to a shelf against one wall. "He'll settle down."

Elsa studied Leroy, Emma's assistant, as he crossed the room to choose a bag of dog treats for the infamous Pickles. She knew he'd been dating her nurse, Audrey, for a while, but for some reason, she couldn't get them to match.

Leroy was brash to Audrey's quiet. Short to her tall, out-there to her organized. A pair that on paper never should have worked, but somehow ....

"Who are you spying on?" Leroy stopped to stare at the computer screen. "Reade stepping out on you, Doc?"

For a minute, Elsa thought he was talking to her, but Emma shook her head.

"No, Leroy. There's a situation we're monitoring."

"A situation?" Leroy pulled a chair close to the desk and sat. "What's going on?"

He leaned closer to the computer screen and jiggled the mouse a few times.

"You are spying!" Leroy pointed at the dots. "They say Killian and Liam." He frowned and stretched the picture. "Why is Liam in an apartment building that's full of dynamite?"

"What?" Elsa snapped, but one look at Emma's guilty expression, and she realized her friend had known. "You knew."

Emma winced. "I knew, but how did he know?" She sent a pointed look Leroy's way.

Leroy rolled his eyes. "Please. This is Swan Harbor."

"Fine," Emma huffed. "Liam's been kidnapped, and the guys are trying to figure out how to rescue him without getting blown up."

"Tunnels." Elsa snapped her fingers, remembering an off-handed comment Rene had made.

"Sure," Leroy agreed. "As long as they have light. Well, that and a hard hat." He stood and grabbed the bag of treats for Pickles and was halfway across the room when he suddenly turned back. "Of course, if the dynamite blows and someone's in them, who knows?"

Elsa's frightened eyes met Emma's. "I can't stand here and not know."

"Killian promised he'd bring Liam back, El," Emma repeated what she'd said earlier. "He promised he'd be careful."

Elsa's thoughts were pinging all over the place. A part of her understood what Emma was saying. And she understood Killian would do everything in his power to save his brother. But Liam was her ....

Liam was her friend, and the man who held her heart. He was also the man with whom she wanted to build a future.

"If the situation was reversed," Elsa put Emma on the spot. "What would you do?"

Emma glanced at a picture of her and Killian taken at their engagement party. "I'd want to be there."

"Are you going to drive me or loan me your car?"

"What do you think?" Emma answered with another question.

Swan Harbor
October 25
12:45 a.m.

LIAM PUSHED UP AND DROPPED HIS HEAD INTO HIS HANDS WHILE he waited for the room to stop spinning.

His stomach churned, and his mouth felt like cotton, but the drums in his head seemed to have quieted. He needed to talk to Elsa. She was probably worried sick. Had she contacted Killian? Did he know what was going on? Were they looking for him?

The room was dark, but a glance at his sports watch told him it was 12:45 a.m. On unsteady legs, Liam pushed up and made his way to the commode room.

A bare bulb lit up the space, and when he looked in the small mirror, he wished he hadn't. The bump on his head had the beginning of two black eyes showing, and his lip was swollen from being slapped.

You're alive, he reminded himself.

He splashed tepid water on his face and left the bulb lit, allowing it to cast a dim light into the room.

The sofa he'd been lying on had once been gold, but was faded and sagging in the middle. Two cushions on the back and a sitting area with overstuffed arms. There was fringe hanging off the edges and around the bottom. Perhaps that had been what prevented his phone from being discovered.

Liam gingerly lowered to the floor and tried to look underneath. This certainly wasn't how he planned to spend his evening, he thought with disgust. He'd wanted to share his surprise.

It had all started the night they'd ended up at Sally's after the painting party at Patty's house.

"Bugger that." Liam pulled Elsa closer. "I just care what you think."

"Oh, I'm happy."

Liam slipped his arm around her waist and led her toward the front room. "You can show me how much when we're alone."

"Perhaps," she giggled. "I'm going to run to the ladies' room. Will you wait?"

"Of course."

"Good." Elsa kissed him, then disappeared.

Liam leaned back against the wall and closed his eyes, wondering how much longer they'd need to stay.

"You look happy."

He opened his eyes to see Rene's amused grin.

"I am but tired."

She chuckled. "Painting can do that to you."

"Agreed."

"Listen," she got right to the point. "I'm not one to beat around the bush, but I heard what you brought Elsa today. That was quite the gift."

Her statement caused a feeling inside he'd not expected. "I heard she created quite the stir."

Rene nodded. "She was pretty angry. Did she tell you what I told her?"

"That there was no money for a new ambulance? Yeah, she told me."

"Not that exactly," Rene corrected. "I told her there was money for a chief paramedic. Are you interested?"

"Bloody hell, yes," he replied without hesitation.

"Coffee here tomorrow at 11:00 a.m.?"

Liam grinned. "See you then."

Rene went into the ladies' room as Elsa was coming out.

"You look tired." Elsa took his hand, and they walked back toward the front of the diner.

"I am." When they rounded the corner, he ran into someone going in the other direction.

Liam studied the man. "Do I know you? You look familiar."

"What are you doing on the floor?"

Liam jumped, and the memory evaporated. "Bloody hell."

"I asked what you were doing on the floor?" the man he'd considered voice one barked.

"Sick," Liam grunted, hoping the man wouldn't look under the sofa.

"Here." Voice one hauled Liam up by one arm. "I brought you a bottle of water."

"Gee thanks."

The man backhanded him, knocking Liam backward on the sofa and breaking his lip open again.

"Watch your mouth," voice one growled, before stomping out and slamming the door behind him.

Liam tugged his shirt out of his pants and wiped off his mouth. It burned like fire, but he didn't think it needed stitches, which was good, considering.

The bass drums were back playing in his head, and his thoughts still felt disjointed. He was positive about one thing, though. It had been voice one's cologne and sweat he'd smelled in his apartment in New York.

"Asswipe." He lay back and allowed the darkness free rein.

Swan Harbor
October 25
1:30 a.m.

THEY'D PARKED THE VAN ON THIRD AVENUE IN THE HCI OFFICE building parking lot. Rusty was being shown how to use the communications equipment The Agency had loaned them. And Killian was taking the weapons he'd need from his bag—38 for his ankle, knife, and extra clips for his belt.

Dylan climbed from the van, and every time Killian got a look at the sheriff's face, guilt rushed through him.

"Look, mate." Killian took the vest Dylan handed him and slipped it over his head. "I feel I need to tell you how sorry I am about all this."

"Would that be sorry that Santora's goons kidnapped your brother or that it ended up happening in Swan Harbor?"

Killian winced. "All of it. Had I known he'd follow me ..."

"Stop it, Killian," Dylan snapped. "I've learned that while we might not like everything that happens around us, things happen for a reason. Do I wish I were home asleep next to my pregnant wife? Yes. But Swan Harbor is your town, and we're here to help you get your brother out safely. Thank you for not going off half-cocked. To be frank, I'm surprised."

Killian gave a half laugh. "I was going to," he admitted. "Until I realized they were keeping my brother in the same building I'd recommended storing the dynamite."

Dylan laughed. "What's that called, 'hoisted by your own petard', or something like that?"

"Something like that."

"Well, I'm glad." Dylan handed him the earpiece. "Are you sure you won't let me go with you?"

They'd argued about this before they'd left the station, and Killian wasn't hep to get into it again.

"We talked about this when we were studying the map, remember? The tunnels are narrow, and I can move faster alone."

Dylan sighed. "Okay. Rusty will be your navigator, and I'll be waiting at the mouth of the tunnel."

"And Simpson and Ricci?"

"They're coordinating with Chief Fowler and the Swan Harbor Police to surround the building."

"Alright." Killian placed the earpiece in, and the commotion on the other end caused his heart to sink. "Bloody hell."

Dylan frowned. "What is it? Does it not work?"

"It works." Killian pointed over his shoulder.

"Oh," Dylan smirked. "I'll just let you take care of that."

"Chicken."

"You betcha."

Killian pulled the earpiece out and went to meet Emma. "I thought I asked you to keep Elsa away?"

She gave him a sheepish look. "I am. Liam is two blocks over that way."

"Emma." He fought to rein in his frustration. "As much as I may have wanted, I didn't go off on my own. We have a plan."

"Does it involve the tunnels?"

"How did you know that?"

"Elsa said something, and Leroy added his two cents."

Her response had his stomach tying itself into knots. "How the bloody hell does Leroy know what we're doing?"

"So, he was right," she murmured, almost to herself. "He said you needed a light."

"I'm taking two flashlights."

"And a hard hat?"

"I'll look into it if it keeps you from worrying." He walked her a few more steps away. "Rusty is guiding my way using The Agency's fancy communication system, and I'm taking an old-fashioned piece of chalk to mark the walls."

"You'll be careful?"

Killian cupped her cheek and kissed her gently. "Face it, Doc. You're stuck with me."

She hugged him, and he could feel the slight trembling in her slim frame.

"Come back to me."

"Count on it. Now kiss me good luck and go take care of Elsa."

Emma kissed him softly. "Good luck," she murmured against his lips, and then kissed him again.

Minutes later, Killian grabbed his flashlight and followed Gray and Dylan into the foothills where he would enter the tunnel.

"Ready?" Dylan shone his light into the narrow opening.

"Aye." Killian tapped his earpiece. "Here I go, Rusty. Get me there."

Killian walked into the tunnel's opening, took a deep breath, and plunged forward.

"Fifty feet in, the tunnel will fork," Rusty's voice came through loud and clear. "Take the tunnel on the left."

Once Killian turned, it grew darker, and he focused on the narrow path in front of him.

"That tunnel will veer to the right and begin a downward slope."

The farther he walked, the closer the ceiling, and Killian had to duck his head periodically.

"At the next fork, turn right," Rusty instructed. "After that, it should be a straight shot to the metal door that leads beneath the building."

Sweat trickled down Killian's back and dotted his upper lip as he made his way to the metal door.

"I found it," he relayed. "It's rusty. Wonder if it creaks like you do?"

"Wanker," Rusty quipped.

"It's locked," Killian groused, even though he'd expected as much. "Hopefully, I can pick it."

"Your undercover skills come in handy," Rusty mumbled.

"My undercover skills got us into this mess," Killian retorted.

"But look at all the fun we're having."

"There is that."

He'd just about given up being able to open the door when he felt something give and the doorknob turned.

"Got it."

"You're getting slow."

"Tosser."

Rusty snickered, but Killian tuned him out. His attention was focused on listening for sounds on the other side of the door.

He pulled the door open an inch, and when he heard nothing but silence, opened it completely. With that done, he withdrew his Glock and stepped inside.

The room was square, roughly 10'x10', with a wooden staircase on the opposite side from where he was standing. There was an opening in the wall behind and when he walked through, he discovered another room identical to the first.

"Bloody hell, Rusty. There's two rooms and two sets of staircases."

Killian heard Gray's succinct response and had to agree. He felt much the same way.

"Our guess is one room holds Liam and the other the goons, right?"

"Gray says he still thinks Liam's in the corner room," Dylan offered.

"Bloody hell, Dylan. Which one's the corner room?"

"Hold on," snickered Rusty.

Killian could hear the shuffling of papers until Rusty returned.

"The door to the tunnel is from an interior room."

Which made it easier for him *if* Liam was in the corner room, as Gray predicted.

"Why is it Gray thinks Liam's in the corner room again?"

There were several minutes of conversation before Dylan answered. "The rooms are the same size, but one has old desks, chairs and a small refrigerator. The other one only has an old sofa. Where would you stash him?"

"Alright. Here I go," he mumbled, testing the first stair. When it held, Killian flashed his light across the ceiling and slowly began the climb. As he neared the top, the staircase swayed, and a creaking noise had him hurriedly searching for a latch.

Here goes nothing, he thought, pushing upward.

TWENTY-EIGHT

Swan Harbor
October 25
2:30 a.m.

Liam woke with a start but lay still, knowing he was no longer alone. He listened. Was he hearing someone else breathing, or was he imagining things?

His heart raced and his body tensed, readying for whatever the thugs who'd grabbed him were bringing this time. Except the sound wasn't coming from the same direction as before.

There was a rustle, and a chill rushed through him.

Rats?

A creak had his body tensing until he heard a soft curse and he had to roll his eyes.

"Took you long enough," he whispered.

"Don't be cheeky, Liam."

Killian flashed the light over him and winced. "Are you alright?"

Liam grunted. "I won't win any beauty contests, but everything is still where it belongs."

"Good to hear. Ready to go?"

"Definitely." He had to twist around until he could push up. "Hey, can you help with these?" Liam held up his hands, which were still tied together.

Killian cut the ties and tossed them aside. "You can walk?"

"My legs are fine," Liam mumbled. "However, I've got a bugger of a headache and probably a concussion." He stood, but when his head swam, he reached for the wall to get his balance. "Any chance you brought some Tylenol?"

"Sorry, no, but Elsa might have some waiting." Killian moved close to the door and listened for a second. "Will that sofa move quietly? We could put it in front of the door to give us more time."

Liam wasn't sure he'd be much help in moving it without falling. "I can try."

But one attempt to lift and they quickly realized it was too heavy to move silently.

"Come on." Killian handed Liam a flashlight. "Rusty's yammering in my ear."

Liam followed Killian to the hole in the floor and flashed his light on the staircase. "Those don't look very safe."

"They aren't," Killian mumbled. "Watch yourself."

"Watch myself, he says," Liam murmured, turning around to take the first step.

"Quit complaining," Killian whispered. "We don't want visitors."

"I'm down here, and you have a weapon," Liam quipped. "Seems like good odds." He took another two steps and when the staircase swayed, goosebumps flew up his spine.

"Oh, brother mine," Killian dropped his voice even lower, "this building is *where* I suggested we hide the dynamite."

"Bugger that, Killian. I'm glad I didn't have that information before."

"Just hurry."

As soon as he'd taken another step, Liam heard an ominous crack and gingerly moved his foot down to the next stair.

"Hurry," hissed Killian.

Liam heard a noise and looked up toward the opening just as the light flashed off. The adrenaline soared through his system, pushing him to reach for the next step. But his foot slipped, then he lost his balance and dropped the rest of the way to the ground.

"Bloody hell," he grunted when he landed awkwardly and twisted his knee.

"Liam, are you alright?" The beam from Killian's flashlight bounced off him.

His knee was on fire, but when he palpated around it, he breathed a sigh of relief. "Twisted my knee. Bloody foot slipped."

"I'm coming, watch out."

The hatch door closed with a whoosh and Liam pushed back, giving Killian room to jump the last few feet.

"Can you walk?" Killian asked, landing next to him.

"I'll make it." Liam pushed up and tried to put weight on his leg and had to grit his teeth to keep from screaming from the pain. "Hold this and give me your knife."

"My knife?"

"Yes."

Liam handed Killian the flashlight, took the knife, and cut several strips of cloth before handing it back.

"You're really rough on shirts."

"Shut up and shine the light on my knee."

It took several tries before he could get the strips tightened around his knee enough to provide support. By the time he was done, the noises above them were noticeable.

"Is that what I think it is?" he barely got out before he heard yelling.

"Yes, let's go."

Liam took his light back and hobbled through another room that looked just like the one they'd landed in.

"We're on our way back," Killian was telling Rusty. "Liam hurt his knee. I'm going to give him the earpiece so I can keep a lookout."

He stopped to wait for Killian just before going through a metal door and took the earpiece.

"We're going through ..." But his blood ran cold when he heard a gunshot.

"Go, go," Killian pushed.

"Rusty, there were gunshots. We're on our way."

"Follow the chalk." Killian slammed the metal door closed.

Liam flashed the light around, using the beam to track the chalk marks Killian had drawn on his way in.

"Liam!" Rusty yelled into his ear. "Did you hear that?"

A muffled sound was immediately followed by the ground under his feet shifting and rocks and debris started falling around them.

"Was that an explosion?"

"Yes!" Rusty screamed in his ear. "Hurry, hurry."

The rocks continued to fall, and in his earpiece, he heard what sounded like all hell breaking loose.

"Rusty! What happened?"

"The building blew. Go!"

They rounded a corner, and the ground felt like it rolled, and Liam's knee buckled. As he fell, the earpiece crackled with another explosion. He landed hard and as his head bounced, the last thing he heard was Elsa screaming his name.

Swan Harbor
October 25
2:45 a.m.

ELSA'S SCREAM BOUNCED AROUND THE VAN AND HER FRIGHTENED eyes met Emma's. They reached for each other's hands and crowded around Rusty.

The commotion coming through the radio was deafening, with multiple voices going at once. All except for the one voice she needed to hear.

"Liam, Killian." Rusty kept adjusting dials. "Come in. Is everything okay?"

Every time he received no answer, Elsa's insides froze a little more.

"They're okay," Emma muttered.

"I know," Elsa agreed, the only acceptable answer.

"Dylan," Rusty tried another voice Elsa had yet to hear since the explosion. "What's going on up there?

When no one responded, he grabbed one of their walkies. "Gray, come in," he repeated several times.

Rusty's eyes met Elsa's when, again, no one answered. "I'll go," she volunteered. "I made Em stop so I could grab my medical bag."

"Do you know where they are? Up the hill behind HCI."

"I do," Emma spoke up. "I watched Killian when he and Dylan left."

"Okay, here, take this." Rusty handed Emma a walkie. "Let me know."

They stopped by Emma's car and grabbed Elsa's bag before starting the walk toward the mouth of the tunnel. Neither said anything, both listening to the chatter coming through the walkie.

"Watch out," someone screeched, and a zip of adrenaline raced straight to Elsa's heart.

She turned frightened eyes and looked back toward the First Avenue Apartment building. The flames could be seen over the trees, as well as the top of the old complex. But as she watched it, the largest explosion yet blew, and the top disappeared.

The ground shook beneath their feet from the combination of dynamite and C4.

"Come on!" Emma took off running and yelling. "Dylan! Gray!" over and over.

"Listen," Elsa shushed her.

They changed their angle and found Dylan banging on his walkie, trying to get it to work.

"Here." Emma handed him the one she'd been carrying. "Where's Gray?"

"He went in there." Dylan nodded toward the opening. "After the last explosion, that happened." He pointed at a part of the tunnel that had fallen.

Elsa's stomach twisted with the additional news as she hadn't considered the tunnel actually collapsing. Her thoughts had run into the more gruesome, like it becoming a fire tunnel.

"Here he comes." Dylan stepped forward to meet Gray.

Before Gray ever said anything, Elsa could tell it wasn't good news.

"There's a cave in," Gray uttered the words she'd feared. "Maybe fifty feet inside."

"Could you hear anything?"

The rising hysteria in Emma's voice matched what was inside her, but Elsa's mind was busy running over the pictures of the tunnels.

"Is the cave in after the fork?" Elsa asked. When Dylan frowned, she added, "When Killian entered, Rusty told him the tunnel forked after fifty feet."

"It's before," Gray told them.

"So, could they have seen the cave in and gone into the other fork?"

Dylan nodded. "It's possible. I wish we could see them."

"We can, but ..." Emma began, annoyance with herself out there for all to see.

"But?" Dylan prodded.

"With all this Santora stuff, Killian has been keeping track of Liam and a few others via an app. But I don't have it on my phone, it's only on my computer."

Gray shrugged. "Is there any reason you can't download it?"

Emma pulled out her phone and searched the app store. Her hands were shaking and the more keywords she tried and the longer she scrolled, the higher Elsa's fear climbed.

"Use your browser," suggested Gray.

The entire time Emma was searching for the app, Dylan was getting an update from Rusty.

"The building is gone, and presumably so are Santora's men."

"I got it," Emma murmured.

"Can you see them?"

Emma stretched the pictures with her thumbs and when she gasped, the acid churned in Elsa's gut.

"There's Killian's phone." She handed the phone to Dylan.

"But not Liam's?" Elsa asked hesitantly.

"No." Emma shook her head, "But El, that means nothing. We know he was with Killian."

"The dot isn't moving." Dylan handed the phone to Gray. "So, do we try to remove the rocks that caved, or try to find them from another tunnel?"

"They could be hurt." Elsa tensed her jaw to keep from screaming as she felt like doing. "A decision needs to be made."

Dylan nodded once and grabbed the walkie. "Rusty."

"What is it?"

"We've got a signal on Killian's phone. The cave in is before the forked tunnels. Is it possible they went that way?"

"Let me check."

It seemed like forever while they waited for Rusty to get back to them, but in reality, it was probably less than a minute.

"Won't work," Rusty came back. "There's an X drawn on that tunnel. Says 'rockslide', 11-2007'"

"Damn," Dylan barked. "Guess we dig."

Swan Harbor
October 25
3:00 a.m.

LIAM OPENED HIS EYES, AND THE FEELING OF SUFFOCATING climbed like bile inside. *Breathe*, he reminded himself, searching for his flashlight.

It was laying a few feet away, and when it wouldn't turn on, he dropped it and reached for his phone. Then he remembered they'd left it behind.

"Killian," he called in a hushed voice. "Killian."

The suffocating feeling rose higher, forcing him to close his eyes and attempt to regroup. There were jackhammers going full force inside his head, which he knew didn't help.

You can do this.

Easy breath in, and he pushed up into a seated position.

Easy breath out, and he picked up the flashlight.

Easy breath in, and he forced the natural inclination to rush down, and slowly unscrewed the cap. He removed the batteries, then returned them before once again screwing the cap back on.

Easy breath out, and he pushed the switch and almost cried when the light came on.

Liam bounced the beam around his tomb, finding the earpiece smashed beneath a rock. The area where he was trapped extended about two to three feet in front of him. Gingerly, he pushed up, his knee complaining, but with the support of the walls, he could move around.

Killian had been behind him, and with a wall of debris between them, it was now Liam's job to find his brother.

He went to work pushing the dirt and rocks aside, constantly yelling Killian's name. The soil was soft and floated in the air and it wasn't long before his eyes were watering, and it was harder to breathe.

Calm down, he warned, changing tactics. Instead of a sweeping motion, he began using a scoop and dump method, enjoying more success. His watch said he'd been working twenty minutes before a hole opened that was big enough he could look through.

"Killian." Liam flashed his light through the small opening. "Killian."

"Liam."

Killian's groan slowed Liam's heartbeat enough for him to set his light aside and resume his scoop and dump.

"How's your head?" Liam asked as he continued to work.

"Hurts," Killian grumbled. "I'd rather you hadn't shared your headache."

"Sorry, brother," Liam retorted. "I didn't share. You picked that up all on your own."

Liam flashed his light back through the hole, careful not to shine it in Killian's eyes. His brother was sitting up and holding his head in hands.

"You're bleeding."

Killian rubbed his hand across his temple and winced when it came away bloody. "No wonder I'm a little woozy."

"Rip the bottom off your shirt to see if you can staunch the flow."

It was another twenty minutes before Liam thought the hole was big enough Killian could climb through.

"Now that I've done all the work," Liam mock- growled. "Can you get your bony arse up and through this hole? I don't know about you, but I'd like to see my lady."

"Quit your complaining." Killian pushed the rest of the way up and located his Glock, slipping it in his holster. "I'm ready."

"Your nap didn't help your disposition."

"Bed was too hard." Killian rubbed his shoulder and stuck his leg through the hole.

"You won't get any complaints from me." Liam took Killian's flashlight and helped him through the rest of the way.

"Alright, left or straight ahead?" Liam shone his light on the pile of debris that had been in front of him and then on the tunnel opening to their left.

"Can you see a chalk mark?" asked Killian.

Liam hobbled forward, brushed at the wall, and shook his head. Then he bounced his light off the walls in the other tunnel.

"There's nothing, but with the walls falling around us, I guess it's possible it's now on the ground."

"Bloody hell," Killian sighed. "Let's try the tunnel to the left. If nothing, I guess we dig. You're quite adept at it already."

"Tosser."

"Wanker," Killian threw back.

The insult caused Liam to snicker.

"Bloody hell," Killian laughed. "What's so funny?"

Liam shrugged and instead of replying, his chuckle grew louder.

"Bloody nutter," Killian quipped.

"Probably," Liam agreed, leaning on the dirt wall to rest his knee. "Feels good though. Try it."

Then, without waiting for Killian, Liam allowed the laughter to wash over him.

Swan Harbor
October 25
4:00 a.m.

Elsa slanted a look at Emma. "Is that laughter?"

Emma frowned. "Hold on."

"What?" Dylan passed a boulder to Gray, who carried it toward the front of the tunnel.

"Listen," Elsa whispered.

Dylan gave them an annoyed look, but stood with his hands on his hips and waited.

"Hear it?" Elsa grinned, her heart flying free and tears immediately springing to her eyes.

Dylan's brows arched. "Is that—?"

"—Laughter," Emma finished. "Which is music to my ears. Except it's—"

"—A bad sign," Elsa added. "Hurry. Could be a sign of hypoxia."

"What are you talking about?" Gray asked when he returned from depositing another boulder in front of the tunnel opening.

"Hypoxia," Elsa explained as they went back to work digging through the debris. "Lower oxygen levels. They've been inside these tunnels for a while. It could lead to confusion, fatigue, fast heart rate, sweating."

"I'll call for an ambulance," Dylan yelled, heading out of the tunnel.

"Killian!" Emma called when she removed a rock and it left a small opening.

"Doc," he replied, "fancy meeting you here."

"Killian," she repeated with concern. "Are you okay?"

"Absobloodyfine," he giggled.

"That makes no sense," Liam quipped.

"So," Killian giggled. "Who cares?"

Emma exchanged looks with Elsa and rolled her eyes. "They're having way too much fun while we've been out here freaking."

"Agreed."

When the hole was big enough, Elsa stuck her head through. "Liam, are you okay?"

He swayed before taking the steps to reach her. "El," he clasped her hand tightly as he advanced. "What took you so long?" Without waiting for her response, he tugged her closer and sealed their mouths.

Elsa squealed, but when their lips touched, she melted. He was alive and breathing, and tasted ....

"Bugger, your lips are sweet, but that burned like fire." Liam stepped away from her.

Obviously, he'd hurt his mouth, she thought, backing out of the hole. It explained the metallic taste of blood.

"Can you guys hurry?" Killian muttered. "My head's killing me."

"Ambulance is on the way." Dylan returned with news that eased some of Elsa's worry.

Liam stuck his face through the hole, allowing her to see just how badly bruised it was.

"Oh, Liam," she cried. "Your face."

"Come get me, Sweet El." He beckoned her, once he'd gotten one leg through. "Let me lean on you."

Elsa tempered her need to rush into his arms and helped him step fully from the tunnel. "Lean on me." She slipped one arm around his waist and helped him hobble to the entrance. "Here, sit."

He slid onto the ground and took several deep breaths of fresh air. "You have an ace in that bag of yours?" he asked when she approached.

She found it lodged in the corner of her bag. "Want me to do it?"

"Let me." He squeezed her hand. "Will you check Killian's head? He and a rock had a meeting of minds."

"If you're sure."

Liam tugged her close for a gentle kiss. "I'm positive. I love you. I'm sorry I worried you."

"I love you too." She tilted her forehead against his, and for a few precious moments, breathed in his essence. "I was so scared."

"I'm here, love."

His words came out like a promise, and all Elsa could think as she went to check on Killian were Lois's words ....

We start with a little hope.

TWENTY-NINE

Swan Harbor General
October 25
9:00 a.m.

"I'm fine, dad," Killian repeated for the fifth or sixth time. "So is Liam."

When Finn said something and Killian rolled his eyes, all Emma could think about was how he was acting like the situation had been no big deal. But to her, it made her think about a few things in her life ... namely, marriage. Maybe she'd been wrong in thinking everything needed to be perfect. That by focusing on the bigger picture, she was missing out on what was going on around her.

"You don't need to do that, dad," Killian was saying. "Alright. Alright. We'll see you tomorrow."

"Your dad's coming?" she asked as soon as he'd disconnected.

"Aye." He grabbed her hand and pulled her onto the bed beside him. "Said he wants to make sure his boys are fine. It's strange having him so attentive. I don't remember that ever being the case."

"It's like my mom." Emma smiled. "She has an opportunity to reinvent herself, and she's taking advantage of it."

"Good for her."

He kissed her and all she wanted to do was relax in his arms. Except something had her pushing back far enough to study him and the evidence of his ordeal.

There was a minor cut on his forehead they'd glued closed. And several on his face and neck, evidence of just how close he'd come to ….

"Hey." Killian brushed his thumb across her cheekbone. "None of that. I'm fine."

His eyes twinkled, and she had to think he was happy, feeling like he'd won, temporarily, anyway.

"Do you have to work today?" she asked, plans for how to spend the day spinning in her head.

"No. Dylan told me to stay away until Monday."

"And your dad's coming tomorrow?"

"Aye. What about your mother?"

"She's coming tomorrow as well," Emma confirmed.

"And Liam and Elsa are here."

Emma laughed. "All we need are my dad and Amber, and we could have a family reunion."

"Is that what you want?"

"One step at a time, Killian. Do you need me to come and get you when you're discharged?"

"No, Doc." He tossed a thumb over his shoulder toward the wardrobe. "Rusty brought Liam's suitcase, my gym bag, and my car."

"Okay, if you're sure. I'm going to clear my schedule."

"Drive safely, Doc. I'll be home after I grab the boxes from the apartment."

"Do you think you should lift anything heavy?"

"I don't need a mother, Doc," he replied quietly. "I'll be alright. Now go."

"Okay, okay."

She left him behind and spent the next few hours rearranging her schedule and making phone calls. But when her stomach growled, and she saw the time, all thoughts of food flew away.

Where was Killian?

Should she call him? Or would he consider that mothering?

Instead, she opened the app on her computer and found his dot, but not at the hospital. Instead, he was at Sally's. And before she'd completely thought through what she would say, hit dial.

When it went straight to voicemail, her heart rate ticked up a notch.

Emma hit redial. It rang three times, and she was prepared for it to go to voicemail when he answered.

"Doc." He sounded strange ... stiff. "What do you need?"

Emma's radar kicked into gear. "Killian, are you okay?"

"I told you, I'm fine doc. Just forgot I needed to take care of something."

"What?"

"Just a few things." He hesitated, and she got the strangest feeling he was parsing out his words.

"Killian," Emma tried again. "Are you sure you're feeling okay? My schedule's clear and I've been waiting to take care of you."

"That sounds nice, Doc," Killian replied, the tenor of his voice making her uncomfortable. "Since you have a little time, could you do me a favor?"

"A favor?"

"Aye." Emma heard him take a breath. "Would you drop my blue suit by the cleaners for me?"

"Your blue suit?"

"That's right. I've got to go."

The phone went dead before Emma could say more.

"His blue suit?" she repeated. "He doesn't have a blue suit."

Swan Harbor General
October 25
1:00 p.m.

DID YOU GIVE HIM TOO MUCH KETAMINE?

Ask him about his phone.

He knew that voice, he thought, struggling to get his thoughts to come together.

Do I know you? You look familiar.

He heard a sound. His eyes flew open, and his heart raced until his brain got the message—you're safe.

"Liam?" Elsa started toward him. "Are you okay?" She laid her hand on his forehead and brushed his hair back, before finally bending to kiss him lightly.

"I'm better now. When I opened my eyes, you weren't here."

"Sorry about that." She continued to run her fingers through his hair, and it felt so good, he almost purred. "I wanted to find out when I could take you home."

"Oh?"

Elsa slanted a look in his direction. "You're not ready to leave?"

"I'm ready to leave, but ..."

"But?"

"Where's home?" Liam finally murmured, curious about her answer.

"Home is—"

The door opened, interrupting her answer.

"Doctor Patterson ... Dan," Elsa amended. "Is Liam ready to go home?"

Liam's eyes met the twinkling brown ones of his doctor's. "How are you feeling?"

"Except for a little headache, sore mouth, and bum leg," Liam acknowledged each. "I've no double vision, confusion, sharp pains, or nausea."

"That's good."

While the doctor asked a few more questions and performed a cursory examination, Liam only listened with half an ear. His focus remained on Elsa's answer to his earlier question.

"Get dressed, and I'll get your release papers," the doctor replied before leaving them alone.

Liam reached for Elsa's hand. "You were saying?"

"I was saying ..."

Her phone buzzed, interrupting her once again.

Liam sighed. "Answer it, love."

"It's Emma."

"Hold on, Emma," he heard her say. "Killian's where?"

Shouldn't he have been still in the hospital?

"He said what?" Elsa frowned, and something inside Liam chilled.

It's not the paramedic that's the problem. Boss wants the brother.

"Hold on." She gave him the phone. "Emma has a question."

"Where's Killian, Emma?" he snapped, his stomach clenching.

"He's at Sally's and sounded a little ... off."

"Off? Why? What did he say?"

Emma laughed, but he heard the nervousness behind it.

"He asked if I would take his blue suit by the cleaners for him."

When's the boss supposed to arrive?

Tomorrow sometime.

Liam's breath caught, and he tried to focus on what he needed to do.

"Emma, listen to me—"

"You're scaring me, Liam."

"I'll explain everything, but not now. Call Dylan and Rusty and have them meet us at the sheriff's department."

"Liam—"

"Trust me. Just go."

Liam studied the man. Do I know you? You look familiar.

"What happened?" Elsa asked as soon as he'd disconnected.

"Killian used one of our codes." Then his mind jumped to the memory of another voice. "I have a question for you, though."

"What?"

"El, remember when we were at Sally's after the painting?"

"Yes."

"Do you remember when I ran into that guy and I told him he looked familiar?"

"Are you talking about Nic?" She hesitated, as if she were thinking about the conversation. "He reminded you he'd been staying at the Beachside."

"Right." Liam remembered Tia mentioning him. Except he could swear he'd seen Nic somewhere other than Swan Harbor. Was he the third voice? "Do I have any clothes?"

"Rusty brought your suitcase earlier."

"While I dress, can you go push the discharge, please?"

"Liam, you're scaring me."

"Trust me," he repeated, just as he'd said to Emma.

Elsa's eyes sent several nonverbal messages before she voiced others. "Okay. But just so you know, you will not leave me behind."

"I'm not asking that of you," and then the fear inside had him revealing, "but Killian's in trouble. We need to go."

As soon as she ran out of the room, Liam went searching for his clothing, hoping they weren't too late.

⋘⋙

Sally's Diner
October 25
1:30 p.m.

KILLIAN LEANED BACK IN THE CHAIR AND TRIED TO APPEAR relaxed. But his insides were going in a million different directions.

Did Emma understand something was wrong?

Had she called Liam? And if so, did Liam remember what he'd been trying to say?

How had Santora slipped into Swan Harbor without being noticed? And why the bloody hell was Nic Nucci involved?

So far, Killian found Nic to be the wildcard. He didn't have the same demeanor as the other members of Santora's gang, 'Ian' had known. There was a nervousness about the way he was holding the gun that said he wasn't as comfortable as he wanted people to think.

"Come on, Santora," Killian pulled the gang leader's attention back to him. "You said if I showed up, you would let the others leave."

"I lied." Santora smiled, showing off the gold caps on his front teeth. "Nic here says the town's too small. I let them go, and everyone will know my business."

Killian fought not to wince, as the other man had a point. Except with Sally, Tia, and Paula tied up on his left and Captain Jack and Sydney on the other side of the room, he needed to do something.

"Your business?" Killian continued to ferret out information. "Which is?"

"To pay you back for destroying my organization, of course," Santora retorted. "That wasn't very nice."

Killian's thoughts ran to catch up, but he couldn't put the pieces together.

"Humor me," Killian murmured. "Because I fail to see how I destroyed your livelihood. From everything I've heard, drugs and weapons are just as plentiful as ever."

"You know what you did," Santora snapped.

Something Liam had said floated around the edges of Killian's mind, but unsure of where he was being led, he searched for another distraction.

"Are you sure you haven't confused me with Jokowitz?" The slight flare of Santora's eyes said he'd struck a nerve. "But you took care of him, didn't you?"

"That idiot." Santora laughed harshly. "He was too desperate for his next fix to want me destroyed.

Which fit, thought Killian. It was what kept Tino under Santora's thumb.

"And Tino," Killian added the name of the man who'd killed Violet into the mix. "He went a little crazy on you at the end, didn't he?"

"Enough!" Santora snapped. "He was a fool over that girl."

"That girl?" Killian arched a brow. "Margherita?

As soon as Killian said her name, he saw Nic flinch.

Finally!

"Imbecile! Tino wouldn't listen and tried to take justice into his own hands."

"Justice?" Killian's mind spun through a few possibilities, but in the end, he couldn't come up with anything new. "So, I was right. Tino came after me because of a female."

"I told you he was an idiot," Santora scoffed. "He had to be taught a lesson."

"So, you tortured him and dumped him on the street?"

Santora shrugged. "No loss."

"And Margherita?" Killian watched Nic. "What happened to her?"

Santora's dark eyes flashed, and for a second, he reminded Killian of a viper ready to strike.

"She was sacrificed for the greater good."

Nic's face lost all color, and the pieces in Killian's head started rolling around.

"Sacrificed?" Killian frowned. "Who killed her?"

"You're playing that card?" Santora laughed. "Come now, Ian ... or should I call you Killian? Trying to lure me into that warehouse was a bit extreme. After all, I didn't kill your little friend."

"No," Killian hummed. "That was on Tino. While I'd love to take credit for the downfall of your business, I'm having a hard time connecting the dots. By the time your warehouse blew, I was gone, remember?"

Santora said nothing, but Killian could tell the information he'd tossed out had caused the other man to think. The possibility he'd gone after the wrong person was not something that would sit well.

He needed to figure out who'd blown the warehouse and tried to lure the crime boss into it. And just exactly how Nic Nucci fit into the picture.

Sheriff's Department
October 25
1:45 p.m.

LIAM HOBBLED INTO THE CONFERENCE ROOM AT THE SHERIFF'S department and gingerly lowered into a chair with Elsa next to him. Dylan and Rusty were sitting across the table. The agents, Simpson and his partner, Ricci, were leaning against a wall, and Emma was pacing.

"Killian's in trouble," he began without preamble.

Dylan sat up a little straighter and crossed his elbows on the table. "What makes you say that?"

"He used one of the codes we'd come up with when he worked undercover," Liam explained. "He told Emma to take his blue suit to the cleaners."

Dylan frowned. "I won't like this, will I?"

"Probably not," Liam acknowledged. "But I think he's telling me Santora has him, and he's not alone."

"How the hell did Santora get into my town and we not know it?" Dylan barked. "We had the entrances into town monitored."

"He had help," offered Rusty. Then added, "Remember the photos delivered to Elsa, and the ones put in Killian's drawer?"

"And the matching bullets," Dylan muttered.

Liam frowned. "Matching bullets?"

Dylan sighed and sent an apologetic look in Elsa's direction. "Yeah. Shawn found one in your tire that matched the one from Elsa's."

Her quick inhalation had Liam grabbing her hand. "So, my flat wasn't an accident? Somehow, I knew that."

"But who's helping Santora?" Dylan continued. "The ones holding you in that building didn't survive."

"While I was being held," Liam went on. "I heard a third voice that was familiar, but I couldn't place it. Then I remembered seeing him at Sally's."

"Who?" Dylan prodded.

"Nic Nucci."

"*What*?" snapped Dylan. "The Nic Nucci that is teaching at Swan Harbor High?"

"Or better yet," Rusty added. "The Nic Nucci who just upgraded our office computers and had time to slip an envelope into Killian's drawer."

"But why?" Elsa asked what they all wondered.

"Revenge." Lee Simpson stepped forward, and the look on his face showed he was annoyed. But, with whom, Liam wasn't sure. "I'd bet money, Nic Nucci is short for Dominic Ranucci. If that's true, he's looking to avenge his sister, Margherita Ranucci, who died last March in a warehouse fire."

Rusty rifled through the files and pulled out one. Then he spread the photos on the table.

"Is this Margherita?"

"That's her," Lee confirmed. "Her and Tino were an item."

"Okay," Dylan circled the conversation back to Killian. "So, it's possible Nic smuggled Santora into town."

"I know it's Santora," Liam pushed. "He's the 'suit.'" When he realized the other men in the room still weren't buying it, he continued. "If it was one of the guys who were higher in Santora's organization, Killian would have said, *'Take my blue jacket.'*"

"Oh okay." Rusty nodded in understanding. "And an underling would have been the pants."

"Yes!" Liam confirmed, speeding the story along. "And if Santora, or any of the goons were alone, he would have said take it to be cleaned."

"But because he said cleaners, Santora isn't alone," guessed Dylan.

Liam nodded. "So, how are we going to save my brother?"

Dylan exchanged a look with Rusty that had Liam's insides clenching. "This is Swan Harbor. Let's give Santora something he will never expect."

Sally's Diner
October 25

2:30 p.m.

Killian glanced at the clock above the counter and calculated it had been almost two hours since Santora had called. And almost twenty minutes since he'd said anything in response to the denial regarding the warehouse fire.

He took inventory of the hostages, worried about how they were handling the situation. Sydney was observing everything around him and, Killian assumed, writing tomorrow's front page story. Captain Jack, who was sitting on Sydney's left, appeared relaxed. However, the twinkle in his eye said he wasn't worried. Paula's chin was resting on her chest, so she was napping or meditating, and Tia's eyes were shooting daggers at Nic.

"Why is he quiet all of a sudden?" Sally whispered, telling him she'd been paying attention to Santora's behavior.

"He's thinking about what I said," Killian muttered. "Aren't you, Santora?" he said a little louder.

The other man turned his beady, black eyes in Killian's direction. "Why would I give any credence to something you've said?"

"Because," Killian tugged the mobster's attention away from Nic. "You know I'm telling the truth. That, in the time 'Ian' worked for you, nothing he did led you to believe he could have orchestrated the warehouse fire. Let's face it. From what I read about that fire, it was quite the coordinated event."

Santora's black eyes glittered with anger. "If not you, then who?"

Killian had been watching Nic, as well as turning over other options. "You said someone lured you there, right?"

"I was supposed to meet with a dealer from South America," Santora surprised him by offering.

"Matías Perez," Killian tossed out, and by the look on Santora's face, he knew he was correct. "I know you'd complained about him trying to shove you out of New York. If that were true, why would you ever assume the meeting would be legit?"

Santora's face turned red. "Why do you think I sent in pretty little Margherita? She was supposed to bring Matías to me."

"Instead, she died, and you were arrested," Killian tsked. "You're getting soft Santora."

"How dare you!" Santora lifted his hand, his 9 mm aimed directly at Killian. "No one dares to talk to me like that."

Before Killian could respond, the diner's front door was thrown open.

"Sally, where's my smoked turkey?" bellowed Leroy.

"Leroy?" Killian mouthed. He looked over his shoulder to see the little man standing next to the door in a blue superman suit, wearing a huge smile.

Then time stood still, as the place filled with smoke. Killian flipped back around toward Santora, to see the 9 mm still pointing directly at him.

"Goodbye, Ian Jones," Santora sneered.

Killian watched his finger press the trigger, and his mind raced for an out. Before he could move, Nic screamed, "No!" and launched his body between him and the bullet.

Nic's gun slid across the floor, and Killian threw himself in the general direction. He heard a pop, and in one motion, grabbed the gun, rolled over, and fired three times.

Tia's screams somehow restarted time, pushing Killian to shout, "Call 911!"

He yanked a tablecloth off a table and pressed it on Nic's abdomen. "Hold on, Nic."

"Hurts," Nic muttered. "I'm sorry ... sorry, but she was my sister."

"Killian." Liam pushed him aside and went to work on Nic. "What happened?"

"He saved my life," Killian explained. "Then I shot Santora. Is he?"

"Oh, yeah," Liam confirmed. "This time, he's really gone."

While Liam worked on Nic, Killian untied Tia. "Are you alright?"

She hugged him. "Physically, I'm fine. Emotionally, I'm so angry I could scream, but I don't want him to die."

"I bet they'll let you ride with him."

"Thanks, Killian."

He then turned to Sally and sent her a crooked grin. "Sorry about the mess."

"Oh, honey." She patted his cheek. "Don't you apologize. This wasn't your fault. Just think of the business I'll have for the next few days. And the stories I have to tell!"

"Killian!" Emma launched herself into his arms and promptly broke down.

"Hey, Doc," he whispered against her temple. "I'm here."

She loosened her arms and stepped back slightly. "Is it really over?"

"It's over, Doc." He cupped her face and kissed her softly. "I told you, you're stuck with me."

"You did, didn't you?"

"I did." He slipped his arm around her and turned them toward the door. "But ... *Leroy*?"

She giggled. "That was Rusty's idea."

"I need to have a talk with my partner," Killian grumbled. "At least Leroy had on the tights. I've seen all his hairy arse I care to."

"Understandable."

Her laughter wrapped around him, and as soon as they walked out of Sally's, Killian tugged her into a corner. He was on the verge of having everything he wanted and needed a minute to celebrate.

"I love you, Doc."

"I love you too."

Then, because he couldn't resist taking a moment to relish, he sunk in and let her carry him away.

THIRTY

Elsa's Mother's Home
October 26
1:00 p.m.

Liam slowly climbed the stairs to Patty Winters' home, took a deep breath, and knocked. He'd second-guessed his decision to stop by alone, especially with her mother's condition. With Elsa, though, he'd discovered he had a touch of old fashion deep inside.

"Well, hello," Patty smiled. "Can I help you?"

"Good afternoon, Mrs.," he hesitated and quickly came back with, "Mrs. Patty. Could I have a few minutes of your time?"

She studied him closely, and he couldn't help but wish he could read her mind. "Sure, you can help me decorate cupcakes."

"Cupcakes?" Liam asked, remembering she'd been making strawberry ones, Olivia's favorite, when she'd gotten burned.

"Sure." Patty invited him inside. "I'm making chocolate ones for Elsa. Those are her favorite."

"Chocolate cupcakes are Elsa's favorite?"

"Oh yes." Patty led him into the kitchen. "I baked twelve, and here's my icing. Doesn't it look yummy?"

Liam dutifully peered into the bowl. "It looks delicious."

"Would you like a taste?"

One look into her guileless eyes and Liam knew he couldn't deny her. He swiped his finger along the rim of the bowl and licked it off. "That's wonderful." He winked.

She giggled like a schoolgirl and handed him an apron. "Here, you don't want to get icing on your clothes."

Liam glanced down at the apron that said, '*Mr. Good Looking is Cooking*' and fought to keep a straight face. "Nice apron."

"Isn't it though?" The entire time she was talking, she was busy separating the cupcakes into two piles and handing him a knife. "I bought it for Max not long after we were married. In fact, he ..."

She told him a story about Elsa's father and how much he enjoyed cooking dinners for his girls. He found his emotions all over the place, because a part of him loved these little peeks into the Winters' family. The other part, though, felt guilty because he was the one privy to the story and not her daughter.

She finished the tale, and while they continued decorating, Liam searched for another topic.

"You met Max when you were in college, right?"

"Yes."

Her expression said she was lost in the past, making him wonder if she remembered his question.

"I thought Max was the most handsome man alive. He was so kind, too."

Patty placed a cupcake on a plate and set it on the table.

"Give it a try."

"Yes, ma'am."

While he enjoyed the cupcake, he worked through several statements regarding why he'd stopped by. Yet, none of them seem right.

She frowned. "What did you say your name was again?"

"Liam. Liam Reade."

"That's a nice name," Patty smiled. "Now, tell me, Liam Reade. What brought you by my place today?"

Liam wiped off his hands and pulled out the ring box that had been burning a hole in his pocket.

"I plan to ask Elsa to marry me tonight," he answered huskily. "I hope I have your blessing."

Patty blinked rapidly and almost reverently took the ring. "It's beautiful," she said of the oval diamond. "It's really a beautiful ring."

"Thank you, and thank you for the cupcake, but I'd better go."

She walked him back through the house and when he stepped out on the porch, she tilted her head. "You know, Elsa will love that ring, but I'm not sure she'll be able to marry you."

Liam's heart sank. "You ... you don't think she'll marry me?"

"No." Patty shook her head. "She's already married to Grandpa Stu. Ta ta."

"Alright then." He grinned with relief when he realized she'd not been talking about his Elsa. "Let's do this."

Siren's Song
October 26
9:00 p.m.

"Are you sure this is alright?" Liam pulled out a chair at a table close to the stage at Siren's.

"It's fine, Liam."

Elsa slipped into the chair and couldn't help but notice the fine tremor in his hand. It had come and gone during their dinner at Captain Jack's with Emma and Killian. But he'd claimed everything was fine when she'd asked.

"Killian's getting an update." Emma settled next to her and nodded across the room where Rupert, Lois, Lance, Lee Simpson, and Gabe Ricci were sitting.

"I heard Nic made it through surgery and is in intensive care," Elsa imparted what little news she had. "I'm happy he's alive, but ..."

Liam tightened his hold on her shoulders. "It's over, love."

"I know." Elsa gave him a watery smile and forced her negative thoughts back. "You were telling me why your father didn't join us for dinner," she reminded him, circling to a conversation they'd had on the walk down the pier.

"Killian and I stopped by earlier and he'd been 'resting.'" Liam made air quotes. "He's supposed to meet us here."

Elsa hummed, finding Finn's absence surprising since he'd come to Swan Harbor to check on his boys.

"Emma, wasn't Ava supposed to join us also?"

"Mom said she got a late start and was tired."

"She's okay though, right?"

"Her health is fine," Emma assured her. "In fact, she just walked in with Anita, Maggie, and Becca. You know," she went on, "I don't think I've ever known her to just hang with friends."

"You said she was reinventing herself, Doc." Killian joined them at their table. "I say bravo for her."

"Bravo for whom?" Finn pulled over a chair from another table.

"Ava," Killian supplied.

"She's not joining us tonight?"

"Mom's over there." Emma waved toward the table where Ava and her friends were sitting. "You'll have to say hello."

"I might do that ... later." Finn smiled at the server who delivered their drinks. "Now, I'd like some assurances that everything with Santora is well and truly over."

"It's over, dad," Liam answered.

"Really," Killian added when his father turned in his direction. "And Simpson was just telling me how Nic got involved."

"Margherita was Nic's sister," Liam explained.

"She died in a fire meant for Santora," Killian added. "Then NYPD arrested him."

Finn frowned. "But if Santora was in prison, why did Nic get involved?"

"For his mother," Killian replied. "She's an attorney in New York and started hearing grumblings and ..."

Killian told of how Dominic Ranucci had taken the death of Ian Jones and turned him into Santora's biggest nightmare. Nic was a talented computer programmer and had been systematically dismantling the organization piece by piece.

"Then he saw me when I was in the City last year," Killian sighed. "And he had to regroup."

"By figuring out a way to move to Swan Harbor?" guessed Liam.

"Not only a way to move here," Killian went on. "But a way to be accepted."

"I can see that," Liam conceded. "When did he show up?"

"March," Emma answered. "Just before Gray and Sadie's wedding."

"Made friends with Gray at some conference," Killian added. "A comment here, another there, and voilà."

"But if Nic was the one who brought Santora into Swan Harbor yesterday, why didn't he just kill him?" Liam followed up.

Killian shrugged. "Not sure. Maybe he chickened out. Maybe he was hoping I would. Bloody fool."

Elsa kept thinking about the look on Tia's face when she'd seen her at the hospital. "Maybe it was Tia who changed him."

"Tia?" Killian repeated. "How the bloody hell did Tia change him?"

"Come on, Killian," Emma teased. "Surely you haven't forgotten the message in all those movies we watched."

Liam laughed. "What movies is she talking about, Killian?"

"The ones that show bad boys are only bad boys until the right woman comes along." Elsa grinned.

Finn laughed, raised his glass, and toasted the table. "She's got you there, my boy."

"Bloody hell," Killian grumbled.

Liam stood and held out his hand. "If you'll excuse us, we're going to dance."

Elsa almost said something about not being asked, but the fine tremor in his hand was back. Besides, she wanted nothing more than to be held.

"That was abrupt."

"I didn't come here to talk about bloody yesterday." Liam nuzzled her temple.

"Why did we come here, Liam?"

He spun her around several times. "For a little dancing, of course."

"And your knee is okay?"

"It's fine," he assured her. "A little cortisone, ice, heat, a wrap, and I'm good."

"If you say so."

As the song neared the end, he tensed and led her back to their table.

"I'll be back." Liam buzzed her cheek and was gone.

Before Elsa could figure out where Liam had gone, Tyler took the stage.

"Tonight, folks," Tyler announced, and the lights slowly dimmed. "We have a special guest. Mr. Liam Reade."

Elsa fought to keep her mouth closed when Liam walked onto the stage carrying a stool and a guitar.

"Liam *sings*?" she whispered, as he ran his fingers over the strings.

Their eyes met. Her heart raced, and she had to hold on to the chair to keep her butt firmly planted.

"For the first time," Liam sang in a husky baritone.

Elsa's heart melted.

As he continued to sing, she realized he'd mashed together multiple songs, using the lyrics to say words he'd struggled with.

We start with a little hope ....

"Show off," Killian muttered.

Emma giggled. "You're just jealous you didn't think of it first."

"Bloody right, I am."

Elsa ignored the noise around her and just focused on the man telling her about their future.

"Forever, it's only you," he hummed. "You are the love of my life. Hold on, close your eyes, and listen to the words. Elsa, love, you are the only one. After all, my love, we're in this love together."

When the song ended, she froze. What am I supposed to do?

Wait!

The heat in Liam's eyes drew her, sending her heart into overdrive. He set his guitar aside and strode in her direction. If she hadn't been paralyzed, she would have thrown herself into his arms.

Liam slowly descended the stairs, his gaze never leaving her.

How did I do?

Did you like it?

Was it enough?

"Oh, Liam," she murmured, taking the last few steps to jump into his arms. "So that's why you were so nervous."

"If only," he mumbled.

His heart raced, and he couldn't quite get his breath, but he had more to say.

"Come here, love."

As soon as she sat, he lowered to one knee, ignoring the slight pain.

"Elsa." Liam held up the ring between them. "The foundation of our future began with the combination of love and hope. From this day forward, we'll build the walls brick by brick. Will you marry me and add another one?"

Fear zipped through Liam as he remembered Patty's words about Elsa not marrying him. Then, their eyes met and in them, he saw the answer to every question he'd ever have.

"Yes," she whispered. "Yes, I'll marry you!"

"Yes?"

"Yes. It's beautiful."

"May I?"

"Please."

"You're the one who's beautiful." Elsa's hand shook as Liam slid the ring onto her finger. Then he pulled her up and kissed her. It wasn't quite the kiss he wanted to give her, but it was enough to let her know exactly what he was feeling.

He knew everyone wanted to congratulate them, but he wasn't ready to share his bride-to-be just yet. On cue, Tyler started the music, and Liam led her onto the dance floor.

"I love you, Liam." Her lips whispered across his neck.

"And I love you."

"That was quite the romantic proposal."

"I wanted to make up for the decidedly unromantic first I love you."

"Oh, stop. I told you everything happens as it should. But this ..."

"Too much?"

"Perfect." A devilish grin crossed her face. "And in Tyler's club too. Were you that sure of me?"

"I was that sure of us."

"Oh, Liam. Sometimes you say the sweetest things."

"Only sometimes," he hummed. "I'll have to work on that."

She chuckled, and knowing their family and friends would swarm as soon as the song ended, he tightened his hold.

"Do you know what today is?"

"You mean besides the best day of my life?"

"Yes, love, besides that."

"Saturday," she quipped.

"Besides that."

"It's October—"

"It was one year ago I wheeled a patient into Queen's Court and saw you for the first time."

"Oh, *Liam*," Elsa sighed. "You remembered the first time you saw me?"

"I do." He pressed his cheek against hers. "It was a sixteen-year-old male who'd been hit while riding his bike."

"Bryce," she murmured, and he could hear the smile in her words. "He was more concerned about his new bike than he was about the possibility of a broken pelvis or shoulder."

Liam laughed. "I remember that. One cop at the scene brought it by the hospital."

"I didn't know that. Was it salvageable?"

"What do you think?"

"I'll take that as a no. Poor Bryce."

"Hey, don't feel too sorry for that kid." Liam chuckled at how they'd all been snookered. "We took it to the bike shop and were told it would be cheaper to buy a new one."

"You didn't?"

"We did," he nodded. "Plus, his was from the past season, so he got an upgrade."

"Well, I for one am sorry Bryce was hurt, but I'll be forever grateful you came into my life."

"Knew you were dangerous even then," Liam mock-growled.

"Sorry?"

"Don't be, love." He twirled her around as the song ended and dipped her into a kiss.

It was only the tinge in his knee that pushed him to lift her back up.

"Thank you for the dance, soon to be Mrs. Reade. Look who's here."

An expression crossed Elsa's face he couldn't read. However, before he could ask, Emma, Sadie, Molly, Ava, Patty, and her nurse, Lilly, surrounded her.

Liam moved back next to Killian. "What's with the disgruntled look on your face? I thought you'd be happy."

"Oh, I'm happy, alright," Killian grumbled. "But you realize what this means?"

"Honestly, I've no clue what you're talking about."

"Come on," Killian said with disgust. "You wrote her a song. That puts pressure on the rest of us."

"Bugger that, Killian. I couldn't let Tyler be the only man who'd written her a song."

Killian nodded. "I can see that, but you cheated. Using lyrics already written."

"Bite me," Liam smirked and waved toward the bar. "Rum?"

⚜

"WHAT'S THAT LOOK ON YOUR FACE FOR, EL?" EMMA ASKED, WHEN it was just them, Molly and Sadie.

Elsa frowned. "What look?" When she noticed her friends weren't buying it, she sighed. "Liam just called me soon-to-be Mrs. Reade."

"So," Sadie shrugged. "You just said you would marry him."

"What if I don't want to give up Winters?" Her heart raced and her stomach tied itself into knots.

"Elsa." Molly patted her on the back. "You have time to decide what you want to do."

"Remember Elsa," Sadie reminded her. "Take back the power."

"Right." Elsa nodded and searched for Liam. "Excuse me ladies."

She wove her way around the tables until she found Liam standing between his father and Killian.

"Excuse us." Elsa took the glass he was holding and handed it to Killian, then tugged Liam into a dark corner.

"I like this." He pulled her against his hard body and nibbled just below her ear, making her knees weak.

Take back the power.

"Wait." Elsa pressed a hand on his chest. "I will decide if I want to be Elsa Reade, Elsa Winters or Elsa Winters-Reade. Do you have a problem with that?"

Liam cupped her face. "Just as long as you marry me, I don't care what your name is. Anything else?"

Elsa made a face at him because he could read her so well. "My mom," she sighed and leaned her head against his chest, fighting the tears threatened.

"What about your mom? Did she tell you Grandpa Stu wouldn't approve?"

She made a noise that came out sounding like a half-laugh, half-cry. "How did you know?"

"I stopped by earlier today and asked for her blessing. She gave it but said she didn't think Grandpa Stu would approve."

"Ugh."

"We could tell her Grandpa Stu is dead, and you're going to marry a much younger and very handsome man."

"Oh, you," Elsa retorted. "We can't do that. But Liam ..."

"What is it, love?"

"Can we get married quickly, before she's ..."

"I'd marry you next week," Liam assured her. "Whenever you want."

"Thank you."

He grinned. "I'm really glad I listened to my heart."

"Me too."

Elsa glanced over his shoulder to see Captain Jack beaming at her. She waved and had to agree he'd been right. Her heart had known and had led her exactly to the place where she was meant to be.

"You listened to your heart. We've got hope. What's next?"

"Whatever we imagine," he smirked, pulling a song title from his song list. "But here's what I'm imagining right now."

Liam pressed her against the wall, and as his lips covered hers, she agreed with another line from his song. Wherever he was, she was home.

EPILOGUE

Siren's Song
October 26
11:30 p.m.

FINN GLANCED AROUND THE ROOM AND COULDN'T STOP THE feeling of pride that zipped through him. Both of his boys had faced their ghosts and come out on top. They'd met strong women, fallen in love, and were building the future he'd always wanted for them.

"Do you enjoy living in Swan Harbor?" he asked his smiling dance partner.

Elsa's blue eyes glittered with happiness. "More than I thought I would. It feels like home."

He laughed. "I have to admit, I never pictured both my sons living in a small town."

"Are you okay with that?"

She was trying to read him, but he'd had years of hiding his thoughts from others.

"It is what it is," he gave a noncommittal response, assuming she would drop it.

"You'd better watch out, Finn. Swan Harbor has a way about it. You never know."

Was he alright with his family moving so far from New York? Especially since it felt as if he'd just gotten back the closeness that had been missing for a few years. But what were his options?

"You talk as if Swan Harbor has a way of," he searched for the right word, "reaching out and drawing people in."

Elsa grinned. "You said it, I didn't."

"That's a fanciful way of looking at it."

"Liam said the same thing."

"Speaking of ..." Finn led Elsa in a couple of intricate steps and moved them away from the watchful eyes of his oldest son.

"You did that on purpose." Elsa laughed up at him. "Was Liam giving you the eagle eye?"

Finn chuckled. "How did you know?"

"He likes to pretend he's tough." She shrugged. "But—"

"—His mother's words still haunt him," Finn finished quietly.

"Yes. It's going to take time."

"And love."

"That too," Elsa conceded.

"You've been good for him, you know?"

She blinked several times before saying, "I love him."

"And he loves you. Welcome to the family, Elsa."

"Thank you."

Then her smile grew, and he could feel Liam standing behind him.

"You couldn't even last an entire song without her," Finn grumbled.

"Sorry, dad." Liam tugged Elsa back into his arms. "Emma's available."

Which was a good thing, he decided, as he had some questions ....

Finn wove his way around the room and was aware of being watched. Which made him uncomfortable, because he was used to slipping in and out of places unobserved. He was a survivor, adapting when needed. Would having a family in Swan Harbor require him to change, as Elsa assumed?

He found Killian and Emma talking to a young man he'd seen before at the diner.

"Dad," Killian greeted him. "Have you met Hayden Patterson? He's a student at Swan Harbor U."

"And works at Sally's, right?"

"My aunt owns Sally's," Hayden confirmed.

"It's nice you're helping your family." Finn smiled. "What are you studying at the University?"

"Computer Science."

"A worthwhile major," Finn acknowledged. "How many more years do you have left?"

"A couple," Hayden sighed as if that was forever, and Finn had to fight off his grin.

"Well, once you graduate," Finn offered. "I have a few contacts in New York City, if you're interested."

"Really?" Hayden's eyes lit up. "Cool, thanks."

"My pleasure. And now," Finn glanced at Emma. "Would you care to dance? You don't mind, do you, son?"

Killian raised a brow. "Doc, be nice to my father."

She laughed, and once on the dance floor, pinned him with her green-eyed gaze. "You're trying to find out why I haven't set a wedding date, aren't you?"

Finn laughed. "You're direct."

"Not always." She lifted a shoulder nonchalantly. "In this case, Killian told me you asked."

"He did?"

"We're trying not to keep secrets from each other," she admitted. "Especially after everything with Santora."

"That's very wise." He organized his thoughts a little more before saying, "You make my son happy."

Emma grinned. "And he makes me happy."

"But?"

She wrinkled her nose. "I swear, if you live in Swan Harbor, forget having secrets."

"You think it's the town?"

"Swan Harbor is," she hesitated a moment, then settled on, "unique."

"Elsa said the same thing." He twirled her around a few times and gave his thoughts time to coalesce. "You two make it sound as if the town is a living, breathing entity."

"There's just something about living here," Emma went on. "That gives you hope there is such a thing as a happy ending."

"Or is it a happy beginning?" He repeated words he'd heard as a child.

"The first day to the rest of your life," she murmured, almost to herself. "I like that."

"Thank you," he laughed. "You may use it."

"I just might. As for setting a date, I will, but ..." Emma took a deep breath as if what she was going to say gave her pause. "My father is coming east next month and then we'll see."

"Does Ava know your father is coming to visit?"

Her eyes flashed with something unknown. "No, I don't think I've told her. But she won't care."

"No?" Finn pushed for a little more information. "No chance to get the parents back together?"

"My father is remarried," Emma offered, her green eyes digging into his dark ones.

"Are you worried about your father's visit?" He moved the conversation away from the mother and back to the daughter.

"Maybe a little."

"You'll be fine," Finn assured her. "You conquered Killian."

"Conquered?" Killian laughed from behind him. "What kind of word is that?"

"One I knew would annoy you," Finn retorted, relinquishing his dance partner.

"Figures," Killian groused. "You always had eyes in the back of your head."

It had come in handy at times, Finn thought. But aloud, told them to have fun and went searching for a drink.

"Club soda with lime," he ordered, leaning against the bar.

He took a sip of the bubbly drink and scanned the room. Should he?

"You're hope," a gentleman about twenty years his senior retorted, mirroring Finn's stance.

"No," Finn quipped, toasting the man with his glass. "I'm Finn. Finley Reade."

"Captain Jack," the older man introduced himself. "And let me clarify, you *have* hope."

Finn studied him. "It's what every good dream starts with. But how did you know?"

"I just know." Captain Jack shrugged. "Are you moving to Swan Harbor like your sons?"

"I hadn't planned on it."

"Huh," Captain Jack grunted and walked away.

Finn found he wanted to shake his head several times to see if the scene would settle. Then he spotted the one dance partner he'd not had the privilege of holding heading in his direction.

"White wine," he heard her request.

He drained the rest of his club soda and stepped up behind her. "Hold the wine for her, will you?" he asked of the bartender, slipping him a five.

Ava King pinned him with her crystal-clear blue eyes. "What do you think you're doing?"

Her porcelain complexion and ruby red lips turned him on more than he could ever remember, but he fought to maintain a neutral expression.

"Please dance with me." He hesitated a beat and pushed, "After all, our children are engaged," knowing her upbringing wouldn't allow her to ignore him.

"Fine."

He led her to the dance floor, pulled her into his arms, and had to fight to keep a semblance of distance between them.

"Are you alright?" he whispered.

Finn could feel Ava fighting the pull between them. "I was doing fine until …"

"Until?" His voice grew husky. "Until I reminded you of how it felt to be close. Until I reminded you of what you're missing. Until—"

"Stop," she pleaded.

"Is that what you really want, love?" Finn continued to seduce with his words. "You can't tell me you aren't reliving those hours we spent together."

"Stop!"

Finn whispered a kiss across her ear and moved back far enough to look into her beautiful face. Their breaths mingled, and it would be so easy to ….

"Oh, Ava."

Her eyes dropped to his lips, and he thought, maybe. Hope bloomed, and then ….

"I can't." She stepped from his arms and ran from the room.

"Bloody hell, dad," Killian and Liam snapped simultaneously.

Finn schooled his features and met his sons' blue eyes.

"What did you say?" Killian took the initiative.

Finn found he couldn't explain and shrugged, feeling much like a cockwomble.

"You'd make us apologize, dad," Liam reminded him. "Maybe you need to listen to your own advice."

"Perhaps I do," Finn sighed. "If you'll excuse me."

When he walked out onto the pier, he didn't see her anywhere. He'd see her at the hotel and turned to go back inside. Then he smelled the pipe and noticed Captain Jack leaning against the wall.

"You feel it, don't you?" the older man posed.

"Excuse me?"

"I said," Captain Jack pushed away from the building and casually strolled forward. "You feel it too, don't you?"

Finn wanted to call him a doddering old fool, but he wasn't doddering and didn't appear foolish.

"Feel what? The arctic air?"

Captain Jack smirked, as if he weren't even going to dignify the response. Then he pointed his pipe in Finn's direction. "Listen to your heart, Finley Reade. It always knows."

Finn watched the Captain walk down the pier and had to wonder at the other man's words. Was there something to Emma and Elsa's thoughts about Swan Harbor? Was he being guided by a force more powerful than him?

Sign up for my newsletter and download an extra Liam & Elsa scene.
A Picnic, A Secret & A Dance
https://sophiebartow.com/bonus-chapters/

Purchase a copy of Ava & Finn's story today.
Kisses, Family & Hope
https://sophiebartow.com/book/kisses-family-hope/

KISSES, FAMILY & HOPE BLURB
SWAN HARBOR'S HOPE STORY BOOK THREE

**Listen to your heart.
It always knows.**

After a health scare, Ava King leaves the running of her family's corporation to others and sets off to find balance in her life. She wants her family, a career, and love. And spending time with her grown daughter Emma, in Swan Harbor, seems like the perfect opportunity. But while there, a mystery behind a charm bracelet leads her to a shocking discovery.

Finley Reade had reinvented himself several times for love. Now, with two grown sons, who have found happiness, he's ready to find the woman to fill the lonely places inside. Ava King is everything he wants, but with her daughter engaged to his son, she's unwilling to give him a chance.

Then, they both encounter Captain Jack, Swan Harbor's eccentric resident. His sage advice has Ava rethinking everything and slowly, she learns to share pieces of her heart with Finn. But secrets from his past threaten to derail any hope for a future with Ava or his sons. He must decide, should he stay and fight for the family he so desperately desires? Or leave everything he loves behind?

Are family and love worth fighting for?

Watch the trailer, read an excerpt, then download a copy of
Kisses, Family & Hope
https://sophiebartow.com/book/kisses-family-hope/

ABOUT THE AUTHOR

Sophie crafts small-town mystery romances that weave intricate plots with richly developed characters. Her female leads are intelligent, resourceful, and resilient, while her male characters, often stubborn, exude sexiness, wit, and a protective nature. She delights in building slow-burn romances, savoring the tension and delaying that first kiss for as long as possible. No matter the trope, every story she writes has a happy ending.

After a fulfilling 30-plus-year career as a speech-language pathologist, working with adult post-stroke and Parkinson's patients, she is enjoying her new journey. With their four children spread out, Sophie and her husband live in South Florida. They share their home with a spoiled dog named Bandit and an equally pampered cat named Irma.

You can find her on her website: **https://sophiebartow.com/**   *Sophiexo*

facebook.com/SmallTownAuthorSophieBartow

x.com/SophieBartow

instagram.com/sophiebartow

goodreads.com/sophiebartow

bookbub.com/profile/sophie-bartow

pinterest.com/SophieBartow

www.ingramcontent.com/pod-product-compliance
Lightning Source LLC
Chambersburg PA
CBHW061112310726
48974CB00002B/501